SOUL READER
The Complete Series
Arcane Souls World

International Bestselling Author
Annie Anderson

Edited by Angela Sanders
Cover Design by Trif Book Design

www.annieande.com

BOOKS BY ANNIE ANDERSON

THE ARCANE SOULS WORLD

GRAVE TALKER SERIES

Dead to Me

Dead & Gone

Dead Calm

Dead Shift

Dead Ahead

Dead Wrong

Dead & Buried

SOUL READER SERIES

Night Watch

Death Watch

Grave Watch

THE WRONG WITCH SERIES

Spells & Slip-ups

Magic & Mayhem

Errors & Exorcisms

THE LOST WITCH SERIES

Curses & Chaos

Hexes & Hijinx

THE ETHEREAL WORLD

PHOENIX RISING SERIES

(Formerly the Ashes to Ashes Series)

Flame Kissed

Death Kissed

Fate Kissed

Shade Kissed

Sight Kissed

ROGUE ETHEREAL SERIES

Woman of Blood & Bone

Daughter of Souls & Silence

Lady of Madness & Moonlight

Sister of Embers & Echoes

Priestess of Storms & Stone

Queen of Fate & Fire

NIGHT WATCH

ARCANE SOULS WORLD: SOUL READER BOOK 1

ANNIE ANDERSON

"Sooner or later, everyone sits down to a banquet of consequences."

— ROBERT LOUIS STEVENSON

1

Waking up in the middle of a cemetery was never high on my bucket list—not that I had a bucket list at twenty-two—but if I had one at all, hanging out in a graveyard wasn't *ever* going to be on it.

Of all the things that could have woken me up, it was the grainy yet damp sensation of dirt on my hands that did the trick.

Not the rain pelting me. Not the lash of wind chilling me to the bone. Not the fact that I was outside when I should be warm in my bed. No, those kernels of awareness came later. It was those simple granules of earth on my fingertips.

My first thought before I took in the world around me was, *Mom's gonna be pissed.* Yes, even being a twenty-two-year-old college senior, I gave a shit what my mommy thought. Especially when my mother was the reigning queen of finding me asleep in my bed with a spent charcoal in my hand and losing her freaking mind. To my credit, I hadn't been the one who decided I should live at home while I went to college. Nor had I been the one who'd insisted on crisp white sheets for a person who was perpetually covered in the remnants of whatever art medium she'd used that day.

Nope, that was on her.

Aching and groggy, it took a full minute to understand that I was, A—outside, and B—in the middle of a cemetery. At night. In a damp, nearly see-through nightgown that had never once graced my wardrobe.

Seemed legit.

Honestly, if I weren't in so much pain—if my gut wasn't roiling with hunger and my head wasn't feeling like someone had taken a pickax to it, I could've sworn I was dreaming. Well, not dreaming exactly. Having a nightmare would be more like it. I mean, why else would I be covered in dirt, sitting on the freshly dug mound of a grave?

It took a hell of a lot of concentration to read the headstone, but I wasn't at all surprised to read my own name: Sloane Emerson Cabot, with my birth and death date right underneath it.

As nightmares went, this was pretty solid. Too bad I had the sneaking suspicion I was in no way dreaming. After what seemed like ages, I moved, struggling to stand on unsteady legs. I stumbled, tripping over my own feet as I plopped back down on the loose earth of another freshly dug grave. I didn't want to look at the headstone, but it was hard to miss. It was double-sized, the granite slab meant for a couple.

The cold finally touched me then. The rain lashed at my face, the pain smashing into me in a wave so vast it threatened to pull me under as I read the names etched into the stone.

Rosalind and Peter Cabot. Right underneath their names was a death date that matched mine.

I heaved, even though my stomach was empty and had been for what felt like a year. When it finally calmed down, I stood again, wobbled, but managed to stay vertical long enough to recognize the cemetery. I passed it every day on my way to school. Whispering Pines Cemetery was three blocks away from my house. In the opposite direction, closer to campus, was the police station.

Dithering, freezing, and hungrier than I'd ever been in my life, I fought with myself.

Should I go see if this was all a bad dream and hope my parents were sitting in their favorite chairs in our living room? Or did I go with my gut, knowing this wasn't fake or a dream or some elaborate prank? Did I go to the police—the only people I could think of who might be able to help me understand this mess?

You could go to Aunt Julie.

That thought streaked across my brain, like a flare in the darkness. Aunt Julie wasn't my aunt, but my mother's best friend. She might know what happened. But Julie was on the other side of town, not two blocks down the street. Cops first. They could call Aunt Julie. They could tell me if this was all one big joke.

Or they could lock you up in an insane asylum. That was an option, too.

No. Someone had done something to me. Someone had hurt me—hurt us. The police would help. They would call Aunt Julie. They would straighten this whole mess out. Or I'd wake up. That was still on the table.

My stomach wrenched, the pain so acute, I stumbled to my knees again. But I had a purpose. I had a place to go and a job to do. So, I got up, pointed my feet to the station, and put one foot in front of the other until I was moving.

My first obstacle was a chained gate, the arched metal moving with the wind. It screeched back and forth, almost like it was laughing at me. I grabbed the padlock, the bulky metal unyielding in my hand one second, and then cracking and breaking into little bits the next. It was true that I might have had a minor hissy fit when I saw the chained and padlocked wrought-iron gate. But my temper tantrum broke the likely rusted-out lock, and I pushed the stupidly heavy gate open. The hinges squealed even more, loud enough to wake the dead. At that thought, I started cackling like I had lost the very last bit of my mind.

But soon, laughing hurt my ribs, and my stomach pitched once more, causing me to catch myself on the trunk of a young poplar tree before I went down again. I stumbled toward my goal—the stone-faced municipal building that was half-jail and half-police station, the courthouse right across the street.

One foot in front of the other, Sloane. Keep moving.

For some reason, I heard that in my mother's voice. It reminded me of all the family hikes we'd gone on, the ones that we seemed to turn into a competitive sport with me losing every single time. Who thought ruck marches in the mountains for time was a family bonding moment? My parents, that's who.

Don't look back, sweet girl. Only forward.

The streetlight was my beacon in the darkness—all I had to do was follow my mother's words, and I'd be okay. It would all be okay. I trudged along, deciding to take a shortcut through the alley instead of following the sidewalk around the block when I retched on the pavement.

The contents of my stomach were a dark viscous liquid that smelled heavily of pennies. I didn't look too hard at what came up, but I didn't have a whole lot of time. I didn't feel so hot.

The brick walls of the alley buffeted the wind and a bit of the rain that seemed to want to lash sideways at me. The shivers didn't rattle my bones so hard, and at that tiny bit of relief, I wanted to curl up in the filth of the neglected lane and fall asleep. But, I only had a little bit farther to go.

Keep going, girl.

I heard the man before I saw him. Smelled him, too. But I was too busy staring at the blue and white Whispering Pines Police Department sign that kept me moving to really realize what the back of my brain was trying to tell me.

My hindbrain was screaming "Danger!" while my stupid front brain only thought about a cheeseburger and a bed and finding my parents. Still, I didn't see him until he was damn near on top of me—the burn of liquor on his breath making me gag. His hands were pale, like the thin fingers of death under his billowing sweatshirt and thick jacket. His face was mostly obscured by the hood, so I didn't catch the red to his eyes or length of his fangs until he'd shoved me against the bricks, their rough exterior digging into my shoulders.

I kicked—my only option since my wrists were caught in his long-fingered grip. He squeezed so hard the bones ground together—but my feeble attempts to injure him were met with a chuckle, eerie enough to keep me up at night.

"You think a fledgling is going to stop me? *Pfft*." His scoff was punctuated by a resounding crack across my face before he yanked my wrists over my head and pulled me up, my feet dangling above the ground. "Your maker should have told you to stay out of another vampire's territory. *Tsk, tsk, tsk*. I suppose I'll just have to send them a message. Your dead body should do just fine."

None of his words made much sense other than "dead body." Those I got loud and clear.

The rest? Not so much.

My stomach took that particular moment to wrench as if someone was reaching into my middle and yanking it out. Given the red-eyed man was currently licking his chops, I had to look down to make sure my flesh was still intact. Without a better option, I brought my knee up, catching him in the middle. He dropped me with a pained "oof!" and I fell to the dirty street. Only then did I rake my hand across his face, my pitiful nails not hurting him too much, but drawing blood all the same.

"You little shit," he growled, backhanding me—knocking me back into the rough bricks. But I barely felt the pain of his blow.

No, I was too focused on the heavenly scent coming from his skin. It smelled like the juiciest steak, and my hunger rose, punching me so hard I felt my mouth water and my gut twist. Before I could fully comprehend what was happening, my teeth were in his throat.

Not at. *In.*

They had punched through his flesh while my body wrapped around him like a barnacle—latching onto anything that would keep the dark, blissfully tangy liquid running down my throat. It was like life was flowing into me, and it was all I could do to keep it.

All at once, images flooded my brain. Flashes of scenes no one wanted to see. Like the man—Jacob was his name— stealing the innocence of a girl who regrettably crossed his path. Or when he snapped the neck of an elderly bespectacled man in a tweed jacket who only asked him for the time. Or a mother and her baby…

Jacob had lived a very long time, and all the while, he'd hurt every single human who'd been unlucky enough to have been in his general vicinity. He hated humans. He hated everyone, and he meted out that hate at any and every opportunity.

I barely felt it when he fell to his knees, or when his ancient heart stopped beating. I drank and drank until there was nothing left. And then I tried to drink a little more. The pair of us were crumpled in the filth of that alley, and I didn't care one bit. All I wanted—no, *needed*—was more of that delicious liquid. My teeth were buried in Jacob's throat, even though there was nothing left of him to take.

Still, I hungered. And still, I took.

I couldn't say for sure when I knew I was consuming his soul—when I knew I was taking everything that he was—to satiate my need. It was definitely during the act itself, but I couldn't say how I knew. But only after I'd consumed the very last bit of his life force, did I fully realize what I'd done.

How I'd changed.

What I had become.

Shakily, I stood—staring down at the blood-soaked nightgown and the filth on my feet and the withered husk of Jacob's body that was quickly crumbling to ash.

Jacob had been a monster, and now, so was I.

My gaze slowly rose to the blue and white sign, that just a few minutes ago, was a beacon in the night, a place to seek refuge. Now it was nothing but a glaring reminder of what I had just done.

I couldn't go to the police. I couldn't go to Aunt Julie. Not if I could do to her what I'd done to him.

All I knew for sure was there was a grave in Whispering Pines Cemetery with my name on it.

Maybe it would be a good idea to just stay dead.

2

ONE YEAR LATER

The benefits of being dead very rarely made up for the whole "not being alive" bit of the utter shitshow I now called my existence. Well, I couldn't say for sure if I was dead or not. My heart still beat, my hair grew. I ate food… sometimes. I used the facilities when I needed them.

Okay, so the eating thing didn't happen as often as it used to. But I didn't burn in the sun and holy water didn't sting. *I'd checked.*

Yeah, I drank blood, and I'd be grossed out for sure if it didn't taste so damn good. But that was a precursor to the real meal—the soul eating part. Not that they were particularly scrumptious, but they were filling, that was for sure.

Taking the life and soul of the vampire who'd attacked me had been what brought me here, and honestly, if it hadn't been for him, I wouldn't be able to kill the fuckers who harmed innocent people. Wouldn't be able to get their asses off the streets before they could kill or hurt someone else. That was the only thing I liked about this life—watching bad guys get what was coming to them.

It certainly wasn't the benefits or pay.

Since that fateful night, I made a habit of combing the streets of Ascension, searching for men like Jacob. Over the last year I'd chowed down on many a soul. To my credit, I only ate bad people, and if what I saw when I drank their blood was anything to go by, well… I was doing the world a favor. I'd get a meal, the world would be safer, and I'd feel a little better about my place in it. Which was why I was planning on planting the rapidly desiccating corpse in my truck in the same cemetery where I'd woken up a year ago.

I couldn't say for certain why I frequented the place. There were plenty of uninhabited woods in this part of the country. Plenty of hills that hadn't seen a soul in about fifty years. I could've buried this guy in one of them, but I didn't.

Now, that wasn't to say that all the people I'd consumed were vampires like Jacob. Not all of them were even a little bit supernatural. Or what was it they called themselves again? *A member of the Arcane world.*

Like that wasn't a mouthful.

Every now and again, I would throw a human into rotation if I caught them doing something they shouldn't. Like attacking women, beating children—that kind of thing. There was one guy who'd kicked a puppy into a wall. I made that guy wet himself before I drank him down.

Truth be told, I wasn't sorry for the lives I'd taken. That probably made me a horrible person, but as a newly formed villain, I just didn't give a shit.

My first order of business after taking Jacob's soul had been to pilfer his ash-laden clothes for his wallet. I'd gleaned enough from his memories to know he only kept cash and had a place in Ascension, a city on the other side of Whispering Pines. Ascension was big—bigger than the college town I'd grown up in—and there I started over, in a way. If one could call squatting starting over.

I had a good reason for being in Whispering Pines on this wretched evening, despite the smell of snow on the air and the bite to the wind. Said reason was currently rotting in the back of my truck, and it was going to take a bottle of Johnny Walker Blue Label, and at a minimum, two bills to get old Gerry to keep quiet about this.

Unlike when Jacob's body crumbled to ash, this body was too new, too fresh to give me the easy way out. My best guess —and about all I had was guesswork—was the younger the person, the fresher the body, the slower the decomp. Jacob, my first soul, had been nearly six hundred years old.

This one, not so much.

To my credit, the human I'd just snuffed out was the literal worst, and if I'd still been human, I would have seriously considered putting a bullet in his brain. Alas, I was not human, and Jeffery Carver Kingston III deserved it. If I could have resurrected him and killed him twice, I would have, but I wasn't that lucky. As it was, I'd have to be careful. Old Jeff here had a family with more money than scruples, and they'd be wondering where he'd gone if I didn't get him planted soon. Not that much could be done if the trail led the cops to a dead woman.

I swiped the expensive booze and hauled myself out of the truck. It wasn't mine, exactly, but I'd confiscated it from a rather unsavory gentleman after he'd been a snack. Finders, keepers, and all that. I'd have to give it up soon enough.

I minced my way around divots in the turf as I crushed over the dying grass to the groundkeeper's office. Gerry Ainsworth was an old, decrepit drunk with exactly zero interest in my comings and goings. After I paid him handsomely with booze and money, he paid me no never mind about what I did with his backhoe.

Usually.

The echo of a game show bounced through the hallway as I made my way to Gerry's office. The old man was just about the only person I talked to nowadays. I couldn't say we were on good terms, exactly, but he didn't ask too many questions.

Except for tonight.

I hadn't even been in the room two seconds—and he hadn't bothered to take his eyes off the screen—before he started in on me.

"You some kind of assassin or something?" he rasped, his voice gravelly, either from his smoking habit, his whiskey habit, or a combination of the two.

A chuckle bubbled its way up my throat. "Or something. I've come bearing gifts."

I met Gerry not long after I woke up at the foot of my own grave. Covered in blood, eyes glowing, and wearing a dead man's hoodie, Gerry had said I looked like a nightmare. Not much surprised the old man, and at sixty-seven, he'd informed me I wasn't the first dead thing to cross his path.

All in all, the conversation was less than comforting, but Gerry didn't call the cops and we'd set up a little bargain. Plus, he was the only person I could really go to when the bodies started piling up.

Gerry peeled his gaze from his show. "What have ya got for me?"

I showed him the box, enjoying when his eyes lit up when he saw the label. His smile was practically beatific when I slapped three hundred-dollar bills on his desk before gently placing the booze on top.

"Keys, please." He didn't reach for the drawer, which I knew held the keys to the backhoe. Gerry and I weren't too big on conversation, so his hesitation was more than a little worrisome.

As strong as I was, I had no interest in digging a grave by hand. No, thank you.

His gaze slid to the left, not quite looking away but also not meeting my eyes. "These people you kill, they're bad, right?"

Coy. I would go with coy. "Who says I kill people, Gerry? Maybe I just like digging in the dirt."

He sat back in his chair, the support brace creaking like it would snap at any second. "I figure, they have to be bad. 'Cause if they weren't, you probably would have killed me by now."

I snickered. "Yes, Gerry, if I were a serial killer, I probably would have killed you by now. But then again, I'd have to find my own backhoe, and those aren't cheap." I held out my hand, uneasiness hitting me square in the chest when he flinched. "Keys?"

"You can't keep doing this, Sloane," he whispered, and if I didn't have such good hearing, I probably wouldn't have caught the fear in his voice. "Someone is going to notice. There's already talk of a vigilante out killing people."

Funny, I hadn't read a word about a vigilante in any local news article. Not at all. And I'd been watching, too.

At my confused expression, he chuckled. "Not in the human news, kid. But the arcane world is small. Big fish go missing? People talk. Someone is going to connect the dots right back to you if you don't cool it."

Doubtful. Real freaking doubtful.

"I hear you."

Gerry gave me a mirthless laugh. "Sure you do, kid." He slapped the keys in my hand. "This is the last time, Sloane. You got me?"

"Fine," I growled, letting a little peek of my other side leak into my eyes. If Gerry knew how this had all gotten started, he might have been a little more sympathetic. Then again, maybe not.

Sympathetic and Gerry didn't really go together.

I swiped a clod of dirt off my forehead before digging a shovel back into the mound to my left. For the zillionth time that evening, I hefted a shovelful of earth from the pile and dumped it into the nearly full grave.

I swear, Sam and Dean made it look so easy.

Sure, I could have used the backhoe, but it just didn't feel right. Not after Gerry's warning. If someone were hunting me, wouldn't I have heard about it?

Where? In your freaking knitting circle?

My bitchy self had a point. I didn't talk to anyone except for Gerry. Where else was I going to learn this shit?

Digging my shovel back into the dwindling mound of dirt, I sighed. It had only been a year, but I was already tired of this shit. Tired of never running out of bad people to drink down. Tired of all the horrible things I saw when I read their blood.

Tired of not having a home, of jumping from one abandoned squatter's nest after the other.

I didn't know why I tried to stay near here. There was nothing left of my childhood home. I'd gone back, even though I'd known I shouldn't. All that had been there was a burned-out shell of a house and not much else.

And the graves of my parents? Those had been real.

My gaze lifted from the fresh mound of dirt to the direction my parents were buried. I'd been the only one who'd woken up that night. I'd been the only one to turn into whatever the hell I was. My best guess? I was some kind of vampire. Even though the ones I'd met—okay, *ate*—didn't look too much like me.

For starters, my fangs were nothing like theirs. No needles for teeth or anything like that. No, when my fangs grew, they just looked like longer, sharper canines. And my eyes never got that eerie red glow, either. Instead, they were more of a vibrant purple. I drank blood—and a lot of it—and I was for sure nocturnal, but otherwise? I felt pretty normal.

Mostly. If by normal you meant a vengeful, supernatural creature with a soul-eating habit, then sure. Normal was my middle name.

I tamped my shovel down on the dirt, smacking the fluffy earth into a hard-packed mound before sprinkling a heavy dose of grass seed. Next was the water. After that, I gathered my supplies, rolled up the hose, and put everything back where it belonged, flipping off the backhoe like it had done me wrong.

Honestly, Gerry was lucky I hadn't shoved those keys up his ass.

Dirty, sweaty, and more irritated than anyone as deadly as I was had a right to be, I climbed back into my pilfered ride and started the engine. The man I'd stolen it from wasn't going to be using it anytime soon.

Or ever, really.

I'd enjoy one last cruise in it before donating it to the local wrecking yard. A shame since it was the nicest vehicle I'd ever semi-owned.

I wanted to think this would be the last time I'd be digging a grave. I wanted to think this would be the last time I'd have to. But I was lying to myself, the same way I'd lied to myself a year ago when I thought the police could have helped me, or that this life was all one big joke.

Denial was a real bitch sometimes.

3

The wind bit into my flesh as I perched on the ledge of an abandoned building the next night. If I had any sense, I would be in a lounge chair sipping a warm drink as I did my nightly surveillance, but apparently, I was a masochist. At nearly four in the morning, it was a little too close to dawn for my liking, and the wind was keeping me awake.

The sun wouldn't burn me, but I would be lethargic in the daylight. Plus, the closer it got to dawn, the closer I was to my internal night-night time. It wasn't like I'd drop dead or anything, but I wouldn't be a picnic to deal with, either. Plus, the closer to daylight it was, the harder I'd find it to do what I was on the godforsaken ledge for in the first damn place.

The building I was spying on had to be an arcane club of some kind. It wasn't like members of the arcane wore a sign or anything, but it didn't take a genius to pick them out of a crowd. Their skin was just a little too pretty, their eyes just a little too jaded, their posture just a little off. They moved with a fluid sort of poise that no human could emulate. Like they were in charge of every millimeter of their bodies.

I said "their," but I fell under the arcane world, too, now didn't I? Which was a fact that I was not at all comfortable with. Every single member of the arcane I'd met had been a sleazeball of the highest order. I wasn't too keen on lumping myself in that group if I could help it.

I watched this club with a fair bit of regularity. I didn't trust members of the arcane world. In my experience—and based on what I'd gleaned from the secrets hidden in their blood—sooner or later, humans always paid the price for their existence. They were their victims, their food, or at times, their playthings.

I couldn't count how many attacks I'd stopped in the last year. Couldn't count how many people I'd stopped from dying. Sure, I wasn't picky about my meals—human, arcane, whatever—but the second I caught an arcaner doing something they shouldn't, I took them out. If I could stop just one girl waking up like I did, well, I was doing something right.

I could feel the bass notes through my feet a building away as the club rocked on into the night. Last call had to be sometime soon, right? Checking my watch, I sighed. Three fifty-five. Last call would be in three... two... one...

The ding of the last-call bell clanged so hard I could hear it over the din of the club. If I were a human, I wouldn't be able to hear the dance music through the heavily insulated walls, but with my freaky ears, I could. I couldn't imagine being on the inside of the building. My head would likely explode from the sheer noise alone.

Shivering, I yanked a cropped strand of hair out of my face and vainly tried to tuck it behind my ear. On top of the thirst for blood, weird purple eyes, and new nocturnal schedule, the ghostly white hair was another tick in the "weird" column.

Honestly, I might as well tattoo "freak" on my forehead and call it a day. If I was going to perch on the ledge of a building like some macabre gargoyle, I should probably be smart enough to at least don a beanie and a sweatshirt. The leather pants were cute and all, but they didn't cover all of me.

I was too busy lamenting the loss of my brunette hair and green eyes—and my solidly packed wardrobe filled with decent winter clothes—that I missed it when the door opened the first time. Club-goers streamed in groups toward the full parking lot, all except a dark-haired woman. Instead of the well-lit lot, she turned down a particularly dark alley. She hunched in on herself like she was fighting the cold, her steps not as smooth as the typical arcaner.

Was she human?

Humans occasionally frequented clubs like this one, but often, they had an escort or were in a padded illusion of safety that only a group could provide. This girl was alone, walking down an alley just like I had before Jacob found me.

I knew, logically, that Jacob hadn't made me like this—that he hadn't been the one to turn me into a monster—but I still blamed him all the same.

Groaning, I stood to get a better vantage on the girl. If I didn't move, I'd lose her, and something in the back of my mind told me to follow. Told me to make sure she stayed safe. That teensy niggle of unease turned into a screeching alarm when I spied a tall man slam out of the club. His head covered in a dark hood, I couldn't quite make out the features of his face, save for the faint luminescence coming from the general vicinity of his eyes.

He tilted his head back, seeming to sniff the air before he whipped it in the direction of the woman.

Shit.

Without much consideration on my part, I promptly hauled

my ass to the fire escape. I'd totally tried that whole "jump off a building" thing a year ago, and there would never be any superhero landings for me. Not anymore.

Jumping off a building hurt. A lot.

I slid down the ladder like this was not my first rodeo—maybe my fourth or fifth—managing to avoid landing on a noisy aluminum trashcan. Barely. I could not, however, avoid the crunch of my thick boots landing on a glass bottle. I supposed I was just fortunate that the damn thing didn't defy the laws of physics and slip out from under my boot like a banana peel. Luckily, my prey was a little too preoccupied with his quarry to pay any attention to me or the seemingly deafening crunch of glass.

A calming breath was in order, but I just couldn't spare the time. I'd lost sight of both the girl and the guy, and as awesome as my sense of smell was, it wasn't like I was part bloodhound. I couldn't just sniff the air like the man had. Out-in-the-open scents dissipated faster than I could smell them. Still, I had a good idea where the guy was headed, so as quietly as I could, I advanced in that direction, praying the shush of my boots didn't make that much of a racket.

The alley smelled of urine, old trash, human waste, new trash, and ozone. Being so close to an arcane club, the ozone smell wasn't exactly surprising. I hadn't seen a lot of it—not outside of my prey trying to get away—but magic had a scent all on its lonesome, and spent magic had a very distinct smell.

The faint strains of a woman's distress reached me as they echoed off the nearby buildings, her fear and pain hitting me square in the gut. Done with worrying about the noise, I sprinted toward my quarry. My fangs had already begun to descend, their sharp points ready and willing to tear into the man's throat.

I hadn't been hungry a second ago, but the thought of

ripping his throat open, the thought of making him cry out instead of her, made me fucking ravenous.

It didn't take too long to catch up to them. The woman was on the ground, scrambling backward in a pitiful little crab walk away from the man as the filth of the alleyway stained her jeans. The thud of the man's boots ricocheted through my chest as he stepped closer to her. Magic bloomed over his hands, and based on that alone, I was fairly certain he was a mage of some kind.

Mages were tricky, crafty little buggers. I hadn't come across too many, the majority of them preferring to do their dirt away from prying eyes. If I let him get a hit in, I would be hurting, so my best—hell, my only—course of action was to knock his ass out before he caught on that I was there.

All of this would have been easy to do if the woman hadn't alerted him to my presence right as I was about to strike. Honestly. Was the deep Scarlet Ohara gasp really necessary?

The man spun, his trajectory now target-locked on me. Unerringly, his magic hit me square in the chest, knocking me into a brick wall, hard enough that I heard it crumble beneath me.

I could tell the spell he'd used was probably meant for someone with a little less power than I possessed, because while hitting the wall stung a bit, it didn't actually hurt—no matter what my back, knees, hips, and skull said.

They were lying bastards, anyway.

Peeling myself out of the Sloane-sized dent in the bricks, I steeled myself for another blow.

But instead of hitting me again, he tried warning me off. "This is none of your business. Back off."

I couldn't see his face any better from this angle than I could at the top of the building. Damn mage tricks. He'd probably spelled his hood so it hid his face.

"Or what? You'll wave your sparkle fingers at me again?" I couldn't stop the taunting chuckle that slipped past my lips. "Nah, I think I'd rather have a snack."

He took a step back, seeming to expect me to lunge again, which revealed who he regularly dealt with. Dumb fighters struck when the opponent could see them. Smart ones did not. No, I zigged when he expected me to zag, coming at him from the side with a solid kick to his knee. I felt more than heard the pop as his knee gave way when I brought my fist down on his temple. Sparkle Fingers managed to move at the last second, so my blow only glanced off the side of his head rather than landing square. Unfortunately for him, he was introduced to the business end of my knee, the sickening crunch of his nose breaking both gross and supremely satisfying. The sight of his eyes rolling back in his head more so.

Blood drip, drip, dripped, and I felt each individual drop as they hit the ground. My hunger slammed into me, but there was no way I could drink this guy down in front of a witness.

As divine as his blood smelled, I was hungry, *not* stupid.

Still, it took a few moments too long for my attention to break from the blood and land on the woman. Shaking myself, I managed to get my bloodlust under control.

"You okay?" I called to the shivering woman. She should be, she was sitting smack-dab in the middle of a puddle. "Did he hurt you?"

She shook her head, her movement a little too manic, a little too wobbly, her long braids half-hiding her face. "N-no. Yo-you st-stopped him. Th-thank you."

I suddenly wished I had something warm to offer her, but all I had was what I was wearing. She probably had a home. I did not. The guy, though, had on a warm jacket. Reaching down, I yanked the fabric off his shoulders, tugging the sleeves free with only a few rips to show for it.

"Here." I offered her the pilfered coat. "You'll freeze."

Still shaking, she just stared up at me. "Wh-why did you help me? Most people would have ju-just walked on by."

Could I explain a year's worth of drama in a single pithy quote?

No, I could not.

The best I could do was give her a shrug. "I'm just not built that way." I offered her a hand up. "Get warm, get home, and for fuck's sake, stay out of alleys. They aren't safe."

Holding out the coat, I impatiently waited for her to slide into it. She blinked at me, belatedly catching the hint and slipped her arms into the sleeves. There, good deed done, and all that. It was dinnertime.

"Off you go. Lighted paths and no alleys, got it?" I advised, turning my head to the blissfully tangy aroma of the mage's blood.

"I really do feel sorry about this," she muttered, and I whipped my head back to her a fraction too late.

Arms banded around my shoulders from behind, as the woman I'd just saved blew a handful of white dust in my face. The powder hit me like a stack of bricks as I lost control over my limbs. Unconsciousness didn't hit me right away, so I saw the regret filling her expression a split second before I was pulled into darkness.

4

After waking up at the foot of your own grave, anytime you woke up in a place you didn't remember bedding down in was a bit of a shock. Hence why I popped up off the cement floor like a fucking jack-in-the-box, ready to fight whoever or whatever was closest. It would figure that instead of being in the middle of a war, I was smack-dab in the middle of a cell.

It was a nice one, as far as cells went, but it was a cell, nonetheless. A concrete floor was beset on three sides by gray cinderblock walls, their faces carved with symbols I couldn't decipher. The back of the gray room held a made-up cot with a plush mattress, pillows, and a duvet. Beside it was a privacy screen, with tiny pink flowers hand-painted on the rice paper panels that hid what I hoped was a toilet. In front of the privacy screen was a small table with a stool nestled underneath, topped with a few books, a tray of food, and a pad of sketch paper.

No pens or pencils were in sight, instead there was a familiar wooden box next to the pad. I knew if I opened it, my favorite brand of charcoals would be inside. I couldn't say why, but just looking at that box made me want to smash it. My mother had bought me a set—grudgingly, I might add—when I was eight. My art teacher, Mr. Sigmund, had reverently showed us his set, and the Japanese brand did not come cheap. I'd begged six months for that set, and when my mother routinely told me no, I saved my allowance for it. I mowed lawns for it, raked leaves, pulled weeds. But the set of charcoals were expensive, and regardless of my little eight-year-old drive, I wouldn't be able to afford them.

She'd surprised me with that very set for my birthday, and I'd burst into tears, hugging her so tight. I remembered how her hair smelled that day, like jasmine and citrus, and the first thing I'd drawn with my brand-new charcoals had been my mother's face. I was eight, and it was in no way a masterpiece, but my mom kept that picture in her pocketbook.

A pocketbook that was likely burned to ash just like everything else we ever had. Just like my parents.

"Do you like them?" a woman asked, and I slowly turned my gaze to the fourth wall. It wasn't a wall at all but a cell door, the bars etched with the same symbols as the walls. Likely the markings were spells meant to keep me in. Keep me trapped.

The woman was sitting on a plain metal folding chair, one leg crossed over the other, her air of confidence ill-fitting her choice of seat. She wore a pristine white pants suit, a black crew-neck top, with a pair of zebra-print stilettos on her feet. I couldn't tell if they were real or a knockoff, but if the red soles and crisp lines of the suit were any indication, then they were likely as real as they got. Her hair was a wavy auburn that was just a shade lighter than true red, with a pair of eyes an odd reddish-whiskey color that reminded me of fresh-spilled blood but could pass for brown to a less-discerning eye.

She wasn't old nor was she young. Really, she appeared my mother's age, the faint kiss of time fanning out from her eyes. She had a tiny little upturn to her nose, which should make her appear cute, but I had a feeling this lady hadn't been called cute *ever*, and she'd probably gut the first dumb bastard to try.

"The charcoals," she prompted like I was simple, "do you like them?"

I flashed my teeth in a failed attempt at a smile. "To be honest?" She nodded for me to continue. "I'm having a hell of a time not smashing them to slivers."

She gave me a smile in return, only hers was genuine and not a bearing of teeth and fangs. "Your candor is refreshing, Sloane. As are your actions." She uncrossed her legs and recrossed them, her left switching places with the right. She settled onto her chair, too, resting her back on the unyielding metal. "When we picked you up, I was under the impression we'd be putting down a mass-murdering Rogue, not a perky blonde with a do-gooder attitude."

Her words didn't smell like the truth—and I couldn't tell you *how* I knew she was bullshitting me, I just did. Still, I had no intention for the word to slip from my mouth, even though it did without consulting my brain.

"Liar."

The woman's smile widened like she was pleased. Then, she sighed like I was giving her a present, the sheer relish on her face enough to turn my stomach. "Oh, I'm going to like you, Sloane."

I couldn't say why, but that statement was not comforting. Not at all.

"My name is Emrys Zane, and I run the Night Watch." At my blinking confusion, she elaborated, gesturing at my cell. "This is the Night Watch. Well, a part of it. Typically, we don't hold many people down here. The ABI carts off the ones they see fit for trial. Very few even see these cells. The Night Watch takes the cases the ABI refuse to, or rather, too scared to take."

"ABI?" I asked, unfamiliar with the acronym.

"Arcane Bureau of Investigation, the arcane world's police. If the ABI are the police, the Night Watch would be the bounty hunters. There are several branches of the ABI, but only one of the Night Watch."

While all this was *super* fascinating, I had a feeling she wasn't holding me here for tea and cookies. That girl in the alley had been a setup. They'd known I couldn't stop myself from helping someone in trouble. They'd *known* I would show up. The question was: why? But I didn't ask, content on letting Emrys carry on with her pitch.

"Do you know about the bounty on your head, Sloane? What it's up to?"

Considering I had no idea I even had a bounty out for me, the answer was a resounding "no."

"Can't say I do. I hope it's big." I wasn't being very nice, but I had the distinct feeling that Emrys wouldn't appreciate subterfuge.

"Three million," she murmured, the quiet words landing like a blow.

"Dollars?" I blurted, shocked anyone would be that desperate to have my head. Then again... I had killed a lot of people over the last year. A lot.

Emrys gave me a grave sort of nod. "Rather remarkable, really. There hasn't been a bounty that high in ages. You know the funny part?"

I shrugged, tossing my hands up, exasperated. "I'm sure you're going to tell me."

Emrys chuckled, before delivering another blow. "The bounty was coded for alive only and would be forfeit upon your death. I find that very interesting, Sloane. Don't you?"

I couldn't for the life of me understand why someone would want me captured alive. Maybe to study me? Torture me? Kill me themselves? None of that spelled happy things.

"Interesting is not the word I would use." I plopped down on the edge of the mattress. "You lied before, why? Did you think I wouldn't smell it, or was it a test?"

"Everything is always a test, dear. Life is a test," she said cryptically. "Yes, I wanted to know if you could sense a lie, but more, I wanted to know if you'd call me on it. You've killed over two hundred members of the arcane, not to mention an unknown number of humans. I wanted to know who I was dealing with."

If she set up the trap, she knew exactly what kind of person I was. And she was wrong. I'd killed over three hundred members of the arcane and roughly a hundred humans. "Liar."

Surprise crossed her face at that one. "No, I did not lie," she insisted, affront clear in her tone. "I have record of only two hundred and six members of the arcane missing, presumed dead, at your hand."

Now, I could confess and let her do whatever she was going to do, but letting her stew in her own misinformation sounded much more fun.

"Your records are wrong." I yawned before falling back on the rather soft mattress. It had been a while since I'd had a good bed to sleep in. Abandoned buildings and comfy home furnishings didn't exactly go hand in hand. Toeing off my boots, I got comfortable, allowing my body to sink into the plush softness. "What I'd really love to know is how many were on your books before I *allegedly* picked them off like the leeches they were? How many I caught doing things they shouldn't? How many with souls as black as night and twice as foul?"

Emrys narrowed her eyes at me, uncrossing her legs so

both spindly heels were on the ground. She could be pissed all she wanted to, I was going to enjoy the pillow and blanket. Snuggling into the bed, I closed my eyes. If I was stuck here, I might as well enjoy it. I had a feeling I wouldn't exactly be skipping once she delivered me to whoever posted that ridiculous bounty.

"And how would you know how dark their souls were?"

I cracked an eyelid, shooting her an "oh, please" look. "You know my favorite brand of charcoals, but you don't know this?" I snorted and turned to my side to really enjoy the mattress. "The sins of every man, woman, and arcaner are hidden in the blood, sweetheart."

I closed my cracked lid, but both my eyes popped open at the screech of the chair skidding. Emrys was on her feet, a mere inch from the bars. I, however, was still in bed, staring at the formerly collected woman, her reddish eyes glowing at me.

"You read their blood, correct? Their souls. And that's why you killed them all. Because they were evil." She may have started it as a question, but Emrys seemed to be working the details out on her own. "A soul reader," she whispered under her breath, the title filled with a reverence I didn't understand.

Maybe I didn't want to understand.

With that, she abruptly turned and strode out of sight, a loud clanging of a metal door sealing shut punctuating her departure. And as much as I would have loved to settle into the plush mattress, I was instead filled with the distinct impression that I should have kept my mouth shut.

My internal clock was reading that dawn was approaching again when the tell-tale squeak of hinges signaled someone's arrival. The meal left for me was cold and congealed and one hundred percent undisturbed.

I had no desire to be drugged, thank you.

But that also meant I was a might bit peckish, AKA, hungry enough to eat a bear.

Unlike the delicate tap of Emrys' shoes, the heavy steps coming my way signaled a *hugely* different visitor. I propped myself up on my pillows, wanting to see the man who was likely here to lead me to my doom. He was dark-haired and tan-skinned, a wealth of stubble on his cheeks and chin, like using a razor was a personal affront. He wore a black shirt, leather pants, and boots, and held himself delicate like he was hurt as he lowered himself onto the chair. Instead of looking at me, he raked a hand through his hair and sighed.

His exhaustion was real enough, but I knew—*don't ask me how*—this was an act. He smelled of half-truths and deception. Unlike Emrys, I decided not to call him on it. A faint scent tickled the air, faint, barely there, but I smelled it all the same. It was a familiar scent, and my fangs descended all on their very lonesome.

But it wasn't just because I was hungry. It was because I knew exactly who he was.

His pale-hazel gaze met my purple one.

The guy from the alley.

5

Sparkle Fingers—as he would be dubbed until I actually knew his name—was a ball of giggles. He exuded happiness and light and exactly zero hostility or malice.

Deep grooves wrinkled the space between his eyes as he regarded me like one would a clump of dog shit on their boot. Honestly? It was like I was staring at my own personal executioner. A personal executioner with a now-crooked nose that seemed to still need some mending.

A very crazy part of me wanted to giggle at him just to see if his head would explode. I mean, what was I going to do? Run away screaming?

I was stuck in this cell with nowhere to run and no place to hide. I hadn't messed with the runes carved in the walls or bars —my gleaned-yet-limited knowledge had warned me not to try. At least the sins I read in the blood I drank was good for something, other than the inevitable spiral into mental illness. Information was always a good thing to have.

Plus, he seemed cranky, and I had no place else to be. Might as well make this shit fun.

"Come to take me away already? Shame. I was just getting cozy." I punctuated my words by wiggling in the mussed covers, showing him just *how* cozy I found them.

Sparkle's frown deepened as he scratched his fingers through the stubble on his cheek. He sniffed and then winced, his hand moving to cover his nose before he thought better of it. "You seem pretty happy with your accommodations. I've never seen someone so pleased to have a bed."

His voice sounded different than when he'd warned me off in the alley, his accent losing its American and landing solidly in British territory. *Faker.*

"How's the nose? Have you had it reset yet?" He opened his mouth to likely bullshit me, but I stopped him. "And before you feign surprise, I know it was you in that alley. You still have blood on you, Cupcake, and you smell delicious." I let my otherness peek out of my eyes as I showed him a bit of fang.

I figured he would startle—it was what every other arcaner had done when they saw my teeth—but his frown only deepened.

"Look, I don't want you here. None of us want you here. But Emrys seems to think you're worth saving, and I'd rather follow her orders than anyone else's. She's willing to say you went rabid and had to be put down." He stopped, shaking his head before shooting to his feet. "She's willing to void a three-million-dollar contract."

Man, this guy was excitable. Sparky started pacing the corridor in front of my cell, and every time he tried breathing through his nose, he would just get more and more pissed off.

"I take it this favor comes at a price?" I called on his third pass because old Sparky wasn't talking, and I was getting bored with the sales pitch.

He stomped back to my cell door, hissing when his skin

made contact with the bars. I could hear his flesh sizzling. I could smell it, too. Not. Appetizing.

"If you think we're just going to void a three-million-dollar contract out of the goodness of our hearts..." He pushed off the bars, his macho show of strength over.

"But it's not 'we,' is it? You aren't doing shit. She's voiding the contract. What I want to know is what's expected out of me? Nothing's free in this world, Sparky, I know that. So, what does she want?"

There were things I couldn't do. *Wouldn't* do. As mercenary a bitch as I was, I wouldn't kill people who didn't deserve it. I wouldn't hurt children, *ever*. And I wasn't going to be anyone's slave. If any of those rules were going to be violated, she might as well truss me up, hand me over, and get her payday.

Because the other option would *not* go well for her.

I told Sparky as much.

"I don't think you understand the gravity of your situation," he began, his condescending tone raking against my nerves.

My chuckle was dark and forbidding. "I think it's you who doesn't understand. I have nothing to lose. Not one thing you could hold against me. I don't have a home or a family or a life. I cannot be bought or bribed or bargained with. She wants to void the contract, fine. That's her choice. What I'm willing to do in return is mine. Now"—Prompted, I got up from my very cozy, very missed bed—"why don't you quit your bullshit posturing, and tell me what she wants in return."

Sparky huffed, slamming himself back onto the chair like a petulant child. I waited, slipping on my boots as he debated with himself on whether or not he was going to sack up and answer me.

"Emrys thinks you're valuable." He spat the words like an accusation. "She wants to recruit you." He let loose a spectacular sneer. "Why she would want a murderer on the team is beyond me. But I follow orders, as will you."

Awww, he doesn't want me in his sandbox. Poor baby.

I couldn't say it, but I agreed with him. I *was* a murderer. If I looked at myself with any rational thought, I *was* the bad guy.

And maybe? They were safer with me in this cage than they would be with me out of it.

Still, giving him shit was much more fun than wallowing. "I kill people who deserve it, and in exchange, I get a little dinner. Would you look so callously at a lion, Sparky?"

His face turned an unhealthy shade of crimson before the door squeaked again. Light, barely-there footsteps were followed by an irritated female voice.

"You were supposed to bring her upstairs, not yak her ear off," the dainty girl with the dark braids and a smokey voice said, her small frame dwarfed by Sparky, even though he was sitting down. In the light, I recognized her as the girl from the alley, her golden skin no longer blueish with the cold. The girl dismissed him, giving him her back as she turned to me. "I'm sorry about him. He's just mad you broke his nose. I'm Dahlia, by the way."

She gave me a weird sort of wave, and then I realized she was doing intricate hand movements of a spell. The runes in my cell began to glow white, the heat of them almost scalding before the markings dimmed. The sound of a key turning in a lock rang through the room, even though it appeared as if she had no key. Then, she gripped the bars that had scalded Sparky's fingers just moments ago and swung the door wide.

Her expression was sheepish when I hesitated to leave the cell. "I really am sorry about drugging you. We thought… Well, we were under the impression you were…"

"A ravenous monster with no control and no scruples?" I quipped. "Yeah, I caught that."

Her wince only grew. "But you saved me. I know I didn't really need saving, but you thought I did. You even gave me a coat when I was cold. Monsters don't do that."

Her mind seemed to be made up—she nodded and stepped away from the door so I could exit. But it wasn't Dahlia I was worried about. Sparky was still sitting in the chair, mulishly staring at me like I was going to rip out her throat at any second. *Idiot.*

Rather than give him the satisfaction of seeing me weak, I strode through the door, giving him my back as soon as I was out. And then he did exactly what I knew he would, the prick.

He pounced.

I could feel the movement before it ever reached me, the rough push of air as he lunged. In this tight of a space, I could feel every breath he took, smell the scent of his rage hit its peak, and this close? I could hear his heart pick up speed at the very last second as his adrenaline kicked in.

So, when he tried to grab me, he clutched nothing but air.

But I wasn't as foolish. In his daze, I latched onto his shirt and slammed him into the gray wall hard enough that the stone hissed with a crack before depositing him ass over tea kettle on the floor. I grabbed his face, smooshing his cheeks and mouth with my fingers, waiting for his eyes to finally focus. When they did, I wanted to make sure he understood. I wouldn't be keeping one eye open. I wouldn't be watching my back. I was the apex predator in this scenario, not him.

And I would not be fucked with.

"The only reason you aren't dead already, is because I was trying to spare your victim from seeing me spill your blood all over the street. Attack me again, and I won't give a shit if the Pope sees, I'll gut you like a fucking fish and lick my fingers clean afterward. Don't test me, Sparky. I don't make the same mistake twice." Then, I may have bounced his stupid head off the floor as I skipped to follow Dahlia.

Okay, the skipping was probably a little petty, but whatever.

The rest of the holding area appeared similar to my cell, but there weren't many, maybe five other small rooms like mine. Only, none of them were furnished. No cot, no toilet, no desk, or screen. Each room was just cinderblock walls filled with the same runes that were in my cell. So, either they didn't get many visitors, or...

"I know how it looks." Dahlia's voice broke me from my musings. "But we don't have very many people as guests in that part of the house. Usually we make the hand off to the ABI. No muss, no fuss. I can't think of a time when there was actually a visitor in those cells."

"So, the house came equipped with a dungeon?"

She swept a handful of braids off her shoulder as she shrugged. "I'm not sure. I think it might have been a lycanthropes moon-called area at one time, but I don't really know the specifics."

My feet stuttered to a stop. "Lycanthropes?"

Dahlia took a few more steps before she noticed I wasn't following. "Wow, you're new. Yes, lycanthropes are a thing. Totally different from weres and shifters, by the way. Lycanthropes are humans infected with a specific type of rabies that mutates their DNA. It makes them turn into these weird half-man, half-animal creatures on the full moon that are *not* cute. Those went pretty much extinct a few decades ago after the ABI cracked down on the mad scientist sorcerer who was trying to 'make' weres."

At my wide eyes due to the veritable fount of information, she waved her hand at me like she was erasing her words from the air. It didn't matter. I'd seen more than a few on my one-woman rampage of Ascension.

Could a year-long culling be called a rampage?

"Don't even ask. Anyway, where was I?" She seemed to think on it for a second. "Right. Weres are arcaners with the ability to shift into a specific animal, and shifters—or shapeshifters—can change into any animal within reason. Both species have their mind intact, but are slightly more animalistic. Except for the lycanthropes. Those guys are coo-coo."

When she was done exploding my brain with info, she gestured for me to get moving, which I did, but with a definite wariness in my step.

"Emrys wants me to show you around the house before your meeting. Plus, the longer we give Bastian to calm down after getting his ass kicked for the second time in twenty-four hours, the better. Man, I've never seen him so cranky."

So Sparky was named Bastian. Short for Sebastian, I was guessing. I liked Sparky better.

"I think he's just mad he doesn't get the payday," I muttered, but I knew that wasn't true. I'd likely bruised his fragile male ego, and as much as I didn't want to, I was going to have to watch my back.

Dahlia snorted, the indelicate sound endearing on the small woman. And she was tiny. I was maybe five eight. She had to be barely pushing five foot even, and that was a stretch. But it wasn't just that she was short, it was how thin she was. I wouldn't have put her past eighteen years old, but I knew she had to be older. She had that look arcaners got when they'd seen some shit.

"Maybe," she mused. "But I think he's more afraid of you. He's one of the strongest of us—outside of Emrys and Thomas. I think he sees you as a danger for the people he cares about."

Shit. Now I felt slightly bad about spiking his head on the ground like a volleyball.

Maybe more than slightly.

6

I didn't say anything else as Dahlia continued leading me up a set of stairs to a thick metal door. At the door, she made a set of complicated hand motions, and the sound of a key in a lock rang out again like when she opened my cell.

With a faint hiss, the door cracked, and she yanked on the metal with all her strength before opening it wide to reveal a sort of opulence I was ill-prepared for. The floors were a dark wood with whorls of grain intricately swirling in each plank, the whole of which practically gleamed against the light of the delicate sconces and lamps dotting around what I assumed was a great room.

A wide staircase lay to my left, the newel post thick and forbidding and topped with a falcon with its wings spread wide. There were bookcases tucked in nooks and crannies, soft furniture that appeared far too expensive for me to sit on, and more that I couldn't see but knew was there just based on this one room.

But really?

It was the architecture that really got me. It was the high

vaulted ceilings and wide windows, the hand-carved moldings and detail. Whoever had built this place had loved it—loved it more than rest or sleep—because it must have taken years to craft all of this.

I should have figured a house with a damn dungeon would be huge, but I still managed to be caught unaware. Somehow, I seemed to feel safer in the dungeon than if I stepped out into the house proper—even with Sparky's boots clomping like a herd of buffalo behind me.

Those stomping feet—and maybe the rage laced in every stomp—were what propelled me out of the dungeon and into the great room. Dahlia hadn't stopped, she was heading up the stairs and I had to run to catch up. And if I managed to slam the heavy dungeon door in Sparky's face, well, it was totally unintentional and not at all on purpose.

My feet practically sank into the plush carpet on the stairs, the delicate pattern swirling up the steps like a wave. Maybe it was the artist in me, but I loved a well-put-together design, and everything about this place had the feel of care, of time. It made me wistful of my parent's house. That wistfulness quickly turned bitter in my chest, and I had to swallow down the hurt and rage and...

Before we reached the top landing, a head poked over the rail. Slitted green eyes and a scowling face stared right at me, rage tinting her features. Her face was positively elfin, despite the septum piercing and heavy eye makeup.

"Stop it. If you're coming up here, you need to ward your mind. It's one thing for me to deal with that bullshit outside," the small woman griped at me, her body coming into full view as we crested the landing. She gestured to the windows, waving at them like she was warding off the outside world. "But if you think I'm carrying your emotions while I'm inside my own damn home, you've got another thing coming. If you're going to be in this house, you need to figure your shit out."

Slightly startled that such a tiny person could be filled with so much rage, I cast a wide-eyed glance to Dahlia.

"Crap. I knew I forgot something," Dahlia groaned. "Don't worry, Harper. I'll get her warded in a few." She then turned back to me. "Harper, this is Sloane, our new recruit."

Harper growled, not sparing me another glance. "I don't give a fuck who she is. Ward her and then tell her to stay out of my rooms. Got it?"

I couldn't help it, I snorted. Harper and I were going to be besties. I just knew it.

"Wow." That was something else. I needed to figure out who pissed in her Cheerios and hand them a medal or something. Their irritation game had to be top notch.

Dahlia sighed before turning back to me. "Harper is an empath. One of the stronger ones. If you're within a mile of her, she can feel your emotions, which doesn't help with the whole sanity bit. I'll let Emrys ward you. Hers are the best."

"Ward me?"

She nodded, chewing on a fingernail. "Emrys is a druid. One of the last in the Americas. Not too many immigrated here, or the ones who did, didn't make it too long on this continent. South America has quite a few more, and Canada has a handful, but she's one of the last of her kind. She can ward you so tight, Harper won't have a reason to bitch at you. Which is good, because if she hates you, it's unlikely that she'll share the Wi-Fi password. Or program your tech. Or do just about anything else that requires any lick of technology. She's our tech wizard."

Dahlia paused, before wiping the air like she was erasing something. "She's not actually a wizard, by the way. She's just awesome at it. She runs comms on jobs and keeps us out of all

CCTV footage. But also? The computers interfere with the whole emotions thing. If she could feel you from her room, you must have been feeling some heavy shit. She'll likely be a complete bitch to you until you get that fixed."

"Get warded pronto. Check." I gave Dahlia a thumbs-up, letting her know I for sure got it.

"Follow me. I'll introduce you to Simon before you meet with Emrys and Thomas."

We turned right down the corridor toward a closed door decorated with "Keep Out" and "No Girls Allowed" signs. Granted, the "No Girls Allowed" sign had a piece of paper attached to it with Scotch tape with the words "Dahlia is okay" hastily written on it, the frayed edge of the paper jagged like it had been ripped out of a spiral notebook. Dahlia pounded on the door with her fist.

We heard a "come in" before she opened the door. The inside of the room was just as messy as I figured it would be. A slender guy decked out in a beanie, glasses, and flannel shirt was sitting on a couch that had seen better days. In his hand was a gaming controller and he was playing some kind of game that required a cat to fight element-wielding foes.

Not what I would expect out of a grown man, but who was I to judge his gaming needs? As long as he wasn't playing some shooter game, I was all for it.

"Simon, pause your silly cat game and meet Sloane."

Simon did not, in fact, pause his game. Instead he ignored my presence altogether while talking to Dahlia like I wasn't there. "She the one who has Harper in a twist?"

His accent was American with a faint British flair, not what I would have expected out of the mouth of a guy who wore flannel like it was his job.

"Don't be rude, Simon."

He grunted back at her, his slight shoulders shrugging. "You know the drill, babe. I don't make the rules."

"They're your rules. Of course you make the rules."

Just then, I felt something at my ankles, a slight brushing, and I glanced down. What I saw might have made me jump out of my skin if I weren't afraid I'd hurt it. A delicate amalgamation of bones in what I could only hope was the shape of a cat, brushed against my legs again like it was marking me. It was creepy as fuck and cute as hell, and I had to fight the urge not to try and pick it up. Its bones were stark white, but its eyes—which were just orbs of green smoke—cast a glow over its whole body.

I had a feeling I was supposed to be scared, but I just… wasn't. Mom had never let me have a cat, and I'd always wanted one. She said she was allergic, but I think she just didn't like that cats walked all over everything.

"Boy or girl?" I asked, instead of doing what I really wanted, which was to scoop it up and try and pet it.

"She's a girl." He paused, his words a little ruffled. "You're not scared?"

Instead of answering that stupid question, I plopped on the floor, crossing my legs as I got a better look at the skeleton kitty. "Can I pet her? What's her name?"

"Isis, and yeah. You sure you're not afraid?"

Dahlia snorted. "Not everyone is going to scream blue bloody murder and run screaming out of the house, Simon. You know that was a one-time thing."

That sounded like a story I wanted to hear, but I was busy letting the bone kitty smell my hand before I ran my fingers over her spine. "Isis, sweetheart, you are a gorgeous kitty. Don't let anyone tell you any different. If they run screaming, chase them and make them cry, okay?"

Isis jumped onto my lap, and I rubbed under her chin as she started to purr. "That's right, you fearsome little beast."

"Okay, you got my vote." Simon paused his game. "Why does Bastian hate her again?"

I snorted, but it was Dahlia who answered for me, "It's either because she broke his nose and kicked his ass, or because she's a mass murderer."

Ouch. Yeah, "mass murderer" was a title I didn't like, but the truth hurt sometimes, right? "Don't forget, I just spiked his head off the concrete and called him Sparky. That won't win me any favors. But at least you like me, don't you, Isis?"

Simon chuckled. "And you brought her in here? You had better take her to Emrys before Bastian finds out and loses the last little bit of his mind."

"That's okay, I'll just hold you and scare him off, won't I?" I said to the cat who was now making herself at home under my chin.

Simon bleated out a guffaw. "How did you know it was Bastian who ran screaming from the house?"

"Common sense? Harper doesn't seem like the kind of girl who would hang out. Dahlia is allowed in, and Emrys is too cool and collected to run screaming from anywhere. Plus, the thought of Bastian running away from a kitty is the best fucking thing I've heard in ages." I cuddled the cat closer, her fragile bones pressing into my bare forearm. "Wanna come with me, Isis? I'll scratch your chin and behind where your ears should be. It'll be fun."

To Simon I said, "I want to steal your cat. She's adorable."

"Can't," Dahlia chimed in. "We're meeting with Thomas, too, and those two don't get along. Put the adorable kitty down. I'm sure Simon won't mind you playing with her later?"

I may or may not have pouted as I reluctantly set Isis on the floor, giving her extra chin rubs before I got up. "I guess, but if she goes missing? I totally took her and probably won't give her back. Cool?"

Simon shook his head. "I've met a few mass murderers in my day. Never met one who likes cats and talks to them like they're people before." He rolled his head on his neck to face Dahlia. "You're sure she's a killer? She seems so… nice."

I let my otherness leak out of my purple eyes, flashing a bit of fang as I answered his question. "I only kill bad people. If that helps you sleep at night, I mean."

Simon's eyes widened, and he shot Dahlia a look as he shoved himself up off the couch. "You'd better get her to Emrys. The last thing we need is Bastian seeing her like that in here. Scoot."

Simon practically shoved us out of the room as he scooped up Isis and held her to his chest. I gave her one last scratch before we were summarily ousted from Simon's room and the door closed and locked.

"Simon is Bastian's little brother," Dahlia informed me. "He's all the family Bastian has left."

Which made my heart hurt for reasons I didn't want to examine.

Harper's voice floated through a closed door to my left. "Get her warded, or so help me, I will pour water on the router and cut the hard line to the house!"

With the threat made against the Wi-Fi, Dahlia latched onto my arm, and the tiny woman dragged me down the hallway.

A meeting with Emrys.

Super.

Dahlia gestured for me to knock on the door before she backed away, like she was saving herself from the portal of my imminent doom. A few steps later, she spun and raced down the hallway back to Simon's room.

Without another option left—other than vaulting the banister and hauling ass out of the house—I knocked, just a gentle three-tap that was not all hesitant or weak sounding. Nope. I was completely and totally not nervous.

Less than a second later, the door flew open to reveal a tall man with jet-black hair and a wicked grin. The strands appeared soft to the touch as they swept the sides of his jaw, tickling the thick stubble there. His grin was a little too perfect, almost sinister, which was at odds with his blindingly white smile and full lips. Maybe it was his cheekbones that were just a little too sharp, or the odd green color of his eyes against his pale-bronze coloring. Or maybe it was because he was just a little too pretty, appeared a little too lethal.

Since he was not who I was expecting, I backed up a step, hoping Dahlia had gotten confused by the boatload of doors in the hall and mixed up where I was supposed to go. A hope that was dashed not a second later when the man's smile grew before he latched onto my arm with an iron grip and hauled me in the room. He let me go in the next instant, the momentum whirling me inside the office like a top.

I was strong—like "could bend metal with my bare hands" strong. This dude made me look and feel like a wimp, and even though he hadn't hurt me, I was one hundred percent certain he could have if he'd wanted to.

"Ah, good. I was wondering what was holding you up. Bastian decided to throw a fit, did he?" Emrys said from behind a stout desk, her eyes trained on a large monitor as she clicked her mouse. "I see you've met Thomas."

Thomas? Did she mean the man who could crush me to a pulp with a flick of his fingers? I turned to look at him, but he'd moved without me noticing. I scanned the room for him, only to find him sitting in a leather wingback with a glass of amber liquid in his right hand and a lit cigar in his left. His eyes had a faint glow to them that reminded me of mine when I got riled.

I had to say, Thomas did not give me the warm and fuzzies.

"Not formally, no," I muttered, feeling awkward and unsure of myself as I stood in the middle of Emrys' office like I was in to see the principal.

"My apologies. Where are my manners?" Thomas said from his perch before setting his cigar down in an ashtray. He stood faster than my gaze could track and then he was in my space, towering over me like a creeper.

Thomas was good looking and knew it. He also knew he was at the top of the food chain.

Message received.

"What manners?" I scoffed, pressing a hand to his chest and gently moving him out of my space. I knew without a doubt in my mind that he was moving of his own accord and wouldn't if he didn't want to be moved. It was tough not to roll my eyes. "I get it. You're stronger and faster and could crush me like a bug should the spirit move you."

"As long as we understand each other," Thomas drawled, catching my hand in his as he bowed his head to give it a light peck. "Thomas Gao, and you are Sloane Cabot."

I nodded before snatching my hand back.

"Quit antagonizing her, Thomas. That is not what you are here for, and you know it."

He sent Emrys a petulant glare before sauntering at a human's speed back to his chair. "If you must ruin my fun, fine."

"Take a seat, Sloane." Emrys gestured to the two leather club chairs across from her desk.

I chose the one farthest from Thomas, a fact he noted if his derisive snort was any indication.

"I called you up here—as I'm sure Sebastian informed you —to formally invite you to be a member of the Night Watch. On a probationary basis, of course. In exchange for your services for no less than one year, you will be provided a room, board, and a stipend for expenses. After your probationary period, you may move to be a full member of the Night Watch and awarded the clearance that provides."

"Whoa, whoa, whoa. I haven't said yes yet. I want to know what it is you do. Because delivering a girl to someone for three million dollars—and it not being the governing body that wants me, but a private citizen—doesn't make me too keen on being a member. It makes me think you're into some seriously shady shit. I might be a mass-murdering sociopath, lady, but I have scruples."

Emrys' lips tipped up like she thought I was cute. "We *didn't* deliver you anywhere. As far as the customer knows, you died and were incinerated by Bastian Cartwright himself after you attacked him. And to be fair, I only took the job, because if we hadn't, someone else would have. People with less *scruples*."

I crossed my arms and sat back in my chair. "You didn't answer my question. You're quite good at that. Not answering questions."

"It used to be my job once upon a time. Now, since you insist on knowing, you will read people for us using your abilities. Not bite, not kill. Just read."

I guessed she meant no soul-eating and no blood-drinking as well.

"That's going to be a problem," I muttered under my breath. "Couple of issues with that. I've never read anyone that I didn't bite first, for one. The 'reading,' as you call it, is involuntary on my part. Two, of the people I've bitten, I haven't left a single one alive. Three, I need to eat. Human food is fun and all, but I need blood to survive."

I may have left off that whole bit about the ones I killed, I also consumed their soul, but if she didn't know, I had no intention of informing her.

"Your maker should be dragged out on the street and shot. What in the bloody hell did they teach you?" Thomas griped, his words laced with venom.

"Maker?" I shook my head. "I woke up on the foot of my own grave a year ago. I don't have a maker, and I didn't choose this."

"All vampires have a maker." Thomas rolled his eyes at me like I was an idiot. "And you have to choose this life. The covenant prevents humans from being selected any other way." His voice was snide, like he was talking to a brainless little girl instead of the cold-blooded murderer I was.

I leaned forward in my seat and let my otherness emerge

from my eyes. He wanted to think I was stupid? Fine. But I wasn't a liar.

"I don't, and I didn't." I could feel my fangs lengthening to their sharp points and digging into my bottom lip.

Before I knew it, Thomas was out of his seat and leaning over me. His fingers dug into the skin of my face as he studied my fangs and eyes. A light dawned on his expression before he let me go. "You're a blood drinker, but you're no vampire."

I knew I was different than other vampires—at least the bottom-feeding assholes I'd come across in the last year. I didn't have the red eyes or weird extra set of needle fangs that they all had.

"You, my dear, are what happens when two species mate that shouldn't."

Staring up at him, I wondered if I could punch him in the balls before he smashed my head in with his bare hands. "Excuse me?"

"If the ABI finds out about her, we're all dead. You know that, right?" Thomas griped at Emrys, before he put his glass to his lips and drank it down.

"I'm handling it. Why do you think you're here? As far as they are concerned, she is a newly minted vampire under your line, and what they don't know, will keep her and all of us alive."

Thomas scoffed. "I like my head attached to my shoulders, thank you very much. Why would I claim this little albatross?"

Emrys steepled her fingers as she rested her elbows on the arms of her chair. She leveled Thomas with an expression so piercing I had to turn away before she decided to look at me like that. "Because I already filed the paperwork, and you have no choice."

A few things made sense as I studied the room. As I stared at the bookcases lining the walls, I reordered the facts as I knew them. One: either my parents weren't human, or they weren't my real parents. Rosalind and Peter Cabot raised me. My first memory was a tea party my mother and I had with a special tea set that I'd gotten that Christmas. I was three. Two: If they weren't human, then I wasn't and never had been. Three: If I wasn't human, and neither were they, why was I here and they weren't? How was I alive?

Emrys and Thomas were still arguing, but they quit when my whispered question reached their ears. "What am I?"

Emrys, once again, answered my question without answering it at all. "You come from the union of a grave talker and a blood mage. Unlike grave talkers, you cannot see the dead, and unlike blood mages, you cannot wield blood magic. Your power is different, and because of the destruction you can cause, because of the secrets someone like you can glean, these two species are discouraged from breeding."

I shook my head, the equation just not adding up. "That doesn't make any sense. I was human. I ate cheeseburgers and argued with my mom about my major. I wasn't strong or fast and sure as shit didn't drink blood. No, someone did this to me. My parents were human. *I* was human."

Emrys' face was filled with pity. "Not if they bound you, dear. Which given the power your mother possessed, is highly likely. Rosalind Sawyer Cabot was a venerated blood mage. If your father was an unregistered grave talker, then they could have bound you and passed you off as a human uninherit. As a human, you could have easily gone to a vampire to turn you."

Thomas groaned and stomped over to a set of glass decanters filled with amber liquid. "What she is failing to say, is that by hiding you and lying to them, our heads will be on the chopping block if anyone finds out what you are."

I'd thought of little else besides what had happened to my parents, to my life, in the last year. The scenarios were many and far-reaching, one just as preposterous as the next. I didn't remember much past falling asleep one night and waking up in that damn cemetery. There wasn't a single clue in our burned-out home, not one scent, not a shred of anything to tell me what happened.

"Did they kill them?" Was that my voice that sounded like broken glass? Were those tears racing down my cheeks?

Thomas scoffed at me, my idiocy too much for him to bear. "You think you'd have been left alive if the ABI had that first inkling you existed? No, Sloane. Whatever happened to your parents? It wasn't the ABI."

My hand swiped at my face, dashing the tears off my cheeks as I sucked in a breath to calm my racing heart.

"That still doesn't solve our most basic problem." I held up a hand to stop Thomas from interjecting more of his shitty commentary. "Besides staying hidden and not bringing down the wrath of the evil government agency upon us, I know. I have to eat. Vampire or not, I'm a blood drinker."

And a soul eater, my mind whispered. *Don't forget that little tidbit.*

"I don't know how to not kill someone. It's one thing to be around lowlifes and monsters day in and day out. I don't know —I don't want to hurt anyone that doesn't deserve it."

Thomas snorted as he settled back in his seat. "Oh, I think the answer to that will arrive in three, two, one..."

At the end of Thomas' counting, Emrys' office door flew open with Sparky on the other side.

In his hand was a ball of electricity, and on his face was an expression of pure murder.

I was screwed.

8

Power crackled on the air, racing across my skin like ants as I contemplated just how fucked my current situation was. I fully expected Sparky to lob that ball of awful at me at his earliest convenience, but he never got the chance.

Emrys stood from behind her desk, batting her glowing palm at him like she was a pissed-off mama cat. Instantly, the ball of electricity in Bastian's hand fizzled and died, the scent of ozone and spent magic high on the air.

Mental note: Do not mess with Emrys. Ever.

Her expression seemed to be carved from stone, three times as rigid and twice as cold. "You called it, Thomas. It looks like we have a volunteer."

"Volunteer for what?" Bastian growled at the same time I squeaked out a "What?"

I shook my head hard. I'd already smelled his blood. I'd already had to force myself not to attack him. If I sank my fangs into his skin...

I swallowed down the saliva gathering in my mouth, hunger

wrenching in my belly. Already my fangs had lengthened, and it was all I could do to hold myself in the leather chair. My nails made little half-moon crescent slices in the leather as I physically restrained myself from launching at his neck and ripping it wide.

My heart tripped in my chest as he took a step inside the room.

"Get him out of here," I growled, my whole body vibrating with the urge to bathe in the warm, succulent bliss trapped in his veins. "I'll kill him. *Please.*"

Tears gathered in my eyes as my stomach twisted again, the hunger a burning agony of need.

It had been months since I'd gone more than twenty-four hours without feeding. After Jacob, I hadn't wanted to feed again—the horror of what I'd done, who I was, too much for me to understand. I had lost my parents, my life, my home. And I was a monster.

I didn't want to be a monster.

But the hunger was too much, and I was too new. The first arcaner I found was feasting on a woman's heart in the back room of a warehouse, the still-warm body of his meal crumpled at his feet. At the time I had no idea, but I now knew the man was a lycanthrope. I tore him apart, drank him down, and ate his soul.

It was the first time I wasn't sorry for killing, and the more arcaners I found in the recesses of Ascension, the less sorry I felt.

But if I killed Sparky, I was pretty sure I'd be sorry. The thought of the lycanthrope's flayed body flashed in my mind, and I shook my head again, my gaze pleading as the tears crested my lids and fell.

"I'll kill him," I whispered, begging now that I knew Emrys meant business.

Thomas knelt at my knees, a faint trace of empathy on his face for a split second before the condescending mask fell back into place. "You won't kill him. I'll be here to teach you. I can't have one of my line murdering arcaners left and right, now can I? If you look like you're taking too much, I'll stop you."

I was under no illusion that his version of "stopping" wouldn't hurt, but if it meant I wouldn't…

"You want to let her feed on me? What the fuck, Emrys?" Bastian growled, the rage in his voice palpable on the air.

"It's your penance for attacking her in the holding area, not to mention your insipid tantrum in my office not a moment ago. I gave you a job to do, and you failed. Miserably. You deliberately went against my orders down there and continue to do so with every single bumbling, rage-filled misstep since I brought her here."

Bastian rocked back on his heels like he'd been slapped. While it was nice for Emrys to stick up for me, I had an inkling why Bastian wanted me gone. Given the way I was holding myself in my seat so I didn't rip his throat out, he'd have to be an idiot not to.

I was a threat to his brother, the last bit of family he had. He knew it. I knew it. We all knew why he was losing his shit like a tantrum-throwing toddler.

And I couldn't blame him. Not one bit.

Still, his reply burned me up from the inside. "She shouldn't be here. She doesn't belong with us."

"Yes, because everyone in this house has such a sparkling reputation?" Thomas quipped, the whites of his sclera veining red as he let his fangs descend.

"I'm not—" Bastian began, but Thomas cut him off.

"Do *not* lie. She is no different than any of us. Even you. And she needs to know how to feed so she is not a danger to you or your brother or anyone else in this house. Shall I ask Simon to volunteer instead?"

Bastian moved forward like he would attack but seemed to think better of it. Appearing to steal himself, he dropped his gaze to me. "I do this, you stay away from my brother."

"No," Emrys whispered, the single word like a barbed threat. "She will be a member of our house. She will dine with us—she will fight with us. You and your fears will not stand in the way of that."

Bastian's jaw hardened enough that I worried for the state of his teeth—or at least I would have had I not caught sight of the fluttering pulse just underneath it. This close, I could smell the drops of dried blood he still hadn't cleaned from his body, but that was nothing close to the scent of the rich lifeblood racing in his veins.

"Fine. If I do this, she cannot feed from anyone else. Not Simon, not Dahlia, or Harper. Just me. Deal?"

Dear sweet mother of all that was holy. Couldn't they just give me a bag of blood or something? I'd rather raid a blood bank than do this.

"Excellent," Thomas purred, a cat that got the canary smile blooming across his lips, putting his previous wicked grin to shame. "Come here, then. I have a feeling if she gets out of this chair, she'll rip your throat out."

That image bounced around my brain, and I winced at the truth of it.

With reluctance in his stride, Bastian approached my chair, kneeling at my feet. I sat there frozen until he smacked the side of my thigh with the back of his hand.

Oh. *Oh.* He meant for me to... Swallowing hard, I widened my legs, and he moved his big body in between them. It was all I could do to not lunge at his throat, but just before I lost what little bit of control I had, Thomas' iron grip landed on my shoulders.

"Some elders believe that a young one should always go for the wrist at first, but I disagree. It is far too easy to rip the delicate skin of a wrist, causing irreparable tendon damage. The throat, however, has a stronger pulse point, meaning it is far easier to feel the slowing of blood flow. Now"—He paused, letting his grip tighten on my shoulders—"you will stop when I tell you to. Understand?"

"I'll do my best," I whispered, unable to let my gaze stray too far from the pounding pulse in Bastian's throat.

"Comforting," Bastian muttered, moving closer as he latched his hands over my forearms on the armrest, pinning them to the seat.

Any other time, I would have balked at being held down, but if I were going to put my fangs in Bastian's neck, I figured I needed the restraint.

"Bite around the jugular, not through it. Yes?" Thomas advised, and I gave him a cursory sort of nod.

And then I struck, unable to hold back for another second as the hunger and heat and scent bombarded me like a battering ram. My razor-sharp fangs pierced Bastian's throat so fast he cried out. By some sort of miracle, I managed not to bite all the way through, stopping just shy of his jugular.

Hot blood filled my mouth, the heady rich nectar flowing down my throat like the sweetest wine. I swallowed once more, letting the power of it fill me, heal me. How had I not noticed when my throat felt like sandpaper? How had I ignored the ache in my joints or the lethargy that filled my limbs? How had I not noticed until all those aches were wiped away, the blood healing so much so quickly. I'd never felt power like this, never drank blood so potent, so strong.

I swallowed again, my hands sneaking out of Bastian's hold.

The fingers of one hand threaded through his hair and the other gripped his shirt, pulling him closer to me as I drank more. A scent I didn't recognize rose in the air, intoxicatingly sweet, incredibly potent. I wanted to roll in it like a cat in catnip, but all too quickly that thought was dashed. Because just like they always did, the images came.

Maybe because I wasn't drinking him dry, maybe because I didn't want to see Bastian's private thoughts and deeds, I didn't see everything like I always had. Instead, I saw flashes, just quick glimpses so fast I almost couldn't make them out. Flashes of… me?

Before I could see anymore, Thomas' grip tightened on my shoulders. Had they been there this whole time?

"It's time to stop, Sloane," Thomas called, his voice seeming so far away even though he couldn't be more than inches from me.

Reluctantly, I pulled my fangs back, wishing I could have more but knowing I couldn't. Only after my fangs had retracted from Bastian's throat did the world turn back on, and I realized the precarious situation I was now in.

Yes, in the time since my fangs pierced Bastian's flesh, my hands found their way to his hair and shirt, but moreover? Bastian's grip was also latched onto me. One of his arms was banded around my back, and the other hand had a full grip on my ass. And he wasn't moving.

Bastian's head rested on my chest, his breathing heavy like he'd run a marathon.

"Lick the wounds," Thomas instructed, and I whipped my head up to stare at him, his wicked grin wide as ever. "I'm serious. It will help the blood clot faster."

I tilted my head back down, my gaze latching onto the eight drops of blood that welled from the puncture wounds. They trickled down his neck, almost meeting the soft cotton of his shirt. Before I thought better of it, I flicked my tongue at the drops, sweeping them up as I passed over the wounds.

At the touch of my tongue, Bastian's grip got tighter, a faint shudder racking his big body. The faintest sort of groan slipped past his lips, and then I finally realized the scent coming from him—what it was.

Desire. Lust. Want.

Not that I understood it at all. Nor could I prevent the low clench inside me that answered the scent's siren call.

The quiet snick of the door closing meant I couldn't ask Thomas, either—not that I could ever see myself broaching the topic with the surly vampire—the room empty now that the danger of me killing Bastian was long gone. For the first time in a year, I wasn't hungry or thirsty, which didn't make any sense at all.

Was it because I had a willing victim?

Was it the strength in Bastian's blood?

And the thought of consuming his soul never once crossed my mind, which was another tick in the unexplainable column. Why did that satiate me before and not now? What was I missing?

We sat there for what seemed like a long time—me watching the wounds heal on his neck as I pondered, and Bastian holding onto me like a barnacle, his breathing slowing by small increments.

It probably should have been awkward, but I was riding high on the bliss of my joints not hurting, my whole body not aching, and the buzzing thoughts pinging around my skull.

Plus... I hadn't hugged anyone in a very long time. It felt almost... nice. That wasn't the right word, but it was as close as I would let myself get.

Bastian rolled his head, his breathing finally slowed enough for him to pull away. His fingers seemed reluctant to pull themselves from my ass cheek. Same with his arm. It was almost as if he didn't want to let me go.

There had to be something with the bite. Maybe I was venomous or something. Yeah, that was totally possible.

But then he shifted away, the loss of his heat leaving me chilled all over as he stood. He moved to walk away and abruptly stopped.

I glanced up, reluctant to see whatever censure or hate or disgust he was going to shovel my way. This was the first time I felt okay in a year and he was going to ruin it.

But instead of censure, all I saw was a carefully constructed blank mask, save for his eyes flashing emerald. "No one else," he rumbled, his voice shattering the quiet. "Only me."

Then he walked out of the room, leaving me to wonder what the hell had just happened.

9

It took far too long to collect myself after Bastian left the room. I had to wonder when I stopped calling him Sparky. Was it when I dug my fangs into his neck that his moniker changed? And what was the deal with the "only me" shit?

Not that I had plans to strike on any other member of the house, but...

My mind replayed the words over and over. *Only me.* Each time, my belly dipped—each time, Bastian's blood thundered through my veins. I was hovering on the edge of hunting him down to ask him what the fuck was going on or hiding from him until the end of time.

Why was I so embarrassed? I was twenty-three not thirteen, and I hadn't exactly been a saint before my world had gone promptly to shit. So why was I acting like a blushing virgin?

Ugh. I'd have to ask Thomas, and I really didn't want to. He'd make fun of me at every turn, but dammit, I needed answers. And at least with Thomas I knew what I was going to get. If I asked Bastian, I had no idea what he'd do. Lash out? Kiss me? Ask me to bite him again?

I threw my arms over my head, hiding my face from the empty room. The scent of Bastian's need was still high on the air and no matter how much I wanted to talk myself out of it, the urge to fill my lungs with it was strong. I had to get the fuck out of here before I did something really stupid.

I shoved myself up from the chair and stalked out of the room, the fresh air of the hall slamming me in the face. It was cooler, the scents of the house less heady and intoxicating. I missed his smell already. How stupid was that? So was the urge to follow his scent down the hall.

My hand still on the doorknob, I stepped back into Emrys' office to get one last breath of him before I shut that nagging urge down. What the fuck was wrong with me? Wasn't I the same girl who spiked his head like a volleyball an hour ago?

Suddenly, a door whipped open, and Harper's scowling face peeked out of the opening. "I thought I told you to get warded?"

"Sorry. Shenanigans ensued, and…" I shrugged by way of answer. "I'll find Emrys and get it done." The thought of what she might be gleaning from me made my face heat with embarrassment. "Sorry," I muttered again, inexplicable tears gathering in my eyes.

The unholy rage left her face for a moment. "It's fine. *You're* fine. Just get it done. This is supposed to be a safe place for me. There aren't many left for people like me anymore."

I did my absolute best not to feel pity—Harper didn't need it and didn't deserve it. What she needed was my respect. I could give her that. "I'll get it done."

"Good." She moved from behind her door to lean on the doorjamb. "And afterward, you can dish about whatever happened in that office, because, *girl*. Whatever went down was hot as *hell*."

My face felt like the surface of the sun. Dear sweet mother, I was not going to talk about that shit. Maybe ever.

"Oh, my god, your face! I had no idea vampires could blush." And then she giggled—the girl who had been nothing but surly since I got here was giggling like a schoolgirl.

Someone shoot me.

I opened my mouth to tell her I wasn't a vampire but immediately snapped it shut. That was information I didn't need to bandy about. Instead, I narrowed my eyes at her and stuck out my tongue. It wasn't her fault she felt that shit, but damn, was tact taboo in this place or what?

"I'm finding Emrys to put the whammy on me, and then… we can never discuss this shit ever again. Nice to meet you, Harper," I called over my shoulder as I hauled ass down the hall and down the stairs.

Following the sounds of voices, I found an opulent dining space off the great room. A wide chandelier made from several globe lights hung in the middle of a giant table, the thing long enough to seat twenty.

While the majority of the house was more of a traditional style, the dining room was more contemporary. A slate-gray rug lay under the table, the thick pile close to a trendy shag. I never understood how to keep shag rugs clean, but damn, did it look soft.

Emrys and Thomas were off in a corner discussing things I wanted no part of. Still, I approached, ready for Harper to never know another thing about my emotions, ever.

"Done already?" Thomas teased. He was quickly rewarded with my face likely turning tomato red—I'd felt the heat as it immediately crept up my cheeks. He had to have smelled

Bastian's desire just like I did, only he knew what it was as soon as it happened. Me, not so much.

"Was I supposed to drain him dry in your absence?" I immediately wished I hadn't asked the question as soon as it fell out of my mouth. Double entendre had never been my strong suit, but I figured Thomas had been around when that shit was invented. As strong as he was, he had to be older than dirt.

Thomas' smile stretched wide. "In a manner of speaking. What do you need?"

Deciding to ignore his dig, I explained the issue. "Harper said I was supposed to be warded? And considering she's yelled at me three times already, I'd like that to be done now-ish if possible."

Emrys' lips tipped up like she knew exactly why I wanted the ward so damn bad. Good god, did everyone in the house know what happened when I drank Bastian's blood?

"Of course. My apologies. In all the commotion, it slipped my mind. Stay still," she instructed, waving a glowing hand in my face before she touched two fingers to my chest.

I felt only warmth, but I heard Harper call a resounding "thank you" across the house so I figured it worked. I wanted to be relieved, wanted to bask in the warmth of having my emotions known only to myself, but then Bastian strode in the room, and I became a ball of I had no idea what. I was a tangled yarn of weird emotions, and I didn't like it one bit.

Emotions sucked.

Big time.

Bastian's neck was completely healed, the skin smooth and unblemished. There wasn't even a scar. I couldn't detect the faintest hint of blood either, not even the old blood that he'd failed to clean off his boots from before. Then I noticed his wet hair, and it dawned on me that he must have showered, washing my scent away while I was busy trying to keep his in my nose.

I couldn't say exactly why this felt like a slap in the face, but it did. My only solace was at least that information was mine alone and not for public consumption. The absolute last thing I needed right that second was some asshole to tell me that I was blushing, or looked hurt, or whatever.

Maybe I was just tired. Right. The sun was just cresting the horizon—or at least that's what my internal clock said. I could blame all this emotional bullshit on that. Except I'd never been so energized in my life, Bastian's blood filling me, nourishing me.

I nearly groaned out loud but managed to stop myself. Still, I got a knowing glance from Thomas who could likely smell my freak-out leaking from my pores.

Fabulous.

"Are you going to eat breakfast with us?" Dahlia's said from my elbow, and I nearly jumped out of my skin. I could have sworn she appeared out of nowhere. "I promise it isn't poisoned."

"I don't know."

Dahlia grabbed my elbow, yanking me to a seat with way more force than a woman that small should have. "You have to. Whenever we aren't on assignment, we always eat one meal together. Granted, we're on assignment so much it's ridiculous, but still. It's been a month since we were able to have a meal together. Even Harper is coming down. Now, Booth and Axel are out of pocket, so you won't get to meet them yet, but it'll be fun."

She practically shoved me into a seat and plopped down beside me.

"Oo-kay. I guess I'll stay."

Dahlia clapped. "You won't regret it. Clementine is the best cook in the state. Makes pancakes made of magic. Fluffy clouds of awesome that just melt in your mouth. Really. You're in for a treat. It feels like forever since we all got to sit down together."

I didn't see any food on the table, but I was willing to wait and see what all the fuss was about. I mean, who could turn down pancakes? Especially ones described with such reverence. It had been a very long time since I'd gotten anything close to a home-cooked meal.

No, Cup O' Noodles did not count, no matter how good they were.

Simon fell onto the chair to my left, and Bastian yanked out the one across from him, slamming onto the seat with a roughness that likely heralded another temper tantrum. Good god, couldn't that man maintain an emotion for more than thirty seconds?

"I need to talk to you," Simon said under his breath, a faint whisper I knew no one but me and Thomas could hear.

I looked down rather than meeting his eyes. "About?"

"My brother, doofus. What do you think?" he hissed back, and I could see his ridged shoulders out of the corner of my eye.

"If he doesn't haul across the table and murder me, sure. I'll pencil you in."

"You'd better." Simon's tone was so different than the one he'd used before. Like I had injured him somehow. I couldn't tell what I had done from then to now that could cause such a fuss except...

Again, I wanted to groan but didn't. Damn Thomas and Emrys for making Bastian feed me. What had they been thinking?

A pretty young woman in a polka-dotted fifties-style house dress swept in from a swinging door, the opening giving a slight glimpse of a kitchen before it swung shut. In her hands were two trays loaded with several serving dishes, and despite how heavy they looked, she appeared to carry them with ease. Her blood-red hair was carefully coiffed into victory rolls, her eyeliner sharp enough to cut steal. On her feet were a pair of heels I would have broken my neck in and save for the fact that she was most certainly not alive, I kind of wished I could take style tips from her.

And by not alive, I meant that her pallor was paler than a ghost, her eyes and the hollows of her cheeks carrying deep shadows, and her head was most definitely stitched on.

What was she, Bride of freaking Frankenstein?

Dahlia answered my unspoken question, whispering in my ear, "She's a revenant. A nice one, but she's still a ghost shoved into a reanimated body. She used to be a dybbuk, but Simon helped expel her. It was a whole thing. She didn't want to move on, so Simon put her in that body, and she works for us."

Dahlia was the queen of information, but I still had questions. "Dybbuk? What the hell is that?"

She put her finger to her lips, shushing me. "It's a possessing spirit. Usually they need help, have unfinished business, so they jump into someone's body. In Clem's case, she jumped into Booth, which was so wrong on every level." She shuddered. "Anyway, that's a story for another time."

What I wouldn't give to ply Dahlia with alcohol and let her spill all the dirt hiding out in her brain.

A clinking glass pulled my gaze from Dahlia to Emrys who stood at the head of the table. "Before we dig in, I have a few announcements. Everyone, welcome our newest member, Sloane. For the time being, I will be partnering her with Simon—"

Even though I was expecting it, I still jumped when Bastian's fists slammed against the table.

"Absolutely not."

10

"I was unaware you were in charge here, Mr. Cartwright," Emrys said, her tone coy, but I still caught the faint thread of threat buried under guile. "Should you be at the head of this table then?"

Bastian stood from his seat, his fists pressed against the wood like he was drawing from the planks. "We all know by now that she is a blood drinker."

Thanks for blurting it out for everyone to hear, Sparky.

"If she's partnered with Simon, what happens when she's injured and needs blood to heal? Or when they're on assignment so long she requires a meal? We discussed that I would be the only person to feed her in this house. If she's going to be partnered with anyone, it should be me."

Out of the two brothers, I would have much preferred to be paired with Simon. For one, I wouldn't be worried about random outbursts. The second reason—and likely more pressing of the two—feeding from Bastian wasn't an experience I wanted to duplicate. It felt dangerous in a way that had the potential for catastrophic consequences.

And he wanted to be partners? Was he high? Other than the blip of him hugging me mid-feeding, Bastian couldn't stand me. He was more likely to stab me in my sleep than be a good partner—not that I'd ever had a partner for anything other than a school project, but still. It wasn't rocket science.

Emrys' silence stretched long enough that I spared her a glance to see if she was preparing to blast Sparky to kingdom come. Her face was a blank mask—a look that was not comforting at all. "So, I can trust you to actually be Sloane's partner, and not treat her like shit on your shoe? I can trust you to feed her when she is injured or in need? I can have faith that you will actually utilize her gifts instead of benching her because of your attitude? If you can promise me that, then absolutely, it makes sense for the two of you to be partners. If you can't, then she needs to pair up with someone who isn't the embodiment of a—what did you call it, Harper?"

Harper entered the room, taking her seat next to Bastian, a malevolent smirk on her elfin face. "A butt-hurt diaper baby with little dick syndrome." She happily reached for one of the still-covered platters. To Bastian, she said, "Sack up, dude."

The table erupted into peals of laughter. Even Emrys and Thomas let out a giggle, but the most surprising was Bastian's booming laugh as he plopped back onto his seat. He laughed until he had tears coming from his eyes, the smile on his face wholly unexpected.

They teased each other like a family—just like mine did before...

I did not laugh—I couldn't. Despite the mirth in the room, I waited for the other shoe to drop, waited for someone to kick me out or tell me I wasn't wanted or that I didn't belong here. Yes, Emrys was sticking up for me, but that seemed like more of a dig at Thomas and Bastian and less for my benefit.

Or maybe I was just looking for ways to sabotage what little hope I had. If I didn't have a home, I couldn't lose one. If I didn't have friends, they couldn't die on me. If I didn't have hope, I wouldn't be crushed when everything inevitably went to shit.

All of this played out undetected from Harper's empath abilities, a fact for which I was supremely grateful. Casting my gaze downward, I hid my face from the rest of the table. I wanted to look at Bastian, wanted to see what was going on behind his eyes, but I couldn't make myself be a part of this hodge-podge family.

"Well, if the state of my manhood is at stake," Bastian rumbled, "I suppose I will just have to rise to the challenge."

Good. This was good. I shouldn't get comfortable here. I shouldn't stick with people who would become fast friends.

I was a killer, wasn't I? Even if I killed bad people, Bastian was right not to want me around his little brother. Killers didn't get friends. Killers didn't get happy families and warm meals and cushy digs and…

Abruptly, I stood, my chair snagging on the shag rug and tipping back in my haste to leave. The crack of it hitting the floor didn't slow me down one bit, and even though the door was easily accessible, and I knew I could leave, I didn't. Instead, I found myself back in my cell, the small quarters somehow more comforting than any other place I'd visited. Without a thought in my head, I pulled the cell door closed.

The runes began to glow as soon as the metal slammed home, the magic locks springing closed. The heat seeped into my palm, and I let the metal go before it could burn me. I couldn't say why that made me breathe easier, being locked in this cell. I couldn't say why I wanted the barrier, but I did. I wanted something to separate me from them. Wanted—no, needed—a way to keep myself away.

From the laughter. From the happiness. From the warmth.

My mom's face flashed in my head—she was smiling wide enough that her crooked canine was visible. She hardly ever smiled that wide because she hated that she'd never gotten braces. A silly thing that my father and I always got on her about when she hid her smile. We were giggling about a misadventure of our family dog, Otis. She'd taken him on a walk, and he'd rolled in the mud—only it wasn't mud but a pile of crap. And then—the big bastard that he was—knocked my mom in the same pile he'd just rolled in.

My mom was so pissed when she began the story, but by the end, my dad and I were out of our chairs laughing at my mom's tale of woe, tears spilling from our eyes. And poor Otis didn't know which human he wanted to inspect because Dad and I were making such a ruckus.

That was two days before the death date on my—*our* —tombstones.

It was the last thing I remembered from before. The last memory I had of my parents, of Otis. Of my home. The last thing I remembered before waking up in the dirt of that stupid cemetery.

Smoke filled my nose as I crawled on my bedroom floor to the window. My skin felt like it was melting off my bones. I reached for the window, but it was too far away. Too far…

My mother's scream pierced the air, the pain reaching my ears as she called my name.

A clanging on metal had my eyes flashing open, my body up and off the cot in an instant. I found myself crouched low to the ground, a feral sort of growl ripping up my throat, the remnant of the dream still at the forefront of my mind.

Bastian stood on the other side of the bars, his large body appearing that much bigger since I was on the floor.

"Remind me never to wake you up when you're in your actual bed. Care to share why you chose the dungeon instead of your room?"

Reluctantly, I stood from my crouch. "Room? I thought this was my room."

"No, members of the Watch do not sleep in the dungeon. Why would you think that?"

My gaze landed on the charcoals, the box a stark reminder of the life I'd lost, and the reason I thought I was supposed to stay down here.

"Do you like them?" His question was reluctant, like he was trying desperately to make conversation. "It was difficult to find anything on you. Neither you nor your parents had any social media to speak of. The only thing I found of any note was a picture of you in a university art class with a box of those. Dahlia said that they might make you feel at home. Reassure you that we weren't the bad guys."

"And all they did was make me angry," I whispered, blinking hard so I didn't start crying. Every time I closed my eyes, I saw the fire racing over the walls of my bedroom. Was that a memory? Or was it just my imagination running wild?

I didn't know, and it was driving me crazy.

"My mom got me a set when I was young. I was saving for them, but they were ridiculously expensive." I shook my head, unable to explain why that box made me want to scream.

"She sounds like a good mum."

My smile was brittle, but I managed to answer him without crying. "She was. She was the best. A little overprotective and overbearing, but dammit, she was a great mom."

"And your dad?"

Mom, I could think about, but Dad was like a knife in the gut every time. Still, I answered, even though my voice was little more than a croak. "The best."

Bastian sat in the chair across from the bars. "Do you know what happened?"

I swiped at my cheeks and nose. "Nope. One day I was living my best life, worried about classes and whether or not I could convince Mom to let me apply for the Fine Arts master's program, and the next, I'm in that fucking cemetery staring at our headstones."

"We all have stories like yours, you know?" His words weren't mean, in fact, they were likely meant to be reassuring. "People we've lost. Wrongs done to us. Bitter wounds that refuse to heal. Thomas was right yesterday. We're not so different."

I stared at my feet rather than meet his gaze. He was right —these people likely had just as much pain as I did. Why else would they be here instead of with a family? Why would they be bounty hunters instead of something else?

"You're probably right."

"As long as you keep that attitude, we'll get along just fine." With a wave of his hands, he completed a set of hand movements similar to Dahlia's, unlocking my cell. "Time for training. Booth and Axel are back, so you're about to be put through the wringer."

Groaning, I shoved my feet into my boots, exiting the cell with the exact same wariness I had yesterday. The difference was, he didn't pounce. I glanced over my shoulder, giving him a steely-eyed glare. "No attacking today?"

Bastian chuckled. "There will be plenty of that in training. First, I'll show you to your room. You can get cleaned up and then we'll head to the gym. If we're going to work together, we'll need to see how we mesh as a combat team. I don't take the easy cases."

"I've kicked your ass how many times in a twenty-four-hour

period?" I prodded, letting him lead the way with the added benefit of not being attacked from behind.

"Twice, if you're keeping score, but I was being gentle. You were a capture job, not a kill."

I snorted. *The ego on this guy.* "Doesn't explain the dungeon attack. You got bested. Twice. Admit it."

"We'll see how much you're crowing after training. Booth has been instructed by Thomas to go full-bore. Your *sire* really is concerned about your fighting abilities. Seems his first impression of you was a bit… *lacking*."

That sounded like Thomas all right. The surly vampire was desperate to be a verified pain in my ass.

Which was why—after a shower and a cursory glance at the ridiculously spacious room they gave me—I ended up face-to-face with the business end of a shifter's fangs.

11

Bastian led me up the set of stairs to the main level and up the grand staircase to the second floor. My feet practically sank into the plush carpet on the stairs, the feeling still odd to me even after my trek on them the day before. My senses felt funny, slightly amped up, and I had to wonder if it was Bastian's feeding that dialed them to eleven.

To the right was the long corridor that led to Simon's room, ahead was a small alcove with Harper's domain, and to the left was Emrys' office. In between the doorways were tiny insets with vases or portraits, but the largest was a painted portrait of a woman in a red dress. The picture was so large, it was a wonder I missed it yesterday.

I paused slightly, studying it. The brunette woman possessed an unearthly level of beauty, her hair coiffed in glam waves of a 1940s movie star, her face turned in profile as she stared off into the distance. Her skin was flawless alabaster, save for a sprinkling of freckles peppering her nose. Her dress floated around her like a cloud, but it wasn't just her hair or skin or dress. It was her eyes, the whiskey color almost bright against her skin. The portrait was done by an expert hand, the colors flowing beautifully together to make her skin almost glow. There was no artist signature at the bottom, which irked me to no end.

Bastian turned right, his gaze directed from the portrait—seemingly on purpose—as he forged down the hall, his face veered away until he'd moved past it.

Was she someone he had lost, someone he hated? Bastian was so closed off, I'd probably never know.

Simon's room was at the end of the corridor, and Bastian stopped three rooms away, opening the heavily carved wood door with a practiced ease. I reluctantly followed only to have my jaw drop once he stepped aside. The walls were a deep teal, the color so rich it almost hurt my heart. At the center of the room was an upholstered king-size bed, the blush-velvet headboard striking against the color of the wall. Dangling above the bed was a brushed-gold geometric chandelier that seemed delicate and modern and made my little artist heart sing. Off to the side, near the giant picture window was an easel with a blank canvas, a drafting table, and a brushed-gold, pin-leg stool with a velvet teal cushion.

"Please tell me you like it?" Dahlia begged, her tiny body shoving Bastian out of the way so she could give me a side-armed hug. "Thomas said artists need the best light, so I switched with you. This room is a little smaller than my new one, but it has a giant window and a fireplace.

This room has a fireplace? My gaze had been so stuck on the art supplies that I missed the sleek hearth, the tile surrounding it reaching all the way to the ceiling.

"Your bathroom is to the right, and you can get to your closet through there." She pointed to a teal door with gold moldings. "I took the liberty of getting your wardrobe started.

Just the basics. Emrys said you didn't have much in the way of things, so I wanted you to feel at home."

I swallowed hard, an emotion hitting me square in the chest that I didn't want to name. It was part pain, part happiness, part misery. It made me want to hug her and punch her in the face all at the same time. I settled on the hug, squeezing her gently so as to not break her tiny bones.

"Dammit, Dahlia," I croaked. "How am I supposed to kick Bastian's ass for the third time if you keep doing nice shit like this?"

She giggled and hip-checked me with enough force that I figured her earlier bouts of helplessness had to be a ruse. "You'll figure out something else to be mad at. So, you like it? You haven't even looked at the bathroom yet."

"Does it have a working shower and toilet?"

She nodded.

"Then I'll love it." I'd been squatting in warehouses and slums for the last year. If the bathroom looked anything like this sort of opulence, I was going to be just fine.

"You say that now, but it doesn't have a soaking tub. I tried to get Booth to put one in, but he said the old plumbing wouldn't support another water line without *blah, blah, blah.* Which really meant he didn't want to do it and figured out a way to bullshit me into accepting the shower-only option. But my new room has the mother of all tubs, and I cannot wait!"

"So what you're really saying is the move was a total sacrifice, but you did it for me because you owe me like a Wookie life-debt or something," I deadpanned, watching as her smile grew wider.

Dahlia put her hand over her heart like she was reciting the Pledge of Allegiance. "Exactly. Total sacrifice. I don't know how I'll live with it, but I will. For you."

"Fabulous," Bastian drawled. "Get cleaned up and meet me

in the gym in an hour. Booth will want to assess your strength before we start." With that, he turned and left, his abrupt departure raising both my and Dahlia's eyebrows.

"That boy needs to get laid. I swear, he gets crankier every day," she muttered, shaking her head. "Here, I'll show you were you get new clothes." She stalked off to the closet, and immediately got to work yanking out underwear and a sports bra, activewear and shoes. "Typically, we train in what we fight in, but if Booth wants to assess you, then he's about to put you through the wringer. Basically, it's going to be a free-for-all to see if you can lift as heavy or do as many push-ups as he can. Comfort is key. Trust me."

Goodie.

After a shower in the biggest freaking bathroom I had ever seen, I donned my new clothes. It had been a long time since something I wore was new or clean or without holes. I was reluctant to leave my leather pants behind, though. I'd stolen them fair and square, and they were still in good shape after a year of hard use.

"Here." Dahlia held her hand out. "I'll have Clem clean them. You'd think it was a chore, but I swear, that woman loves to do laundry. I've never met anyone who loves to fold more than her."

Reluctantly, I handed over the leather, the feeling of it parting from my hands leaving me bereft. I'd washed off what felt like a year's worth of dirt and blood and grime. I felt clean for the first time in a while. Even though I'd done what I could to stay clean, squatting in warehouses hadn't been the best means in which to stay that way. But I'd had little choice. *So, there's that.*

"She'll give them back, I promise. You aren't the only one with an attachment to the old life. When Emrys found me, I'd been eating out of the garbage for six months. There weren't a lot of safe places for witches back then. But our population has grown quite a bit over the last century. Less burnings and trials, I'd bet."

I blinked hard. "How old are you?"

Dahlia swept her braids off her shoulder. "Don't you know you're not supposed to ask a woman that?" she teased. "I was born in 1909. Witches don't typically age as well as I do, but I'm pretty sure I have a little mage blood mixed in there." She said it behind her hand like it was a big secret. "Super taboo back then, not that I know who my parents even are. I was left on the steps of an orphanage as a baby, and those nuns kicked me out the second I displayed an inkling of magic. I lived on the streets until Emrys found me, and I've been here ever since."

I suddenly didn't feel so bad about handing over my leather pants. Scanning the room, I noticed all the little details she'd put into it to make me feel at home, to make it so I would stay. From the bed, to the art table, to the color on the walls. The scent still clung on the air, meaning she'd chosen that color for me, decorating the space exactly like I would want it.

"Thanks," I rasped, trying not to burst into tears at the generosity. Really, I was going to have to punch someone in the face or snap someone's neck to get all these gooey, happy feelings out of me.

"Don't worry about it." She shrugged, heading for the door. "They all did the same for me when I got here. Except for Simon. He only let me into his room, but that was enough. He was dealing with a lot back then. Speak of the devil…" She trailed off as Simon leaned against the doorjamb.

"And he appears," he answered. "Do you mind if I talk to Sloane for a bit?"

"Show her how to get to the gym, would you? I have to read the cards and put some hex bags together." Dahlia yanked his sleeve, and he leaned down. She gave him a raspberry on his cheek before flouncing out of the room, the trails of her bouncy skirt following behind her.

For some reason, I braced myself. Simon wanted to talk to me yesterday, but I'd bounced out of breakfast like a melodramatic teenager. I wasn't all too eager to find out what he wanted to say, but it seemed like my time was up.

Simon pressed on the bridge of his glasses, sliding them up his nose. He adjusted his beanie and fiddled with the cuffs of his flannel shirt. The scent of reluctance wafted toward me, mixed with spent magic and a little fear.

"Out with it," I growled, irritated at his stalling. "If you're going to shatter my happy bubble, at least have the decency to quit stalling, Simon. It's rude."

He opened his mouth to begin, but closed it, his expression just as frustrated as mine likely was.

"You didn't even bring your cat, and to think I was counting on that as a perk of our friendship."

Simon chuckled before sobering. "This is going to sound all kinds of wrong, but if I don't say it, I'll regret it. Just know what I'm about to say has nothing to do with you as a person, and everything to do with my bonehead brother and his fragile, stupid heart."

Oh, I did not like where this was going.

"Don't start with him. Be partners, be friends. Don't start a relationship with him. You think it will work, but it won't. And if you get hurt, if you die on him, he'll..." Simon shook his head, covering his bespectacled face with his hands. "I'm not explaining this right."

"It's okay, man. I don't think your brother likes me, anyway.

And he's cute and all—if you like hot, broody, magic-wielding dolts who don't look before they leap."

Simon peeked from between his fingers. "I am messing this up royally. Okay, so if we could get back to the issue here."

"Which is don't diddle your brother."

"Exactly. Blood drinkers have a way of… charming their sources. Especially if they are a repeat. The more you bite him, the more he'll want to be bitten. The more he'll want you. It's sort of a symbiotic relationship, only it usually involves…"

"Sex?" I wasn't an idiot. I was smart enough to put two and two together. My bite made a normally rage-filled mage into a possessive behemoth with a penchant for grabbing my ass. It didn't mean it had to progress beyond that, right?

Simon blushed so hard the lobes of his ears turned scarlet. Dahlia was over a century old, and Simon had been here since before she had. That meant he was ancient compared to me and blushing like a virgin on prom night.

"Look, I've fed from him once. How about I do blood bags from now on, and we'll see if the attraction fades. If it does, no harm, no foul." I didn't say what would happen if it didn't. Because the both of us had no idea.

Simon reluctantly ended the conversation, his purpose muddied with worry for his brother and his awkwardness about the subject matter. He silently led me to the gym, gave me a mumbled goodbye, and practically sprinted for the stairs.

The wide-open room boasted a climbing wall, tons of weightlifting equipment, and all the accoutrement of a well-stocked gym. A stocky man in a singlet and shorts approached, his hands rubbing together like he was hatching a Machiavellian plan. His long blond hair was pulled into a knot at the top of his head, and I couldn't say why that irritated me, but it did.

I also didn't like the glint to his eyes, or the way his mouth twisted up at the corner, nor was I a fan of the scent of his magic. It smelled of untamed wildness and malice.

He held out one of his beefy hands for me to shake, and stupidly, I took it, assuming that introductions were safe. Booth yanked me to him in a move that was likely intended to dump me on my ass. A fact that was proved correct not a moment later when I was tossed up and over his hip.

Too bad for Booth, landing on my feet was a specialty. So was hitting back. Sailing over his hip, I latched onto his singlet, bringing the fabric up to wrap around his neck. In less than a second, Booth was being choked out by his own shirt, while I yawned dramatically.

Bastian sauntered toward our little tableau, clapping as he struggled to breathe from laughing so hard.

"You should have probably introduced yourself before acting like an asshole, Booth," Bastian advised once his chuckles subsided.

At Bastian's nod, I let Booth go, relishing the wheeze of him sucking in air.

"Hi, Booth. I'm Sloane. Nice to meet you." I said it like butter wouldn't melt in my mouth, trying for a guileless smile. I likely failed, but it really didn't matter. I had a feeling Booth and I weren't going to be friends.

"Pleasure," he wheezed back, on his hands and knees, his hair escaping the tie and hiding his face.

Bastian knelt by his friend, slapping him on the back. "I told you not to. As I recall, I also told you she would hand you your ass."

"Yeah, you did," Booth replied, getting to his feet. "But I had to see what this little lady was made of. I couldn't believe it when Emrys said who she was. I mean, two hundred arcaners? By this little thing? It had to be bullshit."

"Yeah, I'm standing right here," I growled, irritated to no

end that the man was talking about me like I wasn't there. "And it's three hundred."

Booth's gaze shifted to me, the glint in his eyes reminding me of Jacob for a split second. "Oh, is it now? Well, I guess we'll just have to see if you can handle a real opponent then."

12

I was going to kill Thomas. I would drink him down and eat his soul and watch gleefully as he withered to dust.

Booth, the godforsaken shapeshifter who was in charge of my training, was a certified sadist. A fact that was more and more evident the longer my training went on. The first thirty minutes, I was cursing Booth, but I'd since shifted my ire onto Thomas. Booth might be an asshole, but he was the weapon Thomas was wielding, and I was going to get my revenge on him someday.

Booth's razor-sharp fangs snapped, barely missing my arm by millimeters. Since he was so close, I latched onto his thick white fur and launched him across the room, hoping he hit his stupid thick head and passed out. It had been wishful thinking, but it was what I had.

At his returning growl, I figured I was shit out of luck. Especially since Booth wasn't the only person in this house I would be fighting. Bastian's low chuckle was faint enough that I'd be willing to bet he thought I couldn't hear him.

Rookie mistake.

Now I knew he was up in the catwalk area where the climbing ropes were secured, waiting to hit me when I was down. That's what this exercise was supposed to be—an assessment of my skills with more than one opponent. I refused to look up, so I didn't let on that I knew he was up there, keeping a wary eye on Booth instead.

"You think you're funny, but I assure you that if I could use *my* fangs, you'd be singing a different tune." Early in our training, Booth and Bastian informed me I couldn't use my best offensive weapon—a rule I thought was utterly unfair and a waste of time. If we were in a real battle, I was going to use anything I had at my disposal.

Including my teeth.

I felt the rise of magic on the air and smartly ducked. Not a moment later, a ball of fire whizzed by where my head *used* to be. *Rude.*

In the briefing before Bastian and Booth plotted new and inventive ways of kicking my ass, I'd also been informed that creating electricity balls was not Bastian's only talent. Oh, no. The bastard had control of a whole complement of elements.

I was dealing with an elemental mage and a shifter. And the fuckers were working in tandem because Booth decided to strike right when I was distracted, sinking his teeth into my forearm and shaking his head to rip the wound wide.

Motherfucker.

That was it, no more playing nice. Bastian, Booth, *and* Thomas could take their rules and shove them up their asses.

My fingers found Booth's muzzle, and I wrenched, the crack of his jaw breaking audible as I tore his teeth out of my arm. The limb now useless, I struggled to latch onto the damn dog, as he attempted to claw me to ribbons. But I was motivated and pissed right the fuck off. My fingers found his scruff and yanked, pulling him off his giant paws.

Booth was close to two hundred pounds as a human. As a wolf, he was slightly smaller, more compact. But it didn't matter if he were bigger, I'd had my fill of Bastian's blood the night before, so I had no trouble lifting him one-handed so I could stare into his stupid face.

I didn't know wolves could have a contemptuous expression on their furry faces, but Booth proved the rule. I had a feeling if he could close his mouth, my neck would be mincemeat.

"Be happy you will be nursing a broken jaw and not a broken fucking neck. Do. Not. Bite. Me. Again. Not unless you want me to bite you back. I've killed a lot of men for far less."

I was still holding Booth aloft when Bastian approached, a frown marring his pretty face. Well, too damn bad. I wasn't going to be bitten and not defend myself. No way.

"What the fuck did you do?" he thundered, and it was all I could do not to volley the damn wolf at him and watch them both fall like dominos.

"He bit me, so I broke his jaw." Why I needed to explain this was beyond me. "He's lucky I didn't break his stupid neck. How is this training, exactly?"

Bastian rolled his eyes. "Not you. Him. Booth, what in the bloody hell is wrong with you? Her arm is shredded."

I kinda figured that was the point of this bullshit training session—to make me bleed. I mean, not a second ago, Bastian was aiming an electricity ball at my nugget, so the goal couldn't have been to tiptoe through the fucking tulips.

I stared down at said arm. Blood ran down my fingertips to puddle on the floor. I felt more than heard a faint displacement of air, quieter than a whoosh but louder than a breath, and then Thomas was looming over me, his sclera bled to scarlet as his needle-like fangs erupted from the periodontal pockets that held his secondary set of teeth.

His touch was cold as death as he gently took my injured forearm in his hands to examine the wounds.

"Drop the dog, Sloane." His voice was like ice, his gaze never moving from the weeping wounds.

Opening my fingers as instructed, I watched as Booth's limp body fell to the gym floor. Still conscious, the idiot was at least smart enough not to move. The cold finger of fear tickled down my back as Thomas' focus left my arm and landed on Booth.

"You were instructed to test her abilities. To see if she could handle multiple opponents, to see if she had any tactical skills. And although she proved she could best you, you decided on your own to injure her. On purpose and with intent." Thomas' words never rose above a whisper, but they chilled me to the bone. The rage wafting off of him soured the air, and although his ire was not directed at me, I still felt the cold breath of fear. Thomas was trying extremely hard not to murder someone, and I really didn't want it to be me.

"She is of my line, and as such, under my protection. Moreover, she is a member of this team. Your actions shall have consequences—not only with me, but with Emrys as well. I suggest you shift and heal your jaw. You will need to be at a hundred percent if you wish to survive your punishment."

A whine came from Booth's throat—it sounded confused, and I had to agree. None of this made much sense to me. Why was Thomas so angry? Why was a wall of rage coming from Bastian? Why was Booth being punished?

I wanted to ask, but it didn't feel right to. It felt like if I did, they would see just how out of place I felt, just how singular, and then they would try to bring me into the circle.

I couldn't say why that felt wrong, but it did.

"Sloane, if you wish to feed from Booth, you may." Thomas'

voice was pitched so low, I could have sworn I misheard him. "He drew your blood—it is only right that you draw his."

"No." The answer did not come from me. Instead, that single barbed word came from Bastian's throat.

I swallowed hard, the pain finally registering now that the adrenaline was starting to wear off. "No, thank you."

Thomas shrugged as if both my and Bastian's refusal was of no consequence. "Bastian then? You will need healing."

This time it was me who emphatically vetoed that course of action. "If there's a blood bag or something, that would be fine."

I did not need a repeat of the last feeding I had with Bastian —didn't need him closer, especially given Simon's warning. That didn't stop me from meeting his knowing gaze. Nor did it hide the small bit of censure I found there. Did he want to be my personal Capri Sun? Or did he want something else?

"We keep an emergency stash of blood in the infirmary," Thomas answered. "If you wish to drink that swill, be my guest, just inform Axel of what you take so he can keep stocked."

Thomas turned to Bastian. "You will escort her there and stay until she is well again. If the blood does not heal her, you will. Do not presume that I am not holding you accountable for her injuries as well, Cartwright."

Bastian paled slightly, but gave Thomas a stiff nod before guiding me out of the impossibly big gym. Only when we were out of the double doors and down the hall did I broach what had plagued me since Thomas started talking.

"What was that?"

Bastian snorted. "That was Booth acting like the ultimate asshole."

"No, I got that. With Thomas, I mean. What the fuck was that?"

Bastian's steps stuttered—the action faint enough no one but me or Thomas would be able to tell. "*That* was about Amelia. Thomas claimed you, yes?"

I nodded, wanting to hear why Thomas was going full monkey shit over a bite that would heal in an hour or so—sooner if I had blood.

"Amelia was Thomas' progeny, a member like you are. On one of her first missions, things went sideways. She was killed by a Rogue—the woman we were meant to neutralize. Amelia was too new—she could not heal fast enough. Thomas has not made another since."

"That's great and all, but we both know Thomas didn't *make* me, and the only reason he claimed me is because Emrys had already filed the paperwork—whatever that means. He has no reason to... I'm not worth that. What Booth did was—"

"Wrong," he insisted while guiding me down the hall to a tucked away set of stairs. "There isn't another way to say what he did. Booth was only supposed to simulate a capture, not actually injure you. We discussed it before we ever started the iteration. He was never meant to bite you."

I took the stairs gently, the vibrations of the descending steps jarring my arm. Honestly, it was all I could do not to vomit on the slick concrete.

"Then why did he?" I croaked, the pain radiating up my arm to my shoulder. Booth had done some serious tendon damage. Granted, it was nothing I couldn't heal from, but I wouldn't be winning any art contests in the near future.

"That, I don't know," he whispered, his hold more supportive and less guiding. "I'm going to pick you up now." And he did, but the result was less swoon-worthy and more nauseating. The fact that I didn't vomit all over him was a miracle.

He picked up the pace, and in no time, we were in a

brightly lit room with a hospital bed and a rather harried man with glasses inspecting my injuries. He had chin-length brown hair and a hunched quality to his shoulders that made me almost believe he wasn't as big as he actually was. I could only assume this was Axel.

"She's been with us a day, Cartwright. You break her already?" Axel teased, his Southern accent thick as molasses. It wasn't exactly a Tennessee accent. Maybe Texan? He had a winsome smile I would have appreciated better had I not been bleeding out.

"Not me." Bastian set me down on the hospital bed, the paper crackling underneath my ass. "Blame Booth. He tore into her like a complete asshole. No one knows why, but rest assured, Thomas will pull it out of him. That or bash his skull in."

Axel whistled a disbelieving tune. "Booth? That teddy bear?" To me, he said, "Let's see what we're working with here. You have any regenerative abilities I should know about?"

"If you give me some blood—from a blood bag—I should be fine in an hour or so."

Axel rolled his whisky-colored eyes at me. "That stuff? Why don't you take it from the vein?" He didn't let me answer before he pressed on. "No offense, girly, but your arm is shredded. Based on blood loss alone, you've got about five more minutes of you being conscious before I gotta pump some blood into you. Now, you can drink from the blood bags, but that might be a hit to my stash and not leave some for the other members of the house that may need it. Plus..." He trailed off, and I had a feeling I did not want to know why.

But it was Bastian who answered for him, "Plus, if we are going to be partners, you need to trust that I have your back. You taking my blood helps cement that tie. Or at least that was how Thomas explained it to me."

I'd rather take no blood and heal on my own than have a tie to anyone in this house. A fact that was written all over my face if Bastian's answering expression was anything to go by.

"Axel? Give us the room?"

Axel gave me a pitying glance before he got up from his rolling stool. "Sure thing. Try not to kill each other. I just got this place back to normal after Harper's last incident."

Then Axel swept out of the room, leaving me to Bastian and his ridiculous need to feed me his blood.

Sure.

Because there was no way that could go wrong.

13

"Thomas warned me about this, you know," Bastian began, his voice pitched low, his booted feet striding close but not piercing my bubble.

I kept my gaze latched onto his feet and refused to look up. If I caught sight of his neck, of his blood pulsing in that lovely vein, I'd lose it. I wasn't hungry yet, and I wanted to keep it that way.

I cleared my throat, an action that took far too much effort and hurt for some reason. My throat was dry. Why was it so dry? "Warned you about what?"

"He said that, in time, I would want to be bitten. That the thought of you hungry or in pain would make me want to serve myself up so you didn't suffer. That it was dangerous and blissful and would likely cause you to leave us."

His feet moved closer, piercing my bubble. The heat of him washed over me, even though he was a few feet away.

I shook my head, which I instantly regretted because blood loss was a thing and I was losing a lot of it, the healing process taking far too long. Booth must have hit an artery.

"I don't want to be tied to anyone. I don't want a home. I don't want friends." It was a lie—a whole mountain of lies—but it was the truth, too. I didn't want a tie to someone who was going to leave me. I didn't want a home if I was going to lose it. I didn't want friends that would die on me.

"Too bad. Because if you think I'm going to let you leave now, you're dreaming. Now drink, you stubborn woman, or you're going to pass out."

Let me leave? He couldn't make me stay if I didn't want to. I shook my head again—a serious mistake I kept making—and a moan ripped its way up my throat. The room tilted hard, and I barely caught myself on my uninjured hand, stopping myself from falling ass over tea kettle onto the floor.

"Stubborn bloody woman," Bastian growled before he was in my bubble for real, his big body shoving itself between my legs. His giant hand threaded through my short hair, and I found my face pressed to his neck.

My senses were hit like a battering ram. Bastian's heat slammed into me, his pulse thundered in my ears, his scent filled my nose. I hadn't realized I was so cold or so hungry. I shivered—not with want or need, but because the warmth felt so good. Had I always been that cold?

Bastian's grip tightened, shaking me a little. "Drink, dammit, before I slice myself open."

His throat was right there, and I was so hungry. Instinct finally took over as my fangs lengthened and I pressed them into his neck, the gentle pop sounding in my ears as his flesh gave way.

Blood rushed into my mouth, the decadent taste warming me from the inside out. And then it wasn't just Bastian holding me to him, it was me holding him back as I reveled in the healing, the safety, the warmth. All the things I said I didn't want but craved like the touch-starved neurotic mess I was.

Images came, too, but they weren't of Bastian's past or the wrongs he'd done. No, what I saw was our naked bodies tangled in sheets, his teeth nibbling at my collarbone, his body on top of mine, writhing with mine.

Bastian's hand fisted in my hair, and I swallowed, letting the hot nectar flow down my throat. Letting it heal me, letting it fill my whole body with warmth. His grip got tighter, but not pulling, the gentle pressure more of an encouragement than refusal. His scent bombarded my nose, the desire thick on the air as his other arm banded around my back and pulled me closer. His body flush with mine, I couldn't miss the thick ridge pressing against my center, his arousal calling to my own.

I swallowed again, and he answered it with a groan, the deep rumble radiating from his chest and into mine. I felt that groan all the way down to my toes and all the way up to my hair. I felt it like it was hands pressing into my flesh. And then the hand in my hair pulled, yanking my fangs from his neck before his mouth slammed down on mine.

The surprise lasted less than a second, my body overriding my brain, smacking down all my reservations with a single brush of Bastian's lips. My brain wanted to protest—hard—but my body wanted to roll in his scent, wanted to taste the inside of his mouth, wanted to see if I could make him make that delicious sound again. The remnant of his blood was still on my lips, but I did not care and neither did Bastian. His tongue swept into my mouth, a dueling dance that made me pull him tighter, hold him closer.

His scent, his heat, his touch was my whole world, and I wanted to revel in it. Added with the images still flowing from him, it was all I could do not to make those pictures in my head a reality. Somehow my hands found themselves under his shirt, the scalding heat of his skin seeping into my palms as he gave me the most delicious of shudders, pulling another groan from his lips. Dear sweet mother of all that was holy. At that moment I would have given anything to make him make that sound again.

A loud clearing of a throat had the pair of us freezing. Well, it had *me* freezing, my hands stilling on Bastian's skin like I was hiding from a T-Rex. Bastian, however, finished the kiss, his teeth nipping at my bottom lip like he had all the time in the world. When that was done—and the shudder of need slammed into me—he gave me the most beatific of smiles. Half-naughty schoolboy, half-innocent angel, that smile did funny things to my insides. Funny things I did not want to inspect for my own sanity.

"How can I help you, Thomas?" Bastian called, his gaze not moving from mine as he examined my expression.

Thomas' tone was clipped, an irritated sort of chiding one would give a toddler. "You can start by making sure you get your wounds closed. She can't use you if you're dead."

Shit. The scent of Bastian's blood filled my nose, the wounds on his neck still seeping blood.

"Anything else? I was busy."

I had never been so happy that Bastian was enormous. His wide shoulders hid me from Thomas' stare—not that I could have looked at him anyway since Bastian's hand was still fisted in my hair.

"You remember what I told you?" Thomas asked. "About how a vampire's bite was drugging?"

Bastian's gaze did not waver, but his smile died. "Of course. But you and I both know that Sloane is not a vampire."

"If it walks like a duck," Thomas muttered. "Are you capable of being her partner, or shall I pair her with someone who will make sure her wounds are healed prior to shoving his tongue down her throat?"

"Why are you here, Thomas?" I asked, my voice squeaky

like a prepubescent boy, but whatever. I'd just been caught making out with the guy who attacked me... Was that yesterday? Okay, so his censure *might* be warranted.

"I'm here to make sure you don't kill him by accident. Also, I find that I don't like the idea of you two being partners. How do I know he's going to look out for you when he's too busy staring at your ass?" Thomas's tone was sharp enough that I ducked around Bastian's big body to stare at him.

"The not killing him part—as you can see—is not a problem. Unless you think I was draining him dry via his mouth." I shifted Bastian away from me so I could face Thomas. "And I didn't see him distracted when he was lobbing energy balls at my head or planning with Booth to jump me. I think he'll do just fine. But in the off chance he doesn't? I've survived for a year on my own with no home or a single person to look out for me. In that time? I've killed over three hundred arcaners. Wiped out entire packs of lycanthropes by myself. Taken out ghouls and vamps and mages. Alone. The question isn't if he'll watch my back, because I don't need him to. The question, Thomas, is whether or not I'll watch his."

"Bloody fucking hell. You took down the Clayborn pack?" Bastian whispered, the awe in his tone a good sign since I was still staring Thomas down.

The Clayborn pack had been a hodge-podge group of Rogue lycanthropes. It had taken three weeks, but I managed to wipe every last one of those heart-eating murderers off the map. It had been my first order of business after my first feeding, and I gleaned that the man I drank down wasn't the only one, but part of a group of raping, heart-eating, sadists with the sole, single-minded goal of growing their ranks.

"Yes, I did. By myself." My gaze did not waver from Thomas. His entire body was still. I didn't even think he was breathing.

"How?" Thomas growled, the single word like a whip cracking.

"When I woke up on my grave, I didn't know what I was. I was going to the police to see if they could help and cut through an alley. A vampire named Jacob attacked me and I killed him. After that, I didn't go to the police and I didn't feed again, horrified at what I was. I didn't eat for a week. I figured I could starve myself to death because the sun didn't hurt and holy water wouldn't work, and everything else I tried, I healed from. A lycanthrope broke into a warehouse near the place I was holed up—he raped and murdered a woman. I smelled the blood, and I couldn't stop myself. Reading his soul, I found out he wasn't alone, so I hunted them down one by one."

Thomas approached, his movements too fast to track, and he was in my face, barely an inch from my nose. "No. How did you kill them? How did you find them? How did you make them suffer? I want the details."

Stupidly, Bastian put a hand on Thomas' shoulder. Thomas swatted it off so hard I heard the bones crack. Bastian howled in rage and a bit of agony, but Thomas did not move again, his pale-green stare like shards of glass piercing me to the table.

"Tell me," he ordered, his voice like silk.

I felt the pressure of him using his magic on me. Some called it compulsion, some called it the charm, some called it hypnosis. It was all pretty words for the magic vampires had that took a person's will away.

"Not if you're going to try and use that stupid fucking magic on me," I growled, shoving off the table and pushing him away. "You calm down, and maybe I'll tell you. But it was three weeks of bloody work, and the things I saw were..." I shook my head and gave him my back, turning to Bastian to assess his injuries.

Rather than the broken hand I thought he'd have, he

sported a few dislocated fingers instead. Growling, he yanked each back in place like the action wouldn't cause anyone else to puke their guts out on the tile floor.

"I owe you a debt," Thomas whispered, his voice clogged with an emotion I couldn't name. "I will owe you forever. That pack took someone very precious away from me. Someone I will miss for the rest of my exceedingly long life. If there is anything you need of me, I will provide."

Then I felt the displacement of the air and the faintest of whooshing sounds and Thomas was gone.

Bastian flexed his fingers, the motion slow as he tested his healing hand. The blood on his neck had clotted, but the wounds looked angry and painful. Still, he appeared as if the pain did not register.

"The Clayborn pack was the one we were hunting when Amelia died. After her death, they vanished, hopping from city to city, disappearing like smoke as soon as we got close. Thomas has been searching for them for seventy-five years, and you took them out in three weeks."

I didn't know how I felt about that. I wasn't doing anything special other than hunting bad men. At the time it felt like if I was going to be a monster, I might as well kill worse monsters.

"Thomas isn't the only person who owes you, you know."

I rolled my eyes, exasperated at the whole conversation. I didn't want people to owe me anything.

"Awesome. Who else owes me?"

"I do."

My gaze whipped back to Bastian, but he didn't meet my eyes. Shame colored every line of his face as his jaw tightened.

"Why do you owe me?" I was unable to hold the question in any longer.

He lifted his head, spearing me with his sharp gaze. "I just do."

And then he was gone. Without another word, without any explanation, he just left the room, abandoning me to get back on my own.

Some partner he was.

For the first—well, second, but semantics and all that—time since I'd been bitten, I looked down at my injured arm. While still a bloody mess, the skin had knitted back together, the flesh seemingly healed. With nothing else to do besides fret over what the fuck was going on with Bastian, I hopped off the examination table and went to the sink.

I was still reeling from his abrupt departure and Thomas losing it over the Clayborn pack, and all the rest of the changes my life had undergone in the last day and a half. And why did Booth bite me? And why was Simon so freaked?

Well, that one might have made a little more sense now that I'd made out with his brother. As I washed the blood off my hand, I thought about Bastian's lips on mine, his hand in my hair, the scent of him…

Stop it. This is exactly the wrong thing to be thinking about.

As much as my conscience was yelling at me, I couldn't stop the shiver that worked its way through me at the thought of Bastian's hand in my hair, the way he pulled me off his neck and kissed me, the heat of his skin under my palms.

Fuck.

Was it just because he was willing? Was it the blood? Was it the thoughts and images that bombarded me when I read his soul? I could almost feel them again, the memory so vivid. Was that what he wanted? Or because he knew what I was, was that all he was willing to show me?

A cold bucket of libido-killing ice washed over me. He knew I was a soul reader, he could be guarding his mind against me, only showing me those things to hide what was really in his heart. I couldn't say why that felt like a betrayal, why it felt like I'd been stabbed in the chest at the thought, but it did.

But didn't he deserve to hide from me? Wasn't that his right? I was offered his blood, not his soul. I was offered sustenance, not his secrets. Still, the thought of him hiding on purpose hurt me in ways I was not prepared for.

Then I groaned out loud, the sound echoing off the sterile walls and metal cabinets filled with medical supplies. Simon was so right, and I was an idiot for thinking he had no idea. Bastian and I should most definitely not enter into a relationship.

It was going to be blood bags or nothing from here on out.

After I'd washed off all the blood and cleaned up the sink

with cleanser and some paper towels, Axel strode back in the room. Now that I wasn't damn near bleeding to death, I took the time to assess him fully.

When he wasn't hunched on an examination stool, he was quite tall, his broad shoulders held back in a sauntering sort of way that spoke of an easy-going attitude and general jovial nature. His chin-length hair had been brushed back from his face, a streak of gray threaded through it that I hadn't noticed before. He was dressed in jeans, a western-style long-sleeved shirt with snap buttons, and cowboy boots. I'd lived in the South my whole life, and no one in the history of ever, pulled off that look better than Axel.

"Well, I see my med bay is still intact, and you're healed up nice." He picked up my arm to examine the former wound, his hands like ice. "Not even a scar. I'm impressed. Thomas is the only one who can heal that fast from blood consumption, and he's *old*. You're a young thing. How do you heal faster than Thomas?"

"Just lucky, I guess," I muttered before pulling my arm out of his loose hold and blurting the thing that had been on my mind since Bastian left the room. "I need you to get more blood bags." Sighing, I closed my eyes and started again. "I fed from Bastian this time, but I would really appreciate it if you would increase your stock of blood. While it may taste like swill, and it might not work as well—"

"You'd rather drink hot garbage than fall into bed with the man?" Axel cut me off, his assessment blunt but accurate. He tapped his nose. "It smells like mind-numbing lust in this room."

"Essentially." It was a major slight to Bastian, but dammit, I was not risking everything I was when I didn't have that much left to give. I needed to give to me first, for fuck's sake.

Axel's smile bloomed over his face, his teeth impossibly

straight and white. It was a movie-star smile which took his already-blinding hotness to stratospheric levels. Good god, were all arcaners this hot? I didn't remember the Rogues I'd killed being this pleasing to look at.

"Well, I would suggest getting another partner, but there aren't many of us you could feed from. Me and Thomas are out. Undead blood won't nourish you the same way live blood will. Dahlia's anemic, Harper can't stand to be touched, and Simon…"

"Is a no-go because Bastian will go full monkey shit, and I wouldn't touch Booth with a ten-foot pole. So that leaves the bags."

Axel pursed his lips as he folded himself into a chair. "I'll put in an order. You got a preference in type?"

"Not that I know of. And thank you for understanding. I've been alone for a while now, and I kind of like it here. I'd rather not fuck it all up in the first week, you know?"

He nodded sagely, like I was actually talking sense, which made me feel like I was doing the right thing. No more feedings—not from Bastian.

Axel tapped his bottom lip with his index finger. "Emrys said you were a soul reader—not that I've ever seen one of ya'll in the wild. You're supposed to be able to read the blood of a person, right?"

Instantly, I was wary. "Yeah?"

He seemed to pick up on my trepidation because he hunched his shoulders, resting his elbows on his knees. I wondered if he was used to doing that—making himself appear smaller to make people more comfortable. "Emrys said she wanted to wait, but I have a victim I can't identify, and I could really use your help."

"Victim?" I took a small step backward. "What do you mean by victim?"

Axel sighed, running a hand through his hair. "Booth and I just got back from a job. We were hunting down a Rogue that's been responsible for some maulings, but we haven't been able to catch the bastard. Most of the victims have survived, but this one didn't. She's tore up pretty bad, and we can't identify her."

I winced, thinking about drinking blood from a dead body. "And you want my help."

On the one hand, it sounded disgusting as fuck. On the other, I was offered a place here. I couldn't exactly turn my nose up at the first chance to use my abilities in a non-murdery way. I must not have been very good at wiping the *ewwww* off my face because Axel started chuckling.

"You won't have to bite her," he reassured me. "I'll draw some blood with a syringe. You won't even have to look at her if you don't want to."

Swallowing down a fair bit of bile, I nodded. "Okay, sure," I croaked. "If I can help, I will."

"That's the spirit. How much blood do you need?"

I thought back to all the times I'd read a person right before I killed them. Usually, it only took a single pull before I knew every single wrong they'd ever done, every sin etched into their soul.

"A swallow?" I shrugged. "I usually know all I need to after the first pull, so like an ounce?"

Axel got up from his stool and snagged a syringe before heading back to a door that looked like a walk-in freezer. Quick as a whip, he was back with a full syringe which he emptied into a plastic cup.

"Bottom's up," he said, grinning at what was likely my sourpuss face.

Dead blood. I shuddered, and then hauled up my big girl panties, downing the viscous liquid like a shot.

Instantly, I realized I had just done a very bad thing. This wasn't like the flashes of images I got from Jacob or the ephemeral smoke of Bastian's inner thoughts. This was a visceral bombardment of every sense, every thought, every sin. This was hell itself.

Only it wasn't mine.

Time seemed to go backward from the point of her death, her last gasp of breath was in my lungs, the bitter regret racing through her veins. The frantic pawing at her attacker, even though they had already delivered her death knell. The icy-blue glint of the big cat right before it lunged, and on and on it went.

And it wasn't until I saw my face, my parents' faces, did I realize who it was. Whose blood I'd drank, whose life had been stolen.

Aunt Julie.

I wanted to pull out of the read, but I was stuck, the images coming faster, the pain in them as real as if I were there.

But more, it was the visions she saw, the deaths she'd predicted. Including her own. She wasn't human, had never been.

Aunt Julie.

My mother's best friend, my surrogate parent, my friend, my family. The last family I had. I'd considered going to her after I'd woken up, but after Jacob, I'd figured that it would be better if I didn't. Better if I just stayed dead.

And now she was dead.

The visions spun faster, the pain ripping me apart piece by piece. Everything I'd thought was true, everything I'd believed. It was all gone.

A hand on my shoulder caused a tortured moan to leak out of my throat. A bucket was forced in my hands, and as if on cue, I vomited into it. The pain and rage and sorrow coming up with the blood.

I had to get it out, I couldn't let it stay in me.

Aunt Julie.

A warm hand was on my back, but I shrugged it off before tossing more cookies into the bucket until I was shaking and spent, my gut aching with loss and the agony of the knowledge that my last bit of family was gone from this world. My brain just couldn't hang on to anything but the image of the big cat ripping through her flesh, the burning, shredding, torture of claws rending her muscle and skin and bone.

I heaved again, but nothing came up. Tears poured down my face, the sound of my sobs echoing through the sparse med bay like some sort of tortured animal.

"Here, drink this," someone said, handing me a bottle of water. Someone else put a cold washcloth on my neck, and someone else took the bucket away from my hands.

Someone was crying, great, bitter sobs of pain, the sound like the worst kind of torture. It didn't take too long to realize that those sobs—the ones that hurt my heart to hear—were coming from me.

"Sloane, sweetie, I need you to tell me what you saw," Axel urged, his tone soft as silk. "And I'm gonna need you to calm down while you do it. I don't wanna pump you full of benzos, but I will."

An image flashed—one I'd seen before and would never forget—the big cat, its blue eyes flashing as its claws extended. Its white fur matted with blood as it struck again and again, rending flesh and bone, cutting into her like she was tissue paper.

Then a new image—full of fire and pain and my twisted face.

And despite Axel's warnings, despite the comforting hands

and well wishes, I started screaming. I didn't stop until Axel pumped me full of drugs, but even then, I dreamed of Julie's torture, of her memories, of her visions.

Those stayed, and they would cling to me.

Forever.

15

I shuddered, even though it was warm in my house, the heater working double-time to combat the coming winter chill. But visions brought their own form of cold, and no matter the weather, no matter what I did, I would always feel the finger of doom on my back.

One was coming, I knew as much, but I never knew when. I snuggled under my blanket, setting my book down before I lost my page. Visions came every day, but a good book series? Those were rare, and oracle or not, I didn't want the ending spoiled if I accidentally lost my place.

As soon as I put the book down, a premonition slammed into me of a giant home set away from the city. It had a gray façade with elegant architecture and a midnight-blue door. Men were surrounding it, guns in their hands and spells on their belt, their tactical gear loaded down with magical weapons and enough potions to stop a rhinoceros—or an ancient vampire.

They blasted their way through a ward, their numbers too great for the magic to hold, spells firing right along with the guns. They had a singular focus, and it was not one of capture.

This was a kill order.

This was the end of the Night Watch.

A hand on mine had me rocketing out of my drugged sleep, scrambling out of the heavy covers as I practically climbed up the headboard.

"Whoa, girly. No need to climb the walls," a voice called, and I had to blink—hard—to focus on her face. *Harper.*

I wouldn't say I was exactly relaxed after my waking scare, but I did remove myself from the giant headboard. I didn't get any closer to her, though, keeping the large bed between us as she moved to the stool at the drafting table.

"They sent me in here to see if I could help." She held up her hand, wiggling her fingers. "I can affect emotions, not just feel them. I don't use it very often because it bypasses mental warding, but you'd been stuck in whatever hell loop you were in for about half a day. Emrys wanted to see if I could pull you out." She wiped at her eyes with the back of her hand, smearing her carefully applied eye makeup.

She was crying. Why was she crying? Why was she here? What happened to me?

"I'm going on facial cues here since it seems talking is out of your wheelhouse for the time being, but I'm thinking you're confused? Yeah, we all are, kid. Best guess—and this is what I heard from Axel and Thomas—you tried to help him identify a body and it went sideways. Well, more than sideways."

Aunt Julie.

Harper frowned, leaning closer. "Who's Aunt Julie?"

Had I said that out loud? "The body—the woman in the cold room," I croaked. "She is—*was*—my mother's best friend. Juliet Hearst. Aunt Julie."

I didn't tell Harper all I'd seen—all I'd felt. There was no way to put it into words. No way to quantify and measure the agony of her death, the cold ache of her visions, the bitter pill that my entire life had been one lie after the other.

My parents weren't human and had never been. Neither had Aunt Julie. They spelled me, hid me away, lied to me. Because of what I was?

I pressed my eyes closed, the images of her soul hitting me like physical blows. No other reading had ever felt like this. Was it because she was already dead? Was it because she was my family? Was it because despite her faults, Julie had been good?

And she was gone—just like my parents.

A gentle thump radiated through the mattress as Isis jumped onto my bed, the skeleton cat padding her way over the covers to me. Dutifully, I eased from my crouch, allowing the bone kitty to curl up on my lap. Could she sense that I was about to lose it? Or had Simon sent her?

"I've never met a soul reader, so I don't know if knowing someone beforehand makes the reading worse. Given your reaction—and the manner of her death—I'd say reading from the dead is not the best idea."

I gave her a "no shit" look. *Way to state the obvious, Harper.* "I want to see her."

Harper's answering expression was startled and horrified. "Why?"

"Because she is the last of my family, and now she's dead. Because I never got to see my parents or say goodbye to them. I just woke up in a fucking cemetery looking at their goddamn graves. Because I fucking want to, that's why."

She raised her hands in surrender. "Okay, okay. No need to bite my head off. It's just..." She trailed off, wiping another ribbon of tears from her cheek. "I felt what you were feeling, and it was some of the worst pain I've ever..." She shook her head, unable to go on. "I can't do that again, Sloane. I can't pull you out again. I'll go crazy."

Isis began to purr at me, and I absently started scratching under her chin.

"I wouldn't want you to. No one ever needs to feel like that if they don't have to. But I need to see her. If just to say goodbye."

"I'll ask, but I'm telling you, Emrys might lock you up in a padded cell if you lose it again. That was… that was…" She trailed off, shaking her head. With a rueful twist to her lips, she shoved off the stool and strode out of the room.

I wanted to tell her sorry, wanted to take back whatever pain I'd shoveled her way, but the scars were too new and the pain too fresh, so I said nothing. Instead I cooed at a skeleton cat, and prayed my hold on sanity lasted just a bit longer.

Not five minutes later, a quiet rap on my door heralded a visit from Emrys. No longer in a white suit, she seemed almost normal in an eggplant tunic and leggings. Her feet were bare, and it was then that I noticed how short she was. When I first met her, she seemed larger than life and twice as big. Now that everything I had left had been ripped apart, everything seemed smaller. Everything seemed colorless and cruel.

Everything hurt.

"It's good to see you awake, Sloane," she said, sitting on the stool Harper vacated. "I have to say, if this is how it goes after every read, I'm going to have to rethink your purpose here. After what we all saw, my girl, I could not willfully put you through that again—no matter what the gain may be."

Alarm filled me before I stomped it down, letting the pain of losing another home glance off me. I mean, why wouldn't she kick me out? I was no more useful than tits on a bull if I couldn't read people.

I ran my hands over the lush bedding before cuddling Isis closer. Her purr was a balm I would miss greatly. I'd miss the roof over my head and the people. How much would going back to the streets hurt? Would it be worse now since I'd been in such a lavish place? Or since I was here for such a short time, would the memory fade?

A single hot tear scorched down my cheek before I hastily wiped it away.

"Oh, no, Sloane. I'm not suggesting you'd be kicked out," Emrys blurted, moving from the stool to the side of the bed. "I only meant that you'd have a different job. Given the state of Booth's jaw, I figure you could be our muscle. Thomas so rarely goes out in the field anymore."

I gave her a sad imitation of a smile, which was about all I could muster.

"Harper tells me you want to see the body. That the woman was your family?"

A burning sort of ache started in my chest, the flames growing with every breath. All I could do was nod. "Juliet Hearst. She was my mother's best friend. She—she was an oracle."

Not that I knew that information when she was alive. Not that I understood what her last vision meant or why it came about, or if it was true.

This was the end of the Night Watch.

Was it because I was here?

Were people coming for me?

Or had her vision already come and gone with nothing to show for it. I saw in her memories that they often did—a person's decision changed, altering their course and making the vision moot. Was this one of those times?

Or was it the reason she was killed?

Was *I* the reason she was killed?

I was so busy with the thoughts swirling in my head, that I almost missed it when Emrys' face went pale as a sheet.

"An oracle, you said?" Emrys abruptly stood, shoving to her

feet like she had a purpose. "You don't plan on reading her again, correct?"

I didn't have a plan for anything, but the more I thought about it, the more I realized I would need to read her again, need to see if I could glean more from Julie's last moments. She was murdered and I wanted to know by who.

"Sloane?" Emrys prompted, reminding me that I hadn't answered her.

"I don't know. She was murdered by a big white cat, but something about it was familiar and I don't know why. I owe it to her to find out who killed her. Maybe…"

Maybe if I found that person, I'd find out what happened to my parents.

"Maybe we'll get some answers," I finished, heading for the door.

I could do this.

I could.

Right?

Emrys was hot on my heels as I forced myself down the stairs. "May I ask, has it ever been like that for you before?"

I shuddered, hard, and shook my head, not stopping, not slowing down. If I hesitated for a millisecond, I wouldn't have the courage to go back. "Never. I couldn't say if it was because I knew her or because she was already dead when I drank her blood. Truth be told, I'm not all too geared up to find out."

You know why. It was because of what she saw. What she knew. Someone wanted her silent.

That thought came blazing through my brain right as I reached the staircase to the basement. If I read her again, would someone want *me* silent? Could I trust the people in this house? Axel and Booth were chasing a shifter, but how easily could that be a ruse?

How easily could the people in this house lie to my face?

I forced myself to walk down the steps to the med bay, the sterile room more populated than I'd hoped for. Axel was perched on his stool, facing off a harried-looking Bastian and a fanged-out Thomas.

Goodie. Just what I need on this fine morning. An audience.

"Sloane," Thomas breathed as he approached, his sclera returning to white as his fangs receded back into the periodontal pockets that housed them when he wasn't being emotional. He looked like he wanted to hug me, but settled on a reassuring squeeze to my shoulder. "You sure gave us a scare, kid."

I probably should have said something pithy to bolster his spirits, but I just didn't have it in me. My subdued attitude went over like a lead balloon, leaving the men shifting their feet as they struggled to look at me.

They knew something. I could feel the lie on the air as if one had been spoken aloud. They knew something and they were hiding it.

"I want to see her," I murmured, my voice barely a whisper.

They could have their secrets. I'd figure this out by myself, like I always had.

And no one was going to stop me.

16

The three men shifted on their feet again, and it was all I could do not to growl at them.

"I don't think that is a smart plan, Sloane," Bastian advised.

Had I not just been given the worst blow imaginable, I would have marveled at the fact that this was the first time he'd actually called me by name. As it stood, I was just irritated he was in my way.

"You said everyone here has a sad story, right?" I began, my eyebrows raised, my face demanding an answer. He gave me a sharp bob of his head. "How many of you were able to say goodbye to those you lost? Bury them? Shed a tear for their passing? And how many of you woke up to everyone and everything you ever knew gone just like that?" I snapped my fingers right in his face, the loud crack making him flinch. "How many of you had to live through a beloved's death? Felt every tear of their skin, every break in their bones, every feeble fluttering beat of their heart as it withered and died?"

I looked around the room, at their stricken faces. "None? No takers, then?" I speared Bastian with my gaze. "Then how about you stop with the bullshit advice for a problem you've never had and show me her fucking body."

Yes, my words were cruel. Yes, I could have gone about that a little better. But being treated like a feeble little lady in the middle of this shit wasn't going to help me. Finding the fucker who killed Julie was going to help. Finding out what happened to my parents was going to help.

Coddling was just going to drag me down into a pit of despair, and I couldn't let that happen.

Because if I fell in, I wouldn't be able to get back out.

Axel stepped to the side, his hands raised in surrender. "Okay, kid, but it took three times the recommended dosage for a shifter to put you down when you lost it. Don't make me do it to you again."

I followed him as he walked to the large door that had to be a commercial-grade refrigerator and opened it. The room was far larger than I'd expected, maybe ten by twelve feet. It had a wall full of empty slabs, and a lone one in the middle. A black body bag lay on the silver steel table, and despite my earlier bravado, I shivered.

"Now, I know you wanna see her, Sloane, but she ain't pretty." he advised, a gentle concern laced through his words. "The shifter tore into her something awful, and I want you to brace yourself for what you're about to see."

Axel carefully unzipped the bag, the tines parting one by one in the slowest agony ever. I'd seen my fair share of dead bodies. Hell, I'd made more than my fair share, but I never ripped them up. Save for eight puncture wounds—and the occasional throat rippage—my dead appeared mostly as they had in life. Julie was *not* as carefully killed. I knew that much from feeling her death, watching from her eyes as she was slashed and broken.

But seeing it from the outside was worse somehow.

Her face was a bloody mess, half of her jaw missing, her eyes gone from their sockets. Her chest was cut wide, her abdomen empty, the edges of the cavity jagged like...

"Did the shifter... eat her?" I asked, horrified at what I was seeing.

Axel gave me a slow nod. "I think so. He's acting like a wild animal and going for the soft parts. I've never seen a shifter do that—not that wasn't feral and stuck in his animal, anyway. You said it was a big cat?"

I nodded, staring at the lone bit of unmarred skin on Julie's forehead right above her left eyebrow. I bent, pressing a kiss to that bit of skin, her flesh cold against my lips.

Goodbye, Julie. I hope wherever you are, you're at peace.

Rising up from my farewell, I sniffed. Not from tears, those, I feared were gone forever. No, I wanted to know her scent, or rather *his* scent. "The scent patterns in this room are too varied. Do you have any of her clothing?"

Rather than look at Axel, I snagged the zipper and hauled it up, covering her destroyed body as the rest of me went cold. The frost of her skin seeped into my bones, turning me to stone even as I mentally finished my goodbyes.

I didn't need emotions or a conscience. I had no use for pleasantries or niceties. It was time to work.

Hadn't I been doing that for the last year? Hadn't killing Jacob led to the Clayborn pack? Hadn't they led to a nest of ghouls picking off elderly patients of a retirement home? Hadn't those ghouls led to a tiny pocket of Rogue witches stealing children? And on and on and on until I was cleaning up the streets every single day for a year?

I knew how to hunt an enemy, knew how to stalk my prey until they were cornered with no way out.

I couldn't die—*trust me, I'd tried*—so I had nothing but time on my hands. And now with Julie gone, I really did have nothing to lose.

"Yeah, I have them, but I smelled them and all I got was Booth's scent off of them." He strode out of the walk-in fridge to snag a large plastic bag off his desk. "But he's the one who found her and carried her out. You could see if your nose is better than mine."

He handed me the bag, and I opened the zippered top. At first all I got was the scent of decaying blood, bile, loose bowels, and urine and had to shove down a gag. Then the bouquet of other scents wafted out. The earthy tang of shifter —Booth specifically. He was all over her clothes almost masking Julie's light floral signature.

Well, that was a bust.

I zippered the pouch shut and handed it back. "I'll need to see her home then. I'm not getting anything but Julie and Booth."

Axel looked worried. "I don't—"

"No offense, Axel, but I really don't give a shit what *you don't*. I've done nothing but hunt arcaners for the last year. It's what I'm good at. Why don't you just save your misgivings until I'm writhing in pain on your floor. Cool?"

"What about us?" Thomas broke in. "You give a shit what we think, or are you going off half-cocked no matter what we say?"

Bastian, Thomas, and Emrys stood off to the side in a little huddle, but I didn't find censure in anyone's expression. A little pain, a little empathy, a little pity, but no censure.

I pinched the bridge of my nose praying for strength. "I give a shit what you have to say if you're not standing in my way. You going to stop me, Thomas?"

Bastian stepped closer to me, moving in front of Thomas—either to protect me or Thomas, I couldn't figure out which—his face awash in an emotion I couldn't identify. "No one is going to stop you from hunting this bastard down. But we need to do this smart, and forego getting the people around us killed in the name of vengeance. Can you do that, or would you like to be locked down until the end of time?"

Protecting Thomas from me, then.

I pretended to ponder his question. "I don't know. Let me think." I tapped my lip with my index finger. "I'll take door number one, thanks. Any other manly assertions you'd like to make? Those scent patterns aren't going to stay there forever, and I've already lost too much time."

Emrys sighed like I was trying the very last bit of her patience. "I can't believe I'm saying this, but if you're going out into the field, you'll need gear. Thomas will get you outfitted. Meet up at the front door in thirty minutes."

"Are you serious?" Bastian protested. "She's one slippery step away from full-blown feral and you want her out in the field? No offense, but you made it my mission to keep her from killing arcaners and at the first turn you're just giving her what she wants? Am I the only one who sees this?"

Emrys didn't bother sparing Bastian a glance. Instead, she met and held my gaze, an understanding in them that I felt on a visceral level. She gave me the slightest of nods, a gentle bow of her head that spoke of her own loss, her own pain. She recognized it in me. She knew my pain as acutely as I did.

"Mr. Cartwright, do you think I'm a fool?" Emrys raised her eyebrows in challenge. Bastian's deer-in-the-headlights expression was answer enough because she continued, "I thought not. There is a very good reason why I will be accompanying you on this excursion. Rest assured that the responsibility of Sloane's compliance will rest on someone else's shoulders."

Thomas skirted around Bastian and Emrys' tableau and wrapped an arm around my shoulders. "Come on, kid. Let's get you outfitted."

It turned out that Clem of all people was actually in charge of the gear, weapons, and protective clothing that the Night Watch used on a daily basis.

"I don't sleep, so I need to keep busy," Clem explained as her ghostly pale fingers moved like hummingbird wings on a pair of leather pants, the hand stitching a thing of beauty. "As a girl who used to say I'd sleep when I was dead, it's a mighty big adjustment."

Clem was a Southern woman through and through—even though the body she was inhabiting was from California. She told me that little tidbit sotto voce like I'd spill her secrets to the Southern Police or something. But other than the fact that she was a certified chatterbox and well, *dead*, I had no issues with the woman.

She tied off her last stitch and then shook out the garment with a flourish. "I know you had those leather pants, but they just weren't for you, dear. This will protect you better, and Dahlia spelled the leather. Now it will repel killing spells, protect you from poisons, and it's practically bulletproof. I know, I know. Like Thomas, you'll heal from just about anything, but injuries hurt and slow you down."

I accepted the garment. It was a mix of leather and a thick flexible material strategically placed for ease of movement. The leather bits were thick and yet buttery soft. She also handed me a belt with thigh holsters attached.

"Get dressed." Clem pointed to a giant Japanese screen. Apparently, she meant right here, right now. "I'll get your weapons."

Clem might be cute as a button—a very dead button—but she wasn't someone I wanted to cross, so I followed her instruction and got to it. "Weapons?"

"You think I'm going to let you go out into the wild with nothing?" She clucked her tongue at me like I was simple. "Mama Clem has got you covered."

Typically, I would just take whatever weapons my opponents had and use the guns or knives or swords against them. I was decent with a gun, swords were not my forte, and knives were just fun. I thought about this as I slid into the suit Clem had put the finishing touches on. Other than pajamas, it was probably one of the more comfortable things I'd ever worn. It seemed made for me, which made me want to slap myself upside the head because *it was*. I buckled the front closure that secured my meager chest, the material thicker there for added protection.

A pair of low-heeled boots flew over the top of the screen, and I barely caught them before they hit me in the head.

"You coming?" Dahlia called impatiently, and I hurried to zip the boots so as to not keep her waiting.

"Yeah, yeah," I muttered, skirting around the screen and back to Clem who held out a pistol and a weird-handled *thing*. "What is that?"

The top looked like a geometric loop guard for a sword, but there was no metal tine—AKA, the actual sword part —attached.

"Ah." Dahlia grinned. "This is my brilliance, *thankyouverymuch*. I mixed mage and witch magic to make this baby. Hold it in your hand and speak the incantation, *uitta mortis*."

Reluctantly, I did as told—the weight of the handle heavy in my hand for being mostly nothing.

But when I spoke the incantation, the weight shifted, concentrating less on the handle, and flowing out in a ribbon of electric-blue light. It pooled on the ground, waiting for me to flick out the deadly energy.

And then my rusty Latin supplied the translation.

Ribbon of Death.

17

"This is a whip," I said stupidly, stating the fucking obvious. But what was this, *Temple of Doom*? Did I turn into *Indiana Jones* overnight?

Dahlia rolled her eyes at me as she put a hand on her slim hip. "Duh. Okay, so I know that whips are out of style, but it offers a way to strike your opponents from far away, and it's ridiculously cool. Sure, guns and swords are awesome, but you have a magic whip. I mean, that's original."

I raised my eyebrows at her, gently flicking the whip to get a feel for it. I had to admit, it was cool as fuck, and even if it wasn't original, it was at the very least retro. "I'm not mad at it."

"Good, because you have no other choice." Dahlia stuck her tongue out at me. "I made it for you, so no one else can use it. You're welcome."

"Thank you," I replied dutifully. "Thank you both."

"Good. Say the incantation again to get it to contract."

I obeyed, watching as the ribbon of light retracted into the handle before holstering it.

"Now that that's done, it's time to go. Clem, give her some ammo for that Glock and let's get moving."

Clem passed over four magazines, and I shoved them in the specialty-made loops in my belt, checked the mag on the Glock and chambered a round, shoving it in the holster and securing the strap. Glocks didn't have a safety, but the triggers weren't loose, and the strap added protection. If I were going out into the world, I'd need it, and arcaners moved too fast not to have a round in the chamber.

Living in the South all my life, I was comfortable with handguns. I'd shot my first .22 at seven years old. They were tried and true just like climbing mountains, pitching tents, and skinning rabbits. My parents—for all their secrets and faults—taught me how to survive. Taught me how to live in the wild, how to make shelter, how to shoot and prep game.

I wondered what my last year would have been like if I'd actually utilized their teachings and went to the hills instead of the city. Would I be here right now? Or would I be like Julie, torn apart and wishing for another path?

After my weapons check, I followed Dahlia to the front door, the midnight color causing a cold finger of dread to trace down my spine.

"Everyone ready?" Emrys asked, breaking my stare on the doomed door.

I looked around at our group. Bastian, Thomas, Emrys, and Axel joined Dahlia and I at the meeting location. Harper approached, handing each of us a comms device. The tiny black thing was no bigger than a button and was meant to fit in our ear. According to Harper, it used bone conduction and was supposed to be the latest thing in communications gear.

"Do not forget that I can hear everything you say. Thomas ended up on an interlude after some nasty wounds and forgot to take comms off." Harper shuddered like she was reliving the memory. "There are some things you can't unknow or unhear."

Thomas had the good sense to blush—a feat I didn't think possible on his undead skin. "I've apologized a thousand times for that already. How was I supposed to know she was going to be a screamer?" He sighed, pinching his brow. "Please quit using that story as a cautionary tale."

Harper gave him a look that could fry metal. "When I get the sound of you fucking a blood junkie out of my brain, I'll quit mentioning it to any and everyone I give comms to. Until then, you're shit out of luck."

I wanted to laugh for the first time since I'd woken up, and the nearly silent giggle slipped past my lips against my better judgment. Quickly, it turned into an actual laugh until I was practically rolling on the floor. I imagined Harper's face as she scrambled to turn off the comms, having it turn into a slapstick because she was flustered, and the volume turn louder instead of off. I could practically see it in my head.

"Oh, man. I needed that. Never change, Harper. Never."

Harper stuck her tongue out at me, and I blew her a kiss.

Emrys cleared her throat. "We'll all be in the same transport, but here are your teams: Axel and Dahlia, Thomas and I, and Bastian and Sloane. Harper, Simon, and Booth are staying here. Comms check?" We all put the devices in our ears to perform the check, getting a nod from Harper. "Fabulous. Let's roll out."

We followed Emrys as she led us past the front door, down the hall, and to a garage. Among the many cars was a black SUV with dark tinted windows and a ram guard on the front grill. It appeared weighted down as if it were armored, and I realized pretty quickly that it must be. I piled in the third-row seat, Bastian following me, and then we were off.

The drive to my hometown of Whispering Pines was

shorter than I thought it would be. For some reason, in my head I pictured the Night Watch house being farther away than just on the rural outskirts of Ascension. We skirted around the city to get to my little suburb, passing the college I'd gone to on the way to Julie's house. On the other side of town was my childhood home, and I stared in that direction, even though I wouldn't be able to see it. The burned-out wreck called to me even now.

I swallowed, hard, and tried to get my head back in the game. My parents were long dead, but Julie wasn't. Her house had to have some clues. There had to be something there. A scent pattern that was missed, blood somewhere that wasn't Julie's, something. Axel navigated the streets like he'd lived here his whole life, cutting into alleys to avoid being seen.

Evidently there were video cameras on everyone's front porch nowadays, but oh, so rarely did people bother putting a camera on the back entrance, making it vulnerable to attack. Or at least in our case, it made it so some shmuck with a twenty-dollar camera couldn't record something he shouldn't.

Unerringly, Axel found the alley driveway of Julie's former home, the garbage cans set on the curb like it was a normal Thursday night. Did her neighbors know that their friend was dead? Did they hear her being ripped apart? Or were the houses too far apart, the sound too faint for their elderly human ears?

We piled out of the SUV, and I got a good look at the house I'd spent a good portion of my childhood in. A flash of memory superimposed itself on the dark yard. Mom and Aunt Julie cackling at the kitchen table while I drew in the living room. Dad barbecuing on her deck while I played with Otis in the backyard.

But then Axel opened the back sliding glass door, and the memory was shattered. Reluctantly—even though it was my fucking idea—I entered Julie's home. The dining chairs were upended, the table on its side. Blood drips and smears were all over the kitchen. The open-concept space led directly to the living room, the couch cushions a tattered mess of fluff and blood.

I knew from her memories that Julie had tried to fend off her attacker, catching him with the fireplace poker as she fled upstairs. But Julie had been no match for the shifter, and she'd only made it to the top landing before she'd been caught.

Everything I was seeing supported Julie's memories. The blood trails, the scent of her fear clinging to them as if the urgency were still there, a warning to all who entered that the danger had not passed.

Emrys and Dahlia were searching for personal effects to use in case my nose wasn't up to snuff. Axel and Thomas were playing lookout, stationed at the front and back entrances to make sure no one returned to see if there were more victims to be had. And Bastian and I were tasked with identifying scent patterns and looking for clues.

I had a feeling everyone was humoring me. Axel and Booth had been at this a lot longer than I had, and likely had already swept for clues. This excursion was more like they were coddling a toddler who'd thrown the mother of all hissy fits rather than a legitimate mission.

Not that I could blame them. Still, I followed Julie's blood trail from the kitchen where she'd first been struck to the living room where she grabbed the poker. The shifter had scored another hit on the couch, the slashing claw marks telling the tale as they mingled with Julie's blood. She vaulted over the couch, knocking over the console table and lamp, which shattered and cut her arm open. Then she'd hidden behind the couch, readying her weapon.

When the cat pounced, it got a shoulder full of wrought-iron poker. I saw it clearly in her memories, the poker piercing his flesh and fur, the spill of blood splashing on the hardwood floor. But where there should be a puddle, there was none. In fact, it was the one part of this whole space that was free of debris, of blood, of glass.

It smelled of cleanser.

"Well, fuck," I muttered, damn near stomping my feet.

"What?" Bastian's gaze scanned the room, his nose not telling him the same story mine was telling me.

"Julie stabbed her attacker with a poker. You see this spot?" I pointed at the circle of clean space. "The fucker used cleanser to clean up his own blood. And from the looks of it, he took the damn poker with him."

"Fuck."

I nodded in commiseration. I wasn't getting anything but Julie and Booth in here with the teensiest bit of Axel thrown in.

"Are there any droplets away from the scene? He couldn't have cleaned them all, right?"

We followed Julie's blood trail upstairs, but all I smelled was her. This was a bust—just like everyone probably thought it would be.

Rather than pause at the giant pool of blood on the landing, I turned left, walking into Julie's bedroom. Her bed was unmade, the clothes she'd worn the day before draped over the bench at the end of her bed. Nothing in this room had been touched. There were no scent patterns to find or clues to decipher, and it was relieving in a way, because there were no other smells, no fear or blood or death.

Just Julie.

I walked over to the bookcase where a photo of us was displayed prominently. It was my high school graduation, and her dark hair was flying in the wind as I struggled to hold onto my burnt-orange graduation cap, her arm draped over my shoulder. We were both laughing, my mom snapping the candid picture that was just slightly unfocused. On another shelf was a picture of Julie and my mom at my parents' wedding—another candid—my mom in her fluffy wedding gown as the pair of them giggled at something like they had a secret.

These—and any others in the house—were the only pictures left of my parents, of me, left in the world. Sniffing, I went to Julie's closet and snagged the biggest bag I could find. A gray weekender fell off the shelf along with a couple of hat boxes, but I didn't care.

"What are you doing?" Bastian asked, having followed me at some point. His voice was kind in a way that hurt.

I refused to answer him. Instead, I shoved the picture frame in the bag. Crouching, I yanked a photo album off the shelf, flipped through it briefly, and shoved it into the bag. I found three other albums, pilfering those, too, before moving to a jewelry box on her vanity table.

Julie had plenty of expensive jewelry, rubies and sapphires and diamonds glittered from the mouth of the box, but I wasn't looking for any of that. What I was on the hunt for was a cheap opal ring that couldn't have cost more than fifty bucks. It was a giant thing, spanning from the base of her finger to her first knuckle, and I'd always admired it.

She told me once when she was gone from this world, that ring would be mine.

I dug through pricey pieces before finding it at the bottom of a tangle of pearls. Unearthing the piece, I felt a sense of home in that one little bit of cheap jewelry. A sense of happiness that I didn't have before. Slipping the ring on my finger, I breathed a sigh of relief.

"All the money just sitting in that box and you pick out the cheapest piece of jewelry? You are an odd one, Sloane." Bastian's words caught me off guard, pulling my gaze to him.

He stood with his shoulder perched on the doorframe, his arms crossed. He was studying me like he was going to be tested on what he found, his gaze roving over the room, over me, over the ring on my middle finger. Julie had always worn it on her left hand, but since I was left-handed, it went on my right.

"That other stuff isn't mine. I mean, neither are the pictures, but there is no one left to care if I take them. That ring, though, was promised to me. It seems greedy to take the other stuff."

"Like I said, you are an odd one. You could pawn that jewelry and have a tidy nest egg, but to you, that's stealing. I kind of like that about you—that you'd take the sentimental things, even though you have nothing else in the world. I was wrong about you."

Was I supposed to say thank you? I settled on shrugging and staring at my feet.

A startled yell came from downstairs, sending a thrill of unease through me.

And then the pungent scent of smoke filled my nostrils before all the windows in the room blew in.

Smoke filled the bedroom, flames blanketing the curtains and quickly reaching for the ceiling. But that wasn't exactly why I couldn't breathe at present. No, I couldn't breathe because a mountain of a man was currently trying to shield me from no-longer-flying glass, even though I would heal a hell of a lot faster than he would.

"Get off me," I croaked, resisting the urge to shove him off. *Idiot.* I thought it, but didn't say it, trying to conserve the little oxygen in the room. The absolute last thing I needed was me getting all vampy. It was bad enough I could smell the siren call of his blood over the acrid smoke.

Bastian moved off my back, snagging me by the back of my suit and hauling me up. He tucked me under one of his huge arms, moving me bodily as he searched for the exit. His grip was ironclad as he hauled me out of the room—well, until I yanked myself out of his hands.

"I can walk," I growled, landing on my own two feet. "Find the others. Get out of here."

Bastian shouted a protest, coughing from the smoke, but I

was too busy heading back into the inferno that used to be Julie's bedroom. I couldn't leave the pictures behind. With a single-minded mission—that I knew was foolhardy but could not stop—I snagged the bag full of pictures. Fire danced close to the duffle, the flames spreading fast. I snatched the handle before spinning back to the hallway.

The scent of the flames, their heat brought back a niggle of a memory, the thought as ephemeral as the smoke dancing in the air. It was there and gone before I could grab it. Growling at myself I pressed on, trying not to breathe the acrid fumes.

Bastian was halfway down the stairs before he seemed to realize he could go no farther, the downstairs a raging inferno of odd-colored flames. They weren't orange or yellow or any other color I would have thought a flame would be. I'd never seen a green flame before, and despite the fact that it was immeasurably pretty, I knew that magical flames or not, I'd still be a crispy critter if we didn't get the fuck out of here pronto.

I swallowed hard, trying not to think of the team members we left on this floor, while sending a prayer up to any deity that would hear me that they managed to get out intact.

Bastian's own power rose on the air, orange flames coating his fingers as he seemed to press on the magical fire with his ability. Not that it did a whole hell of a lot of good. His magic seemed to make the fire grow instead of diminish, the flames growing hotter second by second.

"There's not enough water in the air to douse the flames, and my magic can't mingle with whatever this is. We need to find another way out." Bastian choked out.

And then it was me hauling him up and away from the flames, guiding him to another room that seemed less smokey. We'd have to jump from a window. If we could even get to one.

There was no doubt in my mind that this was an attack.

Oh, what gave it away, Sloane? Was it all the windows blowing in at once or the magical Molotov cocktail?

I rolled my eyes at myself, praying I remembered the layout of this house correctly. Julie's storage room had a false wall. I'd found it once and got stuck in the attic when I was seven. The attic had a line of transom windows that might have been missed in the blast. They weren't the biggest of windows, but I knew Bastian and I together were strong enough to rip the wall apart if need be.

We just needed a break from the flames.

The storage room was filled with smoke, the wall hidden behind the clutter of a well lived-in house. A sewing table with half a quilt abandoned on its top, crafting supplies, stacks of books and journals and all the things I wished I could go through, but couldn't save. The false wall hissed as I pressed on it, the cool brick a welcome sign in the blisteringly hot room.

"Help me," I ordered, and the pair of us shoved the wall to the side, revealing a wooden staircase. I grabbed Bastian's hand, yanking him behind me before I froze, realizing I'd set the bag down when I shoved the wall aside and almost went back for it. Bastian's hand tightened, stopping me.

"I got it," he yelled over the roar of the flames, holding up the leather bag like he was a harried husband at a crowded mall.

Yes, I was totally going to risk my life—and already had once—to keep those memories. Call me crazy if you want to, but it was the last vestige of my old life and I was keeping it.

Bastian overtook me on the stairs, hauling me behind him as he headed for refuge from the flames. The transom windows were larger than I'd expected, the unbroken glass big enough to fit our bodies through.

If we could reach them.

The attic space was outfitted like a safe room, full of comfy furniture, and a small kitchenette set up like one day the zombies would storm Tennessee and we'd need to hide out to avoid the horde.

"Come on, I'll help you up." He handed me the duffle.

I scoffed. "Yeah, and how will you get up there?" I pointed to the eleven-foot-high transom, the skinny window offering a teensy ledge that no one without a preternaturally skilled body could ever hope to climb.

"Don't argue, and just for once, try to listen to me. I can get out, but not if you're still in this mess. So, for fuck's sake, just let me bloody help you up, woman."

How was I supposed to argue with that?

"Fine," I grumbled. "But if you don't make it out, I will have Simon contact your ghost just so I can kick your ass. You got me?"

"Yes, yes." Bastian bent down, cradling his hands so I could use them as a step. "You'll be terribly heartbroken if I perish."

I looped an arm through the duffle handle, swinging it behind me and completely ignored Bastian's makeshift step. I took three steps back and ran straight at the wall, using my momentum to help me scale the brick. Reaching the window was the easy part, hauling myself up after unlatching it? Not so much. After shimmying my ass into position, I realized that I had the harder job.

I managed to squeeze through the window, spotting Thomas and Axel on the side lawn.

"Here," I called down to Thomas. "Catch." I shoved the duffle through the window, and it landed with a soft thump in his waiting arms.

"Now you, kid," he whisper-yelled, trying to avoid waking the neighbors before we could get the hell out of there.

I shook my head, signaling for them to wait and ducked back into the attic. "Time to go. I think everyone else is out, so come the fuck on. It's going to take the both of us to break this damn brick."

Bastian rolled his eyes at me. "I'm a mage, you silly woman. I can break the wall all on my lonesome. Just—"

"Are we having a meeting?" Thomas broke in, landing almost silently on the high pitch of the roof and scaring the shit out of me. "Or can we exit the current raging inferno that is this house?"

"Sure thing, Thomas. As soon as you convince macho man here that he needs a hand up because there is no fucking way he can scale the damn wall by himself."

Thomas gave us both a stiff nod before he latched a hand to the window ledge and ripped the whole wall away with his bare hand like he was shredding tissue paper. It took two swipes, but there was a Bastian-sized hole in the side of Julie's house.

"Now can we go?" Thomas quipped before jumping off the roof, landing neatly on the lawn with zero problems.

The last time I'd jumped from this high, my whole body had hurt for a week. It figured Thomas could pull off a superhero landing, the bastard.

"Oh, come on, Sloane," Bastian teased, emerging from the giant hole in Julie's house and looping an arm around my waist. "It's only three stories, you wimp."

With that little quip, he shoved off the side of the house, hurtling us toward the ground. But Bastian landed with way more finesse than I had ever accomplished, absorbing the impact with ease.

I ignored Bastian's dig at my totally healthy fear of jumping off a freaking building. "Emrys and Dahlia?"

Axel answered, seeming to slide out of the shadows like a

ghost. "Waiting by the truck. Let's get out of here before the fire department shows up."

I would have followed, but magic was in play and this wasn't some rinky-dink little house fire.

"Are normal firemen equipped to deal with this shit?" I gestured to the green flames that were now licking up the brand-new hole in the attic.

Bastian snorted like I said something funny. "No, but by the time they get here, Emrys and Dahlia will have completed the break?" He said it like a question to Thomas who gave him a sharp nod. "They were just waiting until you got out. Backlash is a bitch, you know."

Backlash?

"Come on, ya'll, the sirens are getting close," Axel advised, leading us around the other side of the house where Emrys and Dahlia were walking around a circle of salt.

The pair of them began chanting in Latin once we rounded the corner, the evidence of our exit all they needed to get started. I felt the faint tremor of the ground shaking underfoot as their chanting got louder, nearly drowned out by the approaching siren. Emrys' palms began to glow as she held them aloft, her magic growing as her voice got louder. When she brought her palms down, the ground pitched in earnest, nearly knocking us all off our feet. Then the flames morphed from green to orange, their heat diminishing.

"Time to go," Bastian reminded us, but I couldn't quit staring at the orange flames that were destroying my last good memories, my last safe place.

It hit me then that Julie's home was never going to be a sanctuary ever again. Never was I going to sit at her table with a glass of wine as I bitched about Mom not understanding art or Dad not wanting me to live on campus. She would never hear me complain about Mom being so adamant about not having social media or giggle with me about some boy I maybe kind of liked but was too nervous to go talk to. She wouldn't give me a hug and a cookie and tell me I was smart to dump that guy or say goodbye to a mean person I thought was a friend. She wouldn't slide art supplies to me under the table—with Mom watching like we were hilarious—when I'd overspent my supplies budget.

This house held so many memories, and they were dying one ember at a time.

Bastian snagged my hand, but I pulled it back. I backed away from him, my eyes still on the house, even as I headed for the alley. They could go if they wanted to, but I had somewhere else to be. Reluctantly, I turned from the house as I picked up speed.

There was someplace else I needed to visit.

The quiet of Meadows Street didn't quite have the same safety that I'd remembered as a child. I'd learned to ride my bike on this block. I'd been pulled down the street by Otis after he caught sight of a squirrel and decided dragging me bodily on the pavement was the best way to catch it. Mrs. Blumenthal fixed me up and helped me limp back to the house. She even gave me a cookie and called my mom to come get Otis because there was no way I was going to chase him down.

My father and I fixed Mr. Ahuja's fence together after that freak thunderstorm two years ago and his kids couldn't come up from Nashville to take care of it. Mr. Rosehill had the best lawn on the block, but was in a war of attrition with Mrs. Gagne over the state of her sycamore tree.

I knew every house. Every neighbor. I knew their pets' names, their kids. I'd lived here my whole life.

But the street felt colder, more somber. The holiday lights had been taken down on all the houses, even though it was the second week in January, and the lack of twinkling lights made the air bitter and the street feel darker.

Then I saw the builder sign in what used to be my front yard, the slap in the face of my memories being destroyed again almost too much to bear. The ruined house was little more than blackened toothpicks, but it still stung that even those would soon be no more. Soon, every single thing I had of my childhood would be gone, and another house would be in its place as if we were never here. As if my father never mowed that lawn. As if my mom never watered the geraniums, or I never swung from the tire in the old oak.

As if our tiny little family were gone forever with nothing to show for it but a trio of tombstones that no one would ever visit.

I twisted the ring on my middle finger, astounded it survived my jaunt through Julie's burning house. I'd never been happier to have a single bit of jewelry in my life. Hell, my ears weren't even pierced. But that one lone ring with its cheap silver band and glittering stone made me feel just a tiny bit less lost.

A teensy bit less alone—even if it was bittersweet.

The score of a single hot tear blazed down my cheek, cooling instantly in the frigid air. I wiped it away with the back of my hand, wishing I were stronger. Wishing I was able to handle all this without turning weepy. Where was the badass who killed without remorse? I'd pay to have her back.

"Now is not the time to wander off, Sloane," a familiar British voice called.

I chuckled mirthlessly. "Any idiot with a working brain cell could figure out where I'd go, Sparky."

Bastian stepped closer, but I didn't look at him. Instead, I stared at the remains of my childhood home, my body decided more tears were the course of action. Stupid tear ducts.

"Exactly. Meaning, that if someone is going around setting fire to places you're in, maybe you shouldn't be alone." His voice was pitched low like a whisper, the wind carrying it away as the heat of him seeped into my skin, even from a foot away.

"Or maybe I should be by myself. I spent a whole year with no one trying to blow me up. One excursion with you lot and it's Molotov central." I tipped my chin back to give him a sideways glance. "You get burned?"

Bastian shook his head. "I'm mostly fireproof. Smoke inhalation, though, will get you every time."

Shifting my gaze back to the burned house, I let myself say goodbye to it. My parents weren't here—I wasn't here. The memories that I had were mine and no one could steal them. Even if so many were clouded in the truths they withheld, my life—our lives—had been wonderful. They gave me every single bit of normalcy and happiness, packing in all the years I had them.

"What if the person who burned Julie's house down did it to us, too? To hide evidence, or to kill us, or..." I shrugged. For what purpose, though? That was what was driving me crazy. *Why?*

Why burn our house down? Why kill us? What were they after? And why was Julie targeted? It was connected, I just couldn't figure out how.

"It's crossed my mind. What was in that house they didn't want us to find?"

I nodded, shivering as the cold began seeping into my bones. Bastian threw an arm over my shoulders, sharing his warmth.

I swallowed hard, gearing up for a hard question. "Do you think they would be ashamed of me? For killing like I do? For..." *The souls I've stolen?* "The things I've done?"

Bastian's arm tightened, pulling me around and to him as

he gave me an honest-to-god hug. I hadn't had one of those in a long time. As tall as he was, my head fit just under his chin, and took the likely rare opportunity to rest my cheek on his chest and absorb the warmth he was offering. I was under no illusion that we were friends—or that he even liked me for that matter—but the touch was welcome as was the comfort.

"I think," he began, but paused as he rested his cheek on top of my head, "that if they knew how many lives you've saved, how many bad people you've taken off the streets, they would be proud. You are not greedy or malicious, Sloane. And that's something—with power like ours—that has to be taught. You had a discipline of right and wrong drilled into you from your first breath. There is no way they could ever be ashamed of you. Ever."

Jesus, who the fuck was cutting onions out here?

I sniffed, tears falling down my face in earnest now. "A simple 'no' would have sufficed. You didn't have to get all mushy on me," I muttered, disgruntled that my tears refused to stay in my eyes were they damn well belonged. "You wouldn't lie about that, would you? About my parents, I mean?"

Bastian gently hooked a finger under my chin, pulling it around so I would look him in the eyes. His were a blazing green threaded through with swirls of glowing gold. "No. I would not." He shook his head slowly, never breaking our locked gaze. "Not about that. Not ever. Do you understand me?"

"Not really," I blurted honestly, and a grin broke out on his face in answer. "But don't worry. There's lots of things I don't understand."

He started chuckling in earnest, the laugh still on his lips as he dropped them to mine. For some reason I wasn't prepared for him to kiss me, the shock of his affection freezing me to the spot. This kiss felt so different from our earlier one. Less frenzied, less angry. It wasn't about feeding or the blood or the thoughts I gleaned from him.

He kissed me because he wanted to. Because he needed to. I felt as much from his touch, the truth in it washing over me as his breath mingled with mine. His giant hands cupped my face, cradling it like it was a precious treasure and then I unfroze, the softness of that touch thawing me into action.

Somehow, I found my hands covering his wrists, the strength and power in them surrounding me with a safety I hadn't felt since I woke up on the dirt a year ago. And despite my misgivings, despite Simon's warnings, despite all the bullshit I spewed to Axel about not going there, I parted my lips and let him in.

Heat enveloped my whole body, a flash fire of want slamming into me as his tongue slid against mine. This wasn't tainted like I'd worried his earlier kisses were—this was a need, pure and simple. Bastian walked me backward until I was pushed against the rough bark of a tree, likely Mrs. Gagne's sycamore. I reveled in the pressure, the weight of his body pressing against mine as our tongues dueled for dominance. His hand fisted in my short hair, and he pulled my mouth from his as he veered south, his lips landing on the tender skin of the underside of my jaw. I shuddered as that flash fire turned into an inferno of need, his answering growl sending me into a tailspin.

Then I was up, my back still pressed against the tree, but now my legs somehow found themselves around his waist, his lips never leaving my skin as he nibbled and kissed and wound me up until I was clawing at him like a woman starved.

I could feel my fangs lengthen, the hunger rising along with my desire, but I didn't want to bite him. I wanted to feel him this way, not the secrets hidden in his blood. I wanted this mindless base need, wanted to taste his lust on the air as his scent filled my nose, wanted all of it enveloping me in all that was Bastian because it felt so much better than anything else I'd experienced ever.

A faint buzzing sound came from his pocket, but the pair of us ignored it, his lips finding mine once again as his evident arousal pressed against my center. I couldn't help it, I moaned into his mouth. His answering groan radiated through me, the vibration waking up every millimeter of my skin, every bit of me.

The buzzing came again, and then I heard Harper's voice over comms—the first of the night.

"What did I say about that shit?" Harper growled, the tinny sound coming from Bastian's earpiece. "And answer your fucking phone, dumbass, before I figure out how to make the damn thing electrocute you."

"Anyone ever tell you that you were the mother of all cock blocks, Harper?" I asked, out of breath and pouting as Bastian let me slide down his front until I was back on two feet.

"Yeah, well, it's a specialty of mine," she sounded off in my ear, the bitter note in her tone making me feel like an asshole.

"Where have you been? You went dark for so long, you missed the attack, subsequent fire, and our daring escape. What happened?" Bastian asked, his smooth voice unhindered like mine was.

"I just got comms up after the whole compound went dark. Even the backups went offline. And something weird happened. Are you—is Simon with you?"

I moved to step away, but Bastian's arm banded around my back, and I was once again plastered to his front. He flashed me a blindingly white smile, knowing I was a put-out disgruntled mess and not giving that first fuck. It was a blissful sort of smile that did weird things to my middle. Weird things I was not at all prepared to feel.

"Right now, no." Bastian squeezed me, his smile growing wider.

"Did he go on the mission with you?"

Bastian sighed. "You know better than that. Why are you asking?"

Harper groaned, her voice wary for maybe the first time since I'd met her, a tone I figured she didn't use all too often. "Because I can't find him. One second everything was fine, and then the house went dark and I felt this blip of emotion that… I can't find him, Bastian, and I don't know what to do."

Bastian's smile froze. Hell, his whole body froze. Then he was moving double-time, my hand in his as he dragged me behind him, heading back the way we'd come.

"Don't move, Harper," he growled, his voice like sandpaper. "I'm coming."

2 0

Bastian's grip was ironclad as he practically ran to the SUV, dragging me behind him. The vehicle was parked around the corner with the whole gang inside, half of them appearing to be sleeping. Bastian pounded on the glass, startling Axel who was snoozing at the wheel.

"You got Harper on comms?" he asked once Axel rolled down the window, panic radiating from his entire body.

Axel shook his head, and Emrys leaned forward to get a better view of us, her odd reddish eyes casting an eerie glow.

"What's wrong?" A flash of concern appeared on her face before it was walled behind the calm façade she usually had in place, but her eyes gave away her emotions just like mine did.

Bastian practically vibrated, he was so wound up. "Harper said comms went offline after a power outage at the house. Full black out, battery and auxiliary power wiped out. She felt a blip of emotion before it was gone, and now she can't find Simon. Power is back online, but..."

Thomas rolled down his window. "Get in the truck, you idiots." He fished an earpiece out of a pocket and stuck it in his ear. "Harper? Can you locate him with his phone or the GPS in his car?"

Harper's scathing voice came over comms as Bastian and I climbed into the back of the SUV. "I would if they weren't right fucking here just like *he's* supposed to be. Don't you think I thought of that? Would I worry every single member of the team unnecessarily, dipshit?"

"Harper?" Emrys cooed, her voice in stereo in the car and on comms. "Take a breath for me. If you can't find him by conventional means, then Dahlia or I will locate him. You are doing all the right things, sweetheart."

The thought of Emrys calming Harper down reminded me of my own mother, the way she would cheer me on when we went on our family hikes, the way she would push me. I liked that Harper had that even if I didn't.

We settled in our seats, and all the while Bastian hadn't let go of my hand. I squeezed his fingers so he knew I was there for him. Simon was Bastian's weak spot, and I wasn't going to let him worry alone. He gave me a quick squeeze back, but didn't look at me, his eyes forward as Axel navigated the sleepy streets.

Harper's exhale breezed through my ear.

"Good girl," Emrys murmured. "Now, lock yourself in your room. We're coming to you. Have you seen Booth?"

"No," Harper answered, "But I didn't look for him. He's supposed to be healing up, right? I figured he'd still be passed out after Axel's drug cocktail of painkillers."

Axel snorted, the SUV accelerating through the dark night, the speed limit a mere suggestion to be ignored. "I gave that boy enough to put down an elephant after Thomas got done beating on him. If he isn't howling for more drugs, he should be dead to the world. Don't you worry none about Booth."

Harper exhaled again, relief in that little puff of air, but I was confused. Why would Thomas beat on Booth? Was it because of me? Because he'd bitten me? Was that what Axel had meant?

"Okay," she whispered. "I'll sit tight. I won't worry about what I can't change. I'll wait for you guys to get here." She said it like she was telling herself rather than reassuring us.

"Good work, Short Stack," Axel crooned through the earpiece. "We'll be there in two shakes of a lamb's tail. Don't you worry about a thing."

Axel flicked the earpiece out of his ear, tightened his grip on the wheel, and pressed the gas to the floor—or at least that's what it seemed like after I was shoved back in my seat from the force. I wasn't the only one who knew something was really wrong, but no one was saying it. So I kept my mouth shut and hoped Simon was going to be okay.

We screamed down the manicured driveway and screeched to a stop in the garage—barely missing a very sleek street bike with an armored guard on the gas tank. We piled out, Axel and Thomas making silent hand gestures at each other before peeling off.

Bastian hadn't said a word in the minutes since we'd explained the problem, and the longer we went on without word from Simon, the more rigid his back got. His neck muscles were so tight, if he tried to move his head, he'd break his whole fucking spine.

Emrys put a hand on Bastian's elbow, stopping him. "Bastian, I want you to go find Clem, make sure she has something to do before she goes bananas. Have her make his favorite or something." He peeled off, likely grateful for something to do. "Sloane, I want you to stay with Dahlia while I collect what I need and get Harper. Do not leave her side, you got me?"

It felt like she was asking me to guard Dahlia for some

reason, and I was more than happy to have a job to do. I felt useless, my knowledge of the house limited, meaning I couldn't help Axel and Thomas with the perimeter check. I couldn't do magic, so I was not needed there. After the fire, I really needed something to do that I was good at, and bodyguard was as good a thing as any. I really wished I could see Simon's room, but that wasn't what she'd asked, so I didn't suggest it.

"Yes, ma'am," I answered, and she was gone, moving so fast I almost lost track of her. Emrys wasn't as fast as Thomas, but she could *move*.

I turned to Dahlia. For the mission, she'd had her braids gathered in a loose bun at the nape of her neck, but she was setting them free. She cracked her neck, her entire body restless as the tension and silence grew.

"You okay?" I asked stupidly. It was obvious she wasn't fine, but I needed to get her talking. She hadn't said a word since before the fire, and I was worried she might be going into shock. Or maybe that was her "mission mode."

Dahlia looked at me, really looked at me for maybe the first time since we got to Aunt Julie's house. Her eyes were wild, fear dancing in them as she seemed to be struggling to keep it all in. "Simon isn't supposed to leave the property—not after he made Clem. If he left—if he..." She shook her head, her teeth pressing into her bottom lip. "There would be no reason we couldn't find him unless someone took him."

"Made Clem? Is that against the rules or something?"

Dahlia nodded. "He was supposed to kill her. Necromancy —well, all death magic—is highly regulated. Reanimating a body, filling it with a spirit? He popped up on a radar he should have avoided. Emrys used all her pull to keep him out of trouble, but he was put on house arrest."

I shook my head. "By who?"

"The ABI. It was all Emrys could do to keep him out of their clutches. Simon wouldn't just leave. He only has a month left on his sentence."

I only very recently discovered there was such a thing as the Arcane Bureau of Investigation, and their scope was still unclear to me. "How long has he been stuck here?"

"Ten years. Simon has been locked down for ten years and he only has a month left. Or *had*." Dahlia began pacing, her long braids swishing against her back as she pivoted. "If it's something stupid and he's not here, I'm going to freaking kill him."

Dahlia was still pacing when Emrys and Harper returned, both of their arms loaded down with spell ingredients. Dahlia hefted a vase off the round entryway table, and Emrys shook out a dark purple cloth that had golden moon designs printed on the fabric. Harper set pillar candles in exact intervals and handed Dahlia a metal bowl and a map.

Emrys turned to me. "Do me a favor, will you? Look over Simon's room. Sniff around, look for clues."

I had a feeling she was either giving me something to do or wanted me gone. But I wasn't going to argue with her— especially since that was all I'd wanted to do since I stepped foot in the house.

Taking the stairs two at a time, I reached Simon's room in a flash. I didn't know much about Simon other than he was Bastian's brother. Well, that and he was apparently a death mage with a skeleton cat and a penchant for pissing off the ABI. Simon's room wasn't much different from the last time I'd been in there. A battered couch in front of an unmade bed, gaming controllers strewn about. Books littered tabletops and nightstands and parts of the floor, some open, some in haphazard stacks that could topple at any moment. The dark curtains were drawn, and a lamp sat lit on an end table with its shade slightly off-kilter. A giant TV was mounted against the wall, a slight film of dust over the dark screen.

On the high-pile rug in front of the TV was a spirit board, but not the cardboard and plastic kid's game one would pick up at a big box store. No, this was a solid-wood affair with hand-carved letters and runes etched around the edges, along with a pair of skulls. The planchet appeared to be made of an iridescent shell of some kind, with a glittering glass viewer. Next to it was a pad and a pen half-covered with a dirty shirt.

But it was the scent that permeated the room that really caught my attention. Beneath the scent of dirty laundry and a stale pizza that had probably been shoved under his bed and forgotten, was the faint traces of the people who had been in this room. Bastian was a mainstay, his masculine flavor all over a battered reading chair. Dahlia, too, she had a favorite side of the couch and her floral bouquet infused that space.

It wasn't those scents on top of Simon's that concerned me.

It was Booth's.

It was fresh, barely an hour old, but it was still here. And that's when a few things became frighteningly clear. Even with Axel in Julie's house, I barely smelled him, but Booth's signature was everywhere. On her couch, on the air, still clinging to everything. If there had been anyone else in that house, I would have known, as much as they touched, as much as damage as they caused, there would have been some trace left behind.

But there wasn't. I only smelled Booth and Julie.

A hot pit of dread opened wide in my belly. I couldn't say why I strode forward to look at the pad of paper. Couldn't say why I peeled the T-shirt back to see the message I knew was written on it.

Beware of Booth. Tell Sloane I love her.

My hand shook as I reached for the pad, a sheen of tears in my eyes blurring the page.

Aunt Julie.

He'd contacted Julie and she'd told him to be careful.

Booth's scent was the only one in Julie's house besides hers.

Beware of Booth.

21

Hot tears fell down my cheeks as I nearly crushed the paper in my hand.

Beware of Booth.

My lips trembling, I backed slowly away from the board.

Did he kill Julie? Did he kill her and then come here and look at me like he'd done nothing wrong, like *I* was the wolf in *his* midst. Did he bite into me knowing he'd tasted her flesh, knowing he'd killed the very last bit of my family?

But Booth had been a wolf when we'd trained. Not a cat.

I vaguely remembered Dahlia's instruction on shifters—that they could turn into any animal—but I couldn't remember if Booth was a shifter or a were.

I had to tell the others. Even if I was wrong—not that I thought I was—Booth had to be located. As far as I knew no one had checked on him, assuming he was still laid up from Thomas' *instruction*. Whatever that meant.

"What's in your hand?" Bastian asked, and I whirled, my

whole body trembling in fear, and knowledge. "What's wrong?"

Slowly, I held my hand out to him, showing him the message Simon had jotted down from the spirit board, unable to tell him all the thoughts swirling in my head.

"It was next to a spirit board. And this whole room smells like Booth. Just like Julie's house. There wasn't another shifter there. I only smelled Booth." I'd thought when I found the person responsible for taking Julie from me, I'd be cold, methodical. I thought it wouldn't burn every single bit of me like I was dying, the loss of her hitting me in new ways. But I wasn't calm, I wasn't collected.

I was a mass of fury and rage and fear and grief. I was barely holding myself together.

"He isn't here, is he? Tell me someone checked on him. Tell me he's here and this is just one big mistake," I challenged him, waiting for him to meet my gaze, waiting for him to tell me I was wrong.

Bastian swallowed, his hazel eyes finally meeting mine. I saw the truth in them, the widened gaze that held the signature of fear.

"Come on. We'll find them. It has to be a misunderstanding. It has to be," he offered, reaching for my hand, but I backed away.

"He killed her. He killed my only family," I whispered. "He took your brother. Why? Why did he do this to us? What did we ever do to him?"

Bastian stepped into my space, his hands cradling my face as he stared in my eyes. "We don't know that, Sloane. Let's tell the others what you've found. Maybe we're wrong."

Maybe we're wrong.

He believed me and didn't want to. I knew why, too. Bastian wanted to believe there was hope for Simon, hope that he would be alive and whole, and unharmed. That this was one big mistake, and we weren't delaying all the grief that was threatening to crash over our heads.

Because if Booth killed Julie, what was stopping him from killing Simon? If he was a monster, was there a rhyme or reason to his murders, or did he kill indiscriminately?

Hesitantly, I gave him a trembling nod and let him guide me out of the room. My fear for Simon ramped up when I heard Dahlia's frustrated groan. Over the banister, I spied the whole gang grouped around the table, the candles alight and casting an odd glow on them all.

"Why can't I find him?" she growled, and the fear that was threatening to crash into me began to crest. The candles that dotted the edge of the table winked out, their flames dying with the end of her spell.

"I think we've got something," Bastian called, pulling me behind him down the stairs. He thrust the pad into Emrys' hands, his rage crinkling the paper. "This was by his spirit board."

Beware of Booth. Tell Sloane I love her.

That message would be burned into my brain until the end of time.

It took Emrys less than a second to read the paper, her trembling hand giving it away, but she didn't raise her head. "Thomas? Check that Booth is where you left him, will you?"

Thomas' eyes widened, his sclera reddening almost instantly. He gave her a swift nod that I doubted she saw before he was gone. His rage-filled scream not a moment later was answer enough. Booth wasn't here.

That didn't explain why Dahlia couldn't find Simon, though. Unless he was…

"What's going on?" Dahlia asked, and Emrys showed her

the paper. The message was powerful enough that speaking it aloud would brand us all.

Dahlia pressed a hand to her chest like she was holding in her heart. Like if she moved wrong, if she took her hand away, her heart would shatter into a million pieces. She stood like that for one long moment before she took a shuddering breath. A single tear fell down her face, and then her expression turned to stone, her jaw visibly clenching.

"None of this explains why I can't find him. Dead or alive, in the next room or in Timbuktu, I should be able to find his skinny ass no matter where it is. Where the fuck is he?"

Emrys offered a comforting squeeze to Dahlia's shoulder, but the witch shrugged it off. I understood not wanting comfort in a time like this. "Maybe he's being cloaked?"

"By Booth?" Bastian scoffed. "Not likely. This is bigger than Booth, I can feel it."

"What about Clem?" I asked, falling onto a nearby chair situated next to a bookcase. "You said he made her, right? Wouldn't the magic in her body be like a link to him or something?"

I knew little about spells or magical items—even less about death magic—but I knew enough about magical bonds to fill a whole library. Every arcaner had a blood tie to their maker or parent. Lycanthropes had one to the arcaner who'd bitten them. Ghouls had one to the death mage who raised them. Vampires to their sire.

If Clem was a spirit inhabiting a reanimated body, she was essentially created by Simon, and should have a link to him in her blood. If she even had blood in her veins. That was definitely suspect, but it was all I had.

Emrys turned to Axel, her hand on his arm. "Ask her if she's willing. Convince her if need be."

I doubted Clem would need convincing, but I didn't say anything.

A quiet meow had me staring at the floor, Isis sat at my feet, and I picked her up, setting the bone kitty on my lap. She rested her head on my chest, fully leaning into me like she needed me to support her this time instead of the other way around.

"I can't purr at you," I told her. "But I can give scratches. We'll find him, sweet girl."

The swish of the kitchen door sounded before Clem appeared in the dining room doorway. Flour covered one deathly pale cheek as well as her black apron which spelled out "Drop Dead Gorgeous" in a glittery purple curlicue font. She marched her way over like a woman on a mission, her odd, icy-blue eyes sharp as a razor as she stomped right up to Bastian.

She seemed like she wanted to slap the shit out of him but managed to hold herself back by the skin of her teeth. "You knew he was gone, and you had me making him apple dumplings instead of helping, you dumb fuck? I ought to kick your simple mage ass up and down this house. I am not some fragile little flower, you macho moron, and you'd better get that into your thick skull before I beat it into you."

Clem then swiftly turned on her heel and marched right to Dahlia on her sky-high heels, dismissing Bastian with a swish of her emerald skirt.

I wanted to hold in my snicker, but with all the stress, with all that had happened in the last two days, I just couldn't. I cuddled Isis closer and busted up laughing, tears trickling out of my eyes as I replayed Clem's words in my head, the tirade getting funnier each time I thought about it.

"Dear sweet lord in heaven, did ya'll break her or something?" Clem asked once my giggles turned into an odd snorting guffaw.

"Or something," Bastian supplied, kneeling at my feet. He warily eyed my arms around the bone kitty, and I nearly busted out in a fit of giggles again once I remembered that Bastian was not a fan of Simon's cat.

I pressed my lips together, holding in my obviously ill-timed mirth. I mouthed a "sorry" to Bastian. Even though he had a faint smile on his lips, I still felt like an asshole. Here I was laughing like a loon while his brother was in a murderer's clutches. I needed a padded cell and an empathy chip installed.

Quickly, I sobered, my mirth dying a swift death. I released one hand free from Isis and reached for his fingers. My family was dead, but he still had Simon, and we'd need to bring him back just so Bastian wouldn't have to feel like I had every day of this past year.

So he didn't go cold like I did.

Outside of our little bubble, Dahlia and Clem were working together to find Simon, but here in this silent little space, Bastian and I held each other's hands and tried not to break down. I wanted to be wrong about Booth. I wanted Simon to be okay and this whole thing to be a misunderstanding. I wanted Bastian's worry to be for nothing.

But I knew I was simply trying to fool myself, so I held his hand and tried to think happy thoughts as I watched Dahlia work.

Dahlia lanced Clem's finger with a slim knife, collecting the slow, black blood in a small metal bowl. Clem's blood smelled of death and magic and… an earthiness I couldn't place until I remembered the day I woke up in a cemetery.

Clementine carried the scent of the grave.

Dahlia snapped her fingers and the candles all lit at once, their flames dancing high for a moment before shrinking to normal size. She dropped some herbs from a vial into the bowl with Clem's blood in it, twisting her hand as she did so. The bowl rose in the air and began spinning on its own as Dahlia dropped more and more ingredients into it—a little salt, some chalk, a drop of her own blood. She snapped her fingers again, the contents igniting in a ball of purple flames.

Clem staggered, nearly falling off her spike heels before Thomas caught her, his reemergence from his search for Booth going unnoticed in the height of the spell. But no one was looking at Thomas at all.

We were all staring at Clem.

Clem's ghostly pale face turned a shade of gray I'd only glimpsed in the long dead. Her icy eyes rolled back in her head, leaving only a white sclera as the orbs began to glow. She started convulsing in Thomas' arms, a thin ribbon of black blood dripping from her nose.

And then she began to speak, the words flowing together in a language I didn't know but sounded familiar. It wasn't Latin, but it was close.

"Blood and death call to you," Bastian translated. "Blood and death call to us all. A master of death awaits you. He awaits you in the hiding place of the soul stealer. He waits for you to bring him home."

Soul stealer? Did she just blurt out my secret all over the fucking table?

Why, yes. Yes, she did.

A flash fire of guilt and adrenaline slammed into me. I'd kind of planned on telling people that little nugget of info around about never, and Clem just spilled all the fucking tea like she was a one-woman tea-spilling machine. My heart tripped inside my chest as I tried not to flinch at Bastian's translation.

Thomas, however, could hear my heart just fine. He leaned around Clem's red victory rolls as he leveled me with a stare so sharp it was a wonder it didn't cut me in two. I cuddled Isis closer, ready and willing to use the kitty as a shield.

All the candles blew out at once, the bowl falling with a metallic clink on the table, and seven pairs of eyes followed Thomas' lead.

"Soul stealer?" Thomas prompted, his eyebrows raised as he awaited an answer.

I was so fucked.

22

In all our scant discussions of what I was, not once did Emrys mention that soul readers could also eat souls. I knew, of course, but I hadn't brought it up because I thought if they didn't know, I wasn't going to tell them. Either that, or it was too taboo a subject, and no one was going to call me out. I was sort of hoping for the second one, but I now knew it was the first.

Maybe I should have confirmed this information—at least to Emrys.

"I'm guessing that ability is not standard issue with soul readers then?" With the lack of head nods and unblinking stares, I shrunk in my seat. "Cool. Umm... Surprise?"

Harper snorted, her eyes wide. "So, you don't just read souls, you eat them?"

I winced. "Only the really bad ones?"

Bastian stood from his crouch, the height disparity not at all comforting with his stony expression. "That was why you wanted to die. Because you consumed a soul and thought what?"

"Pretty much that I was a soul-sucking monster. It was shockingly hard to take myself out, too. Jumping off buildings, getting run over by a bus, starving myself. The list goes on. The only thing I didn't try was cutting off my own head, but it's surprisingly difficult to locate a guillotine nowadays."

"And you failed to mention this at our first feeding, why again?" His lips barely moved as he spoke through a clenched jaw, bald malice and rage lighting his eyes like twin emeralds.

"Hey," I protested, shoving out of my seat, still holding the skeleton kitty. "I distinctly recall me warning that I'd kill you. But then when the feeding started, I didn't read sins in your blood. I just saw *us*. And I didn't have any desire to drain you dry, so I figured it was only really bad souls that were tasty. Still, I requested blood bags, even after both of our feedings just to be safe." I shot my gaze to Axel. "Tell him."

Axel gave me a slow nod. "She did, though she didn't say why."

"A glowing endorsement, Axel, thanks. It's not like I chose this. It's not like one day I woke up and decided, 'hey, let's devour some souls for breakfast.' I was evidently born this way." I pinched the bridge of my nose. "Look, I get that everyone has a hair up their ass about this, but we've got bigger fish to fry. Simon is gone, and if Clem is right, I know where he is. You want to try and figure out how to kill me, great. But let's do it later."

Thomas set a groggy Clem on her feet, steadying her so she didn't go down. "I've never heard of a soul reader actually consuming souls. How can this be?"

"I've heard whispers about soul readers being like you, but they seemed like fairytales," Emrys admitted. "Long ago rumblings full of nonsense meant to scare people away from interbreeding. I understand why you didn't tell us."

"Emrys—" Bastian began, but she cut him off.

"Would you tell strangers about all that Simon can do? Or about Harper? Or Clem? Would you tell them about how Axel and Thomas have been kicked out of every nest they've ever lived in? Would you feel safe enough to let them see the darkness in you? Don't lie—to me or yourself—and answer honestly. Would you?"

Bastian tilted his head back and stared at the ceiling. "No, I wouldn't. So, I should quit being a dick about it. Got it."

His admission was all well and good, but the man wouldn't look at me. I guessed I knew where we were on that front. The sting of rejection—not just from Bastian, but from everyone—washed over me, crushing me with its weight.

At least Isis still liked me.

But I couldn't rely on a cat to get me through this. I was right back to what I felt what seemed like so long ago. I shouldn't get attached to these people. I shouldn't want them to like me, shouldn't try and rely on them any more than I should the damn cat.

I stared straight ahead, no longer meeting anyone's gaze. If I did, I knew they'd see the wound they'd caused, they'd see me bleeding. How many times could my heart be broken, anyway? A handful of times? A thousand? I was once again so happy that Harper couldn't read me anymore. Happy that she couldn't feel this ache in my chest, this pit in my stomach.

Soon enough, I'd be able to turn all of it off. I'd save myself the trouble of wanting things. I'd go back to being on my own, back to the streets where at least I wasn't a burden to anyone else.

"Simon is in an old warehouse close to downtown Ascension." I tried to get them back on task. "I can show you the place myself if you want. If not, I can draw you a map, but I'd feel better if I went along. I know the building and where all the vulnerabilities are."

I walked over to Dahlia and took the whip hilt out of my holster. "You can have this back. I know you made it for a different girl."

But Dahlia refused to take the weapon from me, pushing my hand away. "I made it for you. I don't take back gifts after they're given."

That wasn't exactly acceptance, but it didn't matter. Giving her a sharp nod, I put the hilt back in the holster. I'd leave it in the truck for her when I left.

She'd want it back eventually.

"All right then. Let's roll out in five," Emrys called. "Gather everything you need for a fight. Harper, you're staying here. Clem is given free rein to protect you, so don't sass her when she's back to rights. Engage the Ivory Tower protocol once we leave."

I had everything I technically owned on me—aside from a duffle full of pictures—so I stayed put, but Thomas, Bastian, and Axel peeled off to gather more weapons. Clem shook herself and told us she was headed to the armory. Dahlia left to grab more potion bottles, and Harper trudged upstairs grumbling about a stupid Ivory Tower protocol.

That left me and Emrys still standing at the table. For the longest moment, neither of us spoke, but she broke the tense silence with a whispered apology. "I'm sorry, Sloane. I thought... I don't know what I thought."

My smile was bitter, but I didn't meet her gaze, even though I knew she wanted me to. "I knew this place was too good for the likes of me."

"Oh, no, Sloane. We're really not. All of us have secrets like yours. All of us. Even me."

I met her eyes, tears swimming in mine. "I don't belong here, and you can say I do, but I don't. You should know—just in case I don't get to tell you—Julie saw people attacking the house before she died. They were coming to kill everyone here. At the time, I didn't know what it meant, but I think I do now. If I stay here and someone finds out what I can do, they'll come. They'll come and kill everyone because of me. Like my parents. Like Julie." I swallowed, the pain clogging my throat. "So, after we get Simon back, I'm leaving."

"No, Sloane. You don't have to do that. We'll figure something out."

I shook my head, tears falling down my face faster than I could wipe them away. "I do. You don't need me here mucking things up, and that's the end of it." I swallowed again, trying to stop crying. "I'll meet ya'll in the truck."

And then I left, following my scant memory of how to get to the garage. The SUV sat cold, and I was lucky the thing was still unlocked. I climbed in, sitting all the way in the back like I had before.

Before when Bastian had hold of my fingers.

When he gave a shit.

When I had friends.

Funny how much could change in an hour.

I'd get Simon back. I'd help. And then I'd leave with the knowledge that it would always be better if I stayed on my own. For however long it took to die.

It didn't take too long before people were piling into the SUV, the silence thick as molasses. I put my earpiece back in and looked out the window, reciting the address I knew by heart. I stared out the window and watched the world skate by as we flew down the driveway and onto the highway.

Night still held strong, as it would in this part of winter, and I relished the cold pane of glass against my forehead and the warmth of the interior of the vehicle. I tried to hold onto small comforts, tried to feel things to be thankful for. I'd learned a hard lesson. I'd had a tiny bit of happiness. I'd had a small dose of affection. I'd just have to make those moments stretch and last for however long.

When we entered the city, I began detailing the building. The several entrances and exits, the levels. The pitfalls and booby traps. But my descriptions must not have done the building justice because both Thomas and Axel cussed a blue streak when we rolled passed.

"Are you fucking kidding me, Sloane?" Thomas railed, twisting in his seat to look at me fully. "You spent a year holed up in that dump, and you want to leave us for that? What? Is the mansion not good enough for you?"

I stared straight ahead, the knife in my heart twisting. "You know that's not why, Thomas. You said it yourself. I'm an albatross. I'm the reason you'll all get killed. You're safer without me there. Simon was safer without me there." Finally, I let my gaze meet his. "You said you owed me? Well, you can start by not making me feel like shit because you and I both know that no one wants me in your home. You didn't want me there two days ago, and you don't want me now. So let me go."

I said the words to Thomas, but they were for everyone. They were for Bastian and Dahlia and Axel who looked at me like I was a monster. They were for Harper and Emrys and Simon, too. I wasn't welcome and never would be. They'd finally learned what I'd figured out the first day into this new life. That it would have been better if I'd have just stayed dead.

In a flash, a blur of white bones jumped from the cargo area and onto my lap. Isis curled in on herself, her odd kitty face peering at me with her glowing green eyes.

"What the hell are you doing here?" I asked, secretly relieved to have a friendly face.

Isis meowed in my face, her eyes glowing like twin moons. She reached up on her hind legs and perched her forelegs on my shoulders. Her gaze grew brighter, the green so brilliant I almost couldn't look at it. She meowed in my face again, long and low before a green mist wafted out of her mouth like curling fingers of smoke.

The smoke flowed into my nose and mouth, filling my head with images of the warehouse. She showed me where there were men guarding the entrances, where Simon was, and the biggest problem of them all.

"Booth has Simon," I breathed, my vision still in the warehouse and not in the SUV with the team. "He has him on the third floor in some kind of contraption that will shove him over the edge of the catwalk if Simon moves wrong. But that's not the bad part."

The apparition burned away until the cab came back into focus. I stared at Isis, marveling at what she'd shown me— even if it was pretty much all bad news.

"Not the bad part?" Bastian groused. "What could possibly be worse than someone we trusted holding my brother hostage? You know, other than the fact that you're getting your information from a dead feline?"

I would agree that Bastian had a point, but the bad part was way worse.

"The building is surrounded by ghouls."

Because of course it was.

23

Axel groaned before slamming the SUV to a stop and throwing it into park in an abandoned parking lot, three blocks from the building where Simon was being held. From there, he let out the mother of all growls.

"Of fucking course it is. Any other rays of sunshine you wish to bestow on me? Maybe my father has come back from the grave, or my ex-wife is finally ready to ask me for alimony. Maybe there are rabid alligators and squirrels on PCP in there, too."

As funny as Axel was in the middle of his grown-man hissy fit, I was still focused on the fact that a cat gave me a vision. "Umm... What in the actual all-encompassing fuck did I just...? Why is Isis showing me shit?"

Bastian snorted as he readjusted his weapons. "Isis is Simon's psychopomp. A spirit guide, if you will. He must have sent her a message, and since she likes you, she gave it to you."

I ran a fingertip over her boney spine. "Aren't you a smart girl?" To the rest of them, I asked, "So this is what Simon has seen?"

Thomas turned back around, adjusting knives and weapons as well. "Simon can sense a large majority of the undead. Like most death mages, Simon knows when ghouls are near. Ghouls are the product of death mage magic, so he feels their signature. What you saw might be what he feels, or it could be a mix of what he's seen and what he senses around him."

But what Isis showed me was more than a feeling. It was as if I were flying above everyone and everything unnoticed, like I was looking through a ghost's eyes.

Simon's eyes? Was he already dead? Was this a suicide mission?

I didn't try to explain what I saw—it wasn't like we had the time—and outlined where I thought we should breach. "The third floor is where the catwalk is. If we just wanted to get Simon and get out, I'd breach on the south side where I have a pulley system integrated with the old fire escape. It's hard to get to and they might not know about the secret entry."

The building used to be an old paper factory before it shut down about fifty years ago. The city had been trying to have it torn down for ages, but couldn't get the votes since it was still structurally sound. This wasn't where I had stayed every night —or day—but this was the place I'd gone to when I was scared. It was a place I'd fortified as best I could with scraps and leftover tools.

Yes, it was a shithole. A dump, as Thomas called it, but it was what I had when I had nothing.

That wasn't to say I'd be going back to it when I left them. I had a feeling that Ascension wasn't the place for me anymore.

Harper's voice rang out on comms. "Sloane is right, the third-floor entrance might offer you the best cover, but you should be careful. There are only two heat signatures in the factory, but I'm catching movement on the neighboring rooftops. No heat sig. Could be ghouls or vampires or both."

I wanted to ask how Harper could see the neighboring rooftops, but I decided that some things could just stay a mystery. Knowing Harper, she probably hacked into a defense satellite or something.

"I would advise attacking from the south and taking out any ghouls watching that side," Harper recommended.

"That's as good a place to start as any," Emrys conceded before letting out the mother of all sighs. "Dahlia, you're with Thomas. Axel, you're with me. Bastian, you're with Sloane. Stay sharp. Watch each other's backs. Let's head out, people."

We piled out of the truck, and I led the group to the nearby building. The paper factory was surrounded by a handful of outbuildings, more than a handful of decommissioned warehouses and an old shoe factory. This part of Ascension was left to ruin, the city council always trying to get it wiped out but never managing to seal the deal. Only transients and the homeless hung around here now. But the humans stayed closer to the streets and away from the buildings, likely sensing the things that clung to the shadows, their hindbrains realizing they were prey.

I clung to the walls of an alley as I made my way toward a fire escape a few buildings away. No way did I want to be in an alley, bottle-necked by ghouls. Unlike vampires, ghouls were pack hunters, their strength coming in numbers rather than talons or fangs. Impossibly strong and difficult to kill, they appeared human enough that they could pass you on the street and no one would be the wiser.

Had their diet not consisted of little more than human flesh, they'd fit right in.

My biggest concern was the noise. Like vamps, ghoul hearing was near the top of the pack. It was possible they would hear us coming even from this far away, but we didn't have the time to waste. As silently as I could, I crept up the fire escape stairs, careful to avoid the rusted treads that I knew would either dump me on my ass or squeal like an angry pig. The last thing we needed was every arcaner within a mile radius to know we were here. Surprise was the only damn thing we had going for us.

Once we reached the top of the fire escape, I peered over the ledge of the roof. Immediately, I ducked back down, barely managing not to get spotted by the three huge ghouls patrolling the roof. Reluctantly, I glanced back at Bastian. He'd followed me up this set of stairs, and now we had to figure out a way to silently take these ghouls out. Well, I knew a way, but he wasn't going to like it.

I held up three fingers, telling him how many we had to deal with and pointed to their general position. He jerked his thumb to his chest and held up two fingers, indicating he'd take out two of them, leaving me to take out the third. I picked the closest one, and on his count of three, I launched myself over the ledge. It took three bounds before I was on the behemoth of a man and my fangs in his neck. I had other weapons at my disposal, but I was familiar with these.

All eight of my razor-sharp fangs buried themselves into the ghoul's neck and I ripped, tearing out his throat before he could scream. Then it was just a one, two, twist and his head came off in my hands, his big body withering as it crumpled to the rooftop. It was unlikely he'd shrivel to ash, but at least he was really, really dead.

I looked up to see Bastian battling the second ghoul, the first a smoldering mess of flames on the ground. There were only two ways to kill a ghoul: beheading or fire. Beheading took the least amount of time and was a confirmed kill. Fire took too damn long, and if the ghoul put themselves out quick enough, then we were up shit creek. Groaning, I yanked the spelled whip out of the holster and muttered the incantation to activate it.

The electric-blue tendril of magic bloomed from the hilt, and I wasted no time launching it at the downed ghoul, wrapping it around its neck and yanking off the smoldering remains of his head. Dead checks were an important part of survival. The fact that ripping off someone's head was supremely fun was just a bonus.

Bastian and the last ghoul were circling each other, Bastian with a ball of electricity in his hand and the ghoul missing the lower half of his left arm. Still, the ghoul lunged—one and a half arms outstretched—his teeth bared. Bastian launched his electricity ball, hitting the thing right in the chest. The giant ghoul froze for a few seconds before it let out an unearthly growl and slowly stepped forward.

"Bastian," I whisper-hissed. "Duck." Bastian turned to me, his eyes wide, before he dove for the ground.

I launched the whip at the ghoul's throat, the blue magic wrapping around his neck, and the next instant, I yanked. The crackling whip cut through the ghoul's neck like butter, dropping him like a stone on the debris-strewn rooftop. This ghoul was older than the rest, his giant body crumbling to dust almost instantly. I shrugged. At least clean-up would be a breeze.

"Umm... Sloane?" Bastian called softly. "You know you're still holding a severed head, right?"

I stared down at my right hand, and it turned out Bastian was right. I was, in fact, holding a withering head. *Gross.* Immediately, I dropped the head like its hair was on fire, wiping my fingers on my pants. I suppressed a shudder at the utter ick factor and whispered the incantation to retract the whip before holstering it.

"This building is clear," Bastian muttered through comms.

"We're on a higher floor than the surrounding buildings, so it's possible no one saw our little debacle."

"Except me," Harper said in my ear. "I know I saw it, but Sloane, did you really just rip that ghoul's head off with your bare hands?"

Wasn't that how everyone did it? It wasn't like I had a sword in my hand to ease the job along.

"Status update," Bastian barked, surreptitiously looking over the side of the ledge to see the building below. I followed suit, peeking over the crumbling brick. Even with upgraded vision, I couldn't make out much despite the full moon casting a decent light on an empty rooftop. But I knew better. It had been my experience that ghouls were masters of the shadows, able to blend in and stay hidden, unmoving for hours.

I *hated* hunting ghouls.

Harper grumbled about him spoiling her fun but gave us a quick briefing. "Emrys and Axel have cleared the rooftops on the building to the west. Dahlia and Thomas to the east. There is one more building to clear to the south, and then you have a straight shot to the factory. Since the factory ceiling is mostly glass, I doubt any ghouls are waiting up there, but I don't know about the inside. Footage is not pulling up any movement."

"Can you see Simon?" I asked. "He should be visible on the catwalk, depending on your vantage point."

"That's a negative," Harper replied. "I can't see past the full moon's reflection on the glass."

Fabulous.

"Okay, ladies and gents," Axel called over comms, "converge on the southern rooftop. I see seven ghouls and what looks like a couple of lycanthropes. Do not, I repeat, do not get bitten. I only have one anti-viral in my pack, and I'm saving it just in case Simon needs it."

I wondered if I should tell him I was immune to the lycanthrope virus. Nah, I'd wait to share that little tidbit if I got snacked on.

"Let's move, people," Emrys commanded, and we did.

Bastian rose from his crouch and walked away from the ledge. I followed suit, wondering what the hell he thought he was doing. Yes, the other rooftop was close, but not close enough to jump, and he seemed like he was getting ready to do just that.

"What are you doing?" I hissed, knowing full well what his answer was going to be.

Bastian rolled his eyes. "I'm jumping—what's it look like? You are, too, you wimp."

I shook my head. "I've already dove off one building, thank you. The healing took forever. That roof is over forty feet away. You can't make that jump. I don't care if you think you're a freaking superhero."

A ghost of a smile stretched over his lips before he latched onto my waist, securing me to his side. "Sure I can. You can, too."

Then he took off, running full tilt for the ledge like a crazy person.

I almost screamed but refused to give our position away. Instead, I shut my eyes tight as we sailed over the side of the building, trying desperately not to freak the fuck out. The closest I came to death in this new life was when I jumped off a building. The subsequent fear of falling—well, not to my death because if twenty stories didn't do it, nothing would— was a very real thing.

But gravity didn't work the same way as it had on that rather mournful night. The pull wasn't nearly as strong, and it wasn't a moment later that our feet landed heavily on the rooftop, our momentum leading us into a skid. When I opened my eyes, the fight was in full bloom, and I quickly realized that Axel's numbers were off. There weren't seven ghouls, there were twenty, and there were a hell of a lot more lycanthropes than a few.

A full concentric ring of half-man, half-wolf lycanthropes stood on the outskirts of the melee, their misshapen mouths snapping in anticipation. Dahlia was snapping her fingers, popping heads off like it was a piece of cake. Thomas was swiftly taking ghoul heads with a pair of broad swords that he pulled from who knew where. He sure as shit wasn't wearing them the last time I saw him. Emrys was throwing spells, her glowing hands sending shockwaves to the ghouls to knock them down as Axel took what appeared to be a spelled garrote to the ones that landed at his feet.

Ghouls pretty much handled, Bastian and I got to work on the waiting lycanthropes. Bastian lobbed electricity balls at the dogs, breaking them out of whatever holding pattern they were in. At once, the dogs began their assault, a sure sign that things were not going our way. No pack was this coordinated.

In a heartbeat, my whip was out, the ribbon of death wrapping around one head after the other as it cut through their flesh just as easily as the ghouls. But as awesome as it was, it wasn't working fast enough for my taste. I pulled my gun, hoping the bullets were either silver or at least spelled to do some serious damage. Whip in my right hand and gun in my left, I began firing, the sound like teeny puffs of air rather than blasts of a gun. I wasn't too keen on trying to figure out why my gun sounded like it had a silencer on it, I was just glad someone wasn't going to hear our battle and call the cops.

A ball of fire sailed over my head as the lycanthrope closest to me nearly sank its teeth into my upper arm. The ball exploded against the dog's face, sending embers flying and the lycanthrope rearing back as it clawed at its charring mug. Flames bloomed over its fur, trailing like fingers over its body as the inferno consumed it.

"Move, move, move!" Harper boomed through my earpiece. "Ghouls and lycanthropes are swarming the factory. Get in and get Simon out."

I looked back at the group still fighting and worried if we left them, they'd get killed. But I realized quickly that I didn't have a choice on whether or not I was going to the factory because Bastian scooped me up in his arms and hauled ass to the building ledge. Sailing over the side of the building, I saw a horde of ghouls' racing toward the ground floor bay doors.

Shit, fuck, and damn.

Bastian landed on a metal fire escape and shoved me up the stairs as I tucked the whip and gun back in their holsters. I bounded up the steps as fast as I could, heading for the third-floor catwalk. I grabbed Bastian's hand, yanking him behind me as I picked through booby traps and homemade land mines to the crawlspace above the catwalk.

Paper mills weren't the nicest smelling places, and even though the factory had been decommissioned decades ago, it still had the vague odor of pressed paper. I chose this place because of it, because no matter who followed me home, they would have trouble discerning my scent over the pall of a century's worth of manufactured paper seeping from the walls. But my nose was attuned to the differences in scents, the miasma of chemicals not affecting my nose as it did many other arcaners.

Which was why I shoved Bastian aside as a sword came for our faces once we'd emerged from the crawlspace. The pair of us fell against the rickety safety rail that stopped us from sailing over the side. The metal railing was missing in large chunks, and we were damn lucky to hit a sturdy piece. The sword struck again, and I barely managed to swerve as it came for us. I never figured Booth for a sword man, but he maneuvered the steel like he was born to it, his next strike coming swiftly after his first had missed.

Bastian tossed an electricity ball his way, the shot going wide and exploding against the peeling wall. But even though it didn't hit his target, Booth still ducked, a pause I needed. I yanked my gun and whip free of their holsters, flinging the spelled ribbon out toward Booth. He ducked right where I wanted him to, landing right in my crosshairs as I fired the gun.

But Booth was fast—faster than a bullet—and he moved to the side, the shot hitting him in the shoulder instead of the chest. He staggered back, white fur erupting over his skin, but the shift didn't take him completely.

Bastian moved in front of me, another electricity ball in his hand. "I want you to tell me why. We're your family. We were your pack. You told me as much yourself. You've been with us for half a fucking century, Booth. Why would you take him from me?"

Booth shuddered, his blue eyes glowing bright as he quaked, the phase hitting him hard. "Must take the stealer. He wants her for his own," he growled through his misshapen jaw, the change slowly morphing his features as fur bloomed over his skin. "Must deliver the stealer."

I could only assume the "stealer" was me. I had to say, I was not a fan of the whole "stealer" moniker. Couldn't we come up with a better name that didn't make me sound like the grim fucking reaper?

Yes, this was what I was thinking of instead of realizing that he didn't sound right—not that anyone could sound exactly sane while transforming into a four-legged creature. He sounded like his mind wasn't his own, the monotone making his voice dead. And I was filled with worry about his state of mind, worry about his safety right up until Booth's face morphed into a familiar feline shape.

A shape that tore the last vestige of my family from me.

A shape that murdered Julie.

Booth was the big cat, the white feline with the giant paws that spilled her blood. That took her life.

It was one thing to consider a possibility and quite another to be proven right. Simon's note to *Beware of Booth* was only so poignant out of context. But there was no way to misinterpret this.

My scream of rage and pain could probably be heard for a full city block, and I did not give that first fuck.

"*You.*" I aimed my gun smack-dab in the middle of his forehead. "You took her from me. Why?"

Booth's transformation was completed before my very eyes so I knew he couldn't answer me, but I was *so* tempted to put a bullet in his head and be done with it. Bastian grabbed my wrist, urging me to lower the gun. He couldn't make me. Out of the two of us, I was the stronger one, but I let him push the gun to my side.

"He killed her. He tore her apart," I whispered, the pain of her death rearing up to bite me.

Bastian wrapped a hand around my middle and set me to the side, putting himself between me and the bastard shifter. "I know, but you can't kill him," he muttered, eyeing the giant feline as he rounded the last corner of his shift.

I met Bastian's gaze with a "wanna bet?" expression on my face.

"I don't think any of them know what they're doing. This is bigger than just Booth. We need him alive if we want to know what happened to Julie and why. We need him to find out what happened to your parents."

Bastian walked over to the giant cat before he could get his bearings and punched him right in the temple, knocking Booth the fuck out. Fur melted away from his face almost instantly as Bastian stepped over him.

"Fun fact," he said over his shoulder as he made his way down the walk, "shifters can't sustain their animal form when they're unconscious."

With Bastian's back turned I was sorely tempted to lop Booth's head right off, but only managed to refrain when I heard the call for help down the catwalk. Growling, I booked it down the grated metal path, to find Bastian in a standoff with two ghouls between him and his brother. Simon was unconscious in a wooden chair, precariously balanced on the edge of the catwalk at one of the spots where the guardrail was missing. Blood trailed down his cheek, spilling onto his flannel shirt, his hands tied to the arms of the chair and a rope around his neck and feet. The rope trailed to a rusted-out pulley with the tail end in one of the ghoul's hands.

And beneath us was nothing but air over an open factory floor.

Heavy metal grating echoed through the open factory, the sound of a multitude of booted feet running toward us made a shiver of fear snake its way up my spine. We didn't have the luxury of time.

Peering through the grated floor, I witnessed Emrys' blazing power shove ghouls to their knees as Thomas' swords cut through their necks at a blurring speed. Axel wielded what appeared to be a Morningstar, bashing anything he could reach. Shouts of spells and incantations echoed off the walls. A great big boom sizzled through the air and ghouls went flying back from a very pissed-off Dahlia as she cut a swath through the swarm, the ripping snarl of battle echoing through the factory.

Even with backup, we were out of time.

As soon as Bastian sensed me behind him, he attacked, orbs of fire and electricity flying in the air as I struck out with my whip, severing the first ghoul's head in a snap. I should have gone for the arm that held onto the rope, but dead seemed better than incapacitated.

I was also incorrect in thinking there were only two ghouls up here. As soon as I lashed out with my whip, two more ghouls dropped from the scant rafters. One landed right behind me and the other next to Simon, jostling his chair closer to the edge of the catwalk.

The ghoul behind me banded his giant arms around the top of my shoulders, hauling me back, dragging me away from the fight. I kicked out, trying to get enough momentum to throw him over my back, but the guy was too big. I tried shooting his feet, but his steps were too fast. Even my attempts at kicking his knees did nothing. In my panic, I forgot the one weapon no one could steal from me.

My teeth.

In a flash of inspiration, I latched my fangs onto the ghoul's forearm, burying the sharp incisors into his flesh. He howled in response, but he was mine now. I took a giant pull of his blood, taking his sin for my own. But by my second pull, I knew the problem. This ghoul—this guy—wasn't a monster.

He was spelled.

His blood showed me a nameless, faceless man, a hooded figure as blurry as a dream. The man was a sorcerer or a mage maybe? Or maybe he was something else. Something older, darker, and far more powerful. The ghoul—Martin—had been a morgue attendant, taking what wouldn't be missed when a body went for cremation. He'd never killed a soul in his entire long life until he'd seen an odd purple light two weeks ago.

This ghoul wasn't responsible for his actions, and I could not end his life—not and value my own.

I ripped my fangs from Martin's arm before using his loose grip to my advantage. In a move I'd used many times before, the giant man was up and over my hip, and with a quick twist of his neck, he was incapacitated. A ghoul could survive a broken neck, easy-peasy.

That was a lesson I learned the hard way.

"Don't kill them," I shouted, racing back to Bastian and Simon.

Bastian's fight with the other ghoul was getting closer and closer to Simon, his chair on the razor's edge of toppling over the side. Simon was slowly regaining consciousness, his head lolling as he tried to focus, his glasses askew on his face.

Then there was a flash of white racing passed my feet. A skeleton cat zipped through stomping feet and leapt, landing on Simon's lap. Isis reached up, raking her claws against Simon's non-bloody cheek, waking him up in earnest.

It took less than a second for Simon to focus on the tableau in front of him and the precarious situation he was in. And still I ran, racing toward Bastian and Simon. Raising my gun, I aimed for the ghoul that was so close to knocking Simon off into the wide-open nothing, sending up a last-ditch prayer that the damn man didn't fall wrong.

"Bastian, duck!" I yelled, giving him less than a second to comply before I fired.

The bullet seemed to take an age as it crossed the scant space to its target, ripping into the neck of the ghoul, making him stagger. He swayed closer to Simon, his leg knocking into the precariously balanced chair. And then everything slowed to a crawl.

Everything it seemed, except for Bastian.

Bastian's whole body glowed with a silver light, great swirls of white tendrils surrounded his body as he reached for his brother faster than Thomas had ever moved. His fingers closed over the ropes at Simon's wrist, latching onto him with a single-minded focus of a determined man. Then the world snapped back, Bastian's magic failing, but still he held onto Simon.

But Simon was still going down, and if I didn't do something, they would both fall over the ledge. I dove for Simon as I tossed the tail of the whip, praying it wrapped around the above support strut in enough time and didn't slice through metal with the same efficiency as it had ghoul necks.

I sailed over the edge, reaching for the brothers' joined hands. By some miracle, I latched onto the rope holding Simon to the chair and pulled them with me as we landed in an inelegant pile on the catwalk.

Shaking, I crawled away from the brothers, the act of nearly plummeting to my—well, not *death* but I sure as shit would want it to be.

"A little help down here!" Dahlia called, blasting a rather enormous ghoul right in the face with an orb of magic.

Simon stared at the sea of ghouls and closed his eyes, when he opened them again, his green eyes were all black from pupil to sclera—there was nothing. Then his hands lit with glowing purple magic, the swirls threaded through with inky black. He seemed to pull light and air into himself, the glow of the moon itself dimming. Then all at once, the ghouls fell, crumpling to the ground right where they stood as if they were automatons that had been shut off.

Simon closed his eyes, and then it was like someone plugged the moon back in. Light bloomed through the glass roof once more. Simon's eyes cleared as his magic died, and he looked at his brother.

"How much trouble do you think I'm in?"

And that's when Bastian started laughing.

As it turned out, Simon wasn't in too much trouble. Or at least that's what Agents La Roux and Kenzari told us when we delivered a bound and gagged Booth to them on the steps of the Knoxville ABI building. Agent La Roux was tall and scruffy, his black eyes and hair making him look Italian or maybe French, but his accent spoke of snooty boarding schools. Agent Kenzari was a bronze-skinned pixie of a woman, with chin-length black hair and a stare that saw far too much.

She kept staring at me, and I tried to look anywhere else but in her direction, pretending to inspect the ABI building instead of meeting her piercing gaze.

After reading Booth's blood, I learned a frightening number of things about the Night Watch's resident shifter. First, he had most definitely been the shifter that killed Julie and mauled a string of humans. Spelled or not, I still had a frightening urge to kill him, even after the reading. In his memories I saw the same hooded figure that was in the ghoul, Martin's, with the same odd purple glow. There were other sins, some that made me want to rip his soul from his body and watch him crumble to ash, but I refrained.

Still, I was hesitant to deliver him to the ABI, especially if he planned on spilling the beans about the "stealer" he was sent to find, but Bastian and Emrys convinced me to see their side. Booth had mauled humans and killed a venerated oracle. Plus, he'd kidnapped Simon. If we wanted to keep Simon out of hot water, we'd have to put Booth in it.

It helped that Booth was a babbling mess of nonsense once he'd woken up after the read, his words not forming anything intelligible other than the word "ex" repeated over and over again. Either the hooded man fried his brain, or I had, and the fact that I didn't know did not sit well with me.

Neither did the lives we took.

I wondered if all the ghouls we killed were like Martin, good men plucked from their lives to do someone else's bidding. I hated that I didn't know that, either.

Dawn had come and gone sometime in the last few hours and sitting on the steps in the overcast winter morning was not my favorite pastime. I could barely hold my eyes open as Bastian and Agent La Roux processed paperwork, no one wanting to go inside the building for fear of the "Red Queen's wrath." Another pair of agents scooped up Booth, dragging him inside for questioning. I doubted they'd get anything out of him, and I was kind of sorry about that.

Or I would be if him blabbing didn't mean my death.

Soon, I'd have to figure out a place to stay. It wasn't like I could go back to the paper factory after the recent blow-out. By the time we'd left, there were cop cars heading right for it. If they didn't pilfer what I had stashed there, then someone was going to be watching the place. It wasn't safe.

Agent Kenzari sat next to me on the steps, her piercing gaze practically boring a hole in the side of my face.

"How can I help you, Agent?" I asked, my voice as weary as I felt.

Please leave me alone. Pretty please with sugar on top?

"You can call me Sarina if you want," she chirped, far too perky for this time of day. "You're new, aren't you? You can't be more than what? Twenty-two?"

I sighed. *Small talk it was.* "Twenty-three."

"And you've only been undead for a year? It's impressive you can stay awake. Most new vampires are dead to the world around this time of morning."

If I weren't about to pass out from exhaustion, I would have picked up on her leading questions, but I was just too tired. Instead, I yawned. "Just lucky I guess."

"Can I give you a little tip for the future? Just us girls?" she asked, bumping me with her shoulder.

"Fire away," I muttered, resting my cheek on my propped fist, trying to turn my rigid fingers into a suitable pillow.

"If you want to pass as a vamp, you really should wear some contacts. Those purple eyes are striking, but for the old agents—the ones who know a thing or two—they're a dead giveaway."

Said purple eyes flashed open, and I slowly turned my head to look at the perky agent. "You don't say."

She pointed to her head. "I see lots of things, and from what I see, you are a good person. You do good whenever you can, and that is the only reason I'm helping you. Actually, you remind me of a very dear friend. She's a lot like you—a mix of two lines that are far too powerful."

"I don't know—"

"You're not meant to." She cut me off before she smiled at me, a beatific stretch to her lips that spoke of happiness and contentment, even though her next words were anything but. "We'll need people like you in this world soon enough. Need the strong ones of the old lines to keep this world turning. You're one of the good ones, Sloane. I want you to remember that."

With that, she stood, walking back to La Roux and Bastian as if she hadn't just blown apart my fragile little mind.

Soon, Bastian came back down the stairs, a slew of papers in his hand and an envelope. I figured this was where we parted ways, and I kind of wanted to avoid it.

Rather than waiting for him to tell me I wasn't welcome, I stood, and began heading in the opposite direction of the SUV parked at the curb.

"You're headed in the wrong direction," he called, but I kept walking, picking up my pace and wishing I had a coat against the bitter wind.

Funny, I hadn't felt it before, but now I did.

A moment later, the SUV rolled to a stop next to me, and Bastian got out of the passenger side. Gently, he grabbed my wrist, pulling me to a stop. "I said 'you're headed in the wrong direction.' The car is right here, and it's headed to a place with food and friends and a bed and a roof. It's also headed to a place full of apologies. You didn't deserve the shit we shoved your way. You didn't deserve us doubting you."

He was right, but he was wrong, too.

"I didn't tell you—"

"That was none of my business. We all have secrets, Sloane. I judged you unfairly, and I can promise it will never happen again. You saved my brother's life—even when we treated you like dirt." He shook his head, his expression rueful as he shoved his hands in his pockets. "I owe you more than I can say."

I shivered against the cold, the appeal of a roof over my head almost too good to pass up. Then Julie's vision streaked across my mind. "People are going to be looking for me. I can't—"

Bastian wrapped a blissfully warm arm around my shoulders, effectively cutting off my protest. "Emrys says she has a plan, and when Emrys has a plan, it's best we listen. She'll figure it out." He turned us, steering me toward the passenger seat. "And I'd feel better if you were under a ward, in a place with a lot of people that have more magic than the government deems prudent."

I couldn't really argue with that logic.

"Plus," he murmured in my ear as he opened my door for me, "eventually, I would like to kiss you again, and I can't really do that if I can't find you. It took far too long to locate you the last time."

I stared up at him, mouth agape for a split second before my brain reengaged. "Who says I'd let you?"

Bastian's grin grew wide, rivaling any dastardly smile Thomas had up his sleeve. "I will take that as a personal challenge, Ms. Cabot. Let the games begin."

There was no game playing on the ride home for which I was supremely grateful. I did, however, use Bastian as a pillow and he didn't bitch once, even though Isis was curled in my lap. Simon's cat was stuck to me like glue and had been anytime I was in her general vicinity. I figured it was because I'd saved her human, but with a reanimated skeleton kitty, one never knew.

As soon as we made it back to the house, I trudged up the stairs, intent on a shower and to sleep for about a year. I wasn't particularly settled, nor did I understand all that had transpired over the last few hours, but I couldn't think about those things when I was about to fall off my feet.

Half asleep, I managed to strip, shower, and towel off before falling—literally—into bed. A crinkle of a paper scratched against my face, and I pulled away from the pillow to look at it.

It was a handwritten note, the paper heavy, the scrawl loopy. It took a minute for my eyes to focus enough to read it, the cursive running together, but when I did, I was up and out of bed, backing away from that little slip of paper like it was a damn snake.

I still remember the scent of your parents' skin as they burned. We'll meet again, little one.

—X

Booth wasn't saying the word "ex." He was telling me the bastard's name. Booth had somehow known who he was, and he'd managed to hide it from me. Trembling, I sat at the drafting table and stared at the cream note.

So much for feeling safe.

DEATH WATCH

ARCANE SOULS WORLD: SOUL READER BOOK 2

ANNIE ANDERSON

"Alone. Yes, that's the key word, the most awful word in the English tongue. Murder doesn't hold a candle to it and hell is only a poor synonym."

— STEPHEN KING

1

There were three acceptable reactions to finding a creepy note in your bed from the man who killed your parents.

One: scream your head off and hope someone runs to come save you—*not my favorite option by far.*

Two: smash shit. *On-brand, and really, who can blame me?*

Or three: turn into the ice-cold she-beast that devoured the souls of hundreds of damned arcaners. *I like this one. It has panache.*

I had a solid leaning toward door number two—with the option for three—once I got my shit together. And by shit being together, I meant I needed pants on to deal with this. And maybe a strong cup of coffee and a bag of blood to slake those pesky cravings.

Digging through the ridiculous closet Dahlia had set up for me, I found pajama pants and a top and tossed them on. After that, I began to lose steam as the loss started to creep in.

Man, I knew I should have just started smashing shit.

Anger kept my head above water.

Anger kept me alive.

Anger had hauled my ass through a whole year of being a homeless, soul-sucking monster.

Anger was my friend.

Swallowing hard, I reached for the note. The elegant scrawl blurred a little bit as the emotions started hitting in a one-two punch of bullshit I in no way had the mental capacity to deal with.

What had Mom always told me? *One foot in front of the other, Sloane. Keep moving.*

I couldn't remember my parents' deaths. I couldn't remember how I survived the fire that took them from me, or why I'd woken up days later at the foot of my own grave. All I knew was that they were gone, and somehow, I'd remained. Of course, I'd always had an inkling that something had been amiss. I mean, how the fuck else had I ended up in a granny nightgown taking a snooze on my own grave? It wasn't like I put myself there. But until I read that letter, I didn't *know*.

And the knowledge was a hot poker of loss and grief and rage in my gut.

Add in the fact that the man who'd killed them left me a note inside the first home I'd had in a year. In my bed. In this house, a place where I was supposed to be safe.

The burn in my gut only scorched brighter.

A part of me wanted to do the smart thing, which meant taking this note and giving it to Emrys. She'd know what to do, right? Someone who'd been around since time was a baby likely knew more than I did.

Too bad the other part of me screamed to sniff that letter, to take the scent from it and hunt down the man who'd written his lazy scrawl on the cardstock.

But I knew.

I knew if I opened that door, if I pulled that pin, I would

lose the tenuous hold I had on my soul. I would lose everything, and I didn't have that much left to lose.

So instead of taking the scent for my own, instead of letting vengeance take root in my belly, and instead of doing the smart thing, I stalked out of my room and down the hall, following Thomas' scent pattern to a nook of the corridor I hadn't been down before.

I couldn't say for sure why I picked Thomas instead of Emrys or Bastian. No, that wasn't right. I could totally say why I picked Thomas over my potential romantic *whatever* and a woman that essentially amounted to my boss.

Thomas knew rage.

He knew vengeance.

And he owed me one.

I didn't even get a chance to knock before Thomas had the door open, his eyes flashing red for a moment before fading back to green. Clad in nothing but a pair of black silk pajama pants, I should have swooned or started drooling or something, but all I could do was hand him the note. And if my hand just so happened to be trembling a little, well, then, that was allowed.

Thomas took the note but didn't look at it. No, he stared at my face. I had no idea what he saw there, but I didn't think it was good.

"You smell of Death himself. Why are you handing me a note written in blood, Sloane?"

His whispered words sounded like a bomb going off. Rage ignited in my chest, and it was all I could do to not shriek in his face.

"Read it," I growled through my teeth, knowing full well that if I opened my mouth, I would start screaming and never stop.

With a fair amount of reluctance in his expression, Thomas'

gaze dropped to the card in his hand. It took him less than a second to read the note, and even less than that to vamp all the way out. His sclera went from white to blood-red in an instant, his needle-like fangs peeking out from under his lips. He dropped the card as if it burned him, latching onto my shoulders as if I was a bomb that he was trying to keep from exploding.

At his instant rage, mine ignited as if he'd given me permission to lose it. But whatever he saw next made him move.

In less time than I thought possible, I was up and over Thomas' shoulder, and we were in Emrys' office. I barely got a glimpse of the room before I was bumped off his shoulder and dumped on the leather wingback I'd destroyed with my nails just a few days ago. Then, Thomas, in his ancient wisdom, decided to sit on me.

Cool skin smushed my cheek as Thomas effectively locked me down.

"Thomas, I don't often say this to you, but what the fuck?" Emrys muttered, her tone a mix of baffled and exasperated.

"We have a problem," he replied, the sound of his voice radiating through my whole head from his chest.

"I gathered," Emrys said drolly, the exhaustion in her tone plain as day, even with an ancient vampire using me as a recliner. "Care to share before I have Axel dose you with a tranquilizer?"

"Yes, I fully plan on that, but I'm going to need you to brace yourself, and then I'll get up."

"Bloody fucking hell, Thomas, out with it. I haven't slept in two da—"

Thomas peeled himself from the chair, revealing Emrys in all her tired glory. "Jesus, Mary, and Joseph," Emrys whispered, her odd red irises glowing brightly as she slowly stood from her seat, bracing herself. "Sloane, darling, what's wrong?"

How could I answer her? I'd known something had happened to my parents, but until I'd read that note, I hadn't known it was on purpose. I'd always suspected, sure, but the truth was poison running in my veins, spoiling everything it touched.

"It's this, I think," Thomas replied, handing her the note I'd thought he'd dropped.

The one written in blood.

Whose blood, I had no idea, but everything in me told me I wouldn't enjoy the answer. Everything in me said that the blood on that note would bring me pain and anguish and leave me adrift.

Leave me with nothing.

Emrys didn't break our gaze, even as she took the card from his hand.

"Do you know what you look like right now?" she asked, her expression locked down tight.

Typically unreadable, the druidess held an innumerable number of secrets under that mask, and none of it was comforting. All I could do was grit my teeth as I shook my head. Why in the blue bloody fuck did it matter what I looked like? Why did it matter when she had proof in her hands that my parents were indeed murdered? When she could look at that note and see everything I couldn't bring myself to say?

Nodding to herself, Emrys skirted her giant mahogany desk and held out her hand. When I didn't take it, she latched her fingers on my wrist and gently drew me up from my chair. Leading me to an odd bookcase, she pulled on the spine of a book, and the whole thing moved, pushing back and turning in to reveal an opulent—if a little sparse—room. All that was inside was a bed, a lamp on a lone nightstand, and a full-length mirror.

Emrys tugged me directly to the mirror, turning me to face it, her fingers digging into the skin of my shoulders as if she were trying to hold me in place.

But as soon as I caught sight of my reflection, I understood why Thomas had said I smelled like the dead.

The impossibly white hair and purple eyes were the standard. The fact that my fangs were showing and said purple eyes were glowing like lanterns, also standard—especially since I was a teensy step from losing it.

What was *not* standard was the... I didn't even know how to describe it.

My skin and eyes were radiant, shining with this odd white light that seemed to come from within. But more than that, every few seconds, the figure in the mirror would waver just a little, like a ripple on a pond, and in its place, was what I could only describe as death.

One second my face appeared exactly as I knew it to be. The next, it was as if a skeleton had been superimposed over my features. The creamy-white of the bones winked out every few moments as if it had never been there at all, only to return like a nightmare.

Staring at myself for a solid minute, I tried to get my brain to process what I saw. I was pretty sure my brain broke, remade itself, and broke again in that minute.

I wasn't stupid—contrary to popular belief. It wasn't exactly a leap to suggest that I'd somehow been spelled or hexed or cursed, or whatever the fuck the magic-wielding populace called it. This X, this person who'd taken the time to let me know of his presence, had done this to me somehow. I was sure of it.

He'd killed my parents.

He'd smelled their flesh burn.

He'd…

"Can you fix it?" I croaked, still staring at the mirror and not meeting Emrys' gaze. Both she and Thomas appeared as if they'd seen a ghost. I didn't need another glance at them to see it again.

"I can try, lass."

Emrys left me then, and a few moments later, she bellowed out a curse which had me racing back to the office. She stared at the note as if it had bitten her. Then her gaze slowly drifted back to me.

"That slip of paper should have killed you," she whispered, her face paler than my *Skeletor* one. "It is dark magic, forbidden magic. A blood curse." She said it with a frightened sort of reverence that I didn't think would ever come from her mouth. Emrys was resolute. Steadfast. Indomitable. The fear in her voice made bile crawl up my throat.

"Maybe it doesn't work on people like me?" I offered, the feeble suggestion posed as a question. I didn't know the first thing about people such as myself, and the only person I could think to ask wasn't someone I wanted anywhere near me.

"None of this makes any sense. This"—She pointed at the cardstock—"is foul magic. Made from a member of your line. Spells like this were outlawed in the dark ages. With a working like what I see here, a person could wipe out an entire family with just one spell if they had a mind. I can't think of a single reason in the world you should still be standing here breathing." She swallowed audibly, her face draining of all remaining color. Gently, she sat herself down in her leather chair, a trembling hand covering her mouth.

But there wasn't anyone left in my family—no one that I knew. Mom had told me ages ago that she was an orphan, that she'd lost her siblings early on. Then again, Mom had also implied I was human. That she was, too.

Did this mean that this X had to be someone in my family? If what Emrys was saying were true, then he had to be. *Well, fuck.* That thought had a cold pit of dread opening wide in my belly.

"Can you fix it?" Thomas asked, echoing my earlier question and breaking me out of my thoughts.

By the expression on Emrys' face, I didn't think she could. That single expression told me volumes. She had no idea what was wrong with me, she had no idea why I looked like I did, and she didn't have one single clue as to how to fix it.

She steeled herself then, seeming to shove all her emotions down as she erected a wall of assumed calm.

"I can try," she said again, this time with a resolute power that she hadn't possessed earlier.

But I didn't believe her.

Not at all.

2

So, there I was, sitting in the middle of a pentagram with Emrys chanting around me as I watched Thomas sip whiskey from a cut crystal tumbler. I grumbled as I held the still-bloody heart of a bull in one hand—*locally bred and humanely sourced according to Emrys*—and an ax in the other. All the while, she was in the middle of the thirtieth such spell to reverse whatever this X had done to me.

"Hush, or she'll have to start over," Thomas chided, sipping his drink as if this weren't the last thing Emrys said she could try before she would have to do some really bizarre shit. This was weird enough, dammit, and I was getting worried there would be nothing for me, other than looking like a fucking nightmare until the end of time. Or until I died—whichever came first.

I wanted to toss this bloody bull heart at his face and go eat. Maybe the ax, too, if I was being honest. I doubted I would actually manage to hit him with either—he moved too damn fast —but it would make me feel better. Starving for both solid food and blood, I was pretty close to losing patience. Luckily, Emrys' words were reaching their crescendo. Her voice rose in volume as the candles surrounding me at the points of the pentagram flared high for a moment before blowing out altogether.

Shit.

I'd learned after the fourth spell she'd tried that this was not a good sign. A quick trip to the mirror proved my assumption correct. One second I was Sloane, weird purple eyes and all, and the next…

Growling, I marched right over to Thomas and snatched his whiskey straight out of his hand, downing it in a single swallow. Wordlessly, I held out the glass for a refill. Maybe it was the bloody fingers that no longer held a bull heart or the ax in my other hand, but Thomas quickly filled the tumbler.

After the hours we'd spent researching and trying one spell after the other—each with varying results—her new first order of business would be creating a glamour for me. Mostly so I didn't scare the absolute shit out of people in the house.

"I need a glamour," I muttered, sipping the amber liquid as if it would hold my salvation.

Do soul-stealing monsters get salvation? Doubtful. But I was going to finish this whiskey just to check.

"Whoa, there," Thomas grouched, stealing the tumbler back. "That's a seventy-five-year-old Scotch, not a tequila shot. If you want to be a heathen, go drink something else."

I stuck my tongue out at him, blowing a raspberry like the fully functional adult I was. "Like you wouldn't bathe in the stuff if you could."

Thomas seemed to think about it for a moment before conceding with a shrug.

"You are correct, though. You do need a glamour." Emrys sighed before snatching the Scotch out of Thomas' hand and taking a sip. "At least until I can figure this out."

That was if she could even glamour me. If thirty spells didn't cut it, I had my doubts about whether another would work on me at all—even if it were just changing my appearance.

Emrys' odd reddish eyes began to shine as a crackle of power raced across my skin. Evidently, I didn't need to be in the middle of a pentagram with an animal heart in my hand for this one. *Thank fuck.*

She started to mutter in a language I didn't know as the power died, and then she stomped away, making a beeline for her desk. Her mutterings grew louder as she rummaged through her drawers, searching haphazardly for some item that was supposed to help.

So much for being a functioning member of the team. I mean, how in the hell would I be able to go on missions when I looked this way? How useful would I be if I couldn't read souls *or* go outside? They might as well toss me in the dungeon and throw away the key.

"Ah-ha," Emrys crowed, holding a pendant in her fist like she was making a victory air-punch. "Think you can best me, you wily fuck?" she grumbled under her breath. "I know more than one way to skin a cat."

I really hoped she was referring to this X character and not me. Honestly, I was grateful that she was trying so hard. It had been a long time since someone had gone so far out of their way for me.

Emrys pressed the pendant in between her palms as she hissed in another language I didn't understand, different from the other twelve she'd used so far. Light radiated from between her fingers, almost blinding me before winking out. With an expression of utter satisfaction, she held out the pretty silver pendant with its sizeable oval stone.

"Here, try this out. I might not be able to work any spells on you, but dammit, I can spell objects."

She shook the necklace at me, and I reluctantly took it from her. If this didn't work…

Taking a deep breath, I fastened the silver chain around my neck.

"Holy. Shit," Thomas whispered. "You did it."

Not willing to take Thomas' word for it, I raced back to the mirror. The first thing I noticed was the lack of a skeleton face. But then I realized all too quickly that wasn't the only thing she'd altered. I moved closer to the mirror, as if it would change its answer if I got close enough.

"What the…" I trailed off, trying not to sound unhappy. I didn't look like a creature right out of a nightmare anymore, but…

My purple irises were gone. In their place were vamped-out red ones. And my fangs. Unbidden, my fingers went right for them. Before, my fangs were simply elongated versions of my regular teeth. These needle-like things appeared to be just like Thomas' in the mirror—the weird vampire ones. But as I touched them, I quickly figured out that what I saw in the mirror wasn't real. I might be *seeing* a vampire's fangs, but mine were still there underneath the blanket of Emrys' magic.

Taking a deep breath, I calmed myself enough to retract the fangs, my straight non-pointy teeth reappearing as the vamped-out eyes faded to an odd blue color that was so pale it was barely a hop, skip, and a jump from white.

Well, at least I won't be walking around looking like an Angler fish all the time.

"I figured if I was changing things, it might be a good idea to keep your other status away from public consumption," Emrys offered, her tone soft as if she was trying to keep me calm.

I was totally calm. Totally. The calmest calm to ever calm.

"Knowing what we do now, it wouldn't be smart for you to go out looking nowhere near what a vampire should."

That brought back a recent memory of the tiny ABI agent who'd commented on my eyes. I couldn't afford to be stupid—not about that. I took a deep breath—mostly so I wouldn't freak out about the creepy vampire teeth—and gave her a nod.

"That's smart," I croaked, trying to get my voice to work. "If I'm to be Thomas' progeny, it *would* be better if I actually resembled a vampire."

"Exactly." Thomas interjected. "There's no way she'd be able to walk into a nest as she was and pass for one of us."

I hoped I wouldn't be doing that anytime soon. No offense to Thomas, but being in a room full of ancient killers kind of sounded like a bad idea to me. A really, really bad idea. My first kill in this life had been a vampire, and I'd gleaned no illusions about how vampires treated their prey.

"Go get something to eat and a nap," Emrys instructed, breaking me out of my downward spiral of dark thoughts. "We have a mess to clean up tomorrow. And Sloane?"

I yanked my head up from the close inspection of my still-bare feet. "Yes?"

"I suggest you keep this"—She gestured to the room at large—"under your hat for the time being. I'll be looking into how to fix what that blasted note broke, but I need time."

"Of course," I conceded with a nod. I believed Emrys if she said she'd try. But the operative word was "try." I highly doubted I'd be going without this glamour any time in the near future.

Maybe ever.

And while she was investigating my dilemma, I'd be looking for X—not that I'd be telling her that. Not that I'd be telling *anyone* that. That little tidbit would also be kept firmly under my hat until I found the bastard. Then it would just be him and me and my fangs.

The real ones.

I kept my face downcast. The last thing I needed was for Emrys to figure out my plans and stop me. Keeping my shit tight was of the utmost importance until I was safely behind a closed door.

Without another word, I made my exit, leaving Thomas and Emrys behind me as I navigated the hallways to the kitchen, doing my best to stick to the shadows. Though it undoubtedly would have been funny as shit to scare the life out of Bastian— *I mean, he's afraid of a skeleton kitty for fuck's sake*—I wholly intended to avoid the man.

I chose this course of action for two reasons. One—it would be one thing if we knew each other more than a couple of days, but other than a few shared kisses, a house fire, and a battle, I didn't know him from Adam. And he didn't really know me. There was no way I trusted him to let me do what I needed to do. Bastian wasn't precisely a goodie-goodie, but he wasn't on my level, either. There was no way he'd be down for what I'd have to do to get answers.

And two—because it was totally worth repeating: he was afraid of a fucking cat. The next to last thing I needed was Bastian seeing my un-glamoured face and blasting me to kingdom come. It was bad enough I was the Skelly Queen of the Night Watch every few seconds when I wasn't wearing the spelled necklace. I didn't need singed hair and charred skin on top of it.

After scrubbing the blood from my fingers—I managed to snag a couple of chicken drumsticks from the fridge while largely ignoring the plethora of cabinets and giant sink. If I studied the room too hard, I'd fawn all over the architecture and get caught. Naturally, I ate the drumsticks cold because the only thing better than just-out-of-the-grease fried chicken was cold leftover fried chicken. I stood at the opulent kitchen island, sleepily munching my first meal since I couldn't remember when, before tossing the bones in the trash.

My solid food cravings sated, I picked my way back to my room. I really wanted a nap, but I was under no illusion that I would ever be able to sleep in that bed again. I also wanted to sink my fangs into Bastian's neck, wanted his blood filling my mouth as his scent invaded my nose. I wanted to be held and comforted. I wanted to cry my fucking eyes out. I wanted to mourn my parents and how they'd been stolen from me.

But I wouldn't be doing that, either.

Because as soon as I crested the landing, Thomas was fully dressed and waiting for me.

"Get dressed and be ready to go in ten minutes. We've got a job," he informed me, his face a mask of thunder wrapped in an "oh shit" coating.

Of course we did.

3

It was all I could do not to throw the mother of all tantrums and stomp my foot. I'd been up since the day before yesterday, lived through a house fire, a ghoul battle, finding out my parents were murdered, and Emrys' bevy of spells. Oh, and discovering I was now the female embodiment of *Skeletor*? Yeah, that just added to the tippy top of my "what the fuck" for the week.

Unless someone was about to die a quick and painful death, I wasn't going anywhere. I opened my mouth to say just that, but Thomas cut me off before I could even utter a single syllable.

"Don't. Argue," Thomas growled as he pinched his brow. "I haven't slept either, but you and I are going to Knoxville, and there isn't another way around it. This isn't a message I can deliver via text, and my contact isn't answering her phone."

"What message?"

"I don't know about you, but I don't think the pile of bodies we left in that warehouse is going to go unnoticed for very long. You know, since the cops were descending right about the time we left? Unrest with the ghouls has a way of spilling out through the arcane world. If they think they were slighted or maligned in any way, they typically take it out on their closest rivals, no matter what happened or why. I need to alert my old nest. I owe it to them."

Grumbling, I brushed past Thomas and headed for my room. "You want me to go with you to a nest?" My jaw practically cracked as a yawn hit. "That sounds like the worst idea I've ever heard of. And this is me talking. If I'm the voice of reason in any situation, you should really rethink your priorities."

Thomas gave me a dark chuckle, following me down the hall. "It's a two birds one stone kind of a thing. I have to declare my progeny within the first year. You're already a year old, and if I want to keep the Arcane Bureau of Investigation out of my affairs, I need the queen to sign off on you. With Emrys' glamour, you should be able to pass muster as long as you don't rip anyone's soul from their bodies. Should be a piece of cake."

I was now fully awake, standing stock-still in the middle of the hall as I stared at Thomas. "Are you out of your fucking mind?"

Did I mean to yell that loud enough to wake the dead? No.

Is that precisely what I did? Absolutely.

"What?" he said with a shrug. "It's not as if they're going to make you dine on the blood of the innocent. They won't even look at you too hard. As long as you aren't a feral monster, you should be fine."

This sounded like the worst idea ever concocted in the history of the universe. Huffing, I marched double-time to my room, only to spy Bastian sitting on my bed when I got there.

So much for avoiding the guy.

He startled when Thomas and I busted through the door,

our commotion knocking him out of what appeared to be a solid snooze.

"How long have you been here?" I asked, praying my voice wasn't as accusatory as it sounded in my head.

Bastian yawned as he stood, an imprint of his fist more telling than anything he'd say. He'd been here for several hours, if not all damn day.

"I don't know," he muttered sleepily. "What time is it?"

I had no idea. My internal clock told me night had fallen already, but other than that, I was at a loss.

"It's eleven," Thomas supplied, impatience laced in his tone. "We don't have a lot of time, Sloane. Toss on one of the ridiculous dresses Dahlia got for you, and let's go."

Say what now?

"Dress? You didn't say anything about a damn dress, Thomas."

I'd only just noticed that Thomas was in a black suit with a black shirt and no tie. And back to pinching his brow like I was trying his patience. "I'm taking you to the fucking vampire queen of Knoxville, Sloane," he hissed, his eyes bleeding red but his fangs remaining hidden. "I need you to make a good impression."

I didn't see how stuffing my tomboy ass in a frou-frou dress was going to impress anybody. Thomas seemed to be about a millisecond away from snapping, so rather than arguing, I stomped over to the closet. I hadn't perused the offerings too much in my stay here, the utter lack of time conscious a valid excuse. I hadn't been too interested in fashion prior to my world falling apart. Sure, I appreciated the artistry of it, but jeans and a T-shirt were fine with me.

Blindly yanking a black dress from a hanger, I threw it on, managing to zip it by myself. It was a legit ball gown, one of those lace and chiffon numbers that made everyone resemble a fairy princess. It seemed too delicate a garment for someone like me to wear, with a lace bodice and lined chiffon skirt. Long lace sleeves fit snug to my arms, tied with a black ribbon at my wrists. The deep "V" of the neckline went all the way to my sternum, the nude mesh holding the sides together by a wing and a prayer. And the skirt was something out of a fairytale.

There was no way I wasn't going to mess this up.

I forewent the matching black heels in favor of my lace-up combat boots. *No one will be seeing my feet anyway, right?*

Still grumbling, I stomped out of the closet and hoped Dahlia had supplied me with some makeup, or else I would look like a weirdo. This wasn't the dress for a bare face—even I knew that.

I nearly tripped over my skirt but managed to make my way into the bathroom without injury. Pawing through the drawers, I found a small makeup bag with what I needed. While I was a novice at fashion, I was a master at makeup. It was basically just painting, only on my face. In less than ten minutes, I was done, my eyes screaming drama while my lips were stained the color of blood. There wasn't much I could do with my hair, so this was the best I could do with no notice.

Emerging from the bathroom, Thomas and Bastian's conversation grounded to a halt. Thomas' jaw dropped, but Bastian got an odd, soft look on his face.

"If you tell me I can't take weapons with me, I'm not going," I muttered, planting my fists on my hips. There was absolutely no way I'd be walking into a vampire nest—and in no way actually being a vampire—without weapons. This skirt was enormous. I could fit a Sherman tank under here.

That unfroze Thomas.

"As long as you don't draw them unless you absolutely have to, and you can keep them hidden," he said, nodding to my skirt, his thought following mine.

"Your eyes are a different color," Bastian blurted, and already I felt terrible. There was no way I was telling him why they weren't purple anymore.

Thomas gestured to my necklace. "Emrys made her a glamour so she could pass as one of my kind at presentation. No sense in walking into a nest unprotected."

Bastian nodded, yawning again. "Good call. That would be bad."

"You're staying here and sweeping the house. We need to make sure Booth didn't leave us any surprises. Harper did a cursory inspection, but you and Dahlia will be reinforcing the warding while we're gone," Thomas said, his tone not allowing any leeway. This was an order.

The exhaustion cleared a little from Bastian's expression as his jaw clenched, but he inclined his head.

"I'll go find Clem," I muttered, skirting around the tense tableau between the two men. I had no idea what was going on, and I didn't have it in me to care.

I had enough to deal with.

But I didn't make it more than a foot past Bastian before he caught my hand in his. Glancing over my shoulder, he snagged my gaze with his own.

"Are you okay?"

Such a simple question, and yet it was a shot right to the heart.

"I'm fine." What else could I say? *My whole world fell apart again for the twelfth time since you met me. Care to help me put the pieces back together?*

"You're not, but when you want to talk to me, just know that I'm here. You're not alone anymore, you know."

Shakily, I gave him a nod and turned back to the door, praying I didn't end up having to fix my makeup.

· · ·

Outfitted with only a Glock and a dagger the size of my forearm, I felt barer than naked as I stared at the darkened church. The giant building seemed to melt into the night, the sleepy city of Knoxville buzzing around this dark bit as if it weren't there.

Nestled in what Thomas called Arcane City, the decommissioned cathedral sat like an aging lady, largely ignored yet knowing all the secrets. He'd explained that Knoxville was divided into two parts: the arcane world and the human one. He'd informed me that most places were, unbeknownst to the humans. Arcaners walked among them in secret, blending in, yet staying apart, and had been since the dawn of time. I thought back to the life I'd led prior to waking up in that cemetery and knew he was telling the truth. I hadn't known a damn thing about this world until I'd slammed face-first into it.

This bit, this tiny pocket of Knoxville, was a place no human would dip a toe in. Not because it was dirty or dangerous, but because humans knew when they were being hunted. A leftover signal in their brains that evolution hadn't quite snuffed out sounded when they were being stalked, letting them know they weren't the top of the food chain. Well, that, and I had no doubt this place was warded out the ass.

Vampires clustered around the wide steps of the cathedral leading up to the expertly carved and substantial doors. Thomas had looped his arm through mine and guided me toward them, and I fought the urge to yank up my skirts and sprint away. Not only was I in formal wear, but I was sorely under-armed and at a disadvantage. I knew enough from my time on the streets of Ascension, but not enough about etiquette, social norms, or polite discourse to avoid making a fool of myself.

How to draw, how to paint, and how to fight—those were

in my wheelhouse. Dislodging a ghoul's head in less than five seconds? Absolutely. Not offending an ancient arcaner that could eat me for lunch? That part was iffy.

The vampires appeared to still for a moment as they caught sight of us before seeming to stand at attention. As we ascended the steps, each guard we passed knelt, their heads bowed as if a king was walking by. Mouth agape, I stared first at them and then at Thomas.

Out of the corner of my mouth, I whispered, "What the fuck is going on?"

"I'll tell you later," he murmured back, his voice barely audible. "Close your mouth, Sloane. You're catching flies."

Catching flies, my ass.

Emrys had implied—*or at least I thought she'd implied*—that Thomas had been kicked out of every nest he'd ever lived in. If he'd been kicked out of this nest, why were they bowing?

I snapped my mouth shut, blanking my expression as if this was no big deal. The goal tonight was not to react. Not to Thomas' apparent status, not to the breathtakingly beautiful cathedral, not to anything. I could totally do this.

A pair of guards opened the giant doors, bowing at Thomas as he guided me through. It was an actual struggle not to freeze at the entrance and stare. But man, did I want to. This place—while definitely what I would consider on-brand for a vamp nest—was one of the most magnificent buildings I'd ever been in. I wasn't particularly interested in other churches, but this cathedral was just a beauty. A gallery of pews sat to the left and right of a wide aisle that led to a raised dais. Vampires filled the seats, dressed similarly to Thomas and me, their voices a low buzz of conversation. More people were sitting in the upper gallery, their opulent gowns and sharp tuxedos a happy reminder that Thomas had my back. Had I walked in here with leather pants and a whip on my hip, I had a feeling I would have been just a touch out of place.

Thomas continued his leading, guiding me down the aisle toward a stunningly severe woman sitting on what appeared to be a throne. Skin paler than death, eyes vamped out in a way that seemed permanent, and painted lips the color of blood, she was the most beautiful and yet most frightening woman I'd ever seen. Dark hair was piled on her head in purposefully haphazard curls, a few tendrils snaking out of the complicated up-do to artfully caress her neck. She wore a brilliant green gown that was so simple, and yet so achingly complex, it had to have cost a fortune.

We reached the end of the aisle, and Thomas bowed his head slightly. I copied him, wishing I would have received an etiquette lesson on the hour-long drive here. All I'd gotten was Thomas' clenched jaw and silence.

"You have some nerve," a woman growled, drawing my gaze from what had to be the queen of this nest to her right.

I quickly realized that the voice did not belong to a woman at all but a child. Pale-blonde hair and blue eyes were set in an elfin face of a vampire who had likely been no more than ten when she was turned. And that had to have been centuries ago. This little whisp of a "girl"—*and I use that word lightly*—had the look of a being older than dirt. Dressed in a black lace confection appropriate for a child beauty queen, she stood from her chair.

She then launched herself at Thomas.

I couldn't exactly say *why* I did it. I mean, she had me by centuries, and Thomas could take care of himself. But as soon as her feet left the dais, I had the knife Clem had given me yanked from its sheath and was in front of the man in an instant.

Thomas owed me, not the other way around, but he'd been

kind to me when I'd needed it, and I wouldn't let him get attacked. No way, no how.

It was as if everyone froze. Conversations halted, guards stood stock-still, and even this slip of a thing stood arrested at the end of my blade, which was poised at her throat.

To this tiny—but by no means less deadly—vampire at the point of my knife, I said, "Settle down there, Blondie, or we're going to have a problem."

I had a feeling we probably already had one.

4

londie's expression—which had been full of surprise—quickly stretched into a wide grin. She slid her gaze from my blade to the man behind me. "Oh, I like her. I approve, Thomas. I refuse to let you throw this one back. Did you see how fast she moved?"

Confused but no less wary, I withdrew my blade from her neck and took a step back. Yes, the action gave the illusion that I was standing down, but it still kept me between her and Thomas. Yes, he could defend himself, but something about this place made me think he was more vulnerable here. More at risk. There had to be a good reason he left, right?

"I did. You getting slow in your old age, Ingrid?" Thomas shot back, skirting around me to sweep the small vamp in his arms and give her a hug. Their embrace reminded me of my father's hugs, warm and full of love, and my heart ached a little bit.

"Absolutely not. I'm as fabulous as I've ever been, you fuck."

The curse falling from her childlike mouth startled me for a second before I started snickering. The relief of not having to cut my way out of this nest swept over me. It had been a test—one I hoped I passed.

"You chose well, Thomas. This one will do a magnificent job as your enforcer," the queen said, her smooth voice washing over me.

It was laced in a kind of power I hadn't experienced in my time as an arcaner. It wasn't as if it worked on me exactly, but it flirted with the edges of my brain, seeking entrance. I didn't appreciate being tested like that and couldn't help shooting her a look of contempt, which earned me a no-shit giggle from the queen.

"Yes, you must keep this one. So sound of mind, so strong."

My frown deepened. I didn't enjoy being discussed like I was a slab of beef. But I didn't say anything. We were doing okay for now, and I didn't need to ruin that with my mouth.

"It has been so long since you made a progeny, I thought your days as a sire were over. Tell me—why did you choose this one?" The queen's words were less conversation and more like an accusation. Unbidden of my brain, my hand tightened on the hilt of my dagger.

Thomas stepped away from Ingrid, approaching the queen. "As an uninherit of the Sawyer blood mage line, I felt that Sloane would be a good fit for someone like me. We both are on the outskirts of the arcane world, both without family. It seemed like a no-brainer."

But the queen wasn't looking at him. No, she was looking at me. "And did you turn her before or after her parents were killed in their home and their house burned to the ground?"

Did she just say that to me? Did she just accuse me of murdering my parents?

It was all I could do to re-sheathe my blade, but I did it.

Because when I knocked her ancient ass out, I wanted it to be with my bare fucking hands.

"I will kindly ask you to shut your fucking mouth about my parents." I seethed through gritted teeth. "Your *Majesty*," I added, sneering.

If I hadn't been wearing the necklace that held my glamour, I'd undoubtedly have bright-purple eyes and fangs at the ready. With the glamour, I had no idea what I looked like. Was I vamped out and murder-y? Was I calm, cool, and collected? Who the fuck knew?

All I knew was, if she said one more thing about my parents, I was going to start a fight, and I really didn't give a damn if I was in the middle of a nest of vampires or not.

The queen's smile was unexpected, but I really didn't give a shit. Ingrid, I didn't mind, but this woman had officially gotten on my bad side. "Yes, Thomas. Keep this one. She is magnificent. Such control. Barely a year old and already out of her bloodlust phase. Quite remarkable."

"Yeah, yeah. I'm a goddamn miracle. Could you quit talking about me like I'm a slab of beef sometime in the next thirty seconds? I'm getting annoyed."

"There it is," Ingrid crowed. "Bless Lucifer's bouncing balls; I thought she was going to be a stuffy twat. I knew you wouldn't let me down." She slapped Thomas' shoulder and took her seat next to her queen.

Thomas rolled his eyes at the little vamp as the conversation began buzzing again. He held out his arm for me to approach. "Magdalena Dubois, please meet my progeny, Sloane Cabot."

Magdalena blinked at my name. "She won't be taking the nest's name?"

My brain failed trying to recall how nests worked. I knew there was usually a king or queen with several progenies. But my knowledge was limited to Rogues with no real idea of the hierarchy, or that information just didn't stick when I'd drank them down.

"I haven't discussed it with her, and it was not put forth in her contract, so I doubt it. I don't intend to make a true nest, anyway. You know how well it turned out the last time. Plus, there is only room for one Gao nest in the world."

Magdalena seemed appeased by Thomas' answer. "It is a pleasure meeting you, Sloane," she said.

I honestly couldn't say the same. Test or not, I wasn't too keen on being accused of my parents' deaths, nor was I a fan of the goading way she poked at me. Rather than lie, I bowed my head. Honestly, it was the best I could do.

Thomas let out a dark chuckle, shaking his head at me. I was so happy I amused the man. Well, if he wanted me to be something other than myself, he damn well should have told me.

"I would love to discuss an issue with you privately, Your Majesty. If you would be so kind?" he requested, holding his hand out for Magdalena to take. "Give me a minute, Sloane."

Well, shit.

I did not want to be left alone in the middle of vamp central —especially after the wringer I'd just been put through. Ingrid sauntered off to speak with a nearby vampire sitting in the front pew, while the rest of the nest stared at me as if I was either fresh meat or a bug to be smashed.

After muttering a hasty "excuse me," I walked back down the aisle and out the door, praying the frigid January air would calm me down. It was funny. Before I entered the nest, the air hadn't seemed to touch me at all, but now that I was by myself, it bit into my skin, my lace sleeves doing little against the winter chill.

That's right about the time I noticed I really was alone. The guards that had clustered on the steps before were gone—the buzzing quality of activity now a blanket of silence that sent a shiver of unease racing down my spine. Something told me that they should still be here. Something told me that this silence was wrong.

I barely managed to move in time. The hand that reached for me nearly closed around my hair before I was up with the Glock in my hand. Going for my gun was a stupid move—especially in light of the creatures who'd just decided to play. Seven hulking ghouls were fanned out in a semi-circle, their giant bodies blocking off any escape. There weren't enough bullets in the world to make a dent in these fools. With the cathedral walls at my back, my only options were moving to the dark alley to my left or staying put. And I didn't take a shine to either one.

Not. At. All.

Plus, these guys didn't resemble regular, everyday ghouls, either. Oh, no. They were *made* ones who'd been selected for their size and turned—maybe of their own free will, or perhaps not. Nary a one of these bastards were smaller than six and a half feet tall, and all seven of them were wider than a brick shithouse. There was no way I'd get to the door of the nest—not that I'd choose that avenue, anyway. I'd been a complete fucking fool to grab the Glock.

Guns were loud.

They were messy.

And even though we were in a "hidden" part of Knoxville, I didn't exactly think shooting someone in the face right next to a public street was going to win me any favors.

Still, it was what I had.

The first two bullets went into the center ghoul's eyes, hopefully allowing for enough of a distraction as he fell so I could grab the dagger sheathed under my skirt. In my first stroke of luck of the night, my hand closed around the dagger's hilt before they managed to realize what I'd done. And in my second, I had that blade out and at the ready before they struck. Then it was a whirling dervish of moves and countermoves.

I supposed the fear should have lasted longer, should have made me freeze or something, but it didn't. After the day—*no, the year*—I'd had, I'd been aching to fight someone, anyone. And after the unmitigated rage caused by Magdalena Dubois?

I'd never been so happy to decapitate someone in my fucking life.

The dagger was a bit too short for this task, but I made it work. My blade slashed and stabbed with abandon as I held off the group, while taking the first head at the point of my teeth. It didn't matter what the rest of the world saw with Emrys' glamour, I still had my fangs, and the bastards were sharp.

The only way to kill a ghoul for real was to take the head or burn their bodies to ash, and I really didn't have the time to sit for a bonfire, not with five still-standing ghouls and no backup. But again, the fear I probably should have been feeling never came. No, I was practically giggling as I tossed the first severed head at the next ghoul, the impact of his friend's dome smacking his enough to knock him ass over tea kettle.

This was fun. I'd forgotten how much fun fighting was when I wasn't worried about who lived and who died. When I didn't care for anyone but myself. When all the reasoning I needed was vengeance and the will to survive.

That thought was probably depressing, but at that moment, I just didn't care.

A flash of blonde hair had my giggle dying for a second, until I realized it was Ingrid coming for the assist. Before I could even say anything, Ingrid mowed through the ghouls like a tiny blonde missile, bowling two over before perching on their chests to neatly remove their heads. It was tough not to pout at her taking two heads before I had time to blink.

They had attacked me. It was my fight, and she was ruining my fun. I didn't care if we were on her turf.

Before I could call foul, she'd taken the remaining two down, fluttering her fingers as ghoul heads landed on the pavement with a squelching thud.

And then she was staring at me as if she'd just seen a ghost.

Why on earth would this tiny little assassin look at me like that unless... I slapped my hand to my chest, feeling for my necklace and coming up empty.

Shit.

Well, that secret lasted less than twenty-four hours. The jig was up.

5

Ingrid seemed to be seconds away from blowing her top. She opened her mouth, sputtering in utter horror as she took a few steps backward. I couldn't exactly blame her. Even Thomas had lost his poker face when he saw my new look for the first time. I had a feeling that hardly ever happened. Holding up a finger, I searched the ground for my missing necklace, hoping to stave off her freak-out until I was back to a semi-normal appearance.

The silver metal winked from the still fingers of the first ghoul who'd reached for me. In my haste to get away, I must not have felt him yank on the chain. Stomping over to him, I snatched the pendant from his hand, fiddling with one of the bent O-rings before clasping it back around my neck.

"What the fuck was that?" Ingrid breathed, her voice barely above a whisper.

The ghoul at my feet—the one I'd only managed to shoot— began to stir. I held up a finger again. "Hold, please. I'm sure all your questions will be answered, just…"

How in the hell could I explain what I was about to do?

Figuring I couldn't in the scant time I had before he woke all the way up, I skipped it in favor of getting all the shocking done at once. Ingrid hadn't seemed the excitable sort, and I was really hoping she didn't start screaming her head off.

Stomping on the ghoul's chest, I effectively pummeled his heart before I went for his neck. I needed answers, and the only way I was going to get them was from his blood. It helped that I really didn't give a damn if I took his soul or not. That I had to put on a dress was bad enough, but making me fight in the damn thing was just beyond the pale.

My fangs cut into his cold flesh like a knife through warm butter. His oddly metallic blood was disgusting, leaving a bitter taste on my tongue. But it was his memories that really made my stomach turn. This ghoul wasn't a prince by any stretch of the imagination. A rapist, a murderer, and that didn't cover what he'd done to his own family. This man was nothing like the ghoul I'd refused to drink down in the warehouse.

Huh. Had that only been a day ago?

But this ghoul had seen a flash of purple light and a hooded figure, too, just like the ones who'd been working with Booth. I ripped my fangs from the ghoul's neck, spitting out his disgusting blood on the pavement.

It didn't make any sense.

How had they found me here? And why were they looking for me in the first place? Were they even looking for me? Or was it Thomas they were after?

I knew I wasn't going to get anything out of this guy. The mage or witch or whoever had sent him, knew how to cover his tracks.

And it all led back to X.

Irritated, I clutched the ghoul's head in my hand and roughly snapped his neck. Ripping it from his shoulders took less effort than it took to decapitate a Barbie Doll. No sense in letting him come back for seconds.

"What." Ingrid paused, her voice turning shrill. "The fuck was that?" Wide-eyed was not a look I'd ever peg for the tiny vamp. Childlike or not, Ingrid had seen some shit over the years. I'd bet everything I owned—which wasn't much—that she was roughly the age of dirt.

Shrugging, I let the head drop to the pavement. "I needed answers."

My response did not appease her in the slightest. "And drinking his undead blood was going to give them to you?"

I wiped at my mouth with the back of my hand before shuddering a little. "Not exactly."

All things considered, I probably should have chomped down on that ghoul's soul while I was at it, but I just couldn't bring myself to do it. His blood was like swallowing hot garbage.

"Does Thomas know about this?" she asked, gesturing a hand to encompass me, the rapidly decaying ghoul, and likely all that had transpired in the last few minutes.

I winced as I contemplated just how much to tell her. I figured she and Thomas were close, but if I told her, she could haul off and tell the ABI, and Thomas and I would really be screwed. And it wasn't as if I could kill her. Several centuries old or not, there was no way I'd be able to get past the whole looking like a child thing.

"I do," the man in question affirmed, making both Ingrid and I nearly jump out of our skins. He placed his body in between me and Ingrid, protecting me just as I'd done for him. He glanced at me over his shoulder. "She saw?"

"Oh, yeah," I muttered, nodding. I wanted to say sorry, but this was totally not my fault. Well… I supposed if I hadn't gone off gallivanting by myself, this might not have happened, but it wasn't as if I had a neon sign over my head begging people to attack me. How was I supposed to know?

Thomas' expression was not amused, and I had a feeling I would be paying for this later.

"Are you kidding me?" Ingrid hissed. "Did you really just waltz in here and expect that no one would ever find out?"

Up until I got attacked, she and her queen had been singing my praises. We likely could have skipped on out of here had I not taken that breather.

"Of course I did." Thomas sighed, rubbing the back of his neck, discomfort stamped all over him. "Had Sloane's glamour not come off, no one would be the wiser."

The first order of business: get the necklace fixed so it can't come off willy-nilly. Second: send Thomas a fruit basket or something for tanking his life.

"Even me?" Ingrid's voice was small, as if the kept secret hurt her, her childlike voice practically stabbing me in the heart.

Shit.

Thomas sighed again, pinching his brow. "It's not my secret to tell, Ing."

Now I really felt terrible. Ingrid was someone Thomas really cared about. I couldn't just waltz off and give her nothing, not after what she saw. "Tell her, Thomas. She knows most of it already. And the rest isn't too far of a stretch to figure out."

And this was how I ended up sitting in the middle of the nests' graveyard, under a spelled cone of silence, nursing a blood bag like a Capri Sun as Thomas told Ingrid my sordid little tale.

Ingrid paced between the graves as she plaited her hair, the long strands sifting like silk in her fingers before she brushed them out and started again. "You're telling me you just woke up like this one day?"

I shook my head. "Not exactly. I didn't use to have the skeleton face thing going on, but the rest? Pretty much. One day I was a normal girl, going to college and irritating my mother, and the next, I was a blood-drinking soul eater with a proclivity for killing bad guys. There's a bout of homelessness and some trial-by-fire murder in there, but that's about the gist."

She stopped her pacing, crossing her arms over her narrow chest as she appraised me. "And this X guy—wait, is it a guy?"

"No idea," I muttered. I slurped the last drops of blood from the bag before removing my makeshift straw and sucking up the last of the blood from the tube. I stabbed it into my last bag, disappointed that Axel and Thomas had been right about the bagged blood situation. It was in no way as good as the molten heat that flowed in Bastian's veins—not by a long shot.

But swill or not, this blood was about a zillion steps above the ghoul's, and I was starving.

"His note had a solid penis-wielding flare to it, so I'm going with guy."

She gave my assessment a nod and continued, "So, this X guy is the man who murdered your parents."

Wow, that still hurt hearing out loud.

"I think so." I thought about it for a moment while sipping my beverage. This bag could use some vodka, if I was being honest. "I don't remember who or what killed them, but if he went to the trouble of announcing himself like that, I'm willing to give him the benefit of the doubt."

"Then how did he know you were here?" she asked.

And that was the sixty-four-million-dollar question. One I didn't have an answer to, but I could venture a guess.

"That's a good question, Ing," Thomas said. "I didn't tell anyone outside of my team where I was going. The only other people who knew were you and Mags. I think you have an internal problem."

Thomas' assessment was as brutal as it was accurate. Though, it wasn't as if the Night Watch hadn't been breached before. We were still smack-dab in the middle of the last one.

"Didn't you just tell me one of your own betrayed you? I know with our history, you're hesitant to trust anyone in this nest, but get real." Ingrid knifed her hand through the air, pointing to me. "Someone could have tracked her. This X guy could have tracked you. It isn't out of the realm of possibilities here. Let's not point fingers before we have some hard evidence."

I was piling a lot of trust onto Ingrid's shoulders, so I tried to give her and her assessment a fair shake. But if Thomas was wary of the vampires here, I figured it was smart to keep my eyes peeled.

"I'm not pointing fingers—or at least I'm not trying to. All I'm saying is that you need to keep your eyes open. Keep some important shit under wraps for the time being, or send out false leads. See if there's a leak. If there isn't, no harm, no foul."

Ingrid recrossed her arms, huffing, resembling the eight-year-old girl she most definitely was not. "Fine. But if nothing pans out, I reserve the right to rub your face in it."

Thomas held up a hand as if he was swearing on a bible. "Duly noted."

Softening a bit, Ingrid walked the few paces to hug Thomas, her small head barely reaching his sternum. "I miss having you around. Tell me again why you moved out?"

"Because I enjoy breathing, remember?" He chuckled, giving her a squeeze.

"Oh, that's right." Ingrid huffed before pulling away to level Thomas with an expression full of pure steel. "You stay breathing, you hear me? And keep a lid on that one. All it takes is one idiot with the wrong information to utterly and completely fuck up your whole life."

Thomas' smile turned rueful, and I couldn't help but mirror him. I'd fucked up tonight. I hadn't made sure I was protected, didn't have the right weapons, and hadn't been paying attention. If I ever planned on going outside by myself ever again, I would need to get my shit together.

That was if Thomas let me out of his sight ever again.

"That's the plan," he replied, turning the skull ring on his right hand in a full circle and breaking the makeshift dome of silence.

The ring had been a gift from Simon and made it so nothing living or dead could spy on the wearer. When it came to cool gadgets, I wanted something like that. If I wanted to stay off this X's radar, I'd need all the help I could get.

"And you," Ingrid barked, which made my gaze snap to her. "Watch his back. Do you hear me?"

All I could do was nod. Crossing Ingrid seemed bad for my health.

TWO MONTHS LATER

"Haunting rooftops again, I see," Bastian called from behind me, startling me out of my intense staredown of an inanimate object, namely, a door.

The only thing special about this door was that behind it lay a raging arcane club. The music radiated up from the ground, through the building, rattling my bones even from across the street, but that door was nothing more than a metal barrier to the world beyond. I'd always wondered what went on in clubs like those. Would it be sex and alcohol and dancing bodies—*which wasn't much different from a human club in that scenario*—or would it be darker? Blood and death and all the dark things about the arcane world that I hated? I was smart enough to know that the human world had its darkness, too, but it seemed the more I lived in this world, the more I realized that what I thought was evil didn't even begin to scratch the surface.

"It's a hobby," I muttered, shaking my head to clear the dark thoughts as I stretched from my crouch, my joints protesting loudly. One thing about this life that was the same were the aches and pains. I'd sat in one spot too long, staring at that stupid metal door to that stupid arcane club that wouldn't provide any more answers than the last one had.

My search so far had given me one dead end after the other, and after two straight months of nothing, I was starting to get annoyed. It was bad enough that I had the habit of haunting rooftops *before* the man who'd killed my parents left a note on my pillow.

Now, it was an obsession.

In the last two months—in between bounties and training —I'd been scouring every nook and cranny of Ascension. And my questioning methods hadn't exactly been in line with what I would call pleasant.

Bloody would be a better descriptor.

Hopping off the ledge, I knocked the dark hood from my white hair, letting the spring air cool me down. Sweltering under my lightweight jacket, I yanked it off, trying not to rip the fabric. Clem would be pissed if I ripped another one, and as the house's weapons keeper and person in charge of my solid food intake, pissing her off would not be a smart move on my part. Plus, if Bastian found me, there would be no more sleuthing tonight, and the need to hide my beacon of a hair color was no longer necessary.

I'd need to pick harder to find locations if I wanted him off my ass. Well… I kind of wanted him on my ass, just not while I was in the middle of my special project. I stared down at the skull don't-find-me ring I'd conned Simon into making for me. Leave it to Bastian to find a way to work around Simon's magic.

Bastian stood in the darkness, the faint light barely kissing the high points of his face and leaving the rest in shadow. To everyone else, he was a bruiser with his heavy dark brow and bulking frame. To me, he seemed akin to a big teddy bear—a giant, angry teddy bear, but one, nonetheless.

Even if he was spoiling my stakeout.

"Some hobby," he groused, snagging my hand and reeling me in. "You know, instead of skulking around, you could actually go inside one of those clubs. Take a night off from your 'creature of the dark' persona and actually have fun."

Fun. It was a struggle not to audibly scoff and even harder not to show the derision on my face. I hadn't had *fun* in ages. Hell, I didn't even know what that word meant anymore. And I couldn't remember the last time I'd taken a night off— definitely pre-orphanhood, for sure.

"'Creature of the dark?' What am I, a *Batman* villain? Do I get a cool costume? Is there a car in this deal?"

Bastian's smile gave me legit butterflies, the wide, white pull of his full lips making me all giddy.

Ugh, hormones. Why must you betray me like this?

"No, but it comes with a fabulous house, and our Alfred knows how to make biscuits from scratch."

Just the thought of Clem's cooking made me ravenous. How long had it been since I'd actually sat down at the table and eaten with my housemates? Far too long would be my guess.

"Fair enough," I conceded with a shrug. "Too bad about that car, though."

Truth be told, I'd stolen a crotch rocket from the Night Watch's garage. Well, "stole" was a harsh term. I fully intended to bring it back with a full tank and zero scratches when I was done with it. I had a feeling it was Thomas', and just the thought of damaging the bike made me want to throw up. It wasn't as if I had much in the way of money in my pocket to repay the man, and he was already sticking his neck out for me.

Bastian pulled me closer before making a one-two-step move and spinning me out as if we were dancing instead of just talking. "How about it? Let's go take a night off. Just you and me."

I couldn't remember the last time I'd been to a club, but it was definitely before I was legal to drink, and it was most certainly less cool than any arcaner club. Not that I'd ever been in one of those either, but if it wasn't death and murder, it would probably be okay, right?

"We haven't been alone together in months, Sloane. With Simon getting off house arrest and all those big jobs, it's been crazy. Just one night. The world will not implode if you take the night off, I promise." Reeling me in, our bodies collided enticingly, the gentle rub of his chest against mine doing the bulk of the convincing.

He was referring to the three Fae bounties we'd gone after last month. They had caused so much trouble, I would rather lock myself in the dungeon than go after another of that kind of arcaner again. *Fucking Faeries.*

Bastian dropped a kiss to the bend of my neck, and I had to suppress a shudder. There hadn't been much time for relaxing in the last couple of months and even less time for any kind of romance. Slowly but surely, he was edging back under my skin, making a home for himself there.

It almost made me feel like shit for not telling him about the note. *Almost.*

Then I remembered the shitstorm that followed the "note of doom" and thought better of it. The less Bastian knew, the better.

"If we must," I conceded as if I had no desire at all to see the inside of the club. I totally did, but for some dumb reason, I didn't want Bastian to know that. "One night off couldn't hurt."

After some kind of secret handshake with the doorman,

Bastian led me inside the loudest freaking building I had ever been in in my life. Strobe lights bounced off the walls as the dance music I'd only felt outside pumped through unseen speakers. A mass of bodies writhed on the dance floor while others lingered at the bar or in the booths, yelling to be heard over the din.

The bar was a battered monstrosity with nicks and dents as if it had seen some shit, while the booths were made up of painted black wood and vinyl. There didn't seem to be cocktail waitresses or fancy drinks—just beer in pitchers and baskets of food. I wasn't mad at the modest fare either. The thought of a beer and a basket of fried yumminess—and maybe a blood chaser—seemed like just the thing.

The scent of clean sweat, beer, food, and magic masked everything else, and on top of the noise and light show, I had a hard time figuring out what kind of arcaners we were dealing with. None of them seemed to pay us any mind as Bastian led us right to the dance floor, weaving through the masses to get to the center. The heavy thrum of the bass notes ricocheted through my chest as the heat and music seemed to race down my limbs.

Once Bastian found the perfect spot, he drew me to him, and I quickly learned that he didn't just know how to dance. He knew how to *dance*. I'd never seen a man as big as Bastian have even a lick of rhythm, but all it took was one roll of his hips to realize I'd been sorely mistaken. The sultry beat hit with the punch of a spell, and I quit giving a shit about pretty much anything else except the heat of Bastian in my space and how our bodies fit together. His giant hand found a home on my hip, his fingers flexing just a little, which reminded me of other times...

Times when I had my fangs in his neck and his body in my space and the heat of his blood rushing into my mouth. It reminded me of how good it felt to taste him. To feel his warmth, his soul, to see all the hungry, dirty things he thought about but would never share.

The scent of his need filled my nose as our bodies swayed to the beat, the brush of his chest against mine making my mouth water. I hadn't taken Bastian's blood since our foray in Axel's lab right before a significant facet of my life blew apart. Since then, it had been bad guys and bagged blood for me, which was akin to going from a melt-in-your-mouth medium ribeye to an elementary school cafeteria pizza.

And he smelled good enough to eat.

Something must have flitted across my expression because Bastian's face seemed to mirror everything I had roiling in my chest. The hand at my hip found its way to my hair, and then his mouth was on mine, our tongues dancing rather than our feet.

Did I even have feet? Did it matter?

The heat of the club—of Bastian—wrapped me up in a cocoon. In this tiny spot on the planet, in the circle of Bastian's arms, I was safe. I wasn't wrong or weird or different.

I wasn't a monster.

I wasn't a freak of nature.

And then his mouth broke from mine only to travel to my ear.

"Bite me," he whispered, the words hitting me with the force of a wrecking ball. How I managed to hear them over the music, I had no idea. "Please. I've missed you."

The whole of my belly dipped as everything inside me clenched. I'd dreamt about his blood in my mouth, about our sweaty bodies writhing together as I drank from him. I wanted all of it, all of him, and I couldn't toss up another reason I should keep him at a distance.

All it took was a teensy rise on my tiptoes and a slight turn of my head. Then his neck was right there. Every reason I had, every single good intention, went right out the window. Before I really gave my brain the go-ahead, my fangs were in his neck, pulling deep draws from his vein. It was as if I'd been starving for years and he'd given me my first meal.

His need rose around us like a cloud of ambrosia as images bombarded me: strands of my white hair sifting through his fingers, his mouth everywhere he could reach as we writhed together. I wanted every part of his thoughts. I wanted to do every single dirty, filthy, fucking awesome thing I saw and then some. I wanted us out of this club, out of this city, and on a bed that could take a beating.

But before I could remove my fangs from Bastian's neck to tell him just that, rough hands yanked me away from him.

And the last thing I saw before the shit really hit the fan was a blue ball of magic headed right for me.

Super.

7

The crackling ball of bullshit hit me square in the chest before I even had time to move, the force blowing me off my feet and into the still-dancing crowd. My landing was unforgiving, people kicked and shoved at me as I tried to get a lock on how to move my limbs. The electricity in that spell was enough to take down a rhino, so getting the signals to work took a second—one I really didn't have.

Groaning, I managed to stand, my limbs none too happy about the demand to move. But I didn't get too much down time since another orb of stupid magic was headed right for me. The whole situation pissed me off to no end. I was in the middle of the best time I'd had in months and this asshole ripped it away from me?

No. *Fuck, no.*

My gaze flitted around the room as I dodged the orb—finding Bastian was my highest priority. A close second was finding the bastard who ruined my fun and making them eat their own teeth. My eyes snagged on Bastian, his hulking frame on the other side of a sizable crowd of arcaners swarming toward the exit. His neck was still bleeding, the shine of it making my heart lurch. I hadn't been able to close his wounds. I couldn't say why, but tears pricked my eyes for a second before a surge of heat washed over me.

Bastian was mine. His blood was mine. His body was mine. His safety was mine. Whoever had ripped me from him was going to wish they had never been born.

The mage in question stepped into the light to make himself known, another glittering orb hissing in his hand. The blue magic cast eerie shadows on his face, likely making him appear far more sinister than it should. The guy looked no older than twenty at a push, but I knew he had to be at least a century if not more. Long, scraggly hair pulled into an unfortunate queue at the back of his head, the guy probably snagged a lot of tail in a place like this. With the whole "flannel and ripped jeans and wannabe James Dean but failing miserably" vibe, dumb youngsters of all kinds probably ate it up.

I had never been one of those youngsters, though—even at twenty-three.

"Your kind isn't welcome here. I don't give a shit what your *queen* says. You come into my bar, and use your bloodsucker voodoo on one of my patrons, and you think you're just going to walk out of here? I don't think so."

I knew for a fact I was going to walk out of this bar. The real question was whether or not he would. But mage-dude didn't wait for me to answer. No, he just lobbed that stupid electricity at me like an asshole. Stepping to the side, the magic sailed past me, but he was ready for that. Three more orbs rocketed toward me with the speed of a missile.

Too bad for him, I'd been training.

Before he could throw another one, his wrists were trapped

in one of my hands while the fingers of the other were around his throat.

"Considering I had consent, yeah, I do think I'm walking out of here." I squeezed his wrists together to show him I could crush them if I wanted to. With fear stamped all over his face, my bloodlust and vengeance died a quick death, and I sighed.

Fine. He can live.

"Look, man. I have no problem with you protecting your patrons. But just as a request? Maybe don't shoot first and ask questions later."

And then this fucker did the dumbest thing he could have possibly ever done. Instead of nodding and squashing the situation, he decided to spit in my face.

Fun fact: this wasn't the first time that had been done to me in the last year. It turned out that when certain arcaners found out that they weren't at the top of the food chain, they got a little *testy*. So, I showed them what testy really looked like.

With a quick tightening of my fingers, I crushed the mage's wrists. *Let's see him lob anymore orbs for the next little while.* His whole body went slack—an unfortunate move for him, since I still had a hold of his throat. His eyes popped wide as his lack of oxygen finally registered. And all the while his spit ran down my cheek.

His feet scrabbled for purchase on the floor, but I decided being an asshole was more fun, raising my arm just enough that he could only find the barest of relief.

"Now, what did we learn?" I asked, my voice a deadly calm.

His eyes bugged out of his head as his face purpled. Rolling my eyes, I lowered my arm an inch, letting him get a little oxygen. Not enough, but some.

"Fine, I'll answer for you. You learned not to fuck with

people stronger than you. You learned that you shouldn't escalate a situation with stupidity—especially when you're at a disadvantage. Now, do I need to kill you, or are you going to finally be smart?"

His gaze flitted to the right before he smiled. "Fuck. You."

He might as well have waved a huge red flag in my face to signal that his backup had arrived.

"Sticking with stupidity, I see." And I'd thought it was going to be such a quiet night.

The thing was, I didn't want to kill this guy. He was just an idiot that wanted to make sure his patrons weren't getting violated. That, I totally understood. After my brush with the Knoxville vampire queen, I got it. Had I been anything other than what I was, she could have gotten me to do anything she wanted to. From what I'd gleaned from Thomas, that ability wasn't just limited to her. It wasn't a surprise that a lot of arcaners were iffy around vamps, but this was just ridiculous.

Without much deliberation—mostly to prevent his backup from getting the upper hand—I tossed the mage in the direction I thought they would be coming from. Well, "tossed" was a more polite term for what I actually did. What I really did was spin in a quick circle and shot put his dumb ass as hard as I could.

It was only fair. He'd blown me off my feet once already, and had I been something else, he would have killed me with one of those stupid balls of electricity. Had I actually been a vamp, it might have done some real damage.

When Bastian brought me to this bar, I'd thought we'd have a nice time. Now I was desperately trying not to murder people.

But the small contingent I'd thought the mage had for backup didn't quite encompass all the people at his disposal. By the time I turned to find the exit, there was enough magic headed my way to flash fire a deity. I tried to run, but it seemed as if I'd hit an invisible wall, a spell of some kind holding me in place as the threat rocketed toward me. Just when I thought I was toast, the magic seemed to hit the same wall I was stuck behind, exploding against it with enough force to rock the whole building.

And then I wasn't trapped anymore. Instead, I was behind a very broad back as Bastian put himself between the mages and me. I couldn't explain the sheer amount of relief I felt at seeing him upright and breathing—even if that relief was seriously tempered by the scent of his still-bleeding neck.

Multicolored magic swirled up his arms as the building trembled beneath our feet.

"I suggest you stop this foolishness before you really piss me off," he growled, the sheer power rolling off his body enough to show them he meant every word he said.

I probably shouldn't be as turned on as I am right now, right? I mean, this was a serious situation that required focus and attention so we didn't die. Why exactly did I want to rip his clothes off again?

"Vampires aren't allowed here, and you know it, Cartwright. I don't give a shit who you are, this is still my club." It was the James Dean wannabe speaking, his raspy voice a testament to the fact that I did not, in fact, crush his windpipe.

Pity.

"Tell me—who owns this building, Jarek? Who owns this block? Whose property are you on? You do not own this establishment. I do. And if I want to let my woman feed from my neck, I shall. If I want to grant her entrance onto my property, I shall."

Ho-ly shit. No wonder the doorman had just waved him in. Bastian owned this place?

"This is my club," Jarek insisted. "I get a say at who comes in."

Bastian's magic burned hotter, and I took a small step back. "This is not your club. You manage the bar. This is my club, my bar, my property. And not only did you let loose potent magic in the middle of a crowd, you spit in my woman's face."

I was tempted to just let Bastian lose it on this fool. Really, really tempted.

The best I could do was put a gentle hand on his back and pray that did something. As soon as I did, though, Bastian shot a look over his shoulder. *Nope, that totally did not work.*

Jarek wasn't the only one in deep shit. I had the distinct feeling I was, too.

I lifted my hands in surrender, and Bastian turned back to the mages in front of him. "You're fired. If I see you inside this club again, you're dead." Bastian shifted his gaze to the other men that had come to Jarek's aide. "Be very careful who you consider friends in this town, gentlemen. Quite frequently their stench can carry, landing on any that help them."

That was a carefully worded threat and warning all rolled into one. I had a feeling Jarek wouldn't be welcome in a lot of places in the near future.

"You can't do that!" Jarek protested, the crackle of his power announcing itself.

I took that opportunity to step to Bastian's right—still behind him so he wouldn't get fussy—but with a clear shot if I needed to help. Bastian wasn't just facing off a few mages. Oh, no. He was facing off against the lowly Jarek and about twenty of his closest pals.

But only Jarek was holding an orb of magic. The others appeared as if they were trying to surreptitiously find the exit.

"You don't just get to come in here and kick me out. Not after all these years."

With that, Jarek tossed his orb of magic, his failing wrists making the fact that he could do any spells at all a freaking miracle. Though, this probably would have been more impressive if Bastian hadn't plucked the orb out of the air like he was catching a whiffle ball. The electricity fizzled out as Bastian's fingers closed around it, the faint scent of ozone the only sign that the magic had existed at all.

"I do, and no amount of time in my employ would ever excuse what you did. You just painted a target on your back, Jarek. I'll give you a five-minute head start."

Jarek's face went white as he scrambled back, knocking into his friends as he tried to find the door. His friends bolted for the opposite exit. My guess was they wanted Bastian to follow him and not them. Smart.

And then we were alone, but I was under no illusion the threat had passed.

Bastian turned to face me, his expression thunderous. He drew a handkerchief from his pocket, wiping my cheek.

The relief from that simple gesture was seriously short-lived when he began to speak. "Did you know that certain elements disrupt spells temporarily?"

It didn't matter if his voice was the softest of velvet, my stomach still dropped to my toes.

Slowly, I shook my head.

"What is under that glamour, Sloane?"

8

I in no way wanted to answer that question. In fact, I wanted to find a quiet corner and vomit my guts up before running away and never looking back.

That exact moment was something I'd been dreading for months. Bastian saw me. I knew he had. He'd seen what I looked like now. Oh, no.

Bile rose in my throat as I took a step back. I could totally deny it. *I could.* I could also boss up and tell him and stop fucking hiding.

Both options seemed shitty.

"What did you see?" I croaked, my voice a small, pitiful thing. *Dammit, why was telling him what happened so freaking hard?*

Tears pricked at my eyes, and I couldn't help dropping my gaze to my feet. I wasn't this small, frightened girl. I hadn't been in a long time. So why was I doing this dumb shit now?

Bastian moved into my space, reaching for the necklace that held the spell. And even though I'd had Emrys reinforce the clasp with a fair bit of magic, Bastian still managed to unfasten it from my neck.

And I'd let him.

Stupid, stupid, stupid.

I'd thought I wanted to throw up before. Now, I just wanted to run and hide. Letting my hair fall in a curtain wasn't going to work either because his fingers were in the strands, and he was tilting my face up so he could inspect it.

"What happened?" he asked, the gentleness in the question ready to break me in two.

I did my best to memorize the open expression on his face because I knew once I told him—*and I had no choice but to tell him*—he was never going to look at me the same way again.

But when I opened my mouth to do just that, nothing came out. I hadn't been scared of anything in so long, and this wasn't exactly a small thing. This was—*he was*—important.

"Let me tell you what I know," he began, granting me a reprieve. "The morning after you helped me save my brother, you got that glamour. The spell work has Emrys' signature. You've been avoiding me, my brother, his cat, and everyone else in the house except for Thomas. You work and train until you can barely stand up, and when you aren't doing that, you're out prowling Ascension, searching for something. You refuse to come to me for feedings, to talk, or for anything other than the minimum required interaction so I won't get suspicious."

When he put it like that, I sounded like the biggest bitch on the planet, and he should toss me in the garbage the first chance he got.

"Something happened somewhere in the time we got home to when I woke up in your room, I just don't know what it is. And I won't know, and I can't help unless you tell me."

He was being so kind—so levelheaded—about this that I wanted to crawl under a rock and stay there until I felt less like a slug.

"Wh-when I got home, there was a note on my pillow. From someone named X telling me he remembered what my parents smelled like when they burned. That we would be meeting again soon."

Those whispered words were broken glass as they came out of my mouth. And they hit Bastian as if I'd slapped him. His fingers didn't leave my hair, and his grip didn't tighten, but his face told me that I'd just wounded him worse than if I'd punched my fist into his chest and ripped his heart out. But I wasn't done, and he needed to know the rest.

"Emrys said that the note itself contained a blood curse—one that could take down entire families. She has no idea how I survived or why the curse's outcome is that I look like the Grim Reaper every few seconds. She's done everything she can think of to fix it, and she says she's researching, but..." I trailed off, shaking my head.

I was under pretty good authority that if Emrys hadn't found a way to fix it by now, there likely wasn't a fix to be had.

"And you kept this from me because?" he asked, the words hitting like a punch to the gut, even though they were gentle and soft and no more than a whisper.

How could I tell him that I worried he'd go off half-cocked and get himself killed? That if my parents couldn't save themselves from this X, what was he going to do? That I didn't trust him not to lock me down or keep me out of the fight, or not to run screaming away from the mere sight of me?

"You didn't want me to stop you. Is that it? You thought I would keep you from trying to find this bastard?"

I winced.

"Well, and Simon told me before all this about how you ran screaming from the house when you met Isis." I gestured to my face. "I kinda thought if you saw me this way..." I didn't even attempt to continue. Just saying it out loud made me realize how fucking dumb it was.

Bastian and I didn't have this epic love affair. He hadn't made me any promises or taken vows of forever. We were tied tangentially by my need for blood and the strange kind of possession I felt for him. But it didn't ever feel like enough. The bond wasn't enough. The tie we had to each other was fragile and fleeting.

And I didn't trust it.

That was the real reason I didn't tell him. Thomas owed me. Emrys needed me. But Bastian... He could leave me behind without a blink.

He nodded, his face grave as if he realized something important. "You didn't trust me."

His face wavered as tears of shame filled my eyes, and I couldn't hide because he was still cupping my cheeks, making me face him. "No," I answered. "I didn't."

His warm thumbs wiped the wetness away. "Do you think you might someday? Trust me, I mean? If we had more time?"

My chuckle was dark even as I covered both his hands with my own, pressing them firmer into my skin. "Everything I knew to be true was a lie. Everyone I knew deceived me. What does trust even mean?"

Bastian closed his eyes before resting his forehead against mine. "Trust means that you know I will be here to back you up when you need me. Trust means that I won't hide things from you or lie to you or hurt you on purpose. Trust means that you are safe with me. We haven't known each other long enough for you to believe me, I know that. All I'm asking is that you try. Because what I feel for you, I haven't felt in a very long time. I'm not ready to give that up."

In the circle of his arms with his heat radiating into me, I could almost taste the honesty on his tongue. He meant every single word he said.

"Okay," I murmured, doing my very best not to lie to him. "I'll try." These last few months had been hell, and I didn't think I could do another day of keeping him in the dark.

"Good. Now that I'm in the know, does that mean I might actually see you once in a while? Your absence is hell on a man's self-esteem."

I couldn't help the relieved laugh that burst from my lips. I also couldn't help that I launched myself at him, practically climbing his tall body like a tree and latching onto him as if he would disappear if I didn't wrap him up in my arms and legs as soon as possible.

I was a needy, needy barnacle.

Bastian's laugh was quickly swallowed by my kiss, and the joy in it was a welcome light when I'd been in the dark for so long. It didn't take long for that laugh to peter out or for him to realize that I meant business. Hell, if I could figure out how to manage it, I would have undressed him by the power of pent-up sexual frustration alone.

And when he finally figured out that I was serious? His gloriously strong hands gripped me tighter to him as if he wanted to fuse our skin. His whole body seemed to get warmer as he walked me backward to the closest wall. Then my fingers were under his shirt, exploring the planes of his stomach and higher.

That shirt really needed to go. Probably the pants, too.

When my thumb grazed a nipple, though, I suddenly found my hands out of his shirt and pinned above my head in his much larger one.

He broke the kiss, which ripped a groan from me. I wanted his lips back. I wanted the feel of his skin back. I wanted to fall into him, to roll around in his scent, in his touch until I was sated. Which might be never.

Bastian's green eyes flashed gold as air sawed in and out of his lungs. We were breathing as if we'd just ran for our lives, but Bastian's had the added flare of a man *this* close to coming undone.

"As much as I love where your head is at, I'm going to need you to stop, Sloane." His voice was pure gravel, and there was a slight manic quality to his expression, but I wouldn't be me without pressing my luck. So, naturally, I swiveled my hips—just a little—which made his eyes roll back in his head.

"Stop what?"

A growl ripped up his throat, and he nipped at my neck with his blunted teeth. *Dear sweet lord in heaven, why was that so fucking hot?* There was a solid threat of me combusting right then and there.

"Stop making me lose sense for about ten seconds, so I don't fuck you in a dirty, sticky bar. Let me take you home. Let me have you in a bed. Let me watch you writhe in my sheets as I taste you. Let me make lo—"

I cut him off with a kiss, his hands somehow no longer pinning mine. I was going to let him do all of that, but if he didn't stop talking about what he wanted to do to me, I'd be pushing the issue. Then we really would end up fucking against a wall in a deserted bar.

Was it even deserted? Did it matter?

"Okay," I managed to whisper once I broke our kiss. "Let's go home. And I'll let you do any filthy, dirty, nasty thing you want to me—sexually speaking—in the bed of your choosing. But I'm warning you..." I trailed off, giving my hips one more swivel just to see his gaze go molten.

"Warn me about what?"

I brought my lips right to his, so he could feel every word

that came out of my mouth. "You're going to let me do everything I want to do to you, too. You're going to let me taste you, feel you, fuck you, make love to you." Evilly, I nipped at his bottom lip, which was swollen from all our kisses. "It's only fair."

Somehow, Bastian pressed himself further against me, and I felt every single millimeter of his arousal. Did my eyes roll up into my head? Maybe, but it was so hot to see him so close to losing it. I didn't know how in the hell I was supposed to handle it when his control finally snapped. But boy, did I want to be there when it did.

"Fair is fair, darling," he agreed, nodding to himself. He appeared as if he was shoving all of his lust into a little mental box to be opened at a later date. *Man, did I want to open that present.*

Then he stepped away from the wall, taking me with him. His grip didn't loosen one iota, but we were moving—and fast —like we were racing through time as everything around us sped up. The room, then the buildings and sky sped past us. Then we weren't in the club anymore. We were outside standing next to Thomas' bike, which I'd parked nearly a mile away from my chosen rooftop.

The shock of the movement was probably the only thing that could have pulled me out of my lust haze.

"What the hell was that? How—"

"Mage trick," he muttered, letting me find my feet as he released me. "Let's just say that one isn't exactly aboveboard and may be illegal." He put a finger to his lips, signaling that I was to stay mum about it.

I snorted. Of course, he would use an illegal mage spell to get laid faster. To be honest, I couldn't exactly fault his logic.

"Sure you don't have any other tricks in your arsenal?" I teased, tossing my leg over the sleek motorcycle. "Can you make a portal to another dimension or conjure dark matter or something?" I shoved the black helmet on my head—not because I needed it, but so I didn't get pulled over.

Bastian just shrugged as if he could absolutely do those things if he put his mind to it, and it dawned on me that it was a distinct possibility that he wasn't joking.

"I'll meet you at the house," he said, dropping a kiss to my shoulder before nipping it with his teeth. "Be careful."

Every part of me clenched in answer, and I couldn't wait to feel his mouth on me again.

But as he stepped away, his phone buzzed in his pocket. Groaning, he fished it out and stared at the screen before his gaze immediately found mine.

I had a feeling I wouldn't be getting his mouth back for a very long time.

9

"Say that one more time?" I couldn't believe the bullshit I'd just heard, so there had to have been a mistake. There was no way that…

Bastian moved closer to me like he was going to have to lock me down. What he did not do was repeat himself, and I desperately needed him to.

"Is he—" I couldn't even say it.

His warm hands found my skin, but this time, they were too hot, too rough, too… "There was an attack on the Arcane Bureau of Investigation building in Knoxville tonight. Several agents are dead, and many are scattered to the winds. While that was going down, there was a prison break at our local detention facility. Booth escaped along with about twenty other prisoners. We need to get back to the house so we can help the ABI round up the fugitives."

I'd ripped my helmet off when he told me the first time, so I shoved it back on my head and started the bike. "I'll meet you there."

But before I could put it in gear and take off, Bastian had another too-hot hand on my bare arm. "We'll find him, Sloane."

I wanted to laugh, but I didn't. How many people would die because of that man? How many innocent people had died already? I wondered about the small dark-haired agent who'd given me advice. What had her name been? Sarina? Was she one of those dead agents? Was she hurt? She reminded me so much of Aunt Julie that my heart hurt to think about it.

Damn straight, we were going to find Booth. And this time, I wouldn't let a little thing like decorum stop me. Hell, I'd rip his soul right out of his body in front of a fucking audience if I had to. I'd known good and well I shouldn't have left him alive the last time, and what did I do? I let Emrys and Thomas talk me into being the good guy.

But I wasn't the good guy, and I never had been.

I gave Bastian a stiff nod and took off, letting the city lights race by me as I rocketed toward home.

The drive to the house had been too fast and not fast enough. I wanted to get out there. I wanted to find Booth and tear his soul from his chest, and… Shaking my head, I ripped off the helmet and left it on the seat.

"What the fuck is wrong with your face?" a male voice yelled, scaring the shit out of me. "And why do you smell like death?"

Slowly, I turned to Simon, who was standing at the door to the garage with his skeleton kitty in his arms. Slapping at my chest, I tried to feel for my necklace. I wanted to roll my eyes but refrained. Bastian had taken my glamour necklace off of me, and it was undoubtedly still in his pocket.

Flannel shirt and haphazard beanie on his head, the tall death mage could likely scent the dead a mile away or something. Who knew what powers Simon had? From what I'd gleaned in my short time in this place, Simon and Bastian weren't exactly the norm when it came to their abilities.

"Is there a way we can just skip this whole conversation and pretend you didn't see anything?" I asked as I prayed Bastian got home with my necklace sometime in the next few seconds. The last thing I needed was the whole damn house up in my chili about my stupid face.

Simon stepped fully into the garage and shut the door behind him. I had a feeling I knew what his answer was going to be.

"What in the bloody hell is going on, Sloane?" The threat in his tone was clear as day. He was going to get answers even if he had to pull them out of me with pliers.

Groaning, I eyed the giant bay door, hoping it would open so Bastian could explain to his brother why I looked like the Grim Reaper.

No such luck.

"Cliff's Notes? I touched a letter with a blood curse on it, and now I look like this. I swear I have a glamour, it's just in your brother's pocket. No big deal."

Simon gaped at me for a solid thirty seconds. I wasn't even sure he was breathing.

"Don't we have some fugitives to find?" I prompted, and the mention of our most pressing issue seemed to snap him out of it.

Simon's face took on an air of misery and commiseration. Hearing Booth was out in the world couldn't have been a comforting notion for him any more than it was for me. Not after Booth kidnapped him and tried to kill him to draw me out. Or at least that's what I figured the motive had been. It didn't matter how much blood I'd pulled from Booth during his interrogation. I'd gleaned a slight bit more than fuck all from him.

A part of me wondered if Simon blamed me for his ordeal. It wasn't exactly as if I'd been around in the last couple of months to see if he held a grudge or anything.

"Does Emrys know?" he whispered, and I nodded, which made him breathe a sigh of relief. "And Thomas?"

I nodded again.

"Bastian?"

"He found out tonight. He wasn't keeping it from you or anything."

Simon dipped his head, a frown marring his face before he set his skeleton kitty down. I'd avoided Isis—and damn near everyone else in the house—for months. I wasn't exactly skipping to find out if she would freak out around me now. The last time she'd accidentally wandered too close to Clementine —our resident revenant—there had been several knocked-over vases that paid the price.

But I probably shouldn't have worried. Isis and I were tight. Ever since I'd come to the house, she had taken a keen interest in me, much to Simon's dismay. Isis raced for me, leaping in the air once she got close enough and damn near landing on my chest. My arms closed around her kitty butt, gentle, so I didn't hurt her. Immediately, she started purring as if I was her favorite person on the planet as she rubbed her boney head against my cheek.

Simon's frown intensified, the concern on his face making me a little uneasy. "You know, you're the only person she does that to. She hates Thomas, Axel, and Clem because they're undead. She can't stand Harper or Emrys—something about their magic she doesn't like. She tolerates Dahlia, but only because Dahlia is around her so much. Other than me, Isis is not a fan of almost anyone. Except you."

I shrugged around an armful of kitty, wondering if anyone had told him about just how close Isis and I were. She was the one to show me the way when he'd been taken. Isis was the one who had made sure I knew where he was. She had comforted me when I'd learned of Aunt Julie's death, and cuddling this tiny creature, I felt a relief I usually only got in Bastian's arms.

"You said it was a blood curse? That made you this way? A killing curse, I presume?" Simon edged toward me. An understanding dawned on his face, and he pulled in the air with his nose, scenting me.

I cuddled Isis closer, the urge to run away from Simon flitting through my bones.

"Do you know who death mages make deals with? Who we call upon to do our magic?" Simon asked, a prompt that felt like a trap.

I shook my head, taking a step backward. "No, I don't."

"I didn't either for a very long time. It wasn't until I was well advanced, did I learn the truth about what we do. Everything a death mage does is a trade. A deal. A bargain." With every sentence, Simon moved toward me.

The urge to run grew stronger because I knew he was about to drop a bomb on me—a truth I was positive I was in no way ready for.

"We make the bargains with a deity. He goes by many names in many cultures. But the most common of names is the Angel of Death."

The sound of that name sent a pang of alarm through me for no good reason whatsoever. I didn't want to know this— didn't want whatever he was going to say in my brain.

"That's great information, Simon. Why the fuck are you telling me this?" Reluctantly, I set Isis on her feet, getting ready to make a break for it if I had to. "No offense, but I was under the impression we had shit to do that didn't involve story time about death deities."

Luckily, my reprieve came in the form of Bastian pulling into the open bay door, the headlights of the SUV temporarily blinding me.

"We will be continuing this conversation, dammit," Simon whispered, less like he was talking to me and more like he was talking to himself. Still, I heard him.

Bastian threw the SUV into park and hopped out. Well, it was less hop and more of a sexy step out, but whatever. His gaze found mine, concern stamped all over his face before his eyes cut to his brother. Without a word, Bastian invaded my space, moving in front of me in a protective stance between his brother and me. It wasn't until his big body was between Simon and me that I realized just how close Simon had been.

"Do we have a problem?" Bastian asked, his voice calm and level as if he was discussing the weather. I couldn't tell if he was actually pissed or not, but I in no way wanted to be a sticking point between the brothers.

"There's no problem," I answered, pivoting so I was no longer behind Bastian. "Can I have my necklace back? I'd rather not freak out anyone else tonight."

Bastian peeled his gaze from his brotherly staring match to look at me. Instantly, his face softened a bit. He held out his hand, my necklace dangling from his fingers as if he'd been holding it the whole time. My fingertips brushed his skin as I plucked the necklace from his hand, and even with the knowledge that Booth was out there, that we had work to do, that his brother was standing less than three feet from us, it was as if there was no one else on the planet.

"Excuse me," Simon said, his plaintive barb shattering our tiny moment of peace. "You're just okay with this?" He gestured to my face, and it stung a little that he was being so damn rude.

Okay, it stung a lot.

I fell back a step, quickly fastening the pendant around my neck. If that's how he was going to be, then fine. I could see the writing on the wall. I moved for the garage door that led to the main house.

"Just shut up, Simon," Bastian growled, his innate need to stick up for me softening Simon's blow.

"No, that's not—" Simon began, but I heard a thud, and Bastian cut him off.

I couldn't help but glance back. Simon now had a bloody nose, and Bastian appeared as if he was gearing up to hit him again.

"Shut. Up." Bastian's finger was in Simon's face, the tip lit with crackling magic.

Simon's eyes were pleading, his hands up in surrender. "But—"

"I swear to everything holy," Bastian snarled in his brother's face, "if you say another fucking word, I'm going to make you wish you were never born."

"What's the meaning of this?" Emrys' Irish lilt broke the silence, making all of us whip to attention like good little soldiers.

Simon's chuckle was only slightly nervous, but he answered for us all. "Just a brotherly tiff, Em. Nothing to worry about. You know how it is."

He offered her a shrug that said, "What are you gonna do?" and skirted around his brother to the door. Emrys' gaze narrowed on Bastian and me as if we were the troublemakers of the group. I knew I was, but Bastian was practically a choir boy. Sorta.

"We have a job to do. I suggest you save all tiffs until it's over."

Sound advice.

If only there wasn't this feeling in my gut that whatever Simon wanted to tell me was something I really needed to know.

10

"I want you with Thomas," Emrys ordered as she loaded her belt with potion bottles and other various weapons.

She had been pairing me with Thomas for the last two months, and it was fine before. But now that Bastian knew about me, the urge to have him close by while we were in danger was something of a need of mine.

I opened my mouth to protest, but one look from her odd reddish eyes and I snapped my trap shut.

"And you aren't going after Booth."

That got it open again. "What? You're out of your mind if you thin—"

Emrys shifted her weight, her irises getting the odd glow they got when she was about to zap something to kingdom come. "The pair of you are going after higher-value targets. The ones we cannot afford to lose. As much of a murderer as Booth McCall is, he is not the worst of the worst. I need my strongest hitters out there to find them. A shifter is not my highest priority."

True, Booth was just a shifter, but he had information. He knew who X was. I could feel it. He knew the arcaner who'd killed my parents. His sins were mine to have, mine to take. His soul was mine.

"Who's going after him then?" I challenged, likely to my own detriment.

An evil smile curled the edges of her mouth. "I will. Bastian, Simon, and I will be going after the mid-level targets. Axel and Dahlia will be assisting you and Thomas. Harper and Clem will be staying put. Any other questions about my logistical prowess, or can I continue preparing myself?"

I didn't like any of this. I was being sidelined—big time.

"Be sure to collect extra weapons from Clementine before you go and an earpiece from Harper. Thomas has your assigned targets."

And now I was being shoved off, shooed away like an annoying gnat.

"They know—Bastian and Simon—about this." I gestured to my face, moving my index finger all the way around my mug for "extra" emphasis. "Bastian knows about the note as well." I couldn't say why those words felt like a threat, but they really did. If she was going to shoo me away, I was going to metaphorically flip her off before I left.

Yeah, it was childish, but dammit, compared to everyone else in the house, I *was* the child.

Without another word, I left her with that information and made my way to Clem.

But before I could get to the undead de facto housekeeper, cook, and weapons keeper of the Night Watch, I was waylaid by a tiny, permanently angry empath.

"What the hell is going on with you?" Harper griped, nearly scaring the life out of me. She must have snuck up behind me as I debated the merits of searching for Booth myself.

Turning, I only managed to blink at her. Did she really need me to spell it out?

"Well, Harper, when the man who murdered your last living family breaks out of prison—"

Harper rolled her eyes at me. "That's not what I mean. Your warding is all…" She paused to gesture at the whole of my person. "Off. It's fine right now, but every once in a while, I get a wave of bullshit from you. And then…" She snapped her fingers. "Nothing. What—and I cannot stress this enough—the fuck?"

I was already done with this conversation. Pinching the bridge of my nose, I sighed. "I have no idea. It's not like I can do my own warding. I'll ask Emrys if she can fix it."

"You'd better," she grumped, crossing her arms over her chest.

That's when I finally noticed the fear she was trying so desperately to hide.

"You okay?" I asked, wondering if anyone thought to ask her that. As the resident hermit, Harper rarely ventured out of her rooms, preferring the company of computers to anything living. As an empath, Harper might feel trapped in a house like this—unable to go outside for fear of what she might feel from others. Then again, this might be her one safe spot.

"I'm *fine*," she huffed. "I mean, it's not as if he was my friend or anything. It's not as if we hadn't spent years getting to know each other only for him to betray us all. It's not as if —" She shook her head, turning away from me like just looking at me hurt her. "I know it's selfish. I know what you lost. I know what I'm going through doesn't matter. It's just…"

Under normal circumstances, I'd give someone dealing with this level of bullshit a hug. But touching Harper wasn't ever going to be an option. "It's okay to feel what you feel. There isn't a right way or a wrong way. And I'm sorry that you lost a friend."

"It makes me want all the wards down, you know," she muttered, still facing away. "Even if that means I'll go crazy."

Before I could formulate a response to that, she was gone, stalking off toward her rooms and leaving me behind.

"Are you fucking shitting me?" I growled, chasing a sorcerer up a ladder. This particular ladder led to the tippy top of a water tower that had to be five if not ten stories tall. I was not a fan of heights. I also was not a fan of falling off of said heights.

Landings hurt—a lot.

This particular sorcerer was the last target on our list and a certified pain in my ass. Of the ten arcaners we'd bagged and tagged, this guy was the fucking worst. The first nine hadn't precisely been picnics, but this guy?

It was bad enough that I'd been chasing him for the last twenty-four hours on no sleep, no blood, and no food. But he could do a weird little portal jump thing that made catching the fucker an actual problem. One second, he'd be one place, and the next, he'd be fifty feet away. And he was fast, the spell work or ability or whatever was something he could just do, quick as a whip. I figured he'd tire out eventually, but so far, his energy had seemed endless.

And why was I the one chasing him up a water tower? Oh, it was because this bastard had volleyed spells at us, one after the other, until he managed to hit something. Thomas was somewhere behind me healing from an acid bomb, and Axel was still recovering from an explosion of knifelike barbs that hit him square in the chest. Good thing this sorcerer's aim wasn't better, or Axel would be missing a head and really, really dead.

I was the only one left standing, and it was the principle of the thing at this point. As soon as I caught this bastard, I would be breaking every single bone in his hands and feet before using my last stasis potion.

The hunt prior to this had been almost too easy—especially when compared to this asshole. The detention center and ABI had blood samples from every inmate that made locator spells a breeze. Dahlia found them and spelled Thomas' GPS app to update on their locations as they moved. It was like shooting fish in a barrel... if that barrel was filled with piranhas. All we needed to do was ambush the fugitives and hit them with a stasis spell.

Our only problem was the portal jumper who—no matter how good my aim was—I couldn't hit.

But for the last five minutes, he hadn't jumped through any portals. I hoped he was—*finally*—petering out. I needed food and a bed and not to be chasing this damn sorcerer all over the ass-end of Tennessee.

When I was close to the top catwalk, I smartly—or at least I thought it was smart—ducked. The last thing I needed was to lose my head in the literal sense. A flash of heat skimmed my shoulder, the searing magic burning right through my suit to my skin. The orange jump-suited sorcerer had finally tagged me. Growling, I launched myself the last few feet up the ladder, landing on the catwalk right next to him.

The scraggly-looking man was probably older than dirt but didn't show it. With matted dark hair and wild blue eyes, he stared at me as if I was the boogeyman. His dirt-encrusted fingers weaved more magic, but I refused to get hit with anything else. Before he could complete another spell—or jump for that matter—I caught the side of his face in my hand and bounced his head off the side of the water tower. The sound of his skull making impact was the best thing I'd heard in two damn days.

Let's see you do spells unconscious, you bastard.

My satisfaction ramped up another notch when I poured the stasis potion over his still form. The milky-white liquid snaked around his body, binding his arms and legs together. It also had the added benefit of making it so he couldn't do any magic of any kind or wake up until he got the counter-potion.

Take that, you fuck.

And that was around the time that I realized I was at the top of a water tower with an unconscious prisoner that I needed to haul to the ground.

By myself.

Super.

I was tempted to just sit down until Thomas or Axel or hell, even Dahlia found us. I did not want to shlep this asshole back down the ladder, and I sure as hell didn't want to accidentally drop him, or fall, or… I made the mistake of looking down and had to hold back bile as I scrambled away from the railing.

Yeah, there was no way I was going to be able to do that. I would just have to live up here until the world ended or this water tower collapsed—whichever came first. My legs gave a slight wobble, and I found myself on my ass on the metal catwalk.

Two thuds not only scared the shit out of me, but they also seemed to rock the whole damn tower.

"What, you just going to sit there?" Axel teased, his Texan accent softening the blow of his words, but only a little. Still, the likely harmless taunt grated my last nerve.

Bravado. I would go with bravado. "I didn't see you bagging anyone. Just because I'm having an internal logistical deliberation does not mean that I was resting."

Axel snorted, putting his hands on his jean-clad hips. "Is that what they're calling panic attacks these days? Weird."

I studied his battered cowboy boots, not meeting his gaze. Only Axel would be hunting monster fugitives in western-style boots. "Oh, fuck you."

"Yeah, yeah. That's what all the ladies say."

The man knelt next to me, but I still refused to turn my head. Doing that meant looking out. And looking out meant looking down. Hard pass.

"Now, do you want me to get the perp or you first?"

The question was kind, but I still hated that it had to be asked. And since I had a death grip on the metal grating of the catwalk and likely wouldn't be able to let it go anytime soon, I jutted my chin at the sorcerer.

"Take him. I need a minute."

I needed a crowbar and a sedative, but whatever.

Axel hauled the sorcerer onto his shoulder like he was picking up a bag of feed or something and just freaking jumped. Here I was, trying to even contemplate the *possibility* of getting down and Axel just. Fucking. Jumped off the side of the tower like the landing wouldn't crush an average person.

Another thud of feet landing right next to me had me squeaking like a mouse.

"Am I going to have to blindfold you?" Thomas needled, kneeling at my left.

Asshole.

I might not have been able to look at Axel, but Thomas was close enough that looking at him didn't mean staring out at the horizon. I shot him a scathing glare and was tempted to flip him off for good measure, but I never got the chance. Before I knew it, I was up and over Thomas' shoulder in a fireman's carry, and then he was jumping off the tower just like Axel had.

I didn't even get the chance to scream.

I did, however, get the chance to vomit on his boots once we landed, so, there was that.

11

By the time we got to the ABI detention center, I hadn't quite managed to forgive Thomas for launching me off the tower. Thomas was still in the process of forgiving Axel and Dahlia, who laughed so hard at my up-chuck episode they were rolling on the ground. He'd already told me he would forgive me around about never.

"I didn't see you puking on Bastian when he did it to you," Thomas grumbled for the fifth time as he threw the truck in park. For this mission, we used the giant truck that usually took up residence in the last bay of the garage. The king cab was roomy enough for the four of us, and the extended bed with the shell, made transporting ten immobile fugitives a breeze. We'd had to pass three different checkpoints just to get this far, and I was over all of this rigamarole.

Axel chuckled before socking Thomas in the arm. "That's because she doesn't want to kiss you, dummy. If she did, I suspect she'd be too busy swooning to puke on your shoes."

"Fuck off, Axel," Thomas and I said at the same time. We'd done this at least three times on the four-hour drive from the east ass-end of nowhere Tennessee to the outskirts of Knoxville. But I figured it was because no one had gotten a lick of rest or sleep since the day before last. How we were still awake was a freaking mystery, and I was not handling the lack of sleep very well.

"Please tell me the processing is going to be a snap because I can't take much more of this," Dahlia said, her husky voice laced with sleepy irritation.

"My question is—why are we taking them back to the prison they escaped from?" Axel complained, staring out the windshield at the approaching guards. "Isn't that like putting a bird back in a broken cage?"

He wasn't wrong, but right now, I just did not give that first shit. I wanted these prisoners out of this truck and to be someone else's problem—at least for the next twenty-four hours.

A very tall woman knocked on Thomas' window, the rap of her knuckles practically shaking the whole truck. She had dark hair tied back from her tan face, the braids and dreads a serious complement to her Viking-like appearance. Thomas rolled down the window, ready to speak to the giant woman, but she wasn't looking at him.

No, the very tall, very intimidating prison guard was staring right at me.

Piercing green eyes assessed me as she held her hand out to Thomas for the paperwork. He produced the bounty contracts, and she snatched them out of his hand, never moving her gaze from mine.

I wanted to sink into my seat or turn into a slug or something just to get this woman to stop staring at me. Did I have "criminal" tattooed on my forehead or something?

"Everyone out of the vehicle," she barked and took a few steps back so Thomas could exit his door.

Reluctantly, I followed suit, my tired body revolting at the thought of standing. My feet yowled at me as I made contact with the pavement, but I refused to let this woman see me wince.

Only when I was out of the relative safety of the vehicle did she take her gaze off me and inspect the paperwork. "Twenty fugitives in two days. I have to say, I'm impressed. Only one left on the list. A Booth McCall?"

Thomas shifted forward, his economy of movement putting him between the guard and me, but it was Axel who answered her. His Southern charm was in full force as he reached for her hand. "Yes, ma'am. Our other team is busy rounding him up. Shouldn't be too long now."

The guard nodded, still looking at the paperwork. "A few of these boys were coded 'dead or alive.' You didn't bring me any stiffs, did you?"

Axel chuckled, hooking his thumbs through his belt loops as he seemed to relax. "No, ma'am, we did not. Captured them all alive. They're in a stasis spell, and some of them are a little roughed up, but everybody's breathing."

The guard glanced up then, assessing Axel. In flat boots, the pair of them were eye to eye, and the guard noticed it, too. A faint blush rose in her cheeks as Axel gave her a big old grin. The curvy, giant of a guard was ridiculously pretty with high cheekbones and a pouty lip. If it didn't look as if she could break me in two, I was sure we'd be besties.

"Is that so?"

We had now entered the flirting portion of today's activities, but as long as the armed prison guard wasn't staring at me like she wanted to murder me, I was all for it.

"I have the counter-potions to remove their stasis," Dahlia suggested, breaking the flirty spell Axel had on the guard.

She blinked hard at Axel for a second before moving her

stern gaze to Dahlia. The small witch offered her a velvet bag full of clinking spell bottles. The guard accepted them, nodding as if this was all procedure or something. "I'll ask you to offload the prisoners to the steps. Once we have confirmed identity, we will accept them and cut you the remittance."

Dahlia gave the tall guard a smile. "No problem."

Without much prompting, I hauled my butt to the back of the truck and started yanking on feet. The sooner these guys were back in jail, the sooner I could go to sleep. If I could even sleep.

You heard what she said. They haven't caught him yet. Booth is still out there.

A shiver of unease raced through me, a worry that hadn't been able to take root before. I'd been running my ass off for two days, and all the while, I hadn't spoken to Bastian. As far as I knew, none of us had heard from Bastian, Simon, or Emrys at all.

Thomas and Axel met me at the back of the truck, helping me remove the frozen prisoners from the vehicle.

I wanted to ask, but I just couldn't. It made sense that we hadn't heard from them. They were chasing a shifter through who knew where. A man that could change into any animal at will. I wondered how that stacked up to the portal-jumper and had to admit to myself that their job was likely more complicated by far.

It didn't take long to deposit the prisoners on the steps of the detention center. The giant gray building gave me the major creeps. It resembled an abandoned asylum right out of an awful horror movie. I couldn't even imagine going inside. Asylums made me think of dead people, which made me think of ghosts, which gave me the ultimate heebies.

Bad guys in need of killing? *Sign me up.*

Ghosts? *No, thank you.*

The giant guard barked out a laugh for what seemed like no good reason, pulling my attention to her. She met my gaze and shook her head, giving me a smile for the first time.

At my quizzical expression, she approached, her demeanor considerably less hostile than it had been just five minutes prior. "Sorry about all that. It's just—" She shook her head as if she were debating with herself. "You're wearing a glamour," she muttered under her breath, sotto voce as if this information was just between us.

I took a step away from her, my attention shifting to the checkpoints that I knew I had no shot in hell of getting through in one piece. I was not walking into that prison if I could help it. Only the first couple of gunshots stung, right?

"No, no. Don't worry. It's not a crime to wear a glamour. A lot of arcaners do it if they can't pass as human. But with the prison break and everything, we're all a little on edge." Her lips twisted as her internal debate continued. "Your friends are okay. A little banged up, but nothing a good night's sleep won't cure."

I frowned, shifting my gaze to Thomas.

"No, not him. Your boyfriend and his brother and your boss," she said, making me whip around to face her.

I took a real step back then.

She rolled her eyes and shook her head, seemingly exasperated at herself. She thrust out a hand. "I'm Siobhan Byrne. Psychic, medium, intuitive, whatever. I apologize for overstepping. You just seemed worried about your people, is all."

Reluctantly, I took her offered hand. "Sloane Cabot."

Her giant palm engulfed mine. "Pleased to meet you." But when our skin touched, her pupils dilated for a second as a frown creased her brow. "They'll find him soon, but he isn't the one you seek. Change is coming. Death too. Death is looking for you."

I wanted to move—really, I did—but I just couldn't. Not only was my hand lost in hers, but Siobhan's grip was so tight it was cutting off all the blood to my fingers.

"Death will find you again," she said, her voice taking on a monotone quality that gave me the fucking creeps. "He will find you like the flames found your parents."

Shock pumped ice water through my veins. What the hell did she know about my parents? Siobhan let out a shuddering groan like she was in agony, and to my utter surprise, her grip got even tighter. My fingers felt like they were being crushed under the weight of whatever she was seeing.

And then my hand wasn't trapped anymore. It wasn't trapped because Axel, Thomas, and Dahlia were now in between me and Siobhan, and the giant guard was clutching her head.

"I think it's time to go, don't you?" Thomas muttered, ushering me into the back seat of the truck.

My steps were wooden as I followed his prodding direction, my feelings, my thoughts, all of it on pause as he dutifully buckled me in like a toddler. He then shut my door, climbed into the driver seat, and started the truck.

"You okay?" Thomas asked, his voice a gentle reminder that my emotions should be lambasting my psyche right about now.

I met his gaze in the rearview mirror, and he winced at what he saw there.

"Is she right?" I croaked, the pain starting to bubble up inside me. I couldn't foresee a time in my life when the mention of their deaths would be anything less than the worst sort of torture.

Thomas shook his head. "I don't know."

That was what I was afraid he'd say.

. . .

"You're staying here, and I don't want to hear a word about it. Don't make me make Axel sedate you."

I fought off the urge to flip Thomas off and sneak out, but I was under no illusion that he hadn't already thought of that. I tried not to be put out that Thomas sidelined me for the rest of the mission. No one thought letting me search for Booth was a good idea. I had no doubt it was because if I found him, he wouldn't be going back to the ABI detention center alive. Evidently, Booth had been coded as an "alive only" bounty, just like I had once upon a time.

Thomas and Dahlia had wolfed down a quick meal before heading back out, but Axel and I were told to stay put. I had a feeling Axel's new mission was to babysit me. Rather than get too butthurt about it, I decided to take a shower, get some food, and attempt to sleep, worry for Bastian and Simon making that task seem almost impossible.

I knew I wouldn't be able to get any rest, and it didn't matter if I'd been running for two straight days. But as exhausted as I was, sleep snared me without too much effort on my part, the rest fitful and full of dark things.

Screams.

Fire.

I kept waking up, but sleep clawed at me, trapping me again and again until its hold was too strong for me to break.

My mother was screaming at me, pressing on my chest over and over again. Her hands were hard, weighty like they were fifty-pound dumbbells just chilling on my ribcage. I wanted to answer her, but I just couldn't. Everything hurt. Everything. From my toes all the way up to my hair, every single bit of me felt as if I was being flash fried by a blowtorch, followed by an acid bath.

I couldn't understand her words, either. I was either going deaf or she was speaking gibberish, and I was in so much pain it really didn't matter. It didn't matter when the agony made me want to die.

The room around us was hazy at best. Smoke swirled and bloomed in a halo around her head as an odd purple light whirled up her arms. And she was crying. Or at least I thought she was. A tiny trail of a tear dropped from her eye and hit me on the cheek. I wanted to wipe it away. Wanted to tell her I was okay—I wasn't—but I couldn't do that, either.

Her strong fingers gripped my shoulders, and she pulled me into her arms, hugging me to her chest as if she was saying goodbye.

That's when I saw the flames.

That's when I saw my dad lying in a pool of his own blood in the middle of the living room.

That's when I saw the man in the gray suit, his face shrouded within the shadows, kneeling over my father.

He held a wicked-looking knife in his hand—bigger than a dagger but smaller than a sword—the awful blade coated in my father's blood. He rose from his crouch, an awful laugh bubbling up his throat as the sound danced over the roar of the flames and my mother's sobs.

And he was coming for us.

The trill of a cell phone had me gasping for breath as I shot out of bed like the hounds of Hell were on my ass. I knew the phone had been what woke me up, and I was grateful for the tiny device. The smell of smoke was in my nose, a leftover echo of a dream that was quickly fading from my brain.

I wanted to hold onto it, clutch it in my hand so I could mine it for clues, but the damn thing seemed to be no more tangible than smoke and twice as slippery.

The phone stopped ringing only to begin again, the Night-Watch-issued cell phone blaring an old Deftones song. Groggily, I picked it up, spying Bastian's name on the screen before I answered it.

"Sloane?" Bastian's voice filled my ear, and I breathed the biggest sigh of relief ever.

"Are you okay?" I began, the worry snaking up my throat.

Of course he's fine, Sloane. He wouldn't be calling if he was dead.

"I'm fine, but I need you to get over here." His tone was wary, as if he didn't want to tell me whatever it was he was going to say next.

"Over where?" I held the phone in between my cheek and shoulder as I plucked my pants from the floor and yanked them on.

"Whispering Pines Cemetery," he said, the quiet words hitting me like a haymaker to the chest.

And then he dropped the mother of all bombs.

"We found Booth."

12

Dusk was falling as I dismounted Thomas' bike in the tiny parking lot of Whispering Pines Cemetery. A year ago, I'd woken up in this very graveyard with no memory of how or why I ended up here. Honestly, it still didn't make sense to me.

I doubted it ever would.

The gate to the cemetery was open a crack, the wrought iron creaking back and forth in the slight breeze, the scent of death cloying on the air. Bastian had told me there was no rush. To be careful. But I'd thrown on the first pieces of clothing I could get my hands on and hauled ass to my small hometown.

But as much as I wanted to be sure that Booth was taken down, I had a hell of a time convincing myself to walk through that gate. My hesitation didn't make much sense either. I'd been to this cemetery a hundred times, burying bad guys that were too young to turn to ash. I knew the groundskeeper personally—or as personally as one could know the guy they were bribing to keep his trap shut.

One foot in front of the other, Sloane. Keep moving.

My mother's words often came to me in times like this. Times I didn't want to do the hard thing—and make no mistake, this was going to be a hard thing. I followed her sage advice, ripping the helmet off my head and setting it on the seat before marching toward the gate.

The scent that merely tickled my nose before, now hit me with the force of a battering ram.

Sweeping my gaze over the familiar headstones, my eyes immediately went in the direction of my parents' graves. It didn't matter how many times I'd been here, I always looked there first. Plus, the awful aroma was practically a neon sign pointing the way. I saw Bastian before anyone else, the tall man refusing to blend in with the monuments and headstones. Next to him were his brother and our boss, and beside her was the famed groundskeeper, Gerry. Gerry and Emrys were slightly off to the side, discussing something I couldn't hear, but that wasn't what gave me pause.

Gerry's and Emrys' body language were of two people who knew each other—were friends even. And I likely would have focused on that new bit of information had my advancing steps not brought Booth into view.

Or what was left of him.

Bastian hadn't told me Booth was dead on the phone. Sure, I'd assumed that was the case when he'd insisted that the rush wasn't necessary, but this was…

"What the hell did you do?" I accused. The words were meant to be under my breath, but they cracked like a whip through the quiet night.

I didn't know who exactly I was accusing either, but good fucking god, this man was… Bile crept up my throat, and I had to turn away. I'd seen some awful things in the last year. But what was done to Booth? It was a thing of nightmares.

And I didn't know if I was pissed he'd been killed before I'd gotten my answers, or that I hadn't been the one to do it.

"We didn't do this," Bastian said, his warmth and voice right next to me, seeping into my space like a welcome weight. "Gerry found him like this when he arrived and called us straightaway."

Ah, the aforementioned Gerry. It was a curious thing that Gerry of all people knew to call the Night Watch about what had to have been a ritualistic murder. I couldn't imagine the local cops dealing with this mess. Just from the small glimpse I'd gotten, I knew that Booth was in pieces.

Lots and lots of pieces.

"And he knew to call you because?"

Already I was putting two and two together. A few months ago, Gerry had given me a stern warning about the arcane world finding out about my little hobby. The very next night I'd been ambushed by Bastian himself. It didn't take a genius to figure out that Gerry had ratted me out.

See if I ever buy him whiskey again, the lush.

Bastian sighed. "He keeps us in the loop occasionally. Whispering Pines doesn't have a large arcane population, but Gerry hears things. He's been helpful."

I snorted, refusing to turn to face Bastian. "A tattletale is more like it. He have a reason why the cops aren't here already? Whispering Pines didn't get its name for being a raucous kind of place. Whatever was done to Booth would have caused a stir."

Stir was putting it mildly.

Shuddering, I tried to scrub my brain of the images dancing at the forefront of my mind, but it was impossible. The slight breeze turned into a gust, bombarding me with the heavy scent of decaying blood, bile, excrement, urine, and all the rest of the awful smells a body produced in the throes of death.

"Harper checked for us. There haven't been any calls about a disturbance. Either he was unconscious—which I fucking well hope so—or whoever did this cast a spell so no one heard."

Personally, I didn't hope Booth was unconscious when he died, but that was just me. Booth McCall had taken the last of my loved ones from me. I hoped he felt every cut. For what he'd done to Julie, he deserved it.

Booth seemed to have been cut into sections—hands, elbows, shoulders, feet, knees, hips. The scent of the blood drying on the grass meant that this had to have been done while he was still breathing. But first, he'd been skinned.

And he hadn't been dumped here. Oh, no.

Booth had been meticulously dismembered while he was still alive, his shifter abilities likely prolonging the torture. The only part of him untouched was his head, which rested against a rather familiar headstone.

It should be familiar. It had my damn name on it.

"Do you figure him being on my grave is a message, a gift, or a warning?" I asked conversationally, as if it wasn't a huge deal that the man to steal so much from me was laid out on my grave like a sacrifice.

Moreover, I wondered if X knew I was still alive—if he knew that his blood curse didn't kill me. I wondered if he put Booth on my grave as a taunt. Honestly, it wouldn't surprise me.

Bastian sighed deep enough that it sounded as if his soul was escaping his body.

"To be honest?" Simon said, startling me almost out of my boots. "I'm a bit more worried about the magic used to perform the task than the message. Did you see those sigils?"

Where the hell had he come from? And how had he so soundlessly approached?

Simon gave the pair of us a wide smile, as if startling me was his end goal. *Dick.*

"Don't do that," Bastian chided. "You know shade jumping to eavesdrop is just rude."

Shade jumping?

Simon appeared affronted. "I wasn't eavesdropping. I was listening to a conversation that had to do with the topic at hand."

Bastian rolled his eyes at his little brother. "That you weren't a member of."

"Sigils? I don't remember seeing any sigils. Then again, I was probably too focused on the dead body on my grave."

Simon gave me a solemn nod. "No way was any of this done by hand. The whole place smells of dark magic."

Funny, I couldn't smell anything over the blood.

"Only you can smell that, Simon. Trust me." I shuddered, the scent of Booth's death grating on my brain enough for me to move upwind. Only, when I got closer to Emrys and Gerry—who were still in their familiar huddle—I could sense what Simon had been talking about. It had me wishing I hadn't moved. I'd take the scent of Booth's death over this.

Gagging, I nearly ran away from the scene as I headed for Gerry's office. It smelled of rotting things, dead things. Dark things.

"See," Simon said behind me, the brothers hot on my heels as I sought refuge and air. "Like I said. Dark magic."

Emerging from the groundskeeper's office, Thomas and Dahlia intercepted our little group, preventing my escape. Thomas shook his head at someone over my shoulder—either Bastian or Simon—I couldn't tell which. Honestly, I didn't really care. I needed untainted air and now.

Skirting around Thomas, I marched right for Gerry's office, heading for the bottle of whiskey I knew was stashed in his bottom desk drawer under old rags. Maybe the alcohol would singe my nostrils enough to wash that smell out.

Thomas and Bastian were muttering behind me about something, but I blocked out their voices in favor of my search of alcohol. I located the bottle—nearly three-quarters gone—and cracked the lid. If I chugged the rest, it would be just desserts for the little tattletale.

"She smelled it, didn't she?" Thomas asked, as if me smelling magic was something new.

I swallowed the decidedly cheap whiskey, the burn of it doing the trick of making that smell go away—at least for a little while. "Of course I did. It was like rotting things and…"

A shudder racked my whole body, making the hairs on my arms stand on end. I needed a shower and a blowtorch for my olfactory glands.

"Only magic-users can smell that, Sloane," Thomas instructed, and if he hadn't said it with such condescending conviction, I probably wouldn't have been so irritated.

I rolled my eyes before casting them in Bastian's direction. "Really?"

"Really," Thomas answered for him. "I can't scent what you're describing. I only smell death and blood."

I tried to recall if this was a new trait for me or if I'd had it this past year. I couldn't remember if I'd just scented the ozone of spent magic or the spells themselves, but figured it wasn't that big of a deal. So I could smell this magic? So what? "We all know I'm a freak, Thomas. That isn't exactly new information."

He huffed. "No, but being able to scent out an incredibly rare mind-bendingly complicated kind of magic is. Especially when most arcaners can't."

"I can't smell it, either," Dahlia offered. "But I blame that on my diluted genes and less on you being a magical bloodhound."

At least someone was talking sense. "Oh, what difference does it make?"

Being able to smell the magic that tore Booth apart wouldn't help me find X. It wouldn't help me learn how he'd killed my parents. And who gave a fuck how and why Booth died? It wasn't rocket science. Booth knew shit he probably shouldn't, and now he was dead. This X likely killed him to keep his mouth shut.

It wasn't as if I'd be able to go door-to-door to sniff people to find the elusive X, either. I'd scoured Ascension, Knoxville, Whispering Pines, and everywhere else I could think of for clues. X was a fucking ghost, and being able to smell the magic he used to murder his loose end wasn't going to change that.

But I couldn't say that out loud.

Booth had been with these people for a long time before I got here. He was their friend, their family, and he'd betrayed them. I was the physical embodiment of his betrayal. I was the giant elephant in the room that no one wanted to talk about, and if I told them just how much I didn't give a shit about Booth's death, well...

That would make me heartless, now, wouldn't it?

Maybe I *was* heartless—an unfeeling monster with no remorse.

But just maybe, that was what was necessary to get shit done.

13

The group of them talked amongst themselves for a bit while I downed the rest of Gerry's whiskey. The swill wasn't quite doing the trick anymore, and all too quickly it was gone. Simon and Thomas were still discussing my wonder nose, and I'd parked my ass on Gerry's desk, purposefully messing up the papers there with my ass.

Granted, Gerry had likely done me a favor in ratting me out. I had food in my belly, a roof over my head, and—dare I say it—friends. Still, snitches got stitches and all that.

"Do you know how rare that magic is?" Simon shouted, throwing his hands up. He was probably talking to me, but he wasn't looking at me. He was looking at Bastian, stabbing his finger in his big brother's sternum to hammer home his point. "It's outlawed death magic from the Byzantine Era. There are no books about it. The only way to learn it is from someone who already knew it, and it's damn near impossible to teach. The only way to detect it is if you're a death mage." He gestured to himself with both his thumbs. "*Or—*"

"We fucking talked about this, Simon," Bastian growled, cutting him off and stepping closer to his brother.

Simon's face reddened, and he appeared to be about a millisecond from hauling back and socking Bastian a good one.

"Oh, would you two work out your shit already?" Thomas griped, plopping down on the desk right next to me. "ABI buildings getting raided. Prison breaks. I just got a call an hour ago from my old nest. They got attacked by a bunch of unnested vamps, probably the same damn ones who killed those agents. Whatever is going on with you two needs to be tabled until we can figure this shit out, so knock it the fuck off before I get angry."

That had me hopping off the desk. "Is Ingrid okay?"

I asked about Ingrid and not Mags because, well, I wasn't Mags' biggest fan. Ingrid, though, would always and forever be on my good-guy list.

Thomas rubbed at his temple. "She's regrowing a pinkie finger but otherwise fine. They lost quite a few mid-level members of their nest, though. It was a blow. Luckily, they got backup. If they hadn't…" He shook his head as if the thought hurt him. "She should have called me earlier," he muttered under his breath. "I would have come."

I would have, too. Bounties and sleep be damned. "Do they need any help? Do we need to go?"

Anxiety prickled at my hands and feet—I wanted to be doing something. This X seemed to be in the middle of waging war, and it wasn't some piddly one-on-one shit. This was coordinated attacks. Strategic.

And I had no idea how to fight something like that.

"No," Thomas said, pinching his brow as if he was trying to stave off a headache. "We need to find out who killed Booth. Whoever did it, broke him out of prison, and was likely behind the ghoul attack. He was a loose end in need of snipping."

"Is this magic something we can track?" Dahlia piped up, the small witch practically hidden behind Bastian and Simon as they remained eyeing each other like rabid dogs. Grumbling, Dahlia snapped her fingers in front of Simon's nose, a spark from them zapping him right in the forehead.

"Ow," he grumbled, rubbing the red spot blooming on his skin as he stumbled backward. "What did you do that for?"

Dahlia rolled her eyes. "Pay attention, dummy. Can we track the magic utilizing anything other than Sloane's poor nose? Employing her as our bloodhound isn't going to work and you know it."

Simon gave Dahlia a weighty glare as he continued to rub his forehead. Her eyes twitched a little and she moved to snap her fingers again. "Fine," he conceded, holding up his hands. "I could maybe do a locator working using Booth's blood. But that's a huge maybe."

Footsteps echoed throughout the short hallway to Gerry's office, and Emrys appeared at the door like an angry mama bear. "What's all this?"

"Strategy session and a reprieve from the smell," Simon answered quickly, his tone the picture of innocence.

It was solidly fake innocence, and Emrys wasn't fooled. "I thought I told you boys to table your bullshit. The circumstances haven't changed, you know."

"They're fine," Thomas said, sighing. "Just working out the kinks as we discuss how to locate Booth's killer. Nothing to worry about."

"And when exactly am I going to get my cemetery back?" Gerry asked, his gravelly voice practically echoing through the room. "It's bad enough I've got this one traipsing through here to bury her dead, but now I've got dismemberment to deal with? Ya'll need to keep your arcane shit to yourselves and leave us regular folk out of it."

I leaned to the side, around Bastian's bulk, to give Gerry the coldest of glares. "The first vamp I ever killed was a rapist and murderer, and his hunting ground was less than a block from here. Arcane shit has been in Whispering Pines a fuck of a lot longer than I have, so how about you keep your damn trap shut before I plant your tattling ass in your own damn cemetery?"

Gerry gave me an unbothered stare, like having my boss here was going to save him. Okay, it probably would, but he didn't need to know that. "I thought you only killed bad guys."

"That was before you ratted me out, Gerry. Had I known you were going to be a tattletale, I would have killed you and got my own damn backhoe. Dick."

Emrys sighed as if she was losing—or had already lost—her patience. "Enough, you two. Can we track the magic used or not?"

Simon waggled his hand. "I think so, but it's a huge maybe. If I were to venture a guess, Gerry interrupted whatever spell was being cast. The circle around Booth isn't complete, so technically, I could take a sample of his blood—what little of it he has left—and attempt a working to locate the caster. But…" He trailed off, like he was gearing up for something he really didn't want to say. "I think it might end up as a bust. There's something off about the spell work. It isn't just incomplete. It's backwards."

Grumbling, I skirted around the lot of them, the obvious answer hitting me square in the face.

I could read peoples' souls, right? I'd seen plenty in just a single swallow of Aunt Julie's blood, that I'd viscerally experienced her death. Although I in no way wanted to do that with Booth, maybe—and this was a bigger maybe than Simon's —I could take a taste of Booth's blood and track his killer that way. I'd done it hundreds of times before, hadn't I?

Granted, I did it when the perps were still alive, but…

But what if it's just like Aunt Julie? What if you fall in and can never get out?

That had my feet slowing their role and planting themselves in the manicured grass. The scent of Booth's death and the cloying magic hit me square in the face. Did I want that inside me? Did I want to be trapped in the agony of that death? I wasn't sure I could risk it.

"Please tell me you aren't doing what I think you are."

How did Bastian just manage to sneak up on me like that?

"I don't know. What do you think I'm doing?" I asked coyly, trying to stall for a better answer.

One of his arms came around my front, the heavy weight of it comforting as it rested on my collarbone. "I think," he whispered in my ear, "that you plan on reading him. It's too dangerous, Sloane. The last time you read from the dead..."

He didn't have to complete that sentence. I knew.

"I worry it will be worse for you with his. Who knows what atrocities he's committed? I don't know what you see when you read someone's blood, but I can't imagine that reading him will give you anything but nightmares."

Funnily enough, I didn't have nightmares too often, even with all I'd seen, all I'd read in the blood of deviants and murderers. The only thing I dreamt of was fire and blackness and screaming. And I had a feeling those things had nothing to do with what I gleaned from the blood of the damned souls I consumed.

"I'm not worried about nightmares," I answered, skipping over the rest of my misgivings.

He huffed in my ear as he pulled me closer. "But you are worried about everything else."

"What does Simon want to tell me?" I asked, changing the subject.

Bastian's grip got tighter before he let me go and sighed so heavily that it seemed to come from the tips of his toes. "Simon has a theory about why you are the way you are. It has merit, but it's completely bonkers. And I don't want to cause you undue harm if it turns out to be bullshit. So when I get a chance, I'll be researching the matter. Until then, I planned on making sure Simon kept his trap shut."

"It's bad, isn't it? The theory, I mean."

Bastian chuckled, shaking his head. "Honest?" he asked wincing, and I gave him a nod. "It's not great, but it's not the end of the world, either. It just is. I've been around a long time, and I've seen plenty of things that just are. But you haven't. All the things you've read in the blood of horrible people, you've only seen the worst of us. You've only seen the bad. You haven't seen all the good we are capable of. You haven't seen the wonder, the magic." He approached me again, wrapping me in his arms and pulling me to his chest. "You haven't seen enough to know that beauty and wonder are found even in the darkest of places."

I snorted, cuddling my head against his chest and squeezing him tight. "As beautiful as those words are, it's still a bunch of bullshit. You know that, right?"

Bastian pressed a kiss to the top of my head. "Yes, yes. I'm being an overprotective asshat. Give me a day to research Simon's claims before he drops a bomb on you? I'd hate for you to be forced to react to something that may not be true. You've gone through enough."

Squeezing him tighter, I turned my head to rest my chin between his pecs. Now that I could see his face, it struck me at just how worried he was. Bastian really didn't want to tell me whatever it was that had Simon in a twist. Meaning it had to be pretty bad. And if it was that bad, I probably didn't want to know unless I fucking well had to. "Fine. Twenty-four hours, and then you're spilling your guts. Deal?"

"Deal," he answered readily, like I was giving him a reprieve, and that gave me a healthy dose of pause.

Whatever Simon thought—whatever theory he had—it was probably true. And it was really, really bad.

Fabulous.

Reluctantly, I let Bastian go and took a step back, turning to head for what was left of Booth's body. A drop of his blood wasn't going to hurt, right? Granted, I'd never done a reading with a sample so small, but I could try, couldn't I?

"I thought—" Bastian began behind me, but he stopped himself.

Readily, I filled in the blanks. "You thought you'd talked me out of it?"

"Well, yeah," he answered, rushing to follow me. "Sloane, we don't know what will happen if you do this."

Scoffing, I halted my progress, swinging back to face him. "And we don't know what will happen if I don't. Booth knew X. He knew the man who killed my parents. He killed Aunt Julie. He was at the ghoul attack—he was at the prison break. He knew more information than I could possibly fathom. The last time I read his blood, I got nothing more than shadows. Now that he's dead, he can't fight me. Is this going to suck? Probably. But I can't just sit on my hands because you want the little lady to be safe, Bastian. Whatever it is? I'll heal."

I always did.

Rather than let him stop me, I turned and rushed toward Booth's remains, using whatever speed I had at my disposal. Then, everything seemed to slow down all at once. A flock of carrion birds burst into flight, my movements startling them from stalking their dinner. Their flapping wings moved at a snail's pace as they rose from the ground. Behind them a woman emerged from her crouch, the back of a monument no longer hiding her.

She seemed to be racing for me, her steps caught in this sluggish pocket of time. Her hands waved, flapping just like those birds' wings as she screamed unintelligible words.

I tried to stop—tried to duck—but as my foot made contact with the ground once more, the whole of the earth turned blindingly white as brilliant blistering pain blew me backward.

14

"I don't give a shit if you've been a medical doctor since Christ was a boy, Axel. You aren't taking her out of this room," Bastian growled. His voice had a fierce quality to it that spoke of violence and true death and a little bit of fear.

My eyes fluttered a bit, my lashes sticking together. It was so hard to open them, so I quit. My whole body felt as if it had gone through a meat grinder. I was in a bed, and I was inside, but other than that, I had no idea where I was.

"You're acting real big for your britches, son," Axel snarled. "All my equipment is down there—"

"Then bring it up here if you have to. Do you honestly think I'll let you treat her there while her aunt's body is still in your bloody freezer? If you can't treat her here, then I'll find someone else," Bastian hissed. "You aren't taking her away from me, do you understand?"

Weirdly, I wanted to tell Bastian thank you. As strange and possessive as his demands were, I didn't want to go to the med bay. I didn't want to be that close to Julie. Axel had always brought my blood to me—or Clem had. I hadn't been downstairs since…

"Leave it alone, Axel," Harper growled, her voice so close, it was as if I could reach out and touch her. Well, I could if I could convince my limbs to move. "You're fighting a losing battle in a war that has no purpose. Look. She's already healing. Just go get some blood," she instructed, her tone dismissive. "She'll need it."

Harper's words seemed to cause a chain reaction in my body. I craved blood—needed it in a way I couldn't describe. Everything hurt. Every single part of me felt as if it had been flash fried followed by an acid bath and then been tossed in a barbeque pit for good measure. But before I could say any of that, sounds dimmed, and the world fell away, and I was lost in the dark.

The next time I became aware of my surroundings, warm coppery heaven was dripping into my mouth. A few things became clear instantly, but I chose to ignore them in favor of swallowing the blissful nectar. First, I was naked in what seemed to be a bathtub, the freezing porcelain cooling my overheated skin.

Burned, Sloane. You were burned.

Well, at least my subconscious was paying attention because I sure as hell wasn't.

Second, someone held my mouth open, their gentle grip on my jaw making it so I could drink at all. Over the coppery scent of the blood, I recognized the person almost instantly. I'd know him anywhere. Bastian was feeding me, caring for me, and I needed to see if he was okay. The last thing I remembered was the white-hot heat of a blast, but he had been right behind me, hadn't he?

I opened my eyes by sheer force of will, the compulsion a base need that demanded to be satisfied. They put up a fight, but I muscled my lids open, quickly finding blazing green ones. As I continued to swallow the dregs of a blood bag, I cataloged his injuries—or at least the ones I could see. Bastian had a burn on his cheek, the baby pink of newly healed flesh stark against his tan. He had a stitched cut at his hairline, and his lip was split. Over the blood, I smelled smoke and ozone, and something else I couldn't identify. But all of that took a back seat to the stark worry ravaging his expression.

"You're awake," he murmured, relief easing the lines on his face.

Closing my mouth, I swallowed the last of the blood, and he pulled the bag away from my lips. Hunger clawed at my insides, and as much as I wanted to reassure him I was okay— that I'd be okay—I couldn't. I needed blood. Now.

And though it was not even a moment later, and another bag would be replacing the one I'd downed, I just couldn't wait. While I was all for him feeding me, I needed that blood. I needed it, or I was going to do something really, really stupid. And dangerous. I'd probably done enough stupid, dangerous things for the day.

A sound erupted from my throat as the hunger clawed at me, a keening sort of awful that hurt my own ears.

"It's okay," Bastian crooned. "I have more where that came from."

Before he could bring the bag to my lips, I snatched it away from him, sinking my fangs into the plastic and ripping. Tangy liquid flooded my mouth, and I gulped it down as fast as my throat would allow. All too quickly, it was gone, leaving me bereft before I caught sight of Bastian's pulse thrumming in his neck. He handed me another bag of blood, but it was ash on my tongue once I remembered what his tasted like.

Don't get me wrong, I still ripped into the fresh bag with the same fervor as I had the previous one, but I did it while also eyeing his neck. I didn't want this dead, human blood laced with bitter plastic. Oh, no. I wanted—no, craved—the potent, magic-laced ambrosia that flowed through his veins.

I needed it.

I could tell the exact moment Bastian realized he was out of bagged blood. His throat did this little bobbing thing as he swallowed, a faint trace of fear and lust spicing the air. He craved my bite, but he was scared, too.

Me too, sweetheart. Me too.

All the horrible things that could happen raced through my brain as my fingers found the lip of the tub, and I hauled myself out as he jumped to his feet.

"Sloane…"

I tilted my head so he knew I was listening, the ability to speak just out of my reach. Taking my first step out of the tub, he took one toward me, catching me in his arms when my knees threatened to give out. His spicy, delectable scent got stronger, lust winning out over the fear. That smelled better.

I didn't want him to be scared of me. I wanted him to want me.

That awful keening sound leaked out of my throat again as the hunger became too much for me to hold in. I didn't want him to fear me, but I most certainly wanted my lips at his neck, and his blood in my mouth, and his body surrounding me.

"Shh, sweetheart. Take what you need," he murmured, guiding me to his neck as he lifted me off my feet.

I couldn't say why his permission made the ache in my middle go away, or how I held off my hunger long enough for him to give it to me. All I knew was that I needed his blood, and now, I could have it. Quick as a whip, I struck, my fangs piercing his flesh at the exact moment my legs wound around his hips. Bastian's arms tightened, pressing my body further against his.

The first pull of his blood showed me all sorts of things. Our limbs tangled together as we moved in tandem, his lips on my skin, my flesh pebbling as a gasp erupted from my mouth, his fingers in my hair as we kissed and moved. I'd seen these images before. Nearly every time I'd taken his blood, I'd seen this scene play out almost as if it were a premonition. As if us being together this way was preordained, written in the stars.

My hands pawed at his shirt, the thin material no match for my nails. I swallowed as I made quick work of the pesky fabric, ripping it from between us as if it were no more than tissue paper. My eyes practically rolled up in my head as the warmth of Bastian's flesh made contact with mine.

That single mouthful of his blood eased the ache in my bones, in my throat. It turned off the blistering agony of my healing burns, the flesh knitting itself back together. Everything felt better—everything felt new again. My brain cleared of pain as the heat of Bastian's skin continued to seep into me. It was the best heat. It was safety and lust and protection. Maybe something more—I hoped it was more.

His fingers found their way into my hair, a gentle tug reminding me not to take too much. Without any more prompting, I removed my fangs from his neck, licking the wounds so they would heal on their own. That earned me the best shudder, the vibration of it making everything inside me clench tight.

Without a word, Bastian's hand in my hair became insistent, guiding my face to his as he claimed my mouth in a kiss so hot, it made that damn fireball seem like a puff of smoke. It didn't seem to matter to him that I still had his blood on my tongue. It didn't matter that I was undoubtedly covered in the stuff. It didn't matter because nothing else did except him and me and the closest flat surface—horizontal or vertical, it really didn't matter which. Yanking on my hair, he broke our kiss before tasting the skin of my neck, biting my pulse point with his blunted teeth.

I couldn't stop the whimper that snaked up my throat or the way my hands roamed his skin, or how my hips did their best to grind against him. I wouldn't have stopped them even if I could have. His lips dipped lower as he hitched me higher on his hips, his mouth leaving a trail of biting kisses to my breast. The moan that came out of my mouth once his lips closed around my nipple was loud enough to wake the dead.

And then he moved, one arm releasing me to snap his fingers as his feet made tracks to wherever he needed to take us. I hoped he was going somewhere with a bed.

A big one.

"I need you," I gasped, my hands finding his face before pressing my lips to his again. My back met cool sheets, the coldness of them a stark contrast from the blisteringly luscious heat of Bastian's skin against mine. He settled between my legs, his hand cupping the back of my head as his fingers wound themselves into my hair.

"That's good, love, because I fucking well need you, too." Bastian's words hit me with the sweetest of blows. "I need you today, and I'll need you tomorrow, and on and on until the sun quits burning. I'm yours, you understand?" His green eyes flashed as the seriousness of what he was telling me fell on me like a warm blanket.

Tears stung my eyes before the question I didn't want to ask fell from my mouth. "Promise?"

He nodded, brushing his nose against mine before following suit with his lips. "I promise."

I couldn't help it—not that I thought I'd ever want to help it—I kissed him with every good thing I had left in me. My hands roamed over his skin, letting his heat, his life, his vitality bleed into me. Just like his blood in my mouth, every bit of his energy fueled me. Every single brush of his mouth and caress of his fingers brought me back to life. His mouth moved from mine as he kissed and licked every bit of skin he could reach, his fingers finding my center as his mouth swiftly followed suit. His lips and tongue devoured me as his hot hands clutched me to him, refusing to let me wriggle away.

The man feasted on me, taking everything I had as he wrenched moan after moan out of me. The slide of his tongue, the gentle nibbles of my flesh, sent me into the most delicious frenzy. It was almost too much, too big. What I was feeling couldn't possibly be an orgasm. This was a tsunami and an earthquake and a hurricane all at once. This was… He twisted his fingers inside me, and the dam broke. A flash fire of pleasure erupted over my flesh, and I practically screamed.

Wanting him seemed to be all I could think of—it was in every breath, every kiss, every touch. I wanted him inside me as my fangs pierced his neck. I wanted him invading every part of me. I wasn't sure if I said that out loud or if Bastian could read my mind, but before I could take my next breath, Bastian was kissing me as he rolled us, the taste of my arousal on his tongue making me crave him more.

He sat us up as I reached for his pants. But instead of denim, all I found was him.

God bless mages and magic and whatever sorcery got him naked for me.

My fingers wrapped around his length as a groan rolled up his throat and into my mouth. I'd had the mother of all orgasms, and already I needed him to give me another one. Rising up on my knees, I slicked him through my wetness, not taking him inside. I couldn't say why I wanted to torture him this way, until his eyes flashed that brilliant bright green again.

His growl tore through the room as his fingers found my hair, tightening just enough to make me crazy.

"Give yourself what you need," he whispered against my mouth. "Give me what I need."

And so, I did. Notching his length against my center, I lowered myself onto him, the unbelievably sexy moan that fell from his lips only compounding the bliss of him filling me. I almost couldn't move, the fear I wouldn't be able to take that much goodness, that much pleasure freezing me—right up until his arms banded around my back, his fingers making a home in my hair. Then he nibbled on my bottom lip as he gently thrust upward. My hips moved to answer his, following the rhythm he set. Each retreat was agony, and each return was paradise, the punishing pace killing me and saving me at the same time.

But I didn't bite him yet.

So distracted by every sensation, I nearly forgot about taking his blood. Then he broke our kiss, and all I could smell was our desire. All I could feel was him. All I could see was his face. All I could hear were the noises we made as our bodies glided together and the beat of his heart. My fangs practically ached as the thrum of his pulse rang in my ears.

"Take what you need," Bastian growled, his voice thick and full of gravel.

Without a thought, I struck, piercing the tender skin of his neck with my aching fangs. The bliss of his blood, the feel of him inside me, the groan erupting from his throat. God, it was all too much, too good. Whatever hold I had on my sanity left me then—left us both—our releases crashing over us in wave after wave of molten pleasure.

I couldn't remember how long we stayed connected, or how

many times we came together afterward. It could have been moments or days.

All I knew—deep down in that cold, shriveled thing I called a heart—was that I was in love with Sebastian Cartwright, and if anyone hurt him, they would have hell to pay.

15

I woke up before Bastian did, and like the smart girl I tried to be, I stayed put, studying his sleeping face. Asleep, all the worry melted from his expression. The deep groove between his eyebrows eased, the near-permanent clench to his jaw gone. We'd slept facing each other, my head pillowed on his arm, our legs tangled together along with the bedsheets.

The desire to stay right here in this little bubble of happy filled me. I didn't want to move, or speak, or ask questions. Bastian and I would live here in this room forever and the world wouldn't touch us, and all the bad things would let us be. It was an irrational thought quickly dashed by reality.

"I can feel you thinking," he grumbled, his eyes still shut. His arms closed around me, and I had no choice but to be swept up in them. "No thoughts. Just content, blissed-out afterglow. I must insist on it."

Pressing my nose into the center of his chest, I breathed him in, the crisp hairs tickling my face. "That sounds nice."

I clutched him to me, settling in to never move again, when a god-awful pounding rattled the bedroom door.

"Go away," he called, his arms tightening just a smidge too tight.

"Sebastian August Cartwright," Simon yelled through the door, "you get your ass out of that room this instant. It's bad enough I had to pick the sound warding, but did you really have to use the Faustian defense? You caught my favorite shirt on fire, you ass."

I put a hand on his chest, pushing away so I could look him in the eye. "You set your brother on fire?"

Bastian rolled his eyes. "Only a little, and it's his fault for picking my locks. He could have just as easily sent me a message, but he decided to get cute. I take zero responsibility for his poor planning."

Simon pounded on the door again. "Emrys is insisting that we come to dinner, so put on some clothes and get down there before she decides to test your magic against hers."

At the thought of solid food, my stomach rumbled something fierce, the hungry gurgle probably loud enough to be heard downstairs. I was more than satisfied on the blood front. Bastian's magic-laced offerings had likely powered me up until the end of time. I worried that I might have taken too much from him.

But his skin appeared no worse for wear, and his eyes still had that twinkle of mischief and desire and... Bastian gently clutched my wrist as he reeled me in for a kiss, and for some reason, I didn't care about the possibility of our bubble being popped. I didn't care about anything at all.

A louder bang rattled the door before Thomas' voice echoed through the wood. "Don't make me drag you two out."

I broke the kiss, somehow finding myself straddling Bastian. "Party pooper. We'll be there in a minute."

"Do we have to?" Bastian whined, nuzzling his face

between my breasts as he cupped my ass in his hands, which naturally made everything inside me clench.

Did we have to go? I mean, really? Couldn't we—

My stomach took that opportunity to release the mother of all growls.

"Fine, fine," he muttered, sighing. "I must keep my lady fed." He moved his hands to my hips before lifting me up and setting me on the floor. Then he yanked a robe from the back of his bathroom door, holding it out for me, and I slipped into it. Before I knew it, he was in front of me again, tying the belt. "If I shower with you in here, we'll never leave. Meet you downstairs in ten?"

Can I wash all the blood and sex off me in ten minutes? Looking at the hope and happiness on this face? I was damn sure going to try.

"Deal."

After taking the fastest shower on record and donning jeans and a black T-shirt—one aptly emblazoned with the phrase, "Please don't make me kill you"—I raced down the stairs, my booted feet clomping as I went. Hair still wet and piled on my head, I realized about ten seconds too late that I wasn't wearing any jewelry, as the whole of the dining room came to an abrupt hush. I swear there were practically crickets chirping and everything.

"Dear sweet baby Jesus in a manger, what in the ever-loving fuck sticks is going on with your face?" Clem exclaimed, her thick Southern drawl softening the blow just a tad.

I hadn't bothered to look in a mirror—I hadn't had the time —so I didn't know if I resembled a burn victim, or if it was just the regular old *Skeletor* that was getting Clem's goat. My gaze found Thomas' instantly. "My necklace burned off, didn't it?"

"Oh, most definitely," he answered, a smile creeping across his lips. "As did most of your flesh, your hair, and a few fingers.

As you can tell, it all grew back, and in less than twenty-four hours, too. I know ancients who can't do that. Myself included."

Wincing, I tried to think of a good explanation, but I didn't know any more than they did.

"Well, Clem…" I began, ready to spill the beans—not that I knew exactly what those beans were when the faint trill of someone approaching made me smile.

"I think she's beautiful just like she is," Bastian said from behind me, dropping a kiss to the side of my neck. "There's no reason to wear a glamour at home. You don't wear yours."

He tagged my hand, pulling me behind him to the two available seats. He pulled out my chair before taking his own, and all the while, everyone goggled at us like we were Martians. Okay, I totally couldn't blame them. A couple of months ago, Bastian and I were at each other's throats —literally.

"Point taken, and I agree," Clem replied, setting down a covered platter on the table. "I don't think Sloane needs to wear a glamour at home. I just want to know why she's flickering like a Halloween decoration at the dinner table."

I was glad I wasn't drinking anything because I would have covered Dahlia in it when I busted out laughing.

"A Halloween decoration. Oh, man, that's good." I wiped at the mirthful tears. It was a much better way to think about it. I was a spooky décor piece rather than a monster. I'd totally take it.

"Look who's talking," Harper accused, reaching for the basket of rolls. "You could pass for Bride of Frankenstein's sassy younger sister."

Clem snorted. "Touché, and thank you. That's the nicest compliment anyone's ever given me."

"I aim to please," Harper volleyed back around a mouthful of roll.

Simon tapped his fingers on the table, his impatience ready to erupt from his ears. "So, no one is going to mention the witch in the dungeon, or the fact that Sloane obviously has something wrong with her, or the fact that—"

"Whoa, whoa, whoa." I held up a hand, stopping his tirade. "Can I not get some food in my belly before you start in on everything? I need sustenance to deal with whatever the hell happened to me, the aforementioned witch in the dungeon— glad that's getting some use, by the way—and the veritable mountain of other shit going on. Slow your roll."

Simon glared in my direction, not happy at all that I'd cut him off.

"Exactly. I know you've been dying to discuss this particular quagmire, Simon, but Sloane is right," Emrys scolded, loading her plate with fried chicken and greens. "Can't we have one nice meal with each other before the world falls in?"

He huffed in his chair, crossing his arms like a petulant child.

"What I wanna know is, how in the hell did you keep Simon out of your room so long?" Axel asked, a chuckle laced in his question as he loaded mashed potatoes on his plate. "That boy has been trying to bust in there for hours."

Bastian snorted, passing me a platter of grilled cod. "Faustian defense. Prevents a blood tie from breaking a ward. I knew no one else but my brother would interrupt." He shook his head. "Honestly, after six hundred years, one would think you'd know better."

Shock flooded my limbs as I froze mid-pass to Thomas. I goggled at Bastian for a moment or twelve. "You dirty old man, you. Dating a woman so young. *Tsk, tsk, tsk.*"

I was joking… mostly.

He leaned my way, eyeing my face with amusement. "You've killed more people in a year than I have in six hundred. I figure that makes us about even. Don't you?"

I couldn't fault that logic. The certainty that I was stupidly in love with the man meant that breaking up with him was pretty much off the table. "I'll allow it."

"Dear god, are they always going to be like this?" Harper griped.

"I'm sure I'll piss her off eventually," Bastian answered, his gaze never leaving my face as he leaned back.

"You know this means I'll have to separate you two on jobs," Emrys said through a sigh.

"Oh, no, you won't." Of all the people I expected to say that, Dahlia wasn't the one. Still, she pointed her fork at our fearless leader as if she was ready to stab her with it. "I want my partner back. No offense to Bastian, but he steals all the magical thunder on every single job. What is the point of having two magic-users on the same team? Not just no, but hell no. Let those two have each other, and give me back Thomas, or so help me, I'll—"

"Fine, fine." Emrys held up her hands in surrender. "You can be paired with Thomas. But if they mess up and let high-value targets get away to save each other or some other nonsense, I'll have to reevaluate."

Dahlia pivoted in her chair and pointed her fork at us. "Don't you dare mess this up, you hear me?"

Wide-eyed, all I could do was nod.

"Aww, Dahlia," Thomas said, batting his eyelashes at her. "I didn't know you cared."

She snorted in answer. "Oh, shut up."

After loading my plate with more food than I thought I could possibly eat, I dug in, the inane chatter of friends and family surrounding me. It hit differently than the first night I'd sat in this same chair. It used to grate on me, the feeling of not belonging. I still thought *I* was a freak, sure, but I was wanted here in this family of freaks.

When I had a full belly, and the rest of the table were picking at the dregs of the food, I wiped my face with the napkin before sitting forward in my chair. Simon—who had been nearly silent the whole meal—focused on me.

"Okay. My belly is full, and I'm happy and content for the first time in a year. Let me enjoy it for five more minutes, and then you can introduce me to the witch in the dungeon who tried to blow me up."

"Sloane," Bastian murmured, the plea in his tone a testament to the level of bad coming my way.

"Twenty-four hours was the deal. I figure that's been up for a while now."

"As you wish."

But I didn't wish. Not at all.

16

The dungeon was just as I remembered it—not that I expected much to change in the two months since I'd been here last. Several empty cells encased in rune-covered bars and cinderblock dotted one side of the Night Watch's de facto dungeon.

Bastian had given me a run-down of what happened in the time I'd been lost to my injuries. Evidently, what Simon thought about the circle surrounding Booth's body had only been partially accurate. It had been a backward working, an incomplete circle. However, what he'd thought was a safe space was actually a spell within a spell.

One to kill.

One to neutralize.

And the wrong one was incomplete.

To my astonishment, the witch was not in my old cell. When I'd been brought here a couple of months ago, my cell was furnished with a bed, a toilet, a desk, and a screen for privacy. Evidently, Emrys had thought it would take some convincing to get me to join their ragtag bunch of misfits.

Either that, or they'd wanted me comfortable before I was served up to the person who posted my bounty.

But the witch did not reside in my former home. No, they'd placed her in one of the barren cells with a bucket for a toilet and not much else. The runes surrounding the cell were blazing orange, even though no one was near them. What little I knew about those runes could fill a thimble, but I figured they were glowing because this witch was simply made of magic. They were making her uncomfortable to keep her contained.

At our approaching footsteps, the witch looked up. Mahogany hair fell in messy waves down her back, her face and clothes streaked in soot and blood, an unhealing burn marring her jaw. Hazel eyes flashed for a moment before she winced, the burn of the runes blazing hotter.

Gingerly, she stood, favoring her right leg over her left. "It's good to see you again, Sloane. I was worried about you."

The way she said my name—as if she knew me, as if we'd spoken a hundred times before—grated on my nerves.

"Do I know you?" I asked, settling onto a folding metal chair as Simon and Bastian acted as my sentries. Even Thomas had accompanied us for good measure.

The witch winced, wilting back down to the floor. "I appeared quite a bit different when you knew me. My name is Celeste Warner, but you knew me as Mrs. Ida Blumenthal, the sweet old lady down the street. Sorry for the deception. It was…" She paused, thinking on the right word before settling on, "necessary."

Mrs. Blumenthal? The same lady that helped me with my bloody knees when Otis dragged me down the street?

"Was trying to kill me necessary or just a happy accident?" I remembered her rushing me right before I activated the circle and blew myself to kingdom come. I nearly shuddered at the memory of the pain but managed to hold it in.

Celeste shook her head. "Had I been allowed to finish my circle, none of that would have happened. And in case you don't recall, I was trying to get you to stop. It's not my fault your boyfriend dicked around with time magic." Her gaze shifted from me to spear Bastian with a glare. "You should know better."

Bastian huffed, his cheeks reddening. "Says the woman who used outlawed grave magic to murder a man."

So that's the scent tickling my nose. Funny. It didn't seem too horrible now that Booth's corpse wasn't right next to me.

"Like you wouldn't have done the same," she retorted, giving Bastian a scathing glower. "And Booth McCall deserved to die. With the spell imbued in his flesh, we got lucky. Dollars to donuts he was coming here, ready to kill you all for hiding her. Don't act like that wasn't the end goal." The witch massaged at her temples, as if just talking to us was giving her a headache. "You know, I didn't even want to be there. Had your mother listened to me, I wouldn't have been." She chuckled as she continued to massage her head. "Twenty years in the same house, wearing the same glamour, watching out for you, and it was for nothing. X still found you. He still keeps finding you." Tears gathered in her eyes as she sniffed.

I stood, staring down at the witch as rage prickled my skin. "What do you know about X?"

The laugh that erupted from her mouth was bitter. "I know that he came after you just like he came for my daughter. My Aurora was beautiful. Sweet. Innocent. Never hurt a soul in her short, short life. I did everything I could to keep her hidden. Given who her father was, all the unrest his children were causing, I didn't want her caught up in it. But I couldn't hide her from him." Her lips trembled, her voice growing thick as she continued, "I came home to our house on fire, and Rory..." She shook her head. "I swore I would keep an eye on you. That you wouldn't have the same fate as my girl. I swore to him that I would."

"Swore to who?" I probed. "What are you talking about?"

Frowning, Celeste swiped at her tears, examining me as if she'd never seen me before in her life. "Wow. Your mother really kept you in the dark, didn't she? I swore to your *father*. Azrael."

Bastian and Simon shifted, but I moved even closer to the bars.

"My father was Peter Cabot," I insisted, the hissed declaration coming from clenched teeth. "I don't know what you're playing at, but you've got me mixed up with someone else."

Celeste searched the ceiling for something, maybe patience. "Why do I feel as if I'm on an episode of *Maury*?" Sighing, she brought her chin down, staring me dead in the eye. "Peter Cabot raised you, but he did not provide the genetic material that made you what you are. Just like my daughter, your father is Azrael, the Angel of Death."

"Bullshit."

Celeste's laugh was mirthless. "You'd like to think so, wouldn't you? That everything you knew was real. That you weren't lied to every single moment of your life? I get that. Had your mother listened to me, had she hidden you better, I bet you'd still be in the dark. Still thinking you were human. That she was."

I didn't want to hear this woman lie to me. "Fuck you, lady. Fuck. You." Rage nearly propelled me against the bars, the burn of the runes less important than telling this woman off. "You don't know the first thing about my mother. You don't know the first thing about me."

Celeste struggled to her feet, getting closer to the bars, too. "I know you died that night."

Her words hit me like a fist to the gut, faint images of my mother pressing on my chest filtering through my brain.

"What?" I breathed, but Celeste was on a roll.

"After X slit your father's throat, he came after you, and because she'd bound your powers, because she'd told you nothing of what you were, you were no match for him. Funnily enough, he was probably going to leave your mother alive—just like me and Rory. Leave her to her grief and loss. Leave her alone in the world. But your mother tried to bring you back as a vampire, and it didn't work. She died trying to bring you back, trying to fix her mistake." Celeste shook her head, a bitter sort of pity on her face. "He killed her just like Peter. I know that *I* got you out. I know that *I* took you to your father. I know you're not alive and not undead. I know *lots* of things, Sloane."

The world was spinning, but I seemed to be staying still.

More and more flashes filled my brain.

My father lying in a pool of blood.

A man in a suit with a giant knife.

Purple magic…

Staggering back, I shook my head. "No."

I whispered that word—denying her and her awful statements, but I knew they were true. I knew. My whole body shook with the reality of what she was saying. "Tell me the rest."

"I took you to Azrael, ready to die because I'd failed you. Because I didn't get there in time. Because I didn't stop that bastard from taking you like he took Rory. But Azrael didn't want to let you go—didn't want another one of his children to be lost."

My back met the cinderblock wall as the runes around us glowed brighter, hotter.

"What did he do to me?" The question came out as an accusation, which it most certainly was.

Celeste's expression was a ravaged sort of agony that told me all sorts of things I didn't want to know. *This* was what Simon had figured out. *This* was the truth I didn't want to know. And man, was it going to hurt.

"Azrael did something he couldn't have done for any of his other children. By the time I got you to him, you'd been gone maybe a day, but your mother had attempted to transition you to a vampire. He couldn't make you alive again—you'd been dead too long—but he could imbue you with a piece of himself. He could bring you back by making you like him. You had a fraction of his powers already—they were just bound. So he weakened himself, giving you more so you would come back, so you could live in this realm."

I shook my head, my breaths coming in hurried pants.

"You aren't alive. And you aren't undead. Ask yourself, Sloane, what else is there?"

My mother was screaming, pressing on my chest over and over again. Her hands were hard, weighty as if they were fifty-pound dumbbells just chilling on my ribcage. I wanted to answer her, but I just couldn't. Everything hurt. Everything. From my toes, all the way up to my hair, every single bit of me felt as if I was being flash fried by a blowtorch, followed by an acid bath.

This was death.

I couldn't understand her words, either. I was either going deaf, or she was speaking gibberish, and I was in so much pain it really didn't matter. It didn't matter when the agony made me want to die—made me hope relief was coming.

The room around us was hazy at best. Smoke swirled and bloomed in a halo around her head as an odd purple light whirled up her arms. And she was crying. Or at least I thought she was. A tiny trail of a tear dropped from her eye and hit me on the cheek. I wanted to wipe it away. Wanted to tell her I was okay, but I couldn't do that, either.

Her strong fingers gripped my shoulders, and she pulled me into her arms, hugging me to her chest as if she was saying goodbye.

That's when I saw the flames.

That's when I saw my dad lying in a pool of his own blood in the middle of the living room.

That's when I saw the man in the gray suit, his face shrouded within the shadows, kneeling over my father.

He held a wicked-looking knife in his hand—bigger than a dagger but smaller than a sword—the awful blade coated in my father's blood. He rose from his crouch, an awful laugh bubbling up his throat as the sound danced over the roar of the flames and my mother's sobs.

And he was coming for us.

No, he was coming for her. Pale fingers found her hair, yanking her backward as the sword raked against her throat. Blood poured from her neck as her grip loosened, and I fell backward.

The man examined me, hovering over my rapidly dying body, a gleeful smile on his face as his violet gaze bore into me.

"Give Azrael my best, won't you?" he said before plunging the dagger into my chest.

My legs gave out as I slid to the ground, the rough cinderblock pulling at my shirt. Ragged breaths sawed in and out of my lungs as the runes burned bright around us, their heat searing into my skin.

You aren't alive. And you aren't undead. Ask yourself, Sloane, what else is there?

The answer was so simple and so complicated at the same time. I wasn't alive and I wasn't undead.

I was just dead.

17

"I have to keep my mouth shut for days, but you just let some stranger toss a brick at her head and hope for the best?" Simon shouted, getting in Bastian's personal space.

Is this man seriously upset he didn't get the chance to ruin my entire worldview and the memory of my parents? Because that's just wrong—on a bevy of fucking levels.

Bastian practically growled. "Just because you're the resident death mage doesn't mean it's your responsibility, nor is it even appropriate for you to tell her. And had I known this lady had all the answers, I—"

Simon snarled, cutting his brother off. "You would have done fuck all. You're just glad it wasn't one of us who did the dirty work."

I hated the thought as soon as it entered my head, but Simon wasn't wrong. I was sort of glad Celeste was the one to tell me, and not someone I actually gave a shit about.

"Knock it off, children," Thomas rumbled, his voice a hell of a lot closer than I thought it'd be. His shoulder bumped mine as he settled on the ground. "You can duke it out later when we're not in the middle of a crisis."

I let out a small chuckle, the idea of Thomas calling six-hundred-year-old Bastian a child completely preposterous to me. That and the thought that we would ever *not* be in a crisis. "Oh, out with it, Simon," I insisted. "Anything else you want to add? Am I really a swamp thing that needs to be taken out back and shot or something?"

Really, it wouldn't surprise me at this point. According to Celeste, my father was the Angel of Death. *Because that was a thing.*

"Not that I know of. She had more information than I did. I just had a theory based on Isis, your flickering face, and that story Thomas told me about you trying to die. You kept trying, but you couldn't…" Simon shook his head as he rubbed a hand over his mouth. "I had an errant thought that took root. You'd tried killing yourself and it never worked because you were already dead."

"So, I was a suicidal dead girl," I said, laughing. "The irony there is just beautiful." I puckered my lips and did a little chef's kiss.

Celeste snorted. "No wonder you look like that. How many times have you 'died' in the last year?" She used air quotes and everything, the bitch.

"I have no idea," I replied, picking myself up off the cold stone floor. "It's not like I kept a running tally. I was a little preoccupied with killing bad guys and stopping people from getting murdered on the streets. Excuse the fuck out of me."

She gave me an exasperated stare that could undoubtedly peel the paint off a car. "You're essentially chipping away at yourself every time you do that, stupid."

"Yes, and I totally know exactly what you mean by that.

Don't elaborate at all. I'm sure I'll figure it out." One thing I could say about myself: my sarcasm was on point.

Celeste rolled her eyes so hard I was surprised they didn't roll on out of her head. "Think about it for about a nanosecond. You are the composition of a death deity and a blood mage, only now you have far more death deity essence in you. Every time you 'die,' you're chipping away at the blood mage part of yourself that makes you... well... *you* because the death deity shit can't die. *Duh.* No wonder you look like a walking embodiment of death. You keep fucking around and you will be."

My eyes popped wide as the reality of my situation hit me. Then the nausea landed squarely on my tongue, and I raced out of the dungeon to find the closest receptacle. The downstairs powder room bore the brunt of my reaction, the last truth bomb just a bit too much for me to handle. Heaving in the toilet, I begged my stomach to quit volleying up my dinner. Cool hands found my overheated skin, a wet washcloth on the back of my neck easing some of the worst of it.

"You're going to be all right, love. Just breathe." Bastian's sweet words filtered in my ears, as wetness gathered in my eyes.

How can he want me? I am... I'm a monster.

The tears came in earnest then, the heavy weight of despair practically suffocating me. With my heaves over, he gathered me in his arms, cradling me there as he got comfortable on the ground. "Shh, love. It's okay. You're going to be okay."

"No, it's not," I sobbed, as the truth of it all came crashing over me.

X had already killed everyone I'd ever loved once before. He'd taken everything from me—even my life. He'd tried to kill me over and over again, hurting anyone who'd gotten in his way.

"I don't understand. Why does he want me dead? I've never done anything to him. I've never—" I stopped abruptly and shook my head, the tears falling faster than I could wipe them away. "Why did he rip everything I've ever known away from me? He…" I had to swallow the lump in my throat as the memory of my father, dead, on the floor in a pool of his own blood, flashed in my mind, quickly followed by X slashing my mother's throat.

Shuddering, I tried to wipe the newfound knowledge from my brain.

"He killed them right in front of me, and then he stabbed me." An echo of the agony of his blade piercing my heart radiated from my chest, and I rubbed at the spot. "I think I was already mostly dead by that point, but he needed to make sure."

And he laughed while he did it.

I didn't tell him the worst part of it all. The part I didn't want to think about and would have me avoiding mirrors for the rest of my life—however long that would be.

This X? He looked like me—or like I did now. White-haired, purple eyes, pale skin, high cheekbones.

All too soon I connected the dots.

He'd killed Celeste's daughter, just as he'd killed me. And he used a blood curse to do it when his efforts hadn't panned out like he wanted.

X wasn't *just* family.

He wasn't just *my* blood.

X was my brother.

Scrambling out of Bastian's lap, I staggered downstairs. Celeste had answers and she was going to cough them up one way or another.

Simon and Thomas were hissing in a corner, their

discussion less important than the question I needed to ask Celeste.

"How do I contact Azrael?" The inquiry burst from my lips like a shotgun blast. "You talked to him, right? How do I do it?"

Celeste stared at me as if I'd grown another head. "You want to *talk* to a death deity?"

Did I want to just talk to the man? Absolutely not. I wanted to punch him in the face for taking my choices away from me. I wanted to set his dumb ass on fire. I wanted…

"Yes," I replied, my feigned calm fooling no one. "I want to talk to the man you call my father. I want to hear it *from him* how I came to be what I am. He has answers that I don't."

Totally rational answer. Too bad that was only the half of what I wanted to ask. I'd also appreciate knowing who in the blue fuck gave him the right to make me like this. I was super interested in that answer.

"I don't know if that's a good idea, Sloane," Thomas murmured, his and Simon's conversation dying off at my impromptu interrogation. "Azrael isn't at your beck and call."

I snorted derisively, craning my neck to look Thomas in the eye. "I am one hundred percent positive that I didn't fucking ask you. But just in case I did, wouldn't you want to ask the man who turned you into a monster against your will a question or two?"

Thomas' eyes popped wide in surprise, and he took a step back. "Point made."

"Exactly." Shifting my attention back to our prisoner, I repeated my query. "How do I contact Azrael?" She opened her mouth to respond, but I held up a hand to stop her. "Before you start on some bullshit, please keep in mind that I have reached the *very* end of my rope, I do *not* consider you an ally, and I'm *incredibly* good at getting the answers I seek one way or another. So, you can decide how I get my answers, but please note, that I *am* getting them. Either by you telling me or showing me through your blood—and I *really* don't give a fuck which."

A faint thread of alarm crossed Celeste's face, and she backed up a step. "You're not going to hurt him, right?"

All I could do was laugh. Did she honestly believe I'd be able to hurt Death himself? "I haven't decided, but don't worry your pretty little head about it. If I can't manage to kill myself, I'm thinking I'll have a hell of a time trying to kill him."

She pursed her lips at me as if that rationalization rubbed her the wrong way. "Fine. If you want to pitch a fit like a toddler to your daddy, be my guest." She massaged at her temples as she gave me an exasperated huff. "Find an unwarded spot on the property and call for him with your mind. Azrael is in tune with his children. He'll hear you and come if he can. I don't make any promises that he'll actually come when you call, but summoning him requires a sacrifice I doubt you'd be willing to make."

I frowned at her until it dawned on me. By sacrifice, she meant a real one.

A life.

Yeah, I'd definitely be trying door number one.

"Thank you," I chirped, the picture of politeness, as if I hadn't just threatened to bleed her dry before pivoting on my heel to exit the dungeon. I probably would have been able to follow through with my intended course of action—which was to scream at the sky until Azrael himself showed his stupid face—if I weren't staring down two mages and a vampire.

"What now?" I complained, and if I happened to sound like a whiney brat, well, then so be it.

"Do you really think summoning a death deity is a good idea?" Simon asked, echoing Thomas' earlier question.

"Considering I won't have to kill anyone to do it, yeah, I do." I crossed my arms over my chest as I glared at the death mage. Yeah, he more than likely knew way more than I did on the subject, but I seriously doubted he had put it all together.

"X killed my parents right in front of me before he stabbed me in the chest." I ticked that point off on my thumb. "Then, when that didn't work, he used the Night Watch to find me, putting a three-million-dollar bounty on my head." I raised my index finger. "When that didn't pan out, he got Booth to kidnap you, sending an army of ghouls to do his bidding." Middle finger. "And when that didn't work, he doubled down with a blood curse." My ring finger went up. "Now we have a prison break, a sacked ABI building, and whatever bullshit spell Booth was filled with." All five fingers were up now. "How much fucking collateral damage has his quest to murder me caused? Think about it. I'll wait."

Recrossing my arms over my chest, I waited a full thirty seconds in stone-cold silence.

"Oh, you don't have a retort to that? *Shocker.* But let me break it down further for you. Every single person in this house is in danger because of me. You, your brother, Thomas, Emrys, Dahlia, Harper, Axel, Clem, and even Isis. All of you. Because this is where I lay my head. This is where I found shelter. This is where I found love and acceptance and friends. If you honestly believe that I wouldn't use every single weapon I had at my disposal to protect you, you're fucking dreaming. So yeah, I'm summoning a death deity. You got a problem with that?"

"Anyone ever tell you that you're fucking frightening when you're mad?" Celeste asked, and I whipped my head to glare at her.

"Not twice," I replied before turning back to the men in my way. "Move."

Thomas and Simon did as they were told, but Bastian stayed right where he was. "If you're going to go do something stupid, I'm not letting you go alone."

I pointed my index finger right at his face like I'd seen my mother do a hundred times to my dad. "No funny business. Got it?"

Bastian gave me the Boy Scout salute, as if the man had ever been a Boy Scout a day in his life.

"I promise, 'no funny business,' as you call it. I just want to watch your back." A slight smile curled his lips. "Plus, you don't know where the wards are."

He had me there.

18

The warmth of Bastian's fingers laced with mine helped distract me from the reality of what I was about to do. A few minutes ago, I had plenty of bravado, but as we walked through the high grasses on the edge of the ward, all my earlier confidence seemed to be on sabbatical.

"You don't have to do this, you know," Bastian murmured, gently squeezing my hand in his. "Celeste may know more. We could question her. Maybe—"

"If she had more info, she would have told us. Don't get me wrong, she probably has a ton of answers, just not to the questions I need to ask. She has no more of a way to stop X than we do."

She doesn't know why he made me this way either, don't forget that one.

Bastian seemed to think about that for a moment. "True, but she does have more questions to answer. Like how did you end up on your grave? Why were you just left there with nothing? No answers, no home, no idea what you were or what happened. Who does that?"

Yeah, that was on my list for dear old dad. Just after why his son was trying to kill me, and how I could attempt to kill him first.

Bastian pulled me to a stop when I ignored his griping. "You amaze me, you know? When your case came across our radar, I thought you were just another Rogue. Another monster to be put down. How you survived this last year after what you went through…" He released my hand to cup my face. "You're a goddamn miracle, Sloane."

Funny, I didn't feel like one. But with Bastian's hands on my face, with his beautiful bottle-green eyes staring at me as if I was a treasure? Yeah, I could believe it for a little while.

"You're just saying that because you want back in my pants. Don't lie."

He stepped fully into my space, his front brushing mine as he let my face go to latch onto my hips. "Oh, I definitely want back in your pants, but I mean this, too. You're a fucking miracle."

He lowered his head, gently sweeping his lips against mine, deepening the kiss as soon as I parted my lips. His tongue caressed mine, and I was lost to his safety, to his warmth, to him.

"I was under the impression you needed to talk to me," a deep voice called, shocking the shit out of both of us.

One second, we were kissing, and the next, Bastian had me behind him, a ball of fire in his hand. Well, until the fire in his palm winked out at the same time I heard a snap.

"Was I mistaken?" the voice asked.

How stupid are we? I don't even have a weapon on me—not that I need one, but still.

Peering around Bastian's bulk, I spied a tall dark-haired

man in a black suit. His black hair spilled down to his shoulders, and a long scar marred what I thought was a decently handsome face.

But unlike X, I didn't resemble this man at all.

"Ah, yes." He paused, gesturing to his suit. "This is a comforting depiction of Death for most humans. They expect me to be a dark-suited thing carrying a scythe. I suppose I could go for broke with the hood, but they're dreadfully hot."

A wash of cold dread filled me at his response. Mostly because I hadn't asked him an actual question. Not out loud, anyway. "I didn't say anything."

He shrugged. "Doesn't mean I didn't hear you. You read information in blood—I read thoughts. We each have our own talents."

I touched Bastian's back, trying to comfort him, but he seemed frozen or encased in stone. Bastian stared ahead, unblinking.

"What did you do to him?" I asked, fully stepping out from behind him and moving in front to protect him with my body.

"Nothing. When we're done talking, he'll wake right back up. I simply prefer to discuss your grievances alone."

Grievances. As if my questions were a nuisance. *Asshole.*

"I heard that," he muttered, frowning at me like I was a naughty child.

I narrowed my eyes, crossing my arms. "I meant you to. You turned me into a monster after your son took everything I ever loved away from me. *Grievances.* Death deity or not, you can kiss my ass."

Azrael took a deep breath, likely searching the cosmos for patience. But I had questions, and I was going to ask them.

"Why don't we look alike? I resemble X, why don't I look like you?"

Azrael sighed and snapped his fingers. Instantly, his hair

changed from black to white, his skin lost some of its color, and his dark eyes became violet. "You do, it's just not my favorite form to take." He snapped his fingers again, his original features returning. "You can change your form at will as well." He flicked out a hand, gesturing at my face. "And you can stop with that whole monster nonsense. You're not a monster, Sloane. Never have been."

"Says the man who made me this way. I kill people, Azrael. How am I *not* a monster?"

He chuckled, shaking his head. "Name one innocent person you killed. Name a single one, and I'll agree that you're a monster."

Grumbling because he was right, I crossed my arms.

"Exactly. How many people have you saved because you took out the trash, Sloane? Because you did what I could not? Thousands? Hundreds of thousands? Each life you took had exponential ramifications. Exponential lives saved. And you call yourself a monster? No, daughter, you are not. A warrior, yes. A monster? Never."

As nice as those words were to hear, it didn't stop the betrayal that coursed through my veins. "Is that why you made me like this? To kill bad guys? Is that why you left me alone, left me to wake up with nothing and no one and no memory? So I could what? Be a warrior?"

Azrael flinched as if I'd slapped him. *Good.* I hoped those words hurt just as much as being left alone for a year. Just like waking up to the knowledge that my parents were dead. Did he even realize just how much I'd wanted to die? Just how much I begged for it? Just how many times I tried to make it so?

"It wasn't supposed to be this way," he whispered, his voice a gravelly mess. His gaze was beseeching, but it didn't faze me. One sorry expression wasn't going to erase the damage that had been done.

It wasn't going to take away what I'd lost.

"After I brought you back, I couldn't care for you like I wanted to. I was too run down, too weak. I needed to gather my strength. Celeste was supposed to look after you until I could, but she…" He trailed off, dipping his head to stare at his feet. "She couldn't. Aurora's death changed her. She isn't the same woman she was when she made her vow to me. But I didn't know that until it was too late. By the time I could come to you again, you seemed to be settling in."

Settling in. As if being homeless and alone was a good thing.

"I made sure Gerry kept an eye on you—not that he could do much. When I was able, I did, too. You were finding your way, and it seemed wrong to interfere. And I didn't, until your brother posted that bounty on your head. Then, I had Gerry call his friends at the Night Watch. I knew Emrys Zane would never hand you over like chattel. Knew she would give you a job and a home."

A job and a home were only good if I didn't bring death to their doorstep. They were only good if I could keep them safe. And I didn't know how I'd be able to do that. If X had taken everything once, there wasn't anything to stop him from doing it again. An image played out in my brain. Instead of my father in a pool of blood, it was Dahlia and Simon. Instead of my mother giving me chest compressions, it was me trying to breathe life back into Bastian.

I shook my head, trying to get the scene out of my mind but it stayed there, imprinting itself like a brand.

"Why didn't you just let me die?" I choked out, as I tried to swallow a sob. I was going to lose them. I was going to lose them all.

Azrael gave a slight shake to his head, his gaze getting a far-off quality to it, as if he was staring at something I couldn't see. "You were meant for more—so much more than what you got. Your journey wasn't over yet."

My hands balled into fists at the utter nonsense falling from his lips. "What kind of vague bullshit is that? *My journey wasn't over.* According to who? Who gave you the right to change me? Who gave you the right to make me like this?"

What good was my journey if I always lost the ones I loved?

He snapped his fingers and a pair of black wings unfurled from his back, a wicked scythe in his hand as his eyes blazed purple. He kept the dark hair, though, which I thought was a nice touch. Still, if his end goal was to scare me, it wasn't going to work. My own brain conjured far more frightening things than a pair of wings.

Plus, what was he going to do, kill me? *Too late, Pops, I'm already dead.*

"*I did,*" he insisted, flashing a double set of fangs that looked remarkably like the ones I saw in the mirror every day. "I gave myself the right. Because I see things that you can't or won't see. Because I've been around the block once or twice and know a couple of things you don't. Because you needed to be here."

In the next instant he shrugged his shoulders, and the wings went *poof* as if they'd never been there at all. "I swear, you and your sister are a handful. *No, Dad, don't keep me alive. No, Dad, don't tempt Fate. Please, Dad, save my ass from poltergeists.* Fates, it's as if you both are trying to die at this point."

A tiny buzzing took over my brain for a second before the base functions went back online. "I'm sorry, what? *Sister?* How many siblings do I have? I already know about the spawn of Satan. What is she, his evil twin sidekick?"

Azrael narrowed his eyes at me, likely unamused at the "spawn of Satan" remark. "Living? I believe just the two."

"*You believe?* Again, I ask, how many of us were there?"

"A lot. I'm older than time, Sloane. I've had a lot of kids. Though, I've lost many of them to war they waged with each other over a throne that was never theirs to take."

That shocked me enough to take a step back—which had me running right into Bastian's frozen form. "Please don't tell me I'm supposed to take a throne. I don't want a throne." I started shaking my head. "Nuh-uh, nope, no, not ever gonna happen."

"Don't worry, child. I have no plans to make you do something against your will."

That stopped me, and I met his gaze, narrowing my eyes. "That's not a 'no,' you know. I'm not dumb, Azrael."

He huffed out a chuckle that reminded me a bit of my dad's. "Oh, I know you're not." He sighed, pinching his brow as if I was giving him a headache. "Let me put it to you like this. I have no plans to give up my throne, but in the event I did, would you rather take it, or have the man who murdered your parents do it?"

"That's like asking me if I wanted constipation or diarrhea —either way my problem is still shit."

Azrael burst out laughing, tears of mirth on his face at my crude analogy. "You are so much like your sister, Sloane. I love that about you two. What strong women you've become after the challenges you've faced."

"She's like me?" Was that my voice? All small and childlike?

He nodded, a warm smile gracing his face, as if he was recalling a fond memory. "Same bravery, a few more scruples. She's a homicide detective in a town outside of Knoxville. A good woman."

A murderer has a homicide detective for a sister. That sounded like a disaster waiting to happen.

"But her power is nothing like yours, mostly because she's

still alive. She is formidable, but you… You have yet to tap into what you can do. Your potential is almost limitless. I can teach you. I can help you."

While power seemed like a great thing, leaving the first place I'd called a home in far too long was akin to X's knife in my heart. Reaching behind me, I clutched at Bastian's frozen hand. The flesh was still warm, still a reminder of what I had here.

"You must make a decision. Stay here or come with me to learn all you need to know."

Once again, both my options were shit.

19

"I'll give you time to think about it, but don't tarry too long. My son seems hell-bent on destroying you and your sister—just like he has done to the rest of my children. If I am to teach you all you must know, we don't have time to waste."

Oh, now he's in a rush? Now he wants to twist the knife?

Where the fuck had he been for the last year while I was sucking Rogues dry and digging graves? Where was he when I had no one and nothing but time? And did I still need to drink blood? Did I need to consume souls? How did I stop my face from flickering like a burning-out lightbulb?

There were too many questions and no real answers.

How do I kill X? How do I find him?

"I'll be in touch."

Rather than give me the answers I needed, Azrael gave me a smile instead, snapping his fingers and disappearing in the blink of an eye.

"Goddammit, Azrael," I yelled at the night sky. "You two-faced prick. You could have at least told me how to fix my face, you bastard."

Bastian's hand shook in mine, his body thawing upon Azrael's departure. Once again, I found myself behind his back, and a ball of fire graced his fingertips.

"Where is he?" Bastian hissed, his grip just a touch too tight. He was trembling, his fear not quite under wraps.

I put a quelling hand on his back, wrapping an arm around his middle as I rested my forehead between his shoulder blades. "He's gone. You can stand down."

Shaky breaths sawed in and out of his lungs, the adrenaline of it all causing him to crash a little. "He was so fast. I didn't think he would be that fast. But then again, he's Death."

"Quicker than a blink and just as ruthless as you'd expect," I murmured, reeling at how much and how little I'd learned from the encounter.

Bastian turned, cupping my cheeks in his hands. "Did you get any answers?"

My laugh was bitter as I shook my head, gently pulling my chin from his hold. "No," I replied, turning away from him. "All I got were more questions."

And a choice to make. Don't forget you got that, too.

But what kind of choice was it? I could leave the first home I'd had since my parents died to learn from a man I couldn't stand? Leave my friends, my... *Bastian* to play reindeer games with dear old dad? That sounded like a horrible plan, and a good way to start an apocalypse if I was being honest.

But how could I stay here when X was lurking around the next corner? It wasn't as if he didn't know where I parked my head at night. It wasn't as if he didn't know where I was. It wasn't as if he couldn't take *more* from me. Actually, he *could.* My friends were ripe for the picking if he got a bug up his ass to hurt me even more. How easily had he stolen Simon?

How easily had he infiltrated our home?

I stalked back to the house, the idea of leaving them burning in my gut. Leaving Bastian. A couple of months ago, I'd been all but begging to leave, and now, when I was presented with the choice, the mere thought of it felt like X's sword stabbing me on repeat.

"Sloane?" Bastian called, slowing my steps. "Do you want to talk about it?"

Did I? No, I absolutely did not. What I wanted to do was take him to bed and stay there. What I wanted to do was to kiss every inch of him and pretend the world didn't exist.

I pivoted on my heel, rushing him, though I hadn't meant to. His stunned arms caught me as I jumped, planting a kiss on his lips, which he quickly returned, only breaking it for a moment to answer him. "No, I don't want to talk about it. Can I request a make-out session followed by heavy petting and booze, though?"

"While I'm sure that isn't the healthiest way to deal with your problems, I'm not exactly going to say no." He hitched me higher on his hips. "I do want to talk about it at some point. The time where you had to deal with everything on your own is over. And not just me. Every single person in that house will be here for you—whether you ask for it or not." He swallowed, his Adam's apple bobbing. "I'm not the only one who loves you, Sloane."

My legs tightened around his hips, the urge to kiss him warring in my gut, along with the need to confirm what he'd just said. The uncertainty won out. "You... love me?"

I knew he wanted me, but I sort of figured what I felt for him was too much. Too soon. Too... just *too*.

"I'm pretty sure I've loved you since you bounced my head off the floor like a volleyball."

Chuckling, I shook my head. "Oh, so that's the brain damage talking, then."

Somehow, his hand found its way in my hair, fisting the strands in his fingers, bringing my mouth to his. My eyes fell closed in anticipation, but he didn't kiss me.

"Look at me," he whispered against my lips, and I forced my eyes open. "My mind is perfectly clear. It's not brain damage or me craving your bite, or any other excuse you can come up with to justify why I feel the way I do. I love your grit, your strength. I love your sense of honor, of justice." He sank his teeth in my bottom lip, soothing the bite almost as soon as he gave it. "I love you, and that's not going to change, no matter how many trials we face. Want to know why?"

I had to break his stare, those bottle-green eyes burning all the way down to my very soul. How could I accept such a beautiful gift when just me being here put him in danger?

"Yeah," I croaked, not wanting to hear the rest but needing it all the same. Tears flooded my vision as I brought my gaze back to his.

"Because I'm yours and you're mine, and that'll be true in this life or the next. Until the sun stops burning, understand? I'll repeat this as many times as I have to until you believe it."

The tears crested and fell, streaking down my cheeks, as the sweetest pain hit my chest. "I believe you."

And god help me, I did. Bastian wouldn't let me go without a fight, and there was no way I could stay here if I wanted him safe. But he had to know. I couldn't do what I needed to if he didn't. "You know I love you, too, right?"

Bastian gave me an indulgent smile, as if I was the one just now catching up. "I caught that."

For some reason that had me breathing a sigh of relief. "Good."

"Let's get you that order of heavy petting and alcohol, shall we? Then maybe we can come up with a solution. Yes?"

But I already had a solution—it was just going to kill me to do it. "Sounds good."

At that, he led me through the kitchen, stealing a bottle of vodka from the freezer and a couple of glasses before guiding me to his room. Along the way, I tried to memorize every bit of the house, every nuance of his movements, all the expressions on his face. When we made it to his domain, I didn't bother with the alcohol. I kissed him with every single bit of the love I had in that shriveled organ I called a heart.

His answering kisses were just as intense, just as powerful as mine. They scrambled my thoughts, made me believe that I could stay. Made me contemplate a future where we could be together. Where he would be safe from the danger that clung to me like a death shroud.

In my fevered imaginings, I saw a time where we were safe. Where we were happy.

But then the images of his lifeless stare as I tried to restart his heart flashed in my mind. He and I were never going to get a happy ending, and that only made me kiss him harder. Because if this was the last time I would have with him, I was going to show Bastian just how much I loved him.

My fingers found the hem of his shirt, deftly pulling it up and over his head. I needed his skin. I wanted to touch every inch of him, kiss everything I could reach. I wanted him to feel every ounce of pleasure he'd ever given me—give him *more*, and then some. I wanted his moans, his groans. I wanted his hisses and dirty talk.

I wanted everything.

Before long, we had stripped off all clothing, our frenzy making the night pass far too fast. We tasted each other, loved each other, and when we couldn't hold our eyes open any longer, we slept.

Just like the previous night, I woke before Bastian, but this time I didn't linger. I couldn't allow myself to get caught this time. Moving as silently as I could, I dressed enough to be decent and made my escape, heading straight for my room. The house was silent enough, and I was grateful for the plush carpeting that allowed my stealthy race through the hall.

Once I reached my room, I stopped my sneaking, racing for the closet. Quickly, I located the weekender bag full of old photo albums and Julie's ring. Slipping the cool metal on my finger, I felt a sense of dread wash over me.

He wouldn't know why I left him. Bastian would be in the dark. Was that better or worse than learning the truth? That I was exactly what Thomas had called me those few months ago.

An albatross.

A curse.

And I wasn't going to let him get dragged down with me.

The best I could do was rip a few clothes off the hangers, rummage in the drawers for underwear and socks, and toss the lot into the bag. Then, I dressed in what I figured was a durable outfit. Black jeans and a leather jacket, T-shirt and boots. Who knew where I was going, or how long it would be before I could get fresh clothes? After tying the laces on my boots, I snatched the handle of the duffle with all my worldly possessions and made for the desk.

I had to tell Bastian that I loved him. Had to let him know not to look for me. That I was safe—even if that was possibly a lie.

Unfortunately, I didn't get a chance to do anything of the sort. Especially since the man in question was standing right outside my closet with an expression like thunder. His gaze dropped from my face to the bag in my hand, arms crossing over his bare chest as if he'd run out of his room to chase me down.

"Going on a trip?" he asked, the whispered words slicing through the silence.

I swallowed, regretting getting the bag and the clothes. I should have just gone. I should have run out naked—something, anything. Anything that made it so I didn't have to see his face lose all expression. Anything that made it so I wouldn't glimpse the utter agony right before it turned to stone.

"You could say that."

Bastian pressed his lips together as he slowly nodded. *Oh, man, he's going to lose it.*

"So, love and trust are mutually exclusive for you then? You love me but you don't trust me. Why else would you leave before dusk?"

Blinking back tears, I searched the ceiling for answers. There were none.

"I'm going to get you killed," I whispered, my eyes still aloft, not looking at him. If I spared him so much as a glance, I would wimp out, and for his sake, I couldn't do that. "We've gotten lucky so far, but one of these days, we won't. One of these days he's going to come in here and slit your throat. I'm going to watch you die. I'm going to watch *them* die. Azrael can teach me. He can show me what I need to know. And everyone can live without me. Everyone can be safe."

"What were you going to do? Leave a note? Some pitiful Dear John letter, explaining that talking to me was just too hard or some other toss? Did you think I wouldn't understand?"

"No. I didn't," I said, sighing and giving up my inspection of the ceiling. "Because I figured you'd be arguing with me, just like you are right now. Tell me—how old was my mother?"

Bastian seemed confused at my switch in topic.

"Emrys said she was a venerated blood mage, so how old was she when X slit her throat? How much power did she have —did she waste—protecting me? Do you know?"

He shook his head, but the answer didn't really matter.

"She was old enough to know what she was doing, and X still killed her right in front of me. Every time I close my eyes, I picture you laying lifeless on the floor, and I'm trying to bring you back, but I can't." I inhaled a shuddering breath, tears falling in earnest now. "Simon and Dahlia are dead, I can't find anyone else, and... If I can stop that, I will. If I can keep you from leaving this earth, that's exactly what I'm going to do."

He took a giant step toward me, his warm hands on my arms, infusing me with his heat. "Sloane, you just got your memories back. You just learned who and what you are. You have to take the time to process that before you do something rash."

I tried to contemplate just what that would entail, and a hysterical sort of giggle bubbled up my throat. "Honestly, I don't think there is enough time in the world for that mess."

"I told you that I would stick by you until the end."

And I believed him.

"But what good is that promise if you're dead?"

20

No matter what retort he could come up with—no matter what reason—I still had to leave him. So that's exactly what I did. Skirting around Bastian, I marched right for my bedroom door, squeezing the leather handle of the duffle so I didn't start screaming. Because that's precisely what I wanted to do. I wanted to scream and cry and throw a genuinely juvenile hissy fit.

Instead, I swallowed down my urge to break, the bitter pill shattering my heart, and I hadn't even left yet.

I made it to the landing before Bastian's hand was on mine, pulling me to a stop. "Please, Sloane. Just give me some time. Maybe—"

"There isn't time," I hissed. "He already knows where I sleep. And the attacks keep getting worse. If I don't go now, who knows what will happen? Maybe… maybe if I can get away, he'll leave you all alone." I shook my head, tearing my hand from his, the sheer agony of it burning me up inside. "I have to go."

I wanted to kiss him goodbye. I wanted to stall until the end of time, but I didn't.

One foot in front of the other, Sloane. Keep moving.

My mother's words were the last things I wanted in my brain, her memory stinging just a bit more now that I knew the truth, but her advice was still sound.

Keep moving.

And I did. One step after the other, one agonizing pain after the next. On and on until I was almost to the door.

"Where the fuck do you think you're going?" Thomas growled, barring my way, the midnight-blue door a beacon behind him.

"Yeah," Dahlia called from beside me. "I wanna know, too. It's like every couple months, your ass is trying to ditch us. What? We smell or something?"

Axel stepped up behind her. "Right? I swear, girlie, it's a pain in the ass, and I'm not rightly fond of pains in the asses."

Clem and Simon closed in with Harper trailing behind them, giving Thomas backup at the door. "Fun fact," Harper muttered, "most of the time, your emotions break even Emrys' warding. So, if you thought that living with you was sunshine and roses, you'd be mistaken. But I'd rather have you here on our side and deal with the utter hell going on inside your head than have you out there in danger. And just so you know, I only give a shit about a limited number of people in this world. You're one of them, so how about you stop trying to be the martyr, huh?"

My face was leaking, and I tried to wipe away the mess, but it was a losing game.

"What if you all get hurt because of me? I can't—"

"Oh, fuck what you can't," Harper countered, cutting me off. "You're not special. You think we haven't done this a handful of times with Simon? With Thomas? You think Axel's past is giggles and rainbows? Spoiler alert: none of us made Santa's nice list. We all have a past. We all have demons. One of these days, it'll be my turn to worry about my chickens coming home to roost. Would you let me leave? Would you let me go off half-cocked like a fucking moron?"

She didn't even give me time to say anything because she already knew the answer.

"No, you wouldn't. You'd hogtie me or knock me out or something because I was being a stupid bitch. Am I wrong?"

She wasn't, but I didn't want to tell her that. A faint meow brought my gaze to my feet as Isis wound her skeleton self around my ankles, joining the party. Her glowing green eyes bore into me as if to echo Harper's sentiment. Groaning, I dropped my duffle and picked up the bone kitty.

"Fine, but—"

My words died on my tongue as Isis twisted in my hold, a familiar green mist wafting from her open mouth and into my nose. A couple of months ago, she'd done the same thing, only then, we'd been searching for Simon. A familiar premonition slammed into me: one I'd seen in Aunt Julie's memories.

Night had fallen on a giant home set away from the city, clad with a gray stone façade, with elegant architecture and a midnight-blue door. Men surrounded the house, guns in their hands and spells on their belt, their tactical gear loaded down with magical weapons and enough potions to stop a rhinoceros—or an ancient vampire.

They blasted their way through a ward, their numbers too great for the magic to hold, spells firing right along with the guns. They had a singular focus, and it was not one of capture.

This was a kill order.

This was the end of the Night Watch.

I was too late. I'd let them keep me here too long, and now there wasn't time.

"Get away from the door," I croaked, clutching the cat to me as I tried to find my bearings. Part of Julie-slash-Isis' vision still blinded me as to what was around me. "Men are coming to kill us. Right now. I stayed too long. Oh, god, I stayed too long."

Arms surrounded me, guiding me to a chair. *Bastian.* His warm touch lent me comfort, love, even though I probably didn't deserve it.

"Tell me what you saw. Exactly," Thomas ordered. "Was it like last time?"

"And after you do that," Simon piped up, "tell me why my cat is giving you messages like that. Isis is my psychopomp, not yours."

I ignored Simon's plaintive grumbling to answer Thomas. "Yes, but I've seen this before. Julie saw this the day she died. Men are coming. Tactical gear and spells on their belts. Big ones—ones big enough to bust the wards."

"Harper?" Thomas called.

"Already on it. Engaging Ivory Tower protocol." Harper's voice took on a no-nonsense quality to it, as if she'd been preparing for this shit since the day she was born. "Clem, get Emrys, will ya?"

"Sure thing, Sugar."

Blinking furiously, the world slowly came back into focus, the images of the coming attack flashing like an echo over everything. I cuddled the kitty closer, waiting for my sight to fully return.

"Did you see how many? Where they're coming from?" Bastian asked, rubbing his hands over my chilled arms. Yeah, I was wearing a jacket in the middle of Tennessee spring, but I was freezing.

"Twenty or more. All magic-users. Full tactical gear. *Guns.*" A sob crawled up my throat. "I told Emrys this would happen if I stayed here. I warned her."

Part of me wondered if I called Azrael if he would help. The other part reminded me that he didn't seem too concerned about my welfare—especially since someone couldn't kill an already-dead woman.

"Yes, yes," the woman in question replied as she exited the dungeon door with Clem trailing just behind her. "And I told you then just like I'll tell you now, we'll figure it out." She turned to Dahlia and Simon. "Reinforce the Tower protocol. No loopholes or gaps."

Thomas stood from his crouch. "If these guys are anything like the ones who attacked the Dubois nest, they're going to have ward-piercing arrows. We need to be prepared for a breach. Anything that can cause true death needs to be armored up to the gills."

"Head to the armory then. Use the vests with the titanium plates and protective sigils, gorgets, the works. Clem, get anyone anything they need. You have my permission to pull out the big guns."

Clem nodded her red head, her expression practically carved out of marble.

"Axel, follow her. Any weapon you can carry, yeah?" He nodded and took off, following Emrys' command. "You three, follow me. We'll need potions."

She led us to a bookcase—the entire downstairs was filled with them, hidden in nooks and crannies, anywhere and everywhere. It was like living in a library. Similar to the one in her office, she pulled a book's spine, and an audible click sounded. The case swung into the room to reveal a cache of weapons, potions, and you guessed it: more books. The bottles were varying shades of the rainbow, each with an odd glow that spoke of magic.

Emrys grabbed several at once and dropped them into a black canvas bag with a strange Celtic symbol on it. It was close to a traditional tri-knot only modified slightly, and I had no idea what it meant. She slipped the strap of the bag over her head before grabbing several that had leather thongs attached.

She handed Bastian and Thomas five each. "Stunning, paralysis, and torture potions. Don't miss." To me, she gave the rest. "Tie them to your belt. When you need it, snap the thong, twirl it three times, and launch. The first thing the potion hits is affected, so again, don't miss."

"Here," Axel called, his arms loaded down with weapons. Around his neck was what appeared to be a titanium gorget, the metal reaching just under his jaw and down to his collarbone. It made sense. Being a ghoul, Axel could only die if someone took his head.

I hoped Thomas would be donning something similar with a breastplate for good measure.

Someone passed me the whip Dahlia made just for me, and I strapped it to my thigh. Then it was a flurry of donning weapons and tying potions to my belt. I was more prepared for a battle than I'd ever been, and yet, I didn't feel prepared at all.

Because I'd seen this already. According to Julie and Isis, they were going to breech the wards—they were going to kill us. They were going to take everything away from me.

"Bastian," Harper called from the landing. "Get up here."

Without a word, he grabbed my hand, latching onto it before dragging me behind him. I'd never felt so frightened and so safe at the same time. Or so glad that his brain was following right along with mine. If we had to be in this fight, if we couldn't escape it, I wanted him right next to me at all times.

Just the thought of being separated practically gave me hives.

The pair of us hoofed it up the stairs, and Bastian unerringly led us to Harper's domain. I'd never actually been inside Harper's rooms before then, so I goggled at the wall of screens that displayed every inch of the Night Watch's compound save for the bedrooms and bathrooms. There were no windows in the space, just wall-to-wall screens, a desk filled with tall tumblers and bendy straws, and a cot with a small blanket and a lone pitiful pillow.

Compared to my room, this was practically "a cupboard under the stairs" situation.

"Quit it," Harper barked, yanking my gaze to hers. "I have a huge room next door, but this is where I work. And that's not why I called you up here. Look." She pointed to one of the middle screens.

On it was a handful of men in dark tactical gear—vests, helmets, body armor, the whole nine yards. Potion bottles swung from their belts as they advanced toward the front door. But instead of focusing on the giant guns in their hands or the caustic liquid in those vials, I lasered in on a vaguely familiar face.

"You know him?" Harper asked, and I nodded.

"I don't know from where, but he looks familiar." I glanced up at Bastian, ready to ask him if he recognized the man, but I stopped myself. Bastian's expression was pure, unadulterated rage, and his jaw seemed to be about a millimeter away from snapping in two.

"Jarek," he growled, his bottle-green gaze glowing brighter and brighter as the seconds ticked past.

That name sounded familiar, too, and I sifted through the last few days of shenanigans to place it. "The manager of the club? The one you fired?"

The one who tried to zap me to death for biting Bastian's neck? Yeah, I sounded incredulous, but come the fuck on. This guy didn't have the stones to fight his way out of a wet paper bag, let alone attack the whole of us together.

Man, I should have killed that guy when I had the chance.

21

"What I want to know is how he found us in the first fucking place," Bastian growled. "I thought this house wasn't even on a map."

Harper narrowed her eyes at the screen. "It isn't, and Emrys made it so even satellites can't see the house or the property, and I seriously doubt anyone broke her wards unless..." She trailed off, lost in thought. She shook her head, blinking rapidly. "Please tell me someone was smart enough to sweep Celeste before ya'll brought her here?"

Harper wasn't asking me since I'd been a crispy critter when I got back, but Bastian stared at her blankly as if his entire brain had been switched off. A sinking feeling settled in my gut. I hadn't taken a shine to Celeste—mostly because she'd left me to fend for myself rather than offer me a single iota of help—but I'd sort of figured she was on my side. Her daughter had been taken away from her just like my family had from me.

But what if she didn't blame X like I did?

What if she blamed Azrael?

Oh, shit.

Bastian took off, racing out of the room and down the stairs, with me hot on his heels. But while he stopped at Emrys, I continued on to the dungeon. Shouts sounded behind me, but I kept moving. If Celeste was the catalyst, I needed to snuff her ass out post-haste.

How stupid were we? How easily had I been fooled by a sob story and a tearful tribute to a dead daughter? But had I? In the short time I'd been in her presence, Celeste had rubbed me the wrong way.

What if it had all been bullshit? What if my gut had been right about her?

The runes embedded in the bars and walls burned my flesh as the magic rose high on the air, just before the concussion of a cell door blowing off its hinges nearly knocked me off my feet. As the dust cleared, Celeste sauntered from her cell, a tranquil quality to her face as a swath of black magic billowed over her fingertips. She placed an open palm right on one of the still-burning runes, her flesh sizzling as she smiled. The runes flickered, her hand glowing like they once had.

I didn't understand until the runes dimmed, and her hand grew brighter. She was stealing the magic from the walls. *That can't be good, right?*

A thousand questions flitted through my mind, but the most prominent of them fell from my lips. "Why?"

Silly me, I'd have thought a woman who supposedly devoted her life to keeping X away would give a shit if I lived or died. Or maybe that was precisely it.

I was dead, but I was here.

And her daughter wasn't.

"Why wouldn't I?" Celeste asked, her calm smile such an odd dichotomy from the teary act she'd put on earlier. "I pleaded with Azrael to bring Aurora back when she died, but he refused. I begged him to kill me after you fell, but he wouldn't. But he brought you back, didn't he? He just snapped his fingers and gave you a piece of himself like it was nothing. Got you all cleaned up and handed you back to me with a pat on my head and a 'don't fuck it up this time' pep talk."

I couldn't help it; I pressed my eyes closed at the sheer stupidity of it all. It was as if Azrael had no idea what grief could do to a person, as if he had no clue what a woman with nothing to lose could do.

Moron.

I wanted to haul his ass down here and give him a piece of my mind. "I'm so sorry, Celeste. I wish…" I didn't know what I wished, but her situation was total bullshit. "I don't know how to fix this for you."

But I also didn't know what I was supposed to do. This house was about to be attacked—my friends killed—and she'd been the one that brought them here. Our own personal Trojan horse. And if I were to venture a guess, she was the most formidable of the lot. Giving her an ounce of leeway was going to tip the scales in her favor.

"Oh, but I do. I know exactly how you can fix this for me." The last of the runes winked out, the heat on the air dying like a doused fire. The house itself seemed to tremble in response, the pungent scent of burning metal and flesh permeating the small space.

"You can give that little nugget of Azrael's magic to me, or I can rip it from you. Really, it's up to you. How did you phrase it? Oh, that's right: 'I really don't give a fuck which.'"

A strange crackling sensation raced across my skin as I felt a spell behind me let loose. Smartly, I ducked, allowing whoever was at my back to have an open shot at the crazy witch. The magic hit Celeste but seemed to do nothing more than fizzle out before melting into her flesh.

In no way was that a good thing. In fact, I was pretty stumped on how I was supposed to kill someone that powerful without magic.

"Oh, how sweet. You've come to protect your stray," she taunted, a feigned pout on her face.

Emrys got between Celeste and me, her hand fishing in her satchel as magic bloomed over her fingers. "And you've signed your own death warrant." To me, she muttered, "Get back upstairs. I'll hold her off."

Yeah, no. There was no way I was leaving Emrys to deal with this bitch by herself. Celeste wanted something from me, and I had no doubt in my mind that she'd go through Emrys to get it if she had to.

"Tell me," I called, ignoring Emrys completely and positioning myself in front of her. "Does my father know what you're up to?"

Celeste snorted, rolling her eyes. "I doubt it. Azrael has always had trouble getting into my mind." She tapped her temple, taking a step forward. "You know that's how he picks his lovers, right? When he finds a woman he can't read, he goes gaga over her. Wining and dining. Gifts. The works. I really can't blame the man. I mean, if I heard a world's worth of thoughts, I'd shoot myself in the face. So, it's not a surprise that every time he finds a woman who can't mentally tell him just how mediocre he is by accident, he's all over that. Problem is, he keeps knocking them up and then ditching them for the next bitch he can't read." She tsked, shaking her head. "Rude."

Ouch. My father sounded like a fuck boy.

"So that's a no, then. Cool. Umm." At a loss for words, I called to Azrael in my mind. If he were so in tune with his children as she claimed, maybe he'd hear me.

Did you hear that, Azrael? Your ex-side-bitch is the bad guy. Wanna help my friends and me not die?

I didn't have high hopes that he'd come running.

"Of course, if you just give me what I want, I'd call the whole thing off. Me and my friends would pack up and head home." Celeste took another step toward us, swirls of black flitting over her fingers like live snakes. "And if you don't, I'll make sure every single one of you die screaming just like Booth did." She hummed happily, as if she relished the memory of Booth's torturous death. "He really took a long time to die."

Emrys latched onto my arm. "It's time to go, Sloane."

I agreed with my boss, but it was a question of getting out of here alive. I had a feeling anything we threw at her would just slide right off or get absorbed, or whatever the hell she was doing. If we ran, she'd just zap us, and I had no desire to die screaming. It was one thing to yell at Azrael about keeping me alive, but it was quite another to just hand myself over to a woman working with the man who killed my parents.

I barely nodded my head as I took a step backward. I needed a distraction that could get us the hell out of this dungeon. And again, how stupid was I?

Yeah, Sloane, let's go into a room with only one exit with the bitch who brought these assholes to our door. Sounds like a real good idea. Stellar thinking.

"Funny, I wouldn't think you'd work with the man who murdered your daughter. Tell me—what would Aurora think of you blithely partnering with her killer?"

The taunt had the exact effect, and Celeste wildly blasted off a spell in retaliation. In the commotion, I whispered the incantation to activate the whip, shooting it out as the ribbon of its power unfurled and slicing a cell door off its hinges.

Magic won't work on her? Fine. Let's see how she handles a cell door to the face.

Before she could release another shot, I had that door in my hands and launched it at her, watching with supreme satisfaction as she went down.

"Okay, now we can go," I announced, stowing the whip as Emrys stared at me as if I'd grown another head. "What? I wasn't going to leave you behind. Now let's bounce before—"

An enraged scream cut off my words, and I latched onto Emrys' hand, dragging her behind me as I raced for the dungeon's exit.

I was sort of hoping a cell door to the nugget would have at least bought us five minutes, but it didn't exactly surprise me that I wasn't so lucky. Or that Celeste had decided to toss that fucker right back at us. I had a feeling that damn door was going to hurt me a hell of a lot more than it had hurt her.

Before I could wrench Emrys up the last of the stairs, a hand clutched onto my forearm, yanking me up and through the door. Bottle-green eyes met mine before they drifted past me, giving Emrys a nod of his head.

A large push shoved my back at the same time, and Emrys slipped from my grip. I tried to tug my arm free from Bastian, but his hold was practically an iron manacle. Turning half my body back, I watched as the cell door froze midair, while Emrys gave me a sardonic raised eyebrow. With her newly freed hand, she twisted her wrist, and the dungeon door slammed closed, cutting her and Celeste off from the rest of us.

"Emrys," I screeched, trying to get back to the dungeon, but Bastian's iron grasp dragged me away and shoved me to the ground as a spell whizzed by my head.

It was then that I realized, that while Emrys and I were in the dungeon, a whole other battle had been going on in the living room. Taking shelter behind a tufted leather couch, Bastian and I stared at each other for one long second.

The sound of his voice echoed through my head, the shock of it hitting me with the force of a wrecking ball.

Gods, I love this woman. How did I get so fucking lucky?

It sounded so clear, it was as if he'd said it out loud. Honestly, if I hadn't been watching his face, I would have believed he had.

"I'm the lucky one," I said, pressing a hasty kiss to his surprised lips. "Now, let's stop these bastards before Celeste finds out how to break out of that dungeon."

The surprise morphed into understanding in a split second, and a small smile pulled at his mouth as Bastian gave me a nod. Multicolored magic swirled over his hands and up his arms as his smile grew practically malicious. Without another word, he stood, firing off a ball of electricity with one hand as a maelstrom whipped through the house with the other.

Yep, I was definitely the lucky one.

I just had to stay lucky.

22

iving head-first into the fight, I unfurled the whip at my side, letting it loose on the first intruder with gusto. I was under no illusion that these assholes had come here for anything other than to kill us. For some reason, it didn't matter to me whether or not someone had tricked them into coming. These men were nothing like the ghouls who'd attacked us a couple of months ago.

These men weren't puppets. They hadn't been fooled into coming here.

So I felt exactly zero remorse as the whip sliced through a mage's arm like butter, the crackle of electricity on his no-longer-attached hand dying. He howled in agony for about three more seconds before I struck the whip out again, this time aiming for his neck.

My aim was true enough, and the poor bastard was dead before his head hit the polished wood floor.

The ground beneath our feet began to shake, and books rattled off their assigned shelves as the floor at our feet pitched and swayed. Wood snapped as the flooring buckled and jagged bits rose in the air, hovering for just a moment. And then I saw the mage holding them there, his nose bloody as if the strain was far too much for him. He met my gaze before offering me a sneering smile. He began to squeeze his hand closed but didn't quite manage it. All of a sudden, his eyes rolled up in his head, and his jaw twisted to the left, the sickening crack of his neck breaking reaching me all the way over here. The shards of flooring fell back to the ground like toothpicks.

I wanted to search for who'd saved my ass, but I ended up being too busy getting shot at and spelled that it took a minute. A bolt of electricity slammed me into a wall, white-hot agony racing over my flesh as another jolt hit. Growling through the pain, I attempted to peel myself from the shattered bookshelf jabbing me in the back as I scanned the room to locate where the stupid magic was coming from. Using the wood as a springboard, I sailed toward my assailant. In the commotion, I'd dropped my whip, but that didn't matter.

After all, I was feeling a bit peckish.

My fangs had a hell of a time sinking into his neck, though —what with all the body armor and all—so I settled on ripping his head off his shoulders instead. A knife flashed in my periphery, and I dropped the head in my hands, ducking at the same time. Said dagger caught the crest of my cheek, opening the skin there before I could retaliate. A wide-eyed sorcerer held the blade in a shaking hand as he eyed my face like he wished he could take it back. I suppose I should've felt a sliver of empathy for the guy, but I didn't. All I had coursing through my veins was wrath and a fair bit of malice.

Empathy wasn't on my radar, and it sure as shit wasn't on my to-do list.

My smile was wide as I gave the feeble intruder a push-kick to his knee, snapping it backward as he let out an unholy howl of pain. Catching his blade before it could hit the ground, I whirled, taking his head.

More and more mages trickled in, seeming to come from everywhere, and I took stock. Bastian was blasting a few mages off their feet in between swings of his sword—where he'd gotten it, I had no idea. Simon and Dahlia were on the stairs, holding steady on the first landing before the staircase, leading to the second floor. Black magic swarmed Simon as Isis yowled her displeasure from the upper landing. The man who'd just gotten his head lopped off started to rise, a shroud of dark magic seeming to pull him up by puppet strings. Before I could really comprehend what was going on, the dead man yanked a gun from his belt and began firing at his comrades, his aim top-notch for someone no longer breathing.

Dahlia was right beside Simon, tossing potion vials with one hand as she rotated the other in a magical flourish. Another intruder's neck snapped, and Simon continued his process of raising the freshly dead.

On the lower level, Clem was holding a shotgun, bracing it against her shoulder as she shot a guy in the knee. Not bothering with the body armor, she pumped the shotgun and fired another shot, this time hitting him right in the face. Bloody blowback sprayed her baby-pink 50s-style housedress, and at the sight of the blood, she began cursing a blue streak as she unnecessarily shot the dead guy again.

"You lousy, no-good motherfucker. This dress is vintage!" She shot him again for good measure before moving on to the next guy.

I couldn't see Axel, but I could hear him. Axel's Southern drawl echoed off of the hallways as he taunted an intruder with some insult about farmers and sheep. Thomas was missing as well, but the soundtrack of rapidly dying screams clued me in to his general vicinity.

Everything seemed well and truly handled until the dungeon door blew off its hinges, Celeste and Emrys sailing through it as they continued battling each other. Emrys appeared just as formidable as she always did while Celeste was bloody, her face a half-mask of burned flesh while one arm hung at her side listlessly.

That wasn't to say that she wasn't holding her own.

If anything, she was doing far too well for someone going against Emrys. Large furniture pieces shook before rising in the air and zooming toward Emrys like missiles. Before they could make contact, Emrys waved her hand and stomped a foot. The white glow of spent magic flashed across the hardwood as her foot made contact, the chairs and tables turning to ash. Emrys waved her hand again as if she was gathering the ash, and the burned shards of what used to be the living room furniture rallied together to bombard Celeste.

The ashes hit her like a fist, propelling her through the dining room wall.

But even as I took a deep breath, I knew it wasn't over. I was proved right not a moment later when the remainder of the dining room wall exploded, metal and wood flying into the living room like shrapnel. The explosion took everyone's focus for a split second, and that's when our upper hand turned.

Simon and Dahlia ducked, trying to avoid getting hit by the blast. But as they took their eyes off their opponent, he sliced his hand through the air as if it was a blade. Ice flowed in my veins as I watched twin red smiles bloom on both of their necks, blood welling from their matching wounds.

Dahlia's eyes widened as she clutched at her throat, trying to hold in the blood. Tears welled and raced down her cheeks in those scant moments before her bronze skin paled, and her knees gave out as the life drained out of her.

Simon clutched at his own throat for a single moment

before he reached for his friend, the magic in his fingers snaking through the air toward her. Neither his magic nor his hands reached their target. In the next instant, he, too, fell, following her down the stairs, the pair of them landing side by side, blood pooling in a matching halo around their heads.

An echo of a memory flashed over their still forms. The picture of my father and the image of my greatest fear seemed to merge, the truth of what I saw and what came to be hitting me all at once.

A scream erupted from my throat as I ran for them—to do exactly what, I didn't know—when something cut across my back. White-hot agony raced over my flesh, knocking me to my knees. But at that moment, I didn't care about who was trying to kill me.

All I cared about was my friends.

All I cared about was the slight possibility that I might be able to do something—anything—to fix it.

Another lash raked across my back, and I turned, ready to fight off whoever was keeping me from them. Instead, I ran right into a knife in my gut. I stared at the blade in shock before meeting the gaze of the man who put it there.

"Remember me?" Jarek's smile was wide as he twisted the blade and yanked it up. Pain like I'd never felt bloomed over me, stealing every thought, every breath. I knew without looking that the damage to my middle was enough to kill me if I weren't already dead.

My knees buckled, and the knife slid out as I fell from his grip. Jarek leaned down, putting his face right in front of mine. "You don't look so tough now, do you? Tell me—when you crushed my wrists, did you think I wasn't going to come for you? Did you think I'd just let you get away with it?"

I wanted to tell him to fuck off, but a cough stole my breath. Blood pooled in my mouth, practically drowning me.

"That's okay. You don't have to answer," he said, his snide voice making me want to tear into him, made me want to make it so he never talked again.

A loud boom sounded, and he looked away for a split second. Taking the scant opportunity, I struck, my fangs ripping into his throat faster than he could fight me off. The flavor of Jarek's blood was akin to garbage and bad pennies, but it helped stave off unconsciousness. However, the images that accompanied his death would give me nightmares until the end of time. I would have to tell Bastian what kind of awful shit was going on in his back room.

But that was for later.

Shoving Jarek's rapidly desiccating body off me, I staggered toward Simon and Dahlia. Then a wrenching scream of the worst torment echoed through the room. Without turning, I knew the sound came from Bastian's throat, and the agony in it made me want to break.

But I did turn, searching for the man I loved in the middle of this war. Bastian's sword sliced through the mages like a hot knife through butter. He mowed them down in earnest as he made his way across the room. Explosions rocked the very foundations of the house, but none of that mattered to him. He was a one-man wrecking ball headed straight for his brother.

But his focus cost him.

It cost us both.

I saw the blade headed right for him before he did. It was small, almost dainty. The weapon sailed end over end as it rocketed toward the tender space between the armored plates at his side.

I never knew I could fear something so small. Never realized that such a tiny object could bring about my undoing.

The agony from my wounds left me as I raced for him, ready to take his place if I could. But the world seemed to slow, my feet molasses as they pounded closer but not close enough. The blade reached him before I did, hitting its intended target so much faster than I could.

Bastian met my gaze as he fell, those beautiful bottle-green eyes boring into me as blood bubbled from his mouth. Shock lit his face for a single second before sliding off, his expression falling away as the life slowly left him.

I reached him before he hit the ground, cradling him just like my mother embraced me right before X slit her throat—hugging him to me and praying as I put pressure on the wound.

All the noise faded away as I listened to his heart, the faint fluttering beats petering out as the breaths sawed from his lungs.

"No, please. Please. I'll give you anything. Please," I sobbed. "I love you. *Please." Please don't leave me. Not when I've just found you.* My hands fluttered over his wound, over his chest. Nothing I was going to do would help him.

Bastian gasped, a deep pull of breath that sounded like pure torture, his lips mouthing, "I love you," before they stilled.

Then his chest followed suit.

And his heart stopped beating.

And then whatever soul I had left, left this earth with him.

23

There was a type of pain that couldn't be contained in a single body. No matter how powerful, no matter how old, losing a love like Bastian would destroy even the strongest of souls.

The scream that broke from my throat wasn't a sound that could be quantified or measured. It was torment and regret and misery. It was my soul shattering into a million pieces. Hot tears fled my eyes as I let my grief loose.

Maybe if I screamed loud enough, long enough, someone—anyone—would help me.

But there was no one to pray to and no bargain I could strike. If my father hadn't come by now, he wouldn't be answering my call. He wouldn't be coming for me or the man I loved.

I tried to clutch him closer, but Bastian's weight was ripped from my lap. My eyes popped wide, ready to battle anyone stupid enough to take him away from me, but no one was there.

And I didn't mean there wasn't someone who took his

body. I meant no one as in, not a single soul was in the great room.

No Emrys or Thomas or Axel.

No Clem firing her shotgun.

No Bastian with blood on his lips, his beautiful eyes seeing nothing. No Simon or Dahlia, still as death.

The furniture that I knew for a fact had been blown to smithereens a few moments ago stood pristine in their rightful spots. The bookshelves were filled, each book untouched as if the battle had never taken place. But everything had taken on a shade of gray, as if someone had bled the color from the room while they were emptying it of people. The wall of windows at the back of the house showed a dark world where the moon didn't shine, and the stars had fled.

White motes fell from the ceiling, falling at an unhurried pace as if gravity had no hold on them.

Is it snowing inside?

I held out a hand to catch a snowflake just as I had as a child, the cold flake melting in my palm almost instantly.

This wasn't right. Where was everyone? If I was alive, shouldn't I be in the middle of a war right now? And if I was dead (like, *really* dead), where was Bastian? Where were Simon and Dahlia? If I was dead, shouldn't I be with him? And if I wasn't with them, where in the hell was I?

You know where you are. You've been here before, haven't you?

Images flashed in my brain of a grayed-out version of my living room, snow falling all around me as I sat on my couch. Azrael had come for me there, his crisp dark suit the same as when I'd seen him in the field. He held out a hand and told me to come with him—that he would make it better. That he would make it all go away.

The In-Between.

I was in the In-Between. Not heaven or hell—*if those places even existed*—but a place between worlds, between this life and the next one. Azrael had called it a holding area of sorts, a place where souls searched for the door to leave. This was where souls stayed until they moved on.

He'd told me so much while I'd held his hand, but most of it faded away as if the memory was playing keep-away with me. He'd been kind, so kind as he guided me to a blue door with an evil eye etched into the wood.

The memory faded as the living room flashed into color for a millisecond, sounds of the battle still going strong, a quick cacophony in the silence before snuffing out. The room went gray again, the silence a weighty buzzing around me.

I had to find Bastian and Simon and Dahlia. They were here. *They had to be.*

Because I wouldn't know what to do with myself if they weren't.

Pulling myself to my feet, I searched the great room like a woman playing a very macabre game of Hide-and-Seek. I looked behind furniture and hidden bookcases, but there was nothing but books and weapons to be had.

"Hello? Is anybody here?" I screamed, but no one answered me, the silence suffocating as it bore down on me.

Grief and panic warred in my gut, and I nearly sat down on the couch to breathe through the misery of it. Bastian was just here. Where was he? I had him in my arms.

One foot in front of the other, Sloane. Keep moving.

My mother's mantra stung more here than it ever had before. Because how was I supposed to put one foot in front of the other now? While I was in this gray place?

How was I supposed to breathe?

How was I supposed to find him?

Keep moving. My mother's voice grew insistent, as if she were whispering right in my ear. I spun, but no one was there.

Then her voice called louder, more demanding. *Would he stop looking for you? Would he give a half-ass attempt at searching one room and give up? No. So why are you?*

She was right. Even if my own brain were supplying this pep-talk and not my mother, I couldn't give up now. I had the whole house, hell, the entire world to check. I had nothing but time, and I'd use every second to find him if that's what it took.

Racing to the dining room, I found a small woman with very familiar braids, sitting in her favorite spot at the opulent table. Her face was buried in her hands as she wept, grief spilling out of her.

"Dahlia?" I called. A small measure of relief threaded through me, blooming bright when her head whipped up at the sound of my voice.

"Sloane?" she said, scrambling from her seat to wrap me in a hug. "Gods, I couldn't find anyone. I thought… I don't know what I thought. How are you here? Are you dead, too?"

That was a question I didn't know the answer to—not really. "I don't know. Bas-Bastian—" I couldn't even say it, so I shook my head.

"Oh, no. Poor Simon. I can't imagine how much trouble he's going to get himself into to bring him back."

My heart broke all over again, and I had no idea how I would tell her that Simon was gone, too.

"Dahlia," I began, but she shook her head, stopping me.

"No, he's not." She backed up, running into the table before she stopped. "He's fine. Don't you tell me he's not."

The expression on her face mirrored mine, the ravaged grief of a woman losing her… Oh, no. I'd had no idea. Dahlia *loved* Simon—loved him more than anything. And that realization made what I had to do so much worse.

Swallowing hard, her grief made it so I could barely speak. "He died right beside you. You went together."

She knocked her braids off her shoulder, gritting her teeth against the pain as an expression that could only be described as livid settled on her face. "Well, then where the hell is he?"

I couldn't say why that one sentence made me laugh, but it did —the mirth buoying me out of the deepest grief waters. "I don't know, but I found you. Maybe we can find them. Maybe…" A plan started to form in my mind. "Maybe we can get out of here."

I was the daughter of Death, right? And I'd gotten myself here somehow, hadn't I? Then there had to be a way out.

Dahlia set her jaw and gave me a nod. "Let's go then."

For some reason, I grabbed her hand, not willing to let her go in this weird gray place. If she hadn't heard me screaming at the top of my lungs in the next room, I wasn't willing to chance letting her go.

We set off through the kitchen, searching for our men, the feeling that finding them would be the absolute least of our problems settling in my gut.

Unexpectedly, the kitchen was only mostly empty. A man stood at the sink, silently staring out the blackened window at the nothing beyond.

"Hey," I called, wanting him to turn while I had the pristine white island between us.

Startled, he glanced up, and it was someone I didn't recognize. *Or maybe I did.* Hadn't I taken his head? The man's eyes widened as he advanced, vaulting over the island like a pro. His hands reached for me as if he'd enjoy wrapping those fingers around my throat and squeezing whatever breath I had left out of me.

I let Dahlia go, and on instinct, I reached right back for the man. As soon as my fingers made contact with his skin, he began screaming as if he was burning. Light billowed out of his open mouth and eyes as his skin charred almost instantly. In less than a blink, the man had burned up in my hands like dry kindling, images of his stained soul hitting me all at once. Death. So much death at his hands. He'd lived too long, caring nothing of the people around him as he exacted petty acts of revenge and thoughtless transgressions.

Black grains of ash fluttered from my fingertips to the floor, and all I could think was, *good riddance.*

"Woman, what the fuck?" Dahlia barked. "You grabbed my hand like nothing when you knew you could do that?"

I shook my head. "I didn't know. I've never done that before. But it was similar to when I drank them down topside." *That was precisely it.* Only here, I didn't even need to read their blood to know and to reap horrible souls. "I don't think I can do that to good people. That's why I didn't hurt you."

Dahlia's skepticism was plain as day, but she put her hand in mine.

I repeated Azrael's words to her, hoping they gave her a small measure of comfort in this gray place. "I'm going to fix it."

I just hoped I was telling her the truth.

Abandoning the kitchen, we searched the mudroom and the garage but found no one. Exploring further, we hiked up the stairs, calling their names as we went. Maybe if they heard us, they'd come running.

The world flashed into color again as men I didn't know fought at the top landing, one smashing the other through the solid wood railing before they were gone again, the world losing its color.

Something told me we were running out of time.

"Why were you at the table?" I asked, trying to think of

something—anything that would lead us to them. "Is that where you woke up or…"

"Yeah." Dahlia nodded, squeezing my hand at the memory. "I knew I was dying, felt myself go, and then I woke up in my favorite chair."

I had to wonder if where she woke up was special—if it meant something to her. And if that's where she woke up, then maybe Bastian or Simon might be where they were the happiest.

"Tell me—where is Simon's favorite place?"

Dahlia shook her head. "I don't know. I would say his room, but that was only because he couldn't go anywhere else for so long. Now that he's free, I don't know where that is anymore."

I shrugged, not able to think of a better place to look. "Can't hurt to check, right?"

I didn't know Bastian well enough to assume his favorite place, but I had a few ideas—that was if his preferred spot was in the house. If it happened to be outside, or anywhere else in the world for that matter, I was screwed. And a part of me didn't want to find him first.

If I found him before Simon, something told me it would be very, very bad.

"Let's just check everywhere, yeah?" I muttered, dragging her behind me as I headed for Simon's bedroom.

The door with its jaunty "No Girls Allowed" sign was ajar, and I braced myself for what I might find as I pushed it open. A distressed Simon paced back and forth in front of his beat-up leather couch. He had his beanie in one hand as he ran the other through his mop of black hair.

"Where is she? She should be here," he muttered, shaking his head, still not seeing us. "She was right beside me. She's supposed to be here."

"Simon?" Dahlia called, and the look on Simon's face when he glanced up was a thing of beauty.

He raced for her, and she let go of my hand, allowing herself to be wrapped up in his arms as he peppered her face with kisses. "Oh, my beautiful flower. Where have you been?"

He didn't give her time to answer, her shock at his reaction plain as day. No, Simon just planted a kiss on her lips as if he'd been wanting to do that for ages, sifting his fingers into her braids as if he'd been dying to touch them and hadn't let himself.

I glanced away, the joy in them finding each other almost too much for my battered heart. I turned my back, giving them the privacy they needed.

"I thought I was in Hell," he whispered. "I thought I was back to being remanded to this house forever. Only this time, it was worse because you weren't here."

Was that how I'd view the world if I couldn't find Bastian? Probably.

"Okay, guys, I'm glad you found each other and all, but I need to find…" I couldn't say his name, not out loud, anyway. "I need to find him."

Simon's room flashed in color. Far-away sounds of fighting echoed through the room before silence and gray came back.

No time. We had no time.

"What the hell was that? Where are we?" Simon asked, clutching Dahlia to him as if he'd never let her go.

"The In-Between. Now hold my hand while I look for your brother."

Simon didn't say anything else, he simply grabbed onto my hand as I led us in an odd little march to Bastian's room. We had only spent a few nights—or days, rather—there together, but maybe he would be there. Maybe I'd get lucky.

I opened his door to reveal a messy bed. A messy, empty bed.

The bitter disappointment was hard to swallow, but I refused to stop searching. I let Simon's hand go as I raced for the bathroom, hoping for some nugget of good fortune to smile down on me.

Sitting in the empty tub fully clothed, Bastian slowly looked at me, confusion on his face. "Sloane?"

Relief flooded my limbs, and I dropped to my knees beside

the tub. I reached for him, needing to make sure he was real and not just a fever dream. Our lips collided, and I nearly broke apart, I was so happy.

I found him. I found him.

Bastian broke our kiss. "Wait. Why are you here? I thought I was dead. I thought…"

"You are. I came for you. I don't know how I got here or how to get back, but I couldn't—" I shook my head, unable to describe the sheer agony of losing him. "I found Simon and Dahlia, too. I'm going to get us out of here. I don't know how yet, but I'm going to fix it, okay?"

Bastian brushed my hair off my face, cupping my cheeks. "I know you can, love."

The world flickered into color again, and Bastian's bottle-green eyes began to glow before fading once more. The color stayed longer each time, and I couldn't help but think that was a bad thing.

"We have to go." I got to my feet, and Bastian followed me, clasping my hand in his.

When we got back to the room, Simon and Dahlia were hugging each other, seeming lost.

"Guys?" I muttered, but they stared right through me until I put my hand on their entwined arms. Both of them blinked at me in surprise.

"Oh, thank fuck," Simon muttered. "You left, and we couldn't see you anymore."

The whole of the house seemed to pitch under our feet, and the world flashed into color, the sound seeming to turn all the way up. But it didn't flicker back. Something told me we weren't back. Something told me I needed to move, and now. "Yeah, we need to get the fuck out of here while we still can."

Gripping Bastian's hand, I pulled them from the room, racing back to where I came from. People milled about, no longer fighting but not seeing us, either. Harper sat at the top of the landing, her head in her hands. She was sobbing, and the people around her had their heads bowed, giving her a wide berth. Everyone except Axel, who sat right next to her but not touching—like he wanted to but knew it would cause problems.

Our little group skirted around them, and Harper's head popped up, unerringly finding me.

"Please come back," she pleaded, staring right at me. How she saw me, I had no idea. I wasn't even sure she could see me. It was totally possible she could just feel me.

But with no time, I only nodded, dragging my friends down the stairs with me. At the bottom of the steps, Clem had Simon's head pillowed in her lap, black tears falling from her cheeks as she sifted a hand through his hair. With the other, she clutched Simon and Dahlia's joined hands.

On instinct, I grabbed Dahlia and Simon, guiding them back to their bodies. Fear clouded Dahlia's face, but I gave her an encouraging smile. "It's time to go back now."

Simon only held onto her hand, tugging her into position. "I'll see you on the other side, love. Don't worry."

Reluctantly, she laid down over her body, falling into it. The next second, the gash in her throat closed, and she sat up with a gasp. Simon quickly followed her, falling into his own body and rising a second later.

Clem startled before giving relieved hugs to them both, as Axel and Harper raced down the stairs.

"It's your turn," I murmured, pulling Bastian by the hand to his body. But unlike his brother, he wasn't so easily convinced.

"How are you getting back? What if—"

I raised up on my tiptoes and kissed him. "I think I'll be fine. It's time for you to go."

He dropped another kiss to my lips, reluctantly letting me

go before doing as I asked. He went back to his body, falling into it just as everyone else had, but he didn't rise right away. My heart fell as a blistering doubt slammed into me.

Please, please, please. Please don't let him leave. Please don't take him from me. I'll do anything. Please…

Several long seconds passed, the wait to see his chest moving seeming to take eons. And then Bastian, too, gasped awake. His head whipped this way and that, searching for me as his gaze slid right through me.

"Where is she?" he shouted, but no one answered him.

Emrys knelt at his side. "Where is who?"

"Sloane. She was right there. She brought us back."

Emrys nodded, rising to her feet, drawing the sword from the scabbard at her back. "She'll come when she finds the door."

Emrys moved to a tableau I'd failed to notice. Ingrid and Thomas held a squirming Celeste as the bound woman screeched and thrashed. Ingrid had a hold of Celeste's dark hair, keeping her head still so she could do nothing but stare at Emrys.

When the hell had Ingrid gotten here?

I glanced around, noticing the men and women that milled about weren't mages. They were vampires. Had Thomas called in a favor?

"Do ya have anything to say for yourself?" Emrys asked Celeste, her grip tightening on the hilt of the sword in her hand.

Celeste sneered before trying to spit at Emrys in lieu of answering. Unfortunately for her, Ingrid shook her by the hair, hard, making the spittle land on her chin instead.

"So be it, then." With a flick of her hand, Emrys took Celeste's head, the sword moving so fast I wouldn't have believed it had if Celeste's head weren't dangling from Ingrid's fingers.

Celeste's soul stood where her body had been before it fell to the side, confusion on her vile face as the world fell away, turning gray once more. Everyone around us had disappeared as we landed solidly in the In-Between. Cracking my knuckles, I very nearly smiled, ready to reap this woman so there was no chance of anyone at any time bringing her back. But before I could reach her, Azrael appeared right in front of me.

His back to me and wings spread wide, the Angel of Death was out in full force.

"Azrael," Celeste exclaimed, reaching for him. "Help me. These awful people—"

He took a step back to avoid her hands, his wings retracting to reveal the smooth back of his suit jacket. "Save your pleading for someone who doesn't know the truth, Celeste. Tell me—how does it feel to betray your own daughter?"

"How does it feel to betray your son?" she shot back. "I'm not the only one you left behind, Az."

My father shook his head. "I didn't leave you behind, Celeste. We ended our relationship after you insisted on my son taking my job so I could play house with you. I told you from the beginning, I couldn't do that."

"Essex Drake is twice the man you are," she spat, taunting the man as if she wasn't boarding on a one-way trip to Hell.

Azrael chuckled mirthlessly. "Essex is a sociopath who murders innocents for fun. Just like he murdered our daughter. Just like he murdered her parents," he hissed, tossing a thumb at me. "He sent you on a fool's errand to kill a woman that cannot be killed. You chose the wrong side."

Without another word, he grabbed her by the upper arm. Almost instantly, Celeste's skin blackened like dying embers as light poured from her screaming mouth. I had to admit, her shrieks of pain were nearly as satisfying as if I'd have done it myself.

Azrael's wings reappeared, and he beat them once, a smile on his face as she broke apart. When she was nothing but embers floating in the air, he turned to me.

"You have stayed in my domain long enough. It's time for you to go," he said, gesturing to a door that seemed to appear out of nowhere, with an evil eye etched into it.

"But—"

He held up a hand, shushing me. "I know you have questions, and I'll answer them later. For now, you have to go."

For once in my life, I didn't argue. Why would I? Bastian was on the other side of that door.

As fast as I could, I reached for the knob.

"Sloane?" he called, and I turned back to him. "When you meet your sister, be sure to tell her X's name, will you? Tell her that I'm sorry I didn't give it to her sooner."

Understanding dawned. "You didn't want to kill him."

Azrael met my gaze, his filled with shame. "I should have, but I couldn't. So many people have lost their lives because I couldn't."

I nodded, trying to tamp down the rage boiling in my gut. Betrayal surged in my veins before reason took hold. Could I even fathom taking my child's life? Could I fathom letting that child take others from me? But those were answers I wouldn't be getting—at least not right now.

"Just for grins, what's my sister's name?"

Azrael swallowed, bowing his head in shame. "Darby. Her name is Darby Adler."

Walking through a mystical door from another realm to pop up in the middle of the living room kind of had a way of shocking some people. Which was how I ended up with Emrys' blade at my throat and almost attacked by a tiny blonde vampire. Ingrid realized who I was far faster than Emrys did, skidding to a stop right before she tackled me.

I met my boss' glowing red gaze with a look of irritation, plucking her blade from the side of my throat. "Is that how you say welcome back? Because we need to work on your hospitality skills a bit."

"Jesus, Mary, and Joseph, Sloane," she said before wrapping me up in a hug. "I thought I'd lost you."

I couldn't help hugging her back. It reminded me of one of my mom's hugs, and I had to swallow down my tears.

"Thank you for bringing them back to me," she whispered. "I can't tell you how much I—" Her voice broke, and she squeezed me tighter.

"Yeah, well, don't get used to it. Me bringing them back

was not a freebie invitation to do dumb shit. Finding their asses took work, patience, and a level of fuckery I was not exactly comfortable with."

My tirade had the intended effect of making her laugh, which allowed me to break the embrace. As good as it felt to be hugged, I wanted to find Bastian.

I'd barely gotten out of Emrys' arms before the big man barreled into me, sweeping me up in his embrace. Now that we were in the real world, his warmth seeped into me again, easing my soul. I eagerly clutched him to me, relishing the feel of his skin against mine. Just the breath in his lungs was a wish being granted.

"I was so worried," he whispered against my lips. "I thought you weren't coming back."

Just the thought of leaving made me want to cry, so I shook my head, kissing him with everything I had in me. There wasn't going to be a time where I would be able to leave Bastian. I knew that now.

"I'll always come back to you," I promised once our kiss ended. "Always. Do you understand?"

Bastian chuckled, holding me closer. "You went to Hell for me, Sloane. I think I believe you."

But I hadn't gone to Hell for him. I was pretty sure that little pocket world was a cakewalk compared to what was beyond. Granted, if Bastian had been sent to Hell, I would be on the first train downstairs.

"And don't you forget it."

"What?" a small voice griped. "No hug for me? I come in here and save the day, and not even a 'thank you'?"

I released Bastian to greet Ingrid, who didn't even have a speck of blood on what appeared to be a Catholic school uniform, her pale-blonde hair in plaits. "Hi, Ingrid. Thank you for saving our asses, though I'm pretty sure I missed that part."

Given the state of the living room, or rather the mounds of ashes piled up everywhere, our backup had been busy.

"It's okay. I'll lord it over you later."

I was sure that would be a super-fun time, too.

Several more people joined our little party, and pretty much everyone supplied hugs. Axel nearly broke my back as he squeezed the life out of me. "Remind me to get you any kind of blood you want. I swear, darling girl. I owe you big time."

"No problem, Axel," I croaked, patting his big shoulder. "It was no big deal."

Axel shook his head. "No, girlie. You did a good thing no one else could do, and all of us owe you until the end of time. Anything you need, anytime. Got it?"

"She gets it, Ax," Harper grumbled, shoving him out of the way. "My turn."

She advanced, ready to hug me, but I backed up a step, avoiding her touch. Harper told me once that touch made any warding completely worthless, and I didn't want to cause her harm.

"Don't worry about it," she said, the smile on her face wide and open, a first for Harper. "We're all happy here. It's okay."

Reluctant but unwilling to say no to her, I gave the small woman a hug, careful not to squeeze too tight.

All my friends are safe. They are here and safe and happy, and I can hug them today.

Harper's thoughts spilled into my brain, and I squeezed her tighter, the utter joy in those thoughts breaking my heart just a little.

She let me go first, tears gathering in her eyes, even as she gave me a wide grin. I wanted to say something, but I was attacked by the duo of Simon and Dahlia. The pair swarmed me in squeezes, and I couldn't help the relief at feeling them alive.

"I can't believe that shit worked. I swear, the 'go back into your body' trick only works in movies." Dahlia pulled back to stare at me, smooshing my face in her hands. "I can't say thank you enough."

"All right, all right," Bastian grumbled, peeling Dahlia's hands off my face. "Give Sloane back to me before you break her." He wrapped an arm over my shoulder, tucking me into his body.

Cuddling closer, I met Thomas' gaze through the throng. He gave me a regal nod, mouthing the words, "I owe you," before giving me a two-fingered salute. All I could muster was a tired smile and a shrug, the day's events catching up with me.

If Thomas felt he owed me, I'd let him. Maybe he could pay me back by helping me kill my no-good brother. That would be fun for everyone, right?

What was not a fun time was the clean-up process after the battle. Though Ingrid did know of an arcane company specializing in such things, letting them in the door was a problem. After the note drama on top of the whole siege shenanigans, no one was comfortable with anyone we didn't know coming into the house. Or being on the property. Or being within sniffing distance of the outer border.

So I was stuck helping out. *So much for everyone owing me big time.* Apparently, owing me did not encompass the utter ass pain of putting our house back together.

Fun fact: cleaning blood from hundred-year-old hardwood was a bitch and a half.

Granted, magic had handled most of the grunt work—restoring furniture and walls—but on top of consuming souls like it was my new day job, I was stuck scrubbing the landing like I was Lady fucking Macbeth.

I was about to give up on the whole deal and suggest replacing the flooring when the doorbell rang. The shock of it had me slipping in soapy water and landing on my ass. In the few short months I'd lived here, exactly zero people had ever come to the front door. Other than prisoners and a siege, there had been no visitors at all. I glanced up the stairs, and there was no Harper sticking her head out at the top of the landing to warn me, so I figured it might be fine?

Okay, I was wary as hell, but if anyone was going to answer the door, the person who was already dead was probably the best bet.

Reluctantly, I headed for the door just as the bell rang again, my pace less than urgent. Taking a deep breath, I twisted the knob and opened the door. On the stoop were three people —two ladies and a man. One of the women and the man I knew, but the other—a tall blonde—I did not.

"Agents Kenzari and La Roux, right?" I asked, instead of a more cordial greeting, my tone glacial. I hadn't just made it through an all-out siege followed by a trip to the In-Between to get hauled off to jail. I stepped from the house and closed the door behind me, crossing my arms as I faced them. "How can I help you?"

Agent Kenzari gave me a warm smile, likely intended to ease my nerves, but the effect was dashed by the stone-faced man at her back. Funny, he hadn't seemed so bad a couple of months ago, but now? Now he was a wall of no-nonsense with a "I'll eat you for breakfast" chaser.

"Sloane? Is your name Sloane?" the blonde woman asked, and I shifted my gaze from the agents to her. At my diverted attention, the man edged closer to her, as if he was ready and willing to spirit her off at the slightest provocation.

The woman I didn't know was tall and slender, with shocking cornflower-blue eyes and an open face. It was a face that made me want to tell her my secrets, and I didn't even know the woman.

Get it together, Sloane.

"Maybe. And you are?"

The woman smiled just a little before holding out her hand to shake. When I didn't take it, she frowned a little before her smile came back in full force, a hopeful expression now stamped all over her.

"My name is Darby, and I think you're my sister."

My sister was a homicide detective *and* friends with ABI agents?

Yeah, there was absolutely no way that could go wrong.

GRAVE WATCH

ARCANE SOULS WORLD: SOUL READER BOOK 3

ANNIE ANDERSON

1

"I think you're my sister," the blonde blurted, her brilliant blue eyes pleading for me to believe her.

That wasn't the problem. I believed her—honestly, I did. Given what had transpired over the last few days, I'd pretty much believe anything at this point.

The actual problem was that not only did my long-lost, "totally a cop" sister show up on my doorstep after the biggest battle of my life, but she also brought a couple of ABI agents with her. I had a love-hate relationship with the Arcane Bureau of Investigation. The "love" because they paid the Night Watch boatloads of money to pick up their strays, and the "hate" because I was pretty sure that if they caught a whiff of what I'd been doing over the last year, my ass would be reduced to cannon fodder.

The agents, I knew.

The sister, I did not.

Not to mention, it was difficult to hold up a tough "I'm a badass, and I'll eat you for breakfast" air while being faced with the reality of my whole world being thrown on its ear. Truth be told, this wasn't the first time I had been tossed on my ass, but being confronted by a potentially *not*-evil sibling was on a whole other level.

The blonde—AKA, Detective Darby Adler—was a tall, slender woman in her mid-twenties, standing a few inches above my respectable five seven. Beside her was a tiny, dark-haired ABI agent that I'd met in passing. Agent Kenzari seemed nice enough, but it was the forbidding figure standing at their backs that gave me pause. Agent Bishop La Roux seemed to be contemplating my demise—especially if I replied in a way that he didn't like.

Well, he could try…

"Got to say, I wasn't expecting you to just show up here," I blurted, my mouth running off with the first thing that ran through my brain. After Azrael's parting words, I'd sort of hoped I wouldn't see hide nor hair of my siblings for a little while. What with our douchebag of a brother trying to kill me and all, the thought of a family reunion wasn't exactly on my to-do list. "In fact, I wasn't expecting anyone to show up here. No offense, but the last time people made an unannounced visit, it turned into a bloodbath." A grimace yanked at my lips as the memory of that damn, blasted knife sailing end over end flashed in my brain.

I'd tried very hard over the last several hours to *not* think of that knife. Tried not to remember how it stuck in Bastian's side, his last gasps of breath. Yes, he was currently alive at the moment, but I got a sinking feeling in my gut whenever he was out of my sight. *Neurotic, party of one?*

"And that was yesterday," I tacked on for emphasis. It was not a good time for her to just be showing up on my doorstep.

Not. At. All.

"Oh, I like her." A voice broke in, startling me. It wasn't necessarily the Irish lilt, but more that the voice seemed to have come from what appeared to be an honest-to-god ghost. A no-shit, see-through, messenger from the other side, ghost.

Yes, I'm a walking, talking dead girl, but a ghost? No, thank you.

Was this a new thing I could do because I'd gone to the In-Between? Or was this something else?

My back hit the door in the middle of my scramble to get away, and instantly, I scolded myself. I'd latched onto evil souls in the In-Between with no problem, happy to send them to whatever Hell was waiting for them. But here? Now? I wasn't exactly sure. And that was only if I wasn't in the middle of a psychotic break or anything.

"Holy *shit*. Can you see Hildy?" Bishop asked, clearly aghast. "Is that a family trait or something?"

Family trait? That didn't sound good, but also if the ghost had a name, that likely meant I wasn't losing my freaking mind.

I swallowed hard, trying to get myself under control. "Hildy?"

The man hovered next to Darby, wearing something out of the nineteenth century. Blond curls swept from under a jaunty top hat, the royal-blue ribbon at the base matching his paisley cravat perfectly. His waistcoat was a beautiful, crushed velvet, but his outer jacket had to be some sort of thicker material. Wool, maybe. His eyes were the same crystalline blue as Darby's, only a little more transparent.

"Hildenbrand O'Shea," the ghost offered, moving to the head of the pack. "I'm Darby's grandfather. You can call me Hildy if you like. I kind of like that you can see me. It makes practical jokes a lot more fun." He muttered that last bit *sotto voce* like he fully intended on pulling a joke or five, and I was going to be in on it whether I liked it or not.

The nervous laugh that escaped my throat might have been mildly frantic, but that was neither here nor there. If Darby's eyes were anything to go by, I probably sounded a hell of a lot more hysterical than I'd intended. "You can see him, too?"

Darby shifted on her feet, an uncomfortable sort of shuffling that told me she wasn't exactly keen that this part of her life had been uncovered so quickly. "Yeah, I can see him all right. But not just him." She winced, tugging on the collar of her shirt. "I see all ghosts. It's why I make a good homicide detective. It's easier to solve murders with a little help from the inside."

A homicide detective who can see ghosts? That sounded like a match made in Heaven... or Hell. By how uncomfortable she was acting, I had a feeling it was more of the Hell variety, which I knew well enough.

Sister. I have a sister. And she seems... nice.

I couldn't say why that thought made me feel all warm in my middle, but it was something I wasn't too keen on investigating. A change of subject was in order.

"Well, since no one has screamed the house down that you're not allowed to be here, I figure it's probably cool to let you in." Relaxing, I grabbed the knob. "We're a weird bunch, but it's home, you know?"

I turned just in time to see Bishop wince.

"Yeah, about that," he muttered, scratching at his neck. "I *may* have knocked out your comms for a little bit. Didn't want anyone flambéing us before we even got an introduction. I'll remove my spell in just a second, promise."

He knocked out the comms? Like, did he just snap his fingers and turn all Harper's hard work into dust or something? "Ohh, Harper is going to kill you. Not really," I amended, grimacing. "I know threatening an ABI agent is probably frowned upon. Just..." I shook my head at the sheer stupidity falling out of my mouth. "Come on in."

But as I opened the door, a streak of white bone came

racing out of the house. *Isis.* I'd never had a cat, but I'd had a family dog. Otis was a runner, too, always bolting from the house the first chance he got. But Isis wasn't Otis, and she wasn't exactly running far. Instead of bolting out into the night, the bone kitty leapt into Darby's arms and instantly began a rumble of a purr as she rubbed her head against Darby's jaw.

Why, that little traitor.

"Umm… that's Isis," I muttered, more than a little put out that she was just fawning all over my sister. It was funny when she did it to me because it annoyed the shit out of Simon. It was not cool when it was my turn. Rude. "I thought I was the only one she did that to. Must be Daddy's death juice."

Her face went a little green. "Death juice? Eww, that's just wrong. I do not need to think about our father's sperm, thank you."

That wasn't where I'd been going with that, but… "Okay, so maybe we'll get along just fine."

I couldn't help it—with the stress of the last few days, coupled with meeting my supposed long-lost sister—who could blame me? I dissolved into a snickering mess, bending double as my giggles turned into belly rocking laughter. Wiping tears from my eyes, I led the way into the living room, my mirth dying just as soon as it was borne, once I caught sight of the rather sizable bloodstain still marring the hardwood at the base of the stairs.

Every time I saw that stain, I heard Bastian's scream again. It was why I'd been cleaning it in the first place. Like if I could just get it up, I wouldn't hear that sound anymore. I wouldn't see that damn blade again. I wouldn't remember his shallow breaths as he…

Tearing my gaze from the stain, I tried not to let my whole

body go cold. Tried to remember that he was okay and alive, and breathing and right upstairs talking to Emrys.

He's alive, Sloane. He's not going anywhere.

Blinking away the coming tears, I met Darby's gaze.

"You okay?"

I shook myself, slapping on a false smile as I desperately tried to dispel the ache in my throat. "Fine. We were attacked yesterday. It was—"

"Who the fuck isn't warded in this house? I swear to Christ himself, ya'll better fix it now before I get angry," Harper screeched from the landing, cutting off my hasty explanation. It was just as well. "Honestly. Is it so hard?"

I stifled a laugh, announcing our company. "We have guests, Harper. Maybe take the rage down a notch?"

Like that was going to happen.

Harper's head peeked over the upstairs railing, surprise coloring her face before her eyes narrowed in suspicion as they locked unerringly onto Bishop. "Did you do something to my sensors?"

He gave her a sly grin that was anything but sorry. "Yes, but I'll put them back exactly as they were in just a moment. Care to alert Thomas that we're here?"

"He already knows," Thomas grumbled from the door to the dining room, his voice startling virtually everyone but me. I'd felt his presence long before he spoke, but I seemed to be the only one.

Thomas raked a hand through his black, shoulder-length hair, his pale jade eyes narrowing on Bishop.

"Wait a minute," Darby muttered, her blue eyes going wide. "Thomas? Ingrid's Thomas?"

She knew Ingrid? My respect for my newfound sister shot up about a thousand degrees.

"I take it you're Darby Adler. I can't thank you enough for

coming to her aid. I hate to think that I would have lost her had you not."

So, she not only knew my tiny vampire friend, but she'd also saved her ass? Okay, I was now convinced.

"I didn't do it alone," she muttered, tilting her head in Bishop and Sarina's direction as she tugged on her collar again.

"Wait," Harper broke in, "you guys are the crew that helped the Dubois nest? You realize keeping them alive is the only reason we're alive today. We were getting our asses kicked before they swooped in."

Darby's face went white as she wobbled on her feet. Slowly, she rested her hands on her knees as she sucked in deep breaths, tears swimming her eyes as she did her best to calm down. It mirrored my own internal turmoil so much my heart damn near disintegrated in my chest.

I knelt at her feet, the urge to comfort her insurmountable. "Hey, it's okay. We're okay."

"No, it isn't." She gave me a watery chuckle as she swiped at her cheeks. "It's not okay, and we're not okay. Admitting that isn't weakness, little sister."

I could only blink at the "little sister" comment. "It's weird that that felt good, right? I shouldn't like that at all, but I really do."

And I did. I really, really did. The Night Watch was family—something I hadn't had in a long time. But Darby felt different. More. Like I'd lost a piece of myself, and now it was found.

"How do you feel about familial hugs? My dad—the man who raised me—is pretty big on them. Considering he's my only stable parent, I'd like to pass that on."

What the hell could I say to that? My family had been the same—happy, together, full of hugs and forehead kisses, and family meals. It was like getting a piece of them back. "I could go for that."

She wasted no time, launching herself at me and attack-hugged me with precisely zero regard to decorum. Her grip wasn't just tight, either. It was on a whole other level of strength that made me rethink her fragility.

"I know I'm dead and all, but choking me until I pass out is still pretty uncomfortable," I croaked, and Darby pulled away so fast she nearly dumped me on my ass.

"What?" she barked, her voice cracking like a whip of cop-voice mixed with big sister mixed with mama bear. "Explain. Now."

Confused, I righted myself. "I—I thought you knew. I figured Azrael would have told you since he sent you here."

"He didn't," she said, shaking her head. "Send us, I mean." She jerked her chin at Sarina. "*She* found you. *She* brought me here. Azrael hasn't told me dick. Not even your name before yesterday, and he sure as shit didn't mention that you were... *Dead?* Like really dead or like *un*dead? Because I've never heard of a dead girl just walking around all calm like. I mean, Hildy does it, but..." She whipped her head to the man it seemed only we alone could see. "How do you do that, by the way?"

"Who is she talking to?" Thomas asked, his approach slow and methodical as if he were assessing my sister for brain damage.

Darby's cheeks went pink, her gaze falling to her feet as she realized her mistake. I couldn't imagine being able to see ghosts all the time. Were they everywhere? Did they know she could see them? And was this my fate, too, talking to people no one else could see?

"Her grandfather," Bishop answered, shooting a withering glare at Thomas. "Darby can see and speak to the dead."

Thomas gave me a look of concern before slowly nodding his head.

"I have a couple of other tricks up my sleeve, too," Darby muttered, raising her chin but refusing to look anyone in the eye. *Dammit.*

"The night I became this?" I began. "I died. Azrael tried to bring me back, but I'd been gone too long, so…" I trailed off, not knowing if my story would make her feel any less like a freak. We did share a gene pool, after all.

"He gave you a piece of himself," she guessed. "He brought you back the hard way rather than let you rest."

On the one hand, Darby didn't seem uncomfortable anymore. On the other, she was lighting up like a Roman candle on the Fourth of July. A white light started at the center of her chest, flowing down her arms and pooling in a blinding concentration of power that made her whole body practically vibrate.

"Umm…" I chuckled nervously, staring at the hand still latched onto my shoulder. "Did you know your hands glow a little when you're mad?"

She yanked her hands back, her sheepish expression returning full force. "Sorry. I was just mentally berating our sperm donor for being an absolute fuck stick. I'll try to keep my shit under control."

Somehow, I doubted that was even in the realm of possibilities, but whatever.

"I like her," Harper called from upstairs. "She can stay and don't bother with the ward. If she's anything like Sloane, she'd burn through it, anyway."

Darby shot me a look. "Ward?"

I shook my head at Harper's antics as I dropped an arm around my sister's waist. "Harper's an empath, so emotions are kind of a problem for her. We try to be respectful and ward ourselves, but evidently, our lineage is kind of a bitch on that front."

And that was putting it lightly.

I had a feeling my sister knew exactly what I was talking about.

2

Leading my sister and her ABI cronies upstairs, I felt a sick pit of dread yawn wide in my belly. Sure, it was one thing to meet a sibling, but it was quite another to introduce said sister to the man you were in love with. Not to mention, I was sort of concerned about just leading two ABI agents through the house.

"It's going to be fine, Sloane," Thomas muttered so no one but me could hear, likely hearing my stupid heart beating out of my chest. "I already texted Emrys to let her know. She's waiting for us."

I couldn't say Thomas' pronouncement was the comforting assurance he'd meant it to be, but I marched up the stairs, anyway. At the landing, Harper stood with her arms crossed, eyeing our visitors with her patented skepticism. Well, until Sarina skirted around us all and approached our resident empath.

Harper squinted her eyes as she assessed the agent. "Psychic?" she guessed, tilting her head to the side.

Sarina mirrored her, tilting her head in the same direction as if it would ease the empath's mind. "Oracle."

At the correction, Harper simply shrugged and held out a hand to shake. "Good to meet you."

I wasn't shocked at Harper's quick acquiescence. No, what shocked the shit out of me was the ease at which she held out her hand. I distinctly recalled Harper's aversion to touch. In fact, out of respect, I refused to touch her unless she initiated it for fear of hurting her. Sarina had no such compunction, and as soon as the agent's hand slid into the empath's, a smile dawned on Harper's face that actually hurt my heart, it was so beautiful. I didn't think Harper did that very often—or at least not that I'd seen—and it made me mad and sad all at the same time.

"What the fuck, Harper?" I growled before I thought better of it, my hands almost reaching to touch her but pulling back before I made contact.

Harper's gaze broke with Sarina's, her grin brightening like the coming morning. "I should have done this before. Maybe if I would have done it with Celeste, then none of this would have happened."

A slight wrinkle marred the happiness on her face and pissed me off. "That is not your fault, and you know it."

It made me sick to think that Harper blamed herself for Celeste's actions. None of it had been her fault. It hadn't been any of our faults.

"Someone explain what is going on, please," Bishop barked, hovering at his partner's back like he'd snatch her away at any second.

Sarina gave him a quelling expression before directing her attention back to Harper. "Harper reads emotions naturally through the ambient air, but when she touches someone, she can read nearly every thought, every emotion, everything, and the longer she touches you, the more she can see. Since I'm sort of like her, it isn't as bad as if she were to read another person. Plus, since I'm in the know about all the things, she only has to read me and not the whole group."

"Yeah, but I can't read the future like you can," Harper countered ruefully. "That would have saved my bacon a time or two."

Sarina shrugged. "It has its moments. None that I'd wish on anyone, though."

"Ain't that the truth," Harper muttered, shifting her eyes to Bishop. "You turn my shit on again or what? Given the environment, leaving us unprotected isn't exactly a good thing."

Bishop winced apologetically as he rubbed the back of his neck. "Already done, but do a check to be safe. If you need help beefing up the wards, I'd be happy to lend a hand, too."

I could practically hear Thomas roll his eyes. "Sure, we'd love an ABI agent just moseying on through our security system. No problem."

Bishop's expression turned wounded. "What makes you think after all these years that I would do a fucked-up thing like that? I thought we were friends."

Thomas' eyes went red as needle-like fangs peeked out from under his lips. "Is that what you'd call it?"

"Okay, gentlemen," I growled, sending a steely-eyed glare at Thomas, "let's keep our cool here."

"Yes," Darby agreed, elbowing Bishop in the ribs. "Let's. I don't know how you feel about the ABI, but I'm not a fan." She looked at Bishop and Sarina, giving them a sheepish shrug. "No offense. But my mother runs the Knoxville branch, and well... She's dirty. Like up to her eyeballs in bullshit, sent me to prison for almost a year, body-snatching, baby-killing, *dir-ty*. She's in the middle of this shit, and I'll be damned if she tries a fucking thing on you, so…" Darby shook her head, pinching a brow. "If you need help, I got you. You need backup, I'm down. You need me to bury a body, I know a guy."

I couldn't help the snort that escaped me. "His name wouldn't happen to be Gerry, would it?"

Gerry had been a mighty fine ally once upon a time—you know, before he tattled on me to the Night Watch. I had buried many a body in his cemetery, and all it cost me was a few cases of whiskey. It was the tattling thing that really got to me, though.

Darby blinked at me, clearly stunned. "You know Gerry? How is the old bastard?"

I thought about him being pissed that Booth was in pieces all over his graveyard. "Cantankerous as ever. I can't believe you know the guy that…" I trailed off, shaking myself. *No need to confess your murders to the cop, Sloane. Shut up for once in your life, will you?* "Never mind."

"So, you're a police officer who offers to bury bodies for her little sister? And that doesn't make you dirty, *how again?*" Thomas asked, his jaw clenched as if he were trying to cause a damn scene.

I was about to give him a piece of my mind when Darby beat me to it. "Who says the bodies we'd be burying would be human?" she asked, coyly tilting her head to the side. "I don't police the arcane, but if you don't believe me, why don't you call Ingrid or Mags. They'll vouch for me."

"Mags?" Thomas' face went absolutely ashen as he sputtered, "The vampire queen of Knoxville lets you call her *Mags?*"

Darby waggled her eyebrows at him as her smile turned sinister. "That she does. She owes me. Lots. But that's neither here nor there. Now, weren't we up here to meet someone?"

At her prompting, I pushed through the group, giving

Thomas an extra special shove so he knew I was more than a little pissed at him. I got that he was being protective, but did he need to be an asshole about it?

Three quick raps of my knuckles, and Bastian swung the door wide. It was almost as if he'd been standing on the other side of it, just waiting for me to knock. Dark hair and blazing bottle-green eyes capped a mammoth frame that screamed violence, but all I saw was the way his eyes warmed when they latched onto me. Instantly, I felt like I could breathe again as the weight of worry slid from my chest.

"What's this, love?"

Bastian's quiet rumble was like a warm blanket and a hot drink on a cold day. It was comfort and reassurance. I almost teared up, wanting to tell him everything, but instead, I rolled up on my toes and pressed a kiss to his lips. "I'll tell you in a minute. This is a story only to be told once. Can you get the gang for me? I promise not to start the tale until you come back?"

He narrowed his beautiful eyes at me, but that didn't stop a trace of a smile from pulling at the corner of his mouth. "As you wish, love."

A few minutes later, the lot of us were assembled in Emrys' office, and I started the meeting with a bang. "Okay, everyone, I'd like you to meet Darby Adler. My sister." That last bit felt odd coming out of my mouth, but good all at the same time. "With her, is Agent Bishop La Roux and Sarina Kenzari with the ABI. And there is also a ghost you can't see named Hildy."

Clem gave Darby's ghostly grandfather a finger wave. "Oh, I can see him. How's it going, handsome?"

"Holy Jesus, Mary, and Joseph," Hildy said under his breath, having the good sense to blush, as he pulled at his cravat and eyed our resident revenant with interest.

I made the introductions, but I was sort of at a loss. Though

Emrys had no such troubles. "Can I ask why you're here? It's not often we have ABI agents traipsing through our home. Are ya here in an official capacity?"

Bishop shot a look at Darby and answered, "Absolutely not. As far as the ABI is concerned, we're not here, have never been here, and don't know you except in passing because of bounties. As far as anyone knows, we don't know you."

It was tough to know how to take that, and I wasn't the only one.

"Is that right?" Emrys replied, her odd reddish eyes flashing in affront.

Bishop put himself in front of Darby, practically shielding her with his body. "The ABI was breached three days ago. Agents I'd known for years slaughtered. At the same time, there was a prison break. I know my director is involved. She…" Bishop shook his head, hesitating to say the last bit.

"She's my mother," Darby finished his sentence. "Mariana O'Shea is my mother, and she has infiltrated the Knoxville coven. That's not why I'm here, but I figure this is a two-birds-one-stone kind of deal. I came here to meet my sister. My friends are here to ask for your help."

Darby's expression seemed wounded for a single, solitary moment before she wiped it clean. Like she hadn't realized the agents' plans until just that moment.

Oh. Ouch.

I didn't know what to think about Bishop La Roux, but I sort of sensed that he and Darby were a thing. However, if these two were a thing, he was about to be in the doghouse for the foreseeable future.

"I kind of figured our father would have sent you, but I guess not." I shrugged, trying to get her mind off her douchey maybe-boyfriend. "Hey, speaking of, does the name Essex Drake mean anything to you?" She shook her head, and I snorted. "Well, hold onto your ass. We have a brother, goes by the name X."

"Oh, I know about him. Bastard murderer with a penchant for killing siblings?" she asked to confirm.

"That's the one. Well, Azrael told me to pass along some information. This X? Well, his real name is Essex."

Then that pit of dread I'd been feeling? Well, it decided to turn into a full-on canyon.

Darby turned to Bishop, opening her mouth to tell him something before her eyes narrowed and she snapped it shut. A realization must have dawned, and she gritted her teeth, her hand shining like Christmas morning.

Written all over Bishop was a fair amount of guilt on top of shame.

He'd already known.

And now my sister was pissed.

"You're glowing again," I remarked, and oh, so slowly, she peeled her gaze from Bishop and locked those betrayed eyes on me. I couldn't tell what was going on in her head, but if I had a guess, she was contemplating shooting Bishop in the kneecaps or tossing him off a cliff.

"Did Azrael give you any other details?" she croaked, her eyes filling with awful tears.

I swallowed hard, trying not to snap her dumb boyfriend's neck. That was a thing sisters did for each other, right? "No, just that he was sorry he didn't tell you sooner."

She nodded like I'd said something profound, clearly trying to get herself under control. By the glowing hands, she wasn't doing such a good job.

"I know who he is," Bishop murmured, and the whole room went wired.

"Son, I don't know you," Axel began, his thick Texan drawl doing nothing to conceal the threat in it, "but I'm gonna need you to be real specific on how you know this man and who he is to you."

Bishop skirted one of the chairs in front of Emrys' desk and plopped onto it like he had a right. "He's the second in command at headquarters in a position called 'The Overseer.' He's my boss's boss."

Darby stared at Bishop in silence for a few long moments before she pivoted on a heel and flew from the room, taking her glowing hands and bottled-up rage with her. Hildy whisked after her, shooting a murderous glare at the betraying agent. Bishop followed, taking his life in his own hands as he raced after her like an idiot. I was tempted to trail behind them, but a warm hand on my shoulder stopped me.

"Let them hash it out, love," Bastian murmured in my ear. "We'll worry about burying his body later."

I snorted, wondering if old Gerry had a thing against me burying ABI agents.

"She won't kill him." Sarina sighed, plopping on the chair Bishop had just vacated. "Maim him, sure, but kill? Doubtful. She loves him too much."

I scoffed. *My sister loves that shmuck? Yeesh.*

A faint trace of a smile flitted across Sarina's lips as if she could read my mind. "He only found out a few days ago that they were one and the same," Sarina replied to my derision. "Since then, it's been a little hectic—what, with her almost getting killed about a zillion or so times. I swear that girl is going to give me an ulcer."

That reminded me of an offhanded comment that Harper had made. Darby and Bishop had come to the Dubois nest's rescue, and to hear Thomas tell it, the attack had been vicious.

"Honestly, I don't know how she's still standing with what her mother has been doing," she said, a gust of a sigh following the words as she pinched the bridge of her nose. The scent of her worry filled my nostrils, making me seriously reconsider following my sister. "The level of cloaking that woman has is atrocious. Hiding from me is not an easy feat, and she's doing it without so much as a hitch."

Emrys sat back in her chair, her silence a tangible thing. "You said the director was her mother? You're telling me Mariana O'Shea is Darby's mum? I didn't think that woman was capable of mothering a child, let alone being unselfish enough to produce one in the first place."

"Tell us how you really feel, Emrys. Sheesh," Simon muttered, wincing.

"You've been lucky enough to avoid her thus far, my boy. Trust me. If she'd been in charge when you'd been arrested, you wouldn't be here today. Or you'd be in her pocket doing her bidding just to stay alive."

Sarina nodded, the stark resignation on her face a testament to Emrys' words.

"We're going to need extra protection around the house if we're going against that wretch. Maybe a bloody moat if need be. I never thought I'd see the day," she muttered, shaking her head.

That was not at all a comforting statement, and knowing Emrys, she didn't exaggerate.

This was about to get so much worse.

3

When I woke up this afternoon, I didn't think I'd end up worried out of my mind about another person in my life. Considering the last three days, I kind of figured I'd be topped up on things to be frightened out of my mind about, but there I freaking was.

Swallowing back bile, I stared at the blood coming out of my sister's nose as she wilted in her man's arms. I was still on the fence about Bishop La Roux. It didn't really matter to me whether or not my sister had a thing for the tall death mage—what mattered was his penchant for keeping secrets. But the stark fear on his face and the way he clutched her to him had me tilting a bit.

After Darby stormed out of the room with Bishop in tow, things had gone into hyperdrive. Bastian, Simon, and Dahlia worked together to beef up the warding around the property. Emrys made several phone calls, and what did I do?

I worried.

Well, that and try to contact my bitch-ass father to no avail.

Closing my eyes, I tried to picture him in my mind, tried to call to him.

Come on, Azrael. Just tell us what's going on. Tell us what we're supposed to do. You can't want to follow the rules so bad that you'd…

I was about to say that he couldn't want to follow the rules so bad that he'd let us die, but given his history, that was precisely what he'd do.

You want me to take your throne or whatever, right? How am I supposed to do that if my bitch-ass brother burns my life to the ground? Again.

Since giving answers wasn't in Azrael's wheelhouse, all I got was silence.

A silence that was broken when Harper yelled, "Incoming" from her open office door. "It's Bishop and Darby, and there is an injured girl with them."

But Harper didn't have to tell me. As soon as she said the words, I knew exactly what that feeling was. "Axel, get ready," I hissed at the big man. "The girl is bad off."

I didn't know how I knew it. Didn't know how I translated the dreadful, twisted feeling in my gut into imminent death, but I did. It was the same feeling I'd gotten the moment before Simon and Dahlia died. The exact drop before Bastian had gotten a knife in his chest.

Axel sprang into action, whipping the door open about a millisecond after a dreadful pounding hammered the wood. I barely caught a glimpse of Axel and Darby. My gaze was trained on the battered girl in Bishop's arms as I stood rooted to the spot. I lost sight of them as they headed for the med bay, their retreating backs there and gone as they raced down the steps of the hidden entryway to the lower level. Not a moment later, Bishop reappeared, yelling for Thomas and Dahlia.

He was shouting—had to be. The veins on the side of his neck were bulging, and his face was a mix of pissed off and scared out of his mind, but I could barely hear him. In fact, he sounded like he was underwater. Then he was gone again, slipping back down from where he came.

And me?

I just stood there, the aching truth filling me with a terrible knowledge.

All I could feel was the coming death, but it wasn't at the end of my blade or my fangs, and this little girl didn't deserve it. Worse? Something was stirring in the direction of the med bay that wasn't from the girl at all. No, it had a very different signature. It was like a buzzing that was slowing down, but I hadn't noticed it before. Only once it began to fade did I realize what it was.

That buzz was Darby—Darby's life force or soul or whatever—and it was going quiet. I wanted to howl, wanted to race downstairs, and stop whatever it was that was diminishing her, but I was rooted, stuck. Unable to make my feet do anything but stay right where they were. Thomas and Dahlia hoofed it down the grand staircase, heading for the hidden one leading to the med bay, but before they could traverse those slippery stone steps, Bishop shoved through the door.

And in his arms was my sister, her skin like death, papery and pale. One arm hung limply at her side while the other lay draped over Bishop's shoulder. Bishop's jaw was granite as he carried her to the closest couch, the scent of Darby's blood high on the air.

"What happened to her?" I demanded, my question echoed by the transparent Hildy, who seemed to have popped in from nowhere.

"I'm fine," she insisted as she hung like a wet noodle in Bishop's arms. "Just tired is all."

Tired my ass. She was half-dead, and we both knew it. Hell, Hildy, Bishop, and anyone with a brain in their skull could see it. Did she think I was blind or something? "You know I can smell blood, right? And I have eyes. That hasn't escaped your attention at this point, has it?"

Bishop set her down on a plush couch, and she pried her eyes open with what seemed like a sheer force of will.

"No—though, the blood thing is new," she croaked, cracking a smile. Like that was going to put a Band-Aid on this bullshit. "I'll be fine. Faster if you have any ghosts lying around."

My gaze invariably went to Hildy, and he met it with a roll of his eyes.

"Oh, for fuck's sake," Hildy griped. "This is a damn disgrace. How much of your power did Azrael siphon off of ya, lass? The whole lot? Fucking bastard and his fucking rules. If he had a brain in his head, he'd leave ya with enough to spare, what with you runnin' headlong into danger as ya are." I hadn't noticed before, but Hildy had a thin cane in his hand, the handle a silver skull with emeralds for eyes. And those eyes began to glow, the magic lighting it up in a familiar way, almost like Isis' animated gaze.

Darby held up her hand. "Stop. I'm fine. Don't drain yourself too much."

He didn't answer her, but the glow to his cane grew brighter.

"Quit it. I said I was fine," she hissed, shoving herself off the couch like it took every ounce of her strength to do it.

"Well, at least you're on your feet then," Hildy hissed back, his top hat and cane winking out of sight.

"Okay, what the hell was that?" Bastian grumbled, staring my sister down like she was in serious need of a one-way ticket to a sanitorium. "First, you're pissed, running off to who knows where, then you two come back with a damn near dead girl in tow. Then you heal said girl, but that makes you sick, and now you're talking to people who aren't there? Am I getting this right?"

Simon sighed and rolled his eyes. "You know what grave talkers are, Bastian. Stop being a twat just because you can't see him."

"For fuck's sake," Hildy muttered, snapping his fingers. In an instant, Hildy went from slightly transparent to fully solid as he pierced Bastian with a perturbed glare. "Listen to your brother, mage."

Bastian uncrossed his arms, smiling at the now-solid ghost. "Hildenbrand O'Shea, you dead bastard. How have you been?"

Hildy shrugged. "Oh, you know, just trying to keep my granddaughter alive and my daughter from becoming a blight on the family name. You know, the usual."

"You call the most venerated grave talker in the known histories Hildy?" Simon said, aghast at the audacity of my older sister. "And he lets you?"

She turned to the man in question. "I'm going to need you to spill on all the grave talker deets. Every time people find out who you are, they freak the fuck out. It's weird."

"All in good time, lass. All in good time."

It sounded like a "never" if I ever heard one.

I heard Thomas' footsteps before the hidden door creaked once again. Thomas emerged, the rage blooming on his face a palpable thing. His gaze was trained right on Darby, too, which didn't make a lick of sense. "I'm going to need you to come with me, please. Alone."

"I don't think so," Bishop countered, squaring off against the ancient vampire like an idiot. I didn't know how old Thomas was, but I knew enough not to fight him if I wanted to keep all my limbs attached.

Dahlia slipped from the hidden doorway as well, her

expression pinched with fury. "I want to know what happened to that girl, and I want to know now."

Dahlia's voice had always been quiet, always calm. Like getting riled was beneath her somehow. But this cold, ferocity had even me shaking in my boots. I liked it even less trained on my sister, which didn't make sense. I'd only known Darby a handful of hours, but she already felt like family.

She felt like home.

And that home was being threatened.

"We found her on our way back, crumpled up in a heap right outside the ward," Darby insisted, shaking her head. "I don't think I've ever seen her before today."

"Then why is that child saying your name? Why is she calling for you?" Dahlia hissed, her whole body practically vibrating with rage.

I had to admit that those were some outstanding questions —ones I couldn't even begin to answer.

"No good deed goes unpunished," Bishop muttered. "Fine. We're all going down there. I won't go in the bay, but I'll be damned if you think I'm letting you take my woman off to some underground lair just so you can accuse her of that bullshit. Not just no, but hell no."

I hadn't yet decided how I felt about Bishop La Roux, but I really appreciated how he was protecting my sister right about now—even if it was against people I trusted with my life.

"Works for me," Thomas said, gesturing to the doorway that led to Axel's domain.

Bishop tensed, gently pulling my sister behind him as he headed for the passage. And me? Well, I still couldn't make myself move from the spot I'd been cemented to for the last five minutes.

I tried my very hardest *not* to go down the slippery stone steps to the medical bay if I didn't have to. One, because being that far below ground gave me the willies, and two? Aunt Julie was still down there, her expired shell moldering in a body bag in Axel's freezer. Given that Axel was a ghoul, I tried *extremely* hard to not examine why he needed a freezer in the first place. With all that had happened over the last few months, I still hadn't seen to her body, nor had I really mourned the woman who had been like a second mother to me.

"You don't have to go down there, you know," Bastian whispered in my ear as he wrapped a comforting arm around my middle. I'd been so deep in my thoughts that I hadn't even heard him approach. "No one would even look at you funny. You don't have to be the strong one all the time, love."

I huffed out a mirthless laugh and tilted my head back to shoot him a look. "Would you let Simon go down there alone, knowing he could be potentially attacked?"

Bastian let out a dark chuckle. "I would pity whatever poor fool decided to choose death, but I see your point. Though, I don't see how you've forged this bond so quickly. If I didn't know better, I'd think she'd spelled you."

His thoughts echoed my own, but I couldn't give him a reason why I wanted to protect a woman I'd just met any more than I could rationalize how I knew Dahlia was an ally or that Booth was a flaming danger turd. I just *knew*.

"I can't explain. It's just… she feels like home, you know?"

Bastian pressed his lips together, his brow wrinkling as he studied my face.

"She isn't like him," I insisted, referring to my murderous bastard of a brother. It almost made me gag every time I thought of Essex Drake as my brother. It made me want to rage, and burn things down, and scratch my own skin off.

Because his blood ran through me, too.

Surprise colored Bastian's expression before he locked it down. "I know that, love."

It was then that I realized that tears were gathering in my eyes. Why, I couldn't say, but there they were. "She isn't."

"I can tell you believe that, but there is a darkness in her, too. I know you can see it just like I can. The wrong pressure and she could easily turn to an awful path if she's not careful. Just like you could have but didn't."

Befuddled, I bleated out a shocked laugh. "You don't call over four hundred kills in a year an awful path? I'd hate to see what you think that is then."

Bastian's smile was smug as he pulled me around to face him. "Have you ever killed an innocent person?"

I flipped through my mental Rolodex of kills, full well knowing the answer. "No."

"Have you endangered the lives of good people, let them be slaughtered out of sheer indifference?"

Now I was getting irritated. "Of course not."

"Have you let murderers and rapists and abusers go free to inflict their poison onto their next victim?"

I gnashed my teeth. "You know the answer to that."

His green eyes practically glowed with mirth as he asked his next question. "Then how is your path an awful one, love?"

It really sucked having a wise, older-than-dirt mage as a boyfriend sometimes. How could I compete with half a millennium of experience and life lessons? Fun fact: I totally could not. Rather than tell him he was right, I rolled my eyes. Unerringly, they still found the door that everyone else had easily passed through.

"I don't know what to do about Julie's body," I admitted, my throat burning. "We never talked about what she wanted, and everything I can think of feels disrespectful. And the longer I wait, the more it hurts to do anything at all."

And what did I know about it, anyway? Julie had likely been the one to arrange everything when my parents died. How had she done it all on her own? I didn't have the first clue of where to start, and that made me feel guilty and mad and...

"We'll figure it out, love."

It was the gentle care in his voice that did me in, and I let three tears fall before I sucked in a huge breath.

"You don't have to go down there. You and I can just stay here."

Nodding, I watched the door, praying nothing went wrong down there.

4

It turned out that I had no need to worry. Five minutes after the whole of the house—save for me and Bastian—traipsed down to Axel's lair, the lot of them stomped right back up the steps. Bishop led the way, cradling the young girl in his arms like he thought she might break. Behind him were Darby and Dahlia—both of their faces pinched like they'd seen some shit and were definitely not happy about it.

Bishop set the girl down on the couch much like he had done with Darby earlier, only his expression was three beats past haunted. Something had gone down in that med bay—I had no doubt in my mind. The scent of cold sweat and dried blood and still-healing injuries permeated the living room, the source the beaten pre-teen who was now being covered with a soft blanket by the odd ABI agent. Bishop's fingers curled into fists as he stared at the sleeping child, and if I hadn't peeked at his face, I wouldn't have known he wasn't a millisecond from killing the kid.

"You guys have a gym in this place?" he croaked, his gaze never wavering from the couch.

I squeezed Bastian's hand and lifted my chin in the direction of the training room. Bastian dropped a kiss to my temple and skirted past me. "Sure, mate. It's this way," he said, clapping the agent on his shoulder. "Let's go blow things up and pretend the world isn't shite, yeah?"

Hesitantly, Bishop nodded, letting himself be led away, his fingers still balled into fists. One look at the girl on the couch, and I could see why he was so pissed.

"I thought you healed her?" I blurted, taking in the kid's bruises and swollen features. This was someone's baby, and she'd been shoved to the brink of death.

Darby shook her head. "I don't have enough juice to heal her all the way. I only kept her from dying."

Shock stole my breath as her words filtered through my brain. Ungracefully, I plopped onto one of the club chairs, my gaze trained on the small lump on the couch. Darby had given this child what little life she'd had to spare, damn near killing herself in the process. I wanted to scold her, but I knew enough about myself to know I would have done the same damn thing in her shoes. As admirable as it probably was on the outside, I was really starting to hate the family martyr complex.

A lot.

We sat in silence for a while until Dahlia got a wild hair up her ass, starting an inquisition that didn't need to happen right this second. "Why was she calling for you?" she asked, tapping her bottom lip as she examined Darby with her penetrating stare. "It doesn't make any sense. She doesn't know you, right?"

Darby shook her head. "Not that I know of. Axel said she smelled of witch, but sniffing out witches isn't exactly in my wheelhouse, so…"

Dahlia tapped at her lip again, staring off into the distance.

"Would it be unethical for me to take a blood sample at this point?"

I rolled my eyes so hard I thought they were going to roll on out of my head. "From a child? Dude, you know better."

Dahlia flicked a trio of braids off her shoulder and sighed. "Yeah, I do. I just want to know who she is. I feel like I should know her, and I don't, and it's bugging the crap out of me." She chewed on her bottom lip in deliberation before jumping out of her seat. "I've got it!"

Then she took off down the stairs without so much as a nod toward an explanation.

"I love that girl, but what the fuck?" I muttered, shaking my head.

Dahlia was usually so levelheaded, it freaked me out a little to have her so out of sorts. But everything was out of sorts, wasn't it? Buildings getting raided, ABI agents getting murdered. Prisoners escaping. Attacks on vampire nests. Nothing made sense anymore—not that it ever really did.

"You say that your mom is the ABI director here?" I asked, wondering how deep in the hole the ABI really was. Darby had said her mother was dirty. If that was true, what chance did we have?

She kept her gaze on the child as she answered. "Sort of?" she said with a bit of a hand waggle. "You know the ABI was attacked a few days ago, right?"

Oh, I knew. The last week had been bounties, explosions, and attacks galore. "Of course. We had to round up the fugitives from the prison break. I've never slept so little in my life." I pinched the bridge of my nose, remembering the water tower incident, followed by the stupid graveyard extravaganza of bullshit. "Then I got blown up. It was a whole mess."

Darby's jaw dropped. "I'm sorry, what?"

"Oh, yeah. So, remember I'm technically dead?" *Great lead-*

in, Sloane. That won't freak her out. "Well, I can't exactly die because I'm dead already. So, no worries there, but our brother has—or had—a…" I paused, attempting to explain the last twenty-four hours. "Okay, I don't know exactly who they were to each other. Partner, maybe? Anyway, he had this partner named Celeste, who was this gifted syphoner witch, and she did a number on me. She was also basically a Trojan horse kind of deal and damn near got everyone killed, which is why Harper is freaked you breached the system." I winced again. "Actually, full transparency?" And I had to be really clear here because there was shit she needed to know. Stuff that could change things.

She blinked at me like I was a Martian or something. "Uh, yeah?"

"Technically, a few of us did die," I admitted, pitching my voice low, "but I brought them back?"

She frowned, her brow pulling together in confusion. "What, like a death mage?"

I stuck out my bottom lip, shaking my head. "Not exactly?"

Darby leveled me with a maternal eyebrow raise, coupled with a slight narrowing to her eyes that meant business. "Why are you saying it like a question? Do you not know? Or do you just not want to tell me?"

If we had actually grown up together, I would have been mincemeat with that look. No wonder she was such a good detective. I couldn't help but blurt everything out. "I went to the In-Between and brought them back."

She shifted in her seat, blinking at me. She did that a lot. Though, I did just spill the beans about a completely different dimension, coupled with the fact that I'd single-handedly brought three people back to life. At once. Given the way that Simon kept staring at me like I was the damn boogeyman, well, it wasn't hard to guess that this wasn't anywhere in the realm of normal.

At her continued gaping silence, I continued my blurting, "It's where ghosts live, I think, before they move on. Azrael wasn't exactly forthcoming on the details, but that's what I figure it is. But there's only so much time you can stay there before you get stuck. Simon, Dahlia, and Bastian died, and I…"

"You brought them back," she whispered, finishing my sentence.

Nodding, I dropped my gaze to the twisted fingers on my lap. "I sort of got stuck there, too, but Azrael got me back out. That's when he told me to let you know who our brother is. I think he told me because he knew you were coming. And I think he knows something is coming for us. *He* is coming for us. I think Azrael wanted us to be prepared."

She growled softly under her breath. "It would be nice if he just fucking told us instead of being so goddamn cryptic. It's tough to gauge what's coming if we don't know the whole story. I mean, given what I've gleaned already, this whole thing is a tangle of vines—only the vines are snakes, and the snakes are venomous."

Well, she isn't wrong.

Racing steps sounded before Dahlia emerged from the med bay with a wad of bloody gauze in her fist.

"What in the—" Darby muttered only to be cut off by Dahlia's crow of triumph.

"I found some non-creepily sourced blood," she crowed, as if that wasn't the weirdest fucking thing she could have said. "I need to find this girl's people—either to return her to her home or beat someone's ass, I don't know which."

A small part of me figured it was the latter more than the former, but what did I know?

Dahlia made a beeline for the circular entryway table,

hauling the large vase of flowers off of it. In a matter of moments, there was a purple cloth covering the wood and a gleaming metal bowl in the center.

"What are you doing?" Axel drawled, his head peeking over the banister as he watched Dahlia assemble the ingredients for what I hoped was a location spell of epic proportions.

Dahlia shot him a sly grin that would put a damn demon to shame. "I'm finding the truth. It's better than eating food, sitting on my ass, or pretending to train."

I couldn't help the offended "Hey" that came out of my mouth.

"Don't like my assessment?" My small witchy friend shrugged. "Fine. But I'm not letting a child just sit here without looking for her people."

Then she dropped the gauze in the bowl, along with a slew of other ingredients, and lit the whole lot on fire with a snap of her fingers. A moment later, she extinguished the flames with another snap before pouring the still-burning remains on the tabletop. Curiosity got the better of me, and I peeled myself from my seat to inspect further. Darby must have had the same idea because we paced together to watch what appeared to be a map curl up into smoldering ash.

I didn't know what the remaining bits of paper meant, but Darby did.

"Poppy's a St. James witch," she muttered more to herself than anyone else.

I could only assume the little girl was Poppy, but I didn't understand the significance of being a St. James witch—not really. Shifting to the side, my gaze met frightened brown ones.

"You're not going to send me back there, are you?" Poppy whispered, ducking her nose beneath the top of the couch like she'd hide from us at the first sign of danger.

I knew the answer to that question without so much as a

glance at anyone else. There was no way I'd be handing her over to anyone without a thorough background check and probably a teensy taste of their blood for good measure.

No way in hell.

"If your coven did that to you," my sister growled, blind rage leaking out of her iron control, "then absolutely not. I don't give a shit what anyone says." Then she winced, shooting a defiant look at Dahlia. "No offense."

"None taken," she replied, waving away Darby's words as she pulled her braids into a knot at the back of her head. "If those bitches hurt you, I promise I'm about to go hurt them."

"Damn straight," I echoed, trying to reassure the kid. Poppy's fear hadn't dialed down one iota.

Darby crossed the room, perching on the edge of the couch by Poppy's feet. The blanket she'd been covered with was my favorite, the cloud-like fabric both soft and lightweight. Poppy ran her tiny fingers over it in what seemed like a nervous tick.

"Can you tell me what happened?" Darby cooed softly, and I would have given anything to have had her around when I was new to this world. Cold and alone and scared out of my mind, how much better would it have been with someone—hell, anyone—to give a shit about me when I was scared?

After a bout of a trembling lip, Poppy opened her mouth to answer, only to snap it shut again when a ruckus sounded from upstairs. Stomping feet echoed throughout the room as Harper and Sarina—well, more Sarina than Harper—raced down the staircase.

"Wait for us!" Sarina cried as a disgruntled Harper trailed behind her.

"Oracle," Sarina grumbled, answering a question no one asked aloud. "How many times do I have to say this?" Sarina plopped down on the adjacent love seat, yanking Harper down with her. "Okay, go."

"Stop policing my thoughts, weirdo," Darby chided, and Poppy's eyes grew wide. Darby shot a disgruntled look at Sarina before reassuring the kid. "Don't worry about Sarina. She's a sweetheart, promise."

The agent rolled her eyes as she practically bounced in her seat. "Tell her, kiddo. She'll be pissed, but she's on your side."

Poppy drew back as Harper elbowed Sarina in the ribs. "Quit freaking out the small child, dude. Some oracle you are."

I stared at the ceiling, trying not to start yelling at the pair and their antics. Some psychics they were.

"It's a madhouse in here, kid," Darby muttered. "You get used to it. Can you tell me what happened to you?"

Poppy's tiny fingers reached for Darby's hand, and she freely gave it to her. "I don't know where to start. I don't know…" She trailed off, shrugging. "So much of it doesn't make sense. For weeks people have been acting strange. Not behaving like they used to, not doing their normal things, and when I touch the places they have, it doesn't feel like them."

I sat up straighter. I'd heard of something like that before. These kinds of psychics were called something special. I'd come across a few black-market rings trying to procure psychic slaves to spy on their enemies. They'd been looking primarily for children, wanting to get them young before they could remember their parents. Well, they *had* been before I dismantled their entire enterprise at the business end of my fangs.

"I'm sorry, I don't think I understand. What do you mean?"

Poppy rolled her eyes and shook her head. "Sorry. I—I'm a kind of a…"

"In the arcane world, we call you a diviner. It's psychometry," Sarina murmured, likely reading the pictures in Poppy's head. "The word you're looking for. You touch objects and get an impression or a vision off of them, right?"

"Yeah, that's what Shiloh called it. A diviner." Poppy's gaze dropped to her fingers again. "She's in trouble. I tried to get her out, but with her leg, I couldn't get her to the window."

Darby sat forward on the cushion. "Who is in trouble? Where did you come from?"

Poppy's breath hitched. "Shiloh. She and I were locked in the basement—have been for what feels like a week. I was asking too many questions, and this woman locked me up. I'd never seen her before, but she... hit me, hurt me. When Shiloh saved me, I thought I wouldn't have to go through that again, but there I was—only this time was worse. These people were supposed to be my home—they were supposed to keep me safe."

Tears tracked down Poppy's face, but she wiped them off just as fast as they fell. "I need to save Shiloh. The rest of them can all die for all I care, but she saved me. Put herself in the way of that woman."

"Son of a bitch," Sarina hissed, her eyes getting a far-off quality that put me on edge.

"Let me guess—my mother?" Darby growled, her whole body vibrating as her fingers got a flickering glow to them that I'd quickly learned was a sign she was about to lose it.

Sarina stared at the kid, giving her a nod. "The ring, the one you lifted off of her. Give it to Darby."

The child frowned, her left hand pulling back as if she was trying to hide whatever was in her fist.

Sarina raised her eyebrow at the girl, the no-nonsense pull of it making me sit back in my seat. "She'll keep it safe. Promise."

Poppy's gaze flitted from Sarina to Harper, then to me before landing on Darby. "You have to keep it from the man. It's not meant for him. He'll steal it and make it wrong. You have to keep it safe. If you don't..." She trailed off, shaking her head. "You'll see when you touch it. It's not meant for him, and he shouldn't have it."

"Meant for who?" Darby whispered, but she hadn't needed to ask. We both knew the answer to that question.

Poppy held out her fist, and Darby opened her hand under it. Then the kid dropped a heavy silver ring in my sister's palm, a large black stone practically shimmering in the low light. The thick band had familiar sigils carved into the metal. Sigils that I'd only seen in one place—engraved in the door that led out of the In-Between.

My gut tightened as a familiar buzz overtook my whole body. What the hell was this kid doing with Azrael's ring? And it had to be his, had to be.

"None of this makes any sense," Darby muttered, echoing my thoughts exactly.

"Of course it does," Hildy said, making both Darby and I about jump out of our skins. He'd been MIA while the boys had gone to destroy the training room, so his sudden appearance shocked the hell out of the two of us who could see him. "My daughter's used and abused her power and authority as she's always done. She's infiltrated a covens' home, used them and their power for her own gain. She's gone against everythin' I taught her. Everything." Pain etched lines in his face as a silvery tear trailed down his cheek.

But the "why's" were still a mystery. Why would this woman side with our brother? Why would she go against her own daughter? Why—

Darby gasped as Poppy closed her palm over the ring, latching onto her hand with a white-knuckled grip.

Then the shit really hit the fan.

5

Darby's entire body went rigid as her breath hitched and then stopped altogether. Her eyes were open, but she stared straight through Poppy as if she wasn't there anymore. Before I knew it, I was off my feet, ready to tear Darby away from the child holding her captive.

"Don't," Sarina barked, latching onto my wrist before I could rip my sister away. "She has to see it for herself. She has to know the truth."

Flinging Sarina's hand off me, I barely managed to hold myself back from baring my fangs. "The truth according to who?"

Sarina shook her head at me like I was a simpering child. "Who do you think? You know whose ring that is. I saw it on your face the second you recognized those sigils. Poppy is letting her see the ring's history—information Darby needs if she's to do what she has to."

I'd always thought Sarina was a lovely woman, but right then, I was having trouble not decking the agent. "So, Azrael set this all up, then? What are you, his minion?"

She shook her head again, clucking her tongue at me. "You know better than that, Sloane. You know damn well what it is to be one of us. How is what I see any different from what you see when you read someone's blood? I have no control over the messages I'm given, no more than you do when you taste the flavor of a damned soul. I can't read your mind or future, but I know enough to know that the path you have in front of you is not the same as your sister's."

It might have been childish, but I rolled my eyes and reached for Darby again, the scent of fear and rage and desperation high on the air. Sarina's fingers tightened on my wrist again before I peeled them off, practically grinding my teeth so I didn't crush her delicate bones in my hand. "ABI agent or not, you touch me again, and we're going to have problems."

"You can't touch her. What is meant for her is not meant for you," Sarina insisted, placing herself in between us. "You can flash your fangs and growl all you want, but I'm doing this for you, too. She has to be the one to accept this knowledge. It's her burden to bear, not yours."

I was sorely tempted to bodily move her out of my way or punt her into the surface of the sun—I couldn't decide which—when I felt the whole room go wired. A wall of rage rankled on the air long before the soft shuffle of footsteps whispered down the stairs.

Bastian and Thomas were in this room, their scents reaching me before their steps did, but it was Bishop's unmitigated fury that felt like an actual physical thing.

"What the fuck, Sarina?" Bishop growled from behind me, damn near knocking me out of the way to get to Darby. He reached for her shoulders, yanking her out of Poppy's grip, and that was the exact second I smelled the blood. He cradled my sister in his arms, her skin damn near blue as bloody teardrops fell from her eyes.

My bottom lip started to tremble as I watched Darby continue to wilt, the red of the bloody teardrops so stark on her skin.

Why isn't she breathing? Why is she crying blood? What the fuck is going on?

"Azrael, you get your feathery ass here right now," I yelled, my head tilted back as I shouted at the ceiling. But not only did he not show himself, that cold pit of dread had returned. He wasn't going to come and help.

"We're too warded," Bastian muttered. "He can't hear you, love."

Tears pooled in my eyes as I rounded on the man I loved. "Then summon him or yank him here or drop the war—" I blinked for a second before I raced out the glass French doors that led to the backyard. The weight of the ward was a physical thing, and I knew the instant I crossed it. "Azrael, please. Please ju—"

The air shimmered right in front of me like waves of heat coming up from hot asphalt after a summer rain as my stomach dropped to my toes. Then my father appeared out of thin air. Dark hair, pale skin, black feathers, coal-black suit— the standard fare for the Angel of Death, minus the scythe.

Violet eyes assessed me for a moment, irritation pinching his face. "My ass is not feathery," he scolded, his eyebrow hitched up in parental affront.

I blinked at him for a second, realizing all too quickly that he'd heard me when I'd called for him. He'd heard and ignored me, the dick. "That is not the point, and you know it. Darby needs your help."

His wings shivered a bit before winking out of sight. "No, she doesn't."

"I don't know about you, but not breathing and crying blood sounds like a whole-ass ailment to me. Wanna lend a hand?" Azrael's face hardened, his hair flickering from white to black and back again.

Jesus, fuck. When will I learn to shut my mouth?

Azrael huffed, his gaze moving from me to something over my shoulder. I followed his gaze to see Bastian frantically searching the lawn for me as if I weren't standing right in front of him. "He can't see us. We're not on his plane." I needed a second to digest that little tidbit, but Azrael didn't give it to me. "Your sister is far more resilient than you give her credit for, and she doesn't need my help. Listen to the oracle, will you?"

I was still stuck on the us being "not on his plane" bullshit, but Darby didn't have the time or oxygen for me to ask. "I'd love to listen to her if she were telling me anything, but she isn't. And I have a feeling you know why."

He rolled his eyes, turning away from me as he surveyed the tall grass. "You'll know when the time is right. Now, quit hounding me. She'll wake up soon enough."

Well, this had been a *complete* waste of my time. Now I just needed to figure out how in the hell to get back home.

Azrael shifted back just a little, his wings making another appearance as he prepared to leave. "A storm is coming, kid. And I didn't get to teach you everything I needed to. Just remember, when she asks you for a favor? Tell her yes."

I opened my mouth to yell at him for giving me such stupid, vague-as-fuck advice when my stomach dropped again. The air shimmered all around me as Azrael disappeared—or rather, as I reappeared. One second, I was about to give my stupid father a piece of my mind, and the next, I was engulfed in Bastian's arms and lifted off my feet.

"Don't do that to me again. You hear me?" he growled into

my hair, his hold on me so tight it was almost painful. But under that strength was a trembling sort of fear that I knew all too well. I could practically taste his bitter relief on my tongue. "I thought I'd lost you. Thought I'd be like that miserable bloke in our living room."

I wanted to explain, but we didn't have the time. Darby was going to wake up any minute, and I needed to be there when she did. "We need to go. She'll be coming around soon."

He gave me a startled huff as I slipped from his grasp and latched onto his wrist, dragging him behind me as I marched right back to the house. Azrael hadn't given me anything I could use, nor had he provided even a shred of a goddamn clue as to what I was supposed to be doing. Other than a cryptic "grant her a favor" bullshit, I was at a loss.

"Breathe, baby. I need you to breathe," Bishop pleaded, brushing the blood from Darby's cheeks as he rocked her in his lap.

As if he'd commanded it from the heavens, Darby sucked in a gasping breath. The color started to return to her skin, as more blood fell from her closed lids into her blonde hair, staining it scarlet.

"There you go, baby. Just keep breathing." Bishop's breath hitched as tears ran down his face.

Darby's eyelids fluttered, and for the first time since I saw her in his arms, her skin damn near blue from lack of oxygen, did I take a breath of my own.

"Wh-what happened?" she croaked, the shattered glass of a voice making my stomach drop.

Bishop bent and kissed her forehead, his jaw tightening like he was two steps away from losing it. "You stopped breathing. Your heart stopped beating. You started crying blood. And then Sarina couldn't hear you anymore. She couldn't see inside your mind. We thought... We tried calling

Azrael, but he wouldn't come. God, baby, I thought we'd lost you."

She flinched like he'd slapped her, and I watched a haunted sort of knowledge come over her before she staggered to her feet, ignoring all of us when we insisted she sit back down.

"I need a phone. Now," she ordered, holding out a hand for one, like it was no big deal that she hadn't been breathing a minute ago—like she should be standing at all.

Simon, of all people, slapped his slim Night Watch issued phone in her hand, and without so much as a peep, Darby dialed a number from memory. I practically felt the rings all the way across the room, their trills rattling in my chest as I watched her put the phone up to her ear. When a childlike voice answered, I knew whatever was coming was going to be bad.

"This better be who I think it is, or you're going to have hell to pay," the person on the other end of the line griped, and as much as I wanted to smile, I couldn't. Ingrid Dubois might have sounded like a kid, but the ancient vampire had to be a thousand if she was a day. And I never wanted to find out what kind of hell she could dish out.

"Ing," Darby wheezed, "I need to call in my favor."

When she asks you for a favor, tell her yes.

But Darby didn't ask me for a favor. She'd asked Ingrid. Still…

"About damn time. Jesus. You've held onto the fucking thing for five years. Is this just my favor or the whole nest, because I gotta say, sweetheart, this week has been a fucking doozy."

Well, she's not wrong.

Darby seemed to think about it for about half a millisecond. "The whole nest, both boons from Mags, *and* the *three* favors you owe me. And even then, I might have to take out a marker."

The silence on the other end of the line was deafening, and the weight of it in this room was a physical thing pressing down on my shoulders. "I will say one thing about you, Adler. You sure as shit are a go big or go home kind of girl."

"It's bad, Ing," Darby croaked. "Worse than the attack on the nest."

Bastian clutched my hand tighter in his. Thomas had filled us in on the attack on the Dubois nest. It wasn't just *bad*. It had damn near been a catastrophe. Several mid-level members of the nest had been killed, and Ingrid herself barely made it out intact.

"And this is coming for us all?" Ingrid asked, and Darby looked up at Bishop, her eyes pleading before shifting her gaze to me. She didn't need to ask for any sort of favor for me to back her up. Not with her blue eyes blazing like the Devil himself was knocking on her door.

"If I can stop it, no. If I can't…" Darby trailed off, but I knew. That look on her face told of devastation and death and the end of all good things.

"Consider it done. Thomas will tell you where we are. Meet in three hours, yes?"

She nodded, even though Ingrid couldn't see her, but I could, and there was a bitter defeat in that single head bob.

"Three hours," she agreed and pressed the red "END CALL" button.

Bishop cupped her cheeks as my gut bottomed out. "Tell me. What is it?"

"It's war."

6

War had me watching my sister make one decision after another with no real choices in the matter. It had me standing idly by while she had to choose between her own life—her own safety—and the fate of us all. It had me biting my tongue and trying not to make this whole mess worse for her. It also had me eye to eye with the dirt as we hid in the trees and waited for "the signal."

What that signal might be could be anything from a massive explosion or a hole ripped in the fabric of space. Really, it was a toss-up.

I'd never been to Haunted Peak before, and while it wasn't much bigger than the town I'd grown up in, it did have a few things mine didn't. A giant mountain prison with a lake on top, if it being the main one. The only thing keeping me sane was Bastian's heat at my right and the knowledge that I was free to mow down anyone standing in my way.

"You all right, love?" Bastian murmured, and I shot him an incredulous glare. He knew full well we were way too close to a local ghoul nest who had just as good of hearing as I did to be asking that question.

The same damn ghoul nest that had kidnapped Darby's adoptive father and best friend, J. The same one that was in league with her mother.

The same one that would pounce on us in a hot second if they caught wind that we were here.

Also, being downwind from this vile ghoul nest smelled like malice and dirty socks.

Truth be told, I was not a fan of the current plan. I wasn't too keen on Darby trying to pull the wool over her mother's eyes, no more than I was in favor of her trying to burn herself up just so her mom didn't latch onto a boatload of power. I'd just gotten a glimpse of this woman in my life, and now… Now she might…

Was I all right? No, the fuck I wasn't.

But I didn't get a say—not about this.

Because there wasn't a better plan or another way out. Even if I wanted to take her place—and I really did—I wasn't capable of doing what Darby could. And I couldn't take this away from her, either. Because if it were my family up on the chopping block, I'd be doing the same fucking thing she was. If it were my dad, if it were my best friend, if it were my people, I'd be in her shoes in a heartbeat.

And that just sucked.

My face must have shown the despair, the utter uselessness I felt, because he pressed his shoulder more into me—the best he could do since hugging was off the table. His green eyes warmed in sympathy, and it was all I could do to not start bawling. Over the last three hours I had argued and pleaded and did my best to think of something—anything—else but what we were doing.

A faint rustling to our left pulled my gaze from Bastian to a very small, very ancient vampire. Ingrid was up a tree playing lookout, while the rest of us strategically positioned ourselves in a choke ring just outside the target area. She was also sticking her tongue out at me. If I didn't know better, I'd have thought she was finally regressing to the age she had been when she was turned. But since I was the youngest of us, I pulled the same face, adding an almost silent raspberry for good measure before I faced forward again.

It was the waiting that was killing me. Right then my sister was pretending her way through a pretty dicey situation as she tried to fake out a master manipulator, and here I was just sitting on my ass staring at dirt.

Then I heard an ear-piercing whistle followed quickly by a chorus of bellows and screams. It seemed like that was our cue. Bastian and I popped up from the ground together, weapons drawn and raced toward the ghouls and witches in league with Darby's certified bitch of a mother. Only... only it seemed like the two were fighting each other rather than waiting for us. Witches shot blistering spells at the ghouls as a few of the giant arcaners ripped into the woman with their blunted teeth.

I skidded to a stop as I watched a Knoxville witch wrench her glowing hands apart, the spell working its magic to rip the head clean off a ghoul's neck. Shooting a glance over my shoulder I met Bastian's eyes. He shrugged, lifting his chin at the occupied witches and drew a thumb across his neck.

He didn't have to tell me twice.

Stowing the sword in its sheath, I raced for the witch and latched onto her neck like it was a Capri Sun. Two pulls in and I wanted to wretch at the vileness of her blood, so I yanked out my fangs and snapped her neck for good measure. Darby had said there was a chance that these witches had been conned or spelled, but this one sure hadn't, and the horrors in her blood were deserving of a death sentence no matter who was meting it out.

Spitting the blood on the forest floor, I moved to the next person in my way, uncertain if I would kill them or just knock them out. My internal debate was quickly settled, as a ghoul rushed me with the swiftness of a jungle cat, coupled with the bearing of a linebacker. With a smile on my face, I sliced through his throat without so much as a hiccup, his body beginning to dissolve before his head even hit the ground. I caught sight of Bastian mowing down ghoul and witch alike, taking heads with zero compunction just like I was. But there were so many, the nest larger than I'd thought, and with so many witches in the mix, I quickly lost him in the melee.

I didn't like that I couldn't see Bastian, or that I was so far from my sister, and I absolutely hated that I couldn't wrap up all my friends in fucking bubble wrap and stick them in my pocket so they couldn't get hurt. Honestly? All I wanted was to get to point A—AKA, here—to point B—wherever the fuck Darby was—with no issues and zero injuries. A want that was dashed thirty seconds later when a fireball zipped through the air toward me, while I was busy cutting off a ghoul's head.

I saw the thing about two seconds too late and had to duck to avoid it before the ghoul was properly dispatched. While it was semi-satisfying to see the ball of flames explode against the ghoul's chest, it was significantly less so, once I found myself the target of this witch's next missile. The ghoul bellowed his rage and pain at being set ablaze as I tried to use him as a flailing—albeit on fire—shield.

The results weren't entirely successful.

Sparks exploded against the ghoul's back, the embers catching my right arm and the side of my face in a sear of what should have been white-hot agony that I barely felt. Unerringly, my gaze found the offending witch, a tiny redheaded thing with freckles for fuck's sake. If it weren't for the shit-eating grin that spread across her face, I might have thought she was innocent, but the absolute glee pissed me all the way off. She launched her next attack, another ball of bullshit fire forming in her palm, but I was ready this time. With a swift swing of my blade, I dispatched the ghoul in my way before showing this girl just how fast I could be when I was pissed off. Before she could launch the orb at me, my blade was at her throat.

It was funny, but a few months ago, I would have bit first and asked questions later. But after tasting Bastian's blood, after realizing what evil really tasted like, I couldn't make myself bite the woman. Especially after tasting her coven member only moments before. I didn't want that vile stink in my throat, and I didn't want to know what horrors were hiding beneath her flesh.

Killing her would just have to do. A single flick of my blade and the witch was dead, her body falling in a heap at my feet.

I was almost to the lakeshore just past the tree line when I heard Darby's scream, the sound of heart-rending agony meeting my ears like an echo of my own loss. I knew that sound, knew it so well, I might as well have screamed it myself. Darby was losing someone she loved, and there wasn't a damn thing I could do about it.

But maybe…

My feet flew of their own accord, racing toward that dreadful sound, while my brain tried and failed to catch up to the picture in front of me. Two men were tied to thick wooden stakes buried in the sand: a tall blond man and a slightly shorter dark-haired one. Both had been beaten, the scent of their fear and blood and pain rent high on the air.

But Darby was clutching the blond man to her as his legs gave out and she sank with him to the sand. She screamed and cried but her pleas for help went unanswered, and I knew hope was all but gone when Azrael glided over the sand. For a fleeting second, I thought he might help the man in her arms, but the sadness on his face told the tale without a single spoken word.

In that instant, my heart broke because I knew that resignation, that defeat. I'd seen it on my mother's face when she had known she wouldn't be able to save me, and it was that same damn expression lurking on Azrael's then. It was a helplessness that I, too, felt and had no idea how to remedy.

With a flick of his wrist, Azrael beckoned a fluttering light from the blond man in Darby's arms. The light flickered over the sand, too, as if pulled by a string as Azrael held his arms wide. In a matter of moments, the light speared into his chest, fading out of sight before Darby ever knew he was there. Another scream bubbled up Darby's throat, this one louder and more devastating than the last. The earth rumbled beneath our feet, nearly knocking me to the ground as Darby's pain made itself known.

She pressed a shaky kiss to the man's forehead and stood, and it didn't matter that this man was an unknown to me. It didn't matter that I didn't know if he was her father or her friend. None of it mattered because my sister was dying inside, and I couldn't do a damn thing to help.

A tall woman shrouded in darkness struggled against the hold of a giant Viking-looking Fae. The shadows surrounding the woman moved like ink in water, almost oily as they played Peek-a-boo to the soul underneath. That darkness made my stomach turn, and I didn't have to taste the woman's blood to know who she was.

Darby made a beeline for her mother, an orb of pure light forming in my sister's palm as she assessed the woman dispassionately. Without so much as a blip of emotion on her face, she shoved that orb down her mother's throat and patiently waited while Mariana burned up from the inside out.

It was justice, sure, but it made my skin crawl. My feet decided to start moving again, the bitter detachment on Darby's face a little too close to what I'd done a year ago. She couldn't do what I did—she couldn't fall down that bitter path of revenge and wrath. It would burn her up in the end.

Darby had too much to lose—too much to leave behind. I hadn't, and I didn't want her to torch her whole life. I'd just picked up speed when it seemed like the whole world stopped —the air in my lungs, the birds in the sky, the sounds of the still-going battle. Ghouls mid-strike and witches mid-spell froze, their magic and weapons halting midair. My entire body locked for a moment, my limbs refusing to heed my commands, but something told me to keep going, to keep pushing.

Quicksand had nothing on this. Hell, it was like running in wet cement.

My first thought was that this had to be Darby. Somehow, some way, my sister had stopped the world, stopped time, stopped everything, and half of me couldn't blame her. Oh, how I had wished for it all to stop when I'd realized that my parents were dead. When I understood that it wasn't a lie, and no one was coming back.

When I knew I was alone.

My heart ached in my chest, the echo of grief making it hard to swallow as I pushed forward. Only my next step fell as if there was nothing holding me back, the return of my speed frightening me more than anything else. I raced past the sprawling mansions on the shore and into the trees where my sister held her hands aloft, a group of ghouls caught in the web of the too-potent power thrumming in her veins. A quick flick of her wrists and the ghoul's head popped off, thumping to the ground in a wet sort of splat.

While convenient, the ease at which Darby killed them had bile racing up my throat. Hypocritical, I know. What? Was I the only one allowed to kill without an ounce of remorse? Was I the only one who could take vengeance for wrongs done to me?

While the answer was "No," it was also not a resounding "Yes." Sloane Cabot was dead. Darby Adler was not.

Hildy tried reasoning with her, but what good was a ghost in the face of such pain?

"I know your minds. Your names. Your sins," she murmured, but her voice wasn't just on the air, it was in my head, too. I got a sinking feeling she'd done that on purpose. "Your betrayal has been noted. You are not welcome here. Twenty-four hours. Get the *fuck* out of my town. Get your shit out of Knoxville. Out of my state. If I see you, there is no place in this world or the next safe for you."

"Are you sure you want to be doing this, lass?" Hildy pleaded, stark fear on his ghostly face, but Darby didn't see it. She wouldn't even look at him.

What she did do was shrug, still staring in the distance as witches and ghouls heeded her warning and fled. "Your daughter set this into motion ages ago—all I'm doing is making me and mine safe."

Hildy got right in her face, begging Darby to listen to him. "You're painting a target on your back is what you're doing. Disbanding covens and nests? You realize you're taking the mantle of leader if you do that. Have you thought this through?"

Determination fell over her features, solidifying them into a mask of wrath. "If you think I'm going to let this stand, you're out of your mind. Twenty-four hours is a goddamn gift, and you know it."

She'd given those that betrayed her a day to get out of town.

Was it a gift?

Probably.

Would it bite her in the ass?

Absolutely.

Was I going to be there to back her up?

Without question.

She just had to let me.

7

Funerals were for the birds.

No, that wasn't quite right. While funerals in general were indeed the absolute worst, *Southern* funerals were a level of torture reserved for the deepest pits of Hell. It wasn't just the endless casseroles and impromptu visitors. It was the near-constant gawking and grief-glutting that made me sick to my stomach. Was this what I would have had to deal with if I hadn't died that night along with my parents? A slew of rubberneckers practically doom-scrolling through my life? Given the state of distress lurking in Darby's eyes, I was sort of happy I was left with the direct-to-grave approach.

Over the last few days, I had been keeping an eye out for Darby, helping her arrange her father's funeral, but more than that, I was watching her back and making sure she didn't fly off the handle. She had painted a pretty big target on her back up at the lake, sure, but I was more worried about the thing she *wasn't* talking about—namely the mass of souls she'd absorbed emptying Azrael's ring, executing her mother, and watching her father pass away before her very eyes.

Every so often, in the height of Darby's stress, the house would rattle, or wind would whip inside, or all the power would go out, and we'd have to do damage control. Either Darby's best friend, J, Bishop, or I would usher whatever visitor that had dropped by—totally unannounced—out before they realized that it wasn't nature causing the ruckus. After less than a day, we figured out that keeping visitors out altogether was the best idea.

Darby's skin was a permanent shade of ashen, with twin dark circles under her eyes that resisted the efforts of even the strongest concealer. She tried to sleep—or at least she said she did—but I still heard her rustling in her bed, tossing and turning or screaming herself awake in the middle of the night.

The day of the funeral, the whole of us were acting like skittish cats, waiting for the next shoe to drop, the sense that something was coming high on the air. Or maybe that was just me.

"You ready to go?" I croaked, offering my sister a tall blue mug filled with the strongest coffee I'd ever smelled. I, too, was sipping from my own mug, the daylight hour playing havoc with my sleep schedule. Fidgeting, I pulled at the collar of my blouse as I waited for her to answer.

Instead, she downed half the mug of scalding coffee in one gulp before setting it down to stir in a spoonful of sugar. Her mouth twitched like she was remembering something, and a lone tear streaked down her cheek. Silently, she dashed the wetness away, lifted her mug, and drained the rest of it.

"Not really," she murmured, her voice thick. "I don't think I'll ever be ready."

Yep, definitely preferred the direct-to-grave route. Anything was better than parading my grief around in front of the entire town. Why did people do this? Was it a torture kink or something? The whole thing sounded awful. A service followed by a graveside gathering and then coffee and cake after? It all sounded like a complete nightmare.

We managed to make it through the service without too many issues. Personally, if Darby hadn't insisted on the whole thing, I would have tried to hide her under a rock until she got herself together. Inexplicably, she managed to hold her shit together with only a minor light flickering issue at the church and a small gale at the graveside gathering. Both could be explained away, but I knew it was only a matter of time before she eventually lost her shit.

Bastian was a warm presence at my side as I kept an eye out for my sister. Somehow, he knew just how horrible this was—not just for her, but for me, too. It had only been a year since my family died, only a year since they had been ripped from me, and here I was trying to be strong for a sister I barely knew in a weird little town with far too many arcaners to count.

The wind picked up a bit more as the preacher droned on and on at the graveside, Darby's composure slipping just a little bit more with every extraneous word. Without thought, my feet propelled me to her, and I rested my head on her shoulder for comfort. "Nothing I say can ever make this better. It fucking sucks. And it'll suck for a while." This I knew for a damn fact. "But, you're my big sister, and you know..." I paused, squeezing her withering frame in a sideways hug. "Well, we've got each other. You've always got me to shout at, tell me to go fuck myself, cry, you know...the things big sisters do."

She leaned her head against mine. "I'll remember that. I'm

glad we have each other. Glad I found you." But her voice got thick, and she didn't say another word.

With a nod, I squeezed her shoulder and went back to Bastian, allowing his heat and touch to ease my pain. When it came time to toss dirt on her father's grave, Darby lost what little hold she had on her grief, the ground shaking in her wake as she marched away from the crowd to gather herself. I watched her go, keeping half an ear on the preacher and most of my attention on her.

She picked a bench to sit on, and I slipped through the crowd as soon as it was polite to do so. I didn't want to blow Darby's cover here—being a police officer and all—but I had the distinct feeling that there were far more arcaners in this town than she knew about. A varied few batted an eye when the ground pitched, the majority taking it in stride as if earthquakes were an everyday occurrence and random wind gusts were no big deal. Hell, there wasn't even a stir when the lights in the church went out, or the candles in the sanctuary flared to life of their own accord for a moment before snuffing out altogether.

As soon as I was free of the crowd, I made a beeline for Darby, her fists propping up her chin as tears fell down her cheeks. A man approached her, his crisp gray suit and white hair turning my stomach before I even caught sight of his face. I knew that suit, that hair, that swagger. I'd seen it a year ago as he sauntered over to murder my mother, his steps just as fluid and unhurried as they had been on the day my parents died.

Before I could yell out her name, she stood, facing off against our brother without so much as a nod to her own safety. Her gaze roamed the cemetery, skirting over me as if she hadn't realized I was there before returning to Essex. Her words were muffled, and she turned away, giving him her back.

My feet propelled me faster. She had no idea just how dangerous he was—no idea just how quickly he could strike.

But I did.

As someone who had been killed—technically twice—by this man already, I wasted no time on propriety or social norms. I hauled ass across the graveyard like my life—or rather her life—depended on it.

But by the time I got to her side, Essex was gone, the bastard floating away on a fucking breeze or some shit, and all that was left behind was another freaking note. Propped jauntily in the grass, his lazy scrawl made me rage as I read the words.

Azrael lied to you. Killian isn't where you think he is.
Come find me when you're ready for the truth.
—Essex

The truth? What would he know about the truth?

Darby took one look at that note, and her eye twitched as she ground her teeth before she turned away. I couldn't blame her. I was tempted to scent him out, aching to track him down like the dog he was and… The ground pitched beneath my feet, and it seemed for the first time, Darby actually noticed.

Over the last few days, she'd seemed entirely unaware that she'd been wreaking havoc, but now—when it was all too impossible to contain—she realized the issue. Or it was because both of us got knocked on our asses. That could be it, too.

With my butt on the grass and my rage nearly exploding out of my ears, I peered at the too-fancy cardstock and my brother's bullshit scrawl. I didn't believe a single word on that paper. Whatever this was, it had to be a trap of some kind. Essex was fucking famous for those. How many people had he killed, how much death had been met out by his hands? I didn't trust Azrael as far as I could throw him, but Essex? I'd rather cut off my own arm and solder it to my forehead than believe a single word he had to say.

Darby reached for the cardstock, but I smacked her hand away before her fingers could make contact. The last time I'd touched one of Essex's notes, I'd turned into a flickering *Skeletor* party decoration. That fate was not going to befall my sister. No way, no how. Plus, anything that came from him was highly suspect and sure to be filled with booby-traps.

"Are you okay?" Stupidly, that was the first thing that came out of my mouth, the annoying epithet making Darby grind her teeth—she was likely so tired of hearing it.

She rolled her eyes, rubbing the hand I'd smacked, seeming to come back to herself. "Of course I'm not okay. Are you okay?"

Was I?

No, I could honestly say that I was not. And why would I be? The man that murdered my parents just strolled through this cemetery without a care in the world. He just fucking walked in here. There weren't any sirens or a disturbance in the force. Nothing held him back, and no one kicked him out. And nothing was stopping him from doing it again. There was nothing to keep him out or prevent him from walking right up to us and slitting our throats next.

"No," I croaked. "No, I'm not okay."

Warm hands closed around the top of my shoulders, pulling me to my feet. Bastian's bottle-green gaze bore into me, but all I felt was my too-hot skin prickle as my jaw clenched so hard, I thought I was going to break my teeth. His fingers threaded through my hair, and he pressed my face into his shoulder.

"Your face, love," he whispered when I resisted, and it dawned on me that Darby wasn't the only person losing it today. "Breathe, Sloane. Tell me what happened."

Darby let out a snort. "Our bastard of a brother is what happened. See for yourself."

But Bastian didn't look. Instead, he pulled back, cupping my face in his hands as he looked me over. "I will in a moment," he murmured.

How do I protect her? How do I keep her safe? And will she even let me?

Bastian's mouth didn't move at all, but I heard his voice in my head all the same. It was what settled the storm in me, the turbulent waves crashing in my head quieting just a little so I could think.

"I'm okay. We're all okay," I lied, sucking in deep breaths, so I didn't just fucking lose it all over this overly crowded cemetery.

Bastian's mouth twisted, but he let me get away with my bald-faced lie, breaking his gaze away to stare at the cardstock in the grass. His grip on me only got tighter as his jaw clenched, the truth of the situation coming to light far faster than I thought it would. My grip on him got tighter as well, and rather than plan and strategize or comfort Darby or get us the hell out of there, I dropped my forehead, resting it against his chest. The welcome beat of his heart echoed through my whole body, and I breathed in his scent.

He was here and alive. I was here with him—not so much alive, but close enough. The world was still turning, my sister was still breathing. We were okay, right?

Right?

Pulling my face out of Bastian's chest, I met his gaze, and a flicker of a smile spread across his lips. "Back to normal already. I suppose this is unnecessary then."

He reached into his pocket and pulled out a necklace with a familiar purple stone. It wasn't the same glamoured necklace that had been burned off me a few days ago, but it was a close enough replica that I had to do a double take. I took the chain from his fingers, fastening it around my neck as fast as I could. I had a feeling I'd be needing it soon enough.

I felt more than heard Thomas and Bishop approach, with Darby's best friend J and his boyfriend Jimmy trailing closely behind.

Thomas took one look at the note on the ground and rolled his eyes. "You know that's a trap, right?"

I narrowed my eyes at him. "No shit."

8

The evidence bag plastic did nothing to hide the note's intended purpose. I stared at it as it rested on Darby's coffee table, the offending paper tucked safely inside so it couldn't poison us or kill us or whatever it was intended to do. Crammed on the couch, I sat half on top of Bastian, while Thomas' shoulder pressed into mine, and Simon perched awkwardly with Dahlia on his lap. Five people weren't meant for this piece of furniture, but since all the other chairs and most of the floor was occupied, I kept my trap shut. After Essex's appearance at the cemetery, most of us decided to skip the reception at Darby's father's house in favor of a strategy session at hers.

Too bad there had been zero strategy and a hell of a lot of silence.

Darby and Bishop sat in a cerulean velvet armchair with gold nail head trim and a jaunty winged back, her legs rested on the armrest, and Bishop had her head tucked under his chin. Her eyes were closed, and one would think she was sleeping if it weren't for the little tremors rattling the house every so often. Well, that and about every sixty seconds or so she would clench her fists so hard her knuckles turned white, and the lamps would buzz and flicker like they were about to explode.

She wanted out of this house. She wanted to be out on the street searching for the witches who betrayed her, or maybe she wanted to take some ghoul heads. Hell, I was pretty sure she'd be happy with just going back to work, but that wasn't an option, either. No, her options were hamstringed by the souls rattling around in her body and our asshole brother lurking in the shadows somewhere.

What am I supposed to do, Azrael? I mentally pleaded for him to hear me. *So, yeah, those souls didn't kill her right away or anything, but this isn't good. No one save for a deity is supposed to have that much power.*

But as was his norm, Azrael not only refused to show his face, but he also didn't illuminate any answers, either. Of course, I had an idea of what could be done, but I didn't think anyone was going to like it.

I sure as hell didn't.

"So, no one is going to say anything about the penchant for earthquakes this house has?" Harper griped from the floor, her head resting on Sarina's lap. "Or the fact that this one is so juiced up she might as well power a nuclear reactor?" She hooked her thumb at Darby as she stared at the ceiling. "I mean, I'm all for trying to gather oneself and hiding away, but holy shit, girl, you light up like Vegas every twelve minutes, and a single temper tantrum from you is going to break the planet."

Eyes still closed, Darby snorted. "Tell me how you really feel, Harper. Don't hold back."

"That *was* me sugarcoating it, sweetheart. You don't want to hear everything I have to say."

As someone who had been on the other end of a Harper tongue-lashing, I winced. Darby opened a lone eye, spearing Harper with an irritated half-glare.

"Maybe I do." Darby opened the other eye and sat up. "Maybe I want to know what you're holding back."

Oh, this has disaster written all over it.

Harper mirrored her, rising from her Sarina pillow to stare Darby down. "You have too much power running through your veins, no outlet, and you're shaking the fucking planet. Not to mention, no one has said a peep about whether or not the souls roiling under your skin are being put to rest, or what's going to happen now that you've essentially blew up two Knoxville factions. Your father died and that is awful. Truly, I feel for you, but you have too much going on to just sit here and wallow, especially when you're waving a red fucking flag in front of your brother."

Harper stood, and I was too stunned that all my fears were just spewing out of her mouth to do anything else but just sit there.

"I feel them whispering under your skin, and I know you do, too. Those souls aren't at rest, and they aren't at peace. You're just another prison for them, and Essex Drake just walked up to you like you were a cute little toddler. I have to wonder why he's not terrified of you, and when I think about that too hard, I get scared."

Exactly zero things about what Harper said were wrong, and Darby seemed to know it, too, because she stared at my small friend and simply nodded. "I'm scared, too. But I don't know if I can fix it or even how I'm supposed to. Azrael is MIA again, and… I don't trust myself to go up against Essex. I don't trust myself to walk out in public or say hi to my neighbors or go back to work. I'm just trying to breathe here."

Squeezing Bastian's hand, I offered the solution I'd been

mentally deliberating for about forty-eight hours. "Why can't we put the souls back in the ring? Your body can't hold them without causing seismic activity, right? And you're not absorbing them like normal. Then, why can't we just shove them back in the ring, pawn it off to Azrael, and have his feathery ass deal with it?"

I had a feeling things wouldn't go that smoothly, but it was at least a start toward a fucking solution here. Too bad it didn't solve our most basic of problems.

Bastian squeezed my hand in return, leaning in to whisper in my ear, "You're leaving something out, love. I can feel it."

I pulled away from him and gave him an "I'll tell you later" look. Oh, I was leaving a whole host of shit out. Namely, that I had a feeling that Azrael wouldn't help at all, and I'd have to somehow take the damn thing down to the Underworld myself—not that I knew how to get there. Or—and this was a far likelier scenario—Essex was just waiting for us to do this very thing so he could steal the ring and enact whatever plan he had stashed up his sleeve.

Bastian's jaw tightened, his eyes going gold for a moment before fading back to green. Yeah, I wasn't getting anything past him.

"As if he would even help," Darby muttered, resettling on Bishop's lap.

I stood, mirroring Harper as we both stared at Darby. "Then he doesn't help. But you can't keep those souls inside you forever. Because sooner or later Essex is just going to tap you like a keg and suck them out, and then we're just as fucked as we were two damn days ago."

That came out harsher than I'd intended, but it was the truth.

Sensitive to her grief? No.

A truth she needed to hear before she burned from the inside out?

Definitely.

Every part of Darby felt too big, too powerful, too much. And she wasn't holding it together—not that I expected her to, given what she lost—but this wasn't the kind of power you could just let fester.

Darby rose from Bishop's lap, she, Harper, and I an irritated triangle of women. It took me less than a second to realize that if Darby was pissed off enough, she could probably blow me off the map, but I stood firm.

"You know they're right, D," J said from his perch on the floor. He was cuddled up next to the giant Fae I'd met on the battlefield, his injuries all healed up from Darby's overabundance of power. "You can't keep all that bottled up forever. If it doesn't kill your body, it sure as hell will kill your mind."

Darby's smile was rueful, a bitter twist to her lips that was almost a sneer. "You think I don't know that? You think I can't read all your thoughts, feel all your emotions? You think I don't feel your ideas just buzzing in the back of my mind?" She blinked furiously as a tear slipped from her eye. "I know I can't do this forever. I can barely handle today."

"Then what do you plan to do about it?" Thomas asked from his place on the couch, a cut crystal tumbler in his hand that was only half-full of top-shelf whiskey. "Because all I see is a scared child who runs the risk of turning out just like the parents she hates so much." The room was already pretty quiet, but a hush fell over it that added a whole other weight to the air. "If you're the woman I think you are, I would hope the safety of those around you would be your top priority."

Everyone tensed as the tremors that had only occasionally

popped up, rumbled through the house hard enough to leave a crack in the living room wall.

"But I suppose choosing to throw a temper tantrum is more your speed then?" Thomas taunted before sipping his whiskey like he didn't have a care in the world.

"Really?" I squawked. "Antagonizing her? This is your plan?"

Thomas turned his chin to spear me with a bored glare. "It worked on you, didn't it?"

I couldn't recall a time where Thomas' antagonism had done anything but piss me off and confuse the shit out of me, but if it would work on Darby, I wasn't going to complain.

Much.

But Thomas' hard truths had the desired effect as the ground settled. All eyes were on Darby as she gritted her teeth and clenched her fists, her anger held at bay by a wing and a prayer. But soon her hands unclenched, and her jaw relaxed, and she gave Thomas a rueful sort of nod.

"Okay. I will agree something needs to be done, but I don't trust Azrael, and I don't believe Essex, and I don't know what will happen if I extract these souls. So, if we could figure that out, that would be great. In the meantime, I think everyone should head home."

Personally, I thought that was a horrible idea. Leaving her unprotected after Essex had made contact seemed like the worst idea ever. Plus, Bastian and I had been staying in her guestroom, and the fact that she was sending us home rankled a bit. I didn't like the fact that she would be by herself, nor did I like the idea that I might be abandoning her.

When neither Bastian nor I moved, Darby pierced us with a glare. "I mean you, too. You've stayed here for two days. I don't need a babysitter anymore."

"The hell you don't," I protested. While everyone else was

hurrying to their feet to go, I stayed rooted to the spot. "Essex is still out there—"

"And I've got back up here if he decides to pick a fight. You have a life and a home that doesn't include me. It's about time you went back to it."

It wasn't like I could stay there if she wanted me to go, but I still didn't like it. It felt like I was leaving her to the wolves. "This is a horrible plan you know"

"Probably. But at least my house will be empty."

As someone who hated it when there were far too many people around, I could totally understand. That didn't mean I liked it.

"Fine. But I swear to everything holy, if something happens while I'm gone and you get killed, I am retrieving you from the Underworld and kicking your ass."

Again, not that I knew how to do that, but I'd figure it the fuck out.

"Promises, promises," she muttered, smiling, the pull to her lips just as fake as the mirth in her voice.

This was a horrible idea, but I was going to do it, anyway.

I just hoped it didn't come to bite me in the ass.

Upon our reluctant departure from Darby's house, the tense energy coming from Bastian multiplied tenfold. The entire ride home was filled with tense looks and an even thicker silence, no one saying so much as a peep in the hour-long drive. I knew as soon as we got home, he would ask the questions brewing behind those bottle-green eyes, but I didn't know if I could answer him. He would want to know what I'd been leaving out at Darby's house, and the truth of it would piss him all the way off.

The SUV pulled into the drive, Bastian at the helm. His knuckles were nearly white as he held onto the steering wheel, but he managed to peel them off one by one without ripping the whole thing off Hulk-style. Everyone else hopped out of the car, but he stayed right where he was, staring at his hands as they fisted on his lap.

Yep, there was no way I was getting out of this interrogation. No way, no how.

The garage door rolled closed, the mechanical clank of it

locking almost making me jump out of my skin. Then he rotated in his seat to stare at me. "Well, love, I'm all ears."

Oh, so we're doing this here then. Super.

Rather than answer him, I got out of the car and headed for the garage door. I didn't make it two steps past the SUV before my back was pressed into the still-cooling metal, and he was in my space, pressing his big body into me.

"I don't know if this has escaped your attention, but I wasn't asking." Bastian's expression was cool and calculating, but I saw the worry and fear and bitter agony behind the mask. It tempered all my resistance, leaving me with coy sass rather than unmitigated rage at being pinned down.

"Enlighten me then. What do you want to know?" It was a stupid question, sure. I knew the answer, but stalling seemed like my best course of action.

"I want to know what you're hiding. I want to know what you didn't say at Darby's house. I want to know why you think not telling me is a good idea. When has keeping the other person in the dark ever worked out for us?"

His fingers curled around the back of my neck as he tilted my head up so I could not escape his gaze as it dropped to my lips. "And I want to know why you don't want to tell me."

The heat of him radiated through my body, and it warmed a part of me that had been cold since seeing that stupid note. As high-handed as it was, it still made me feel protected, which was stupid and girly and... "You know the answer to that. You're going to freak out, and then I'm going to freak out, and then it's going to turn into a big, huge mess that I can't fix when I already have a pile of messes that I can't fix in my back pocket. I just wanted five minutes where nobody expected me to fix their problems."

He dipped his nose so it brushed mine. "No one expects

you to fix everything. Especially not me. Now, tell me what is going on."

I sighed, basking in his heat for a moment before I broke everything. "You're going to freak out."

"Then I'll freak out. And then after that, we'll deal with it together."

I shook my head, breaking the tense stare-down and thought long and hard about how I could tell him the truth. Swallowing thickly, I let it all out. "Azrael isn't going to help. And she can't keep those souls inside her. They have to be brought to the Underworld, and if Azrael isn't going to help, the only person I could think to take them—is me." I flicked my gaze back to him, and almost wished I hadn't.

The change that came over him was immediate. His eyes flashed gold, the burning orbs boring a hole into my soul.

"No," he whispered with a vehemence that shook me to my core.

"What do you mean no? There isn't anyone else—"

He pressed further into me. "It is not going to be you."

I broke our stare-down, my eyes falling to his lips, his jaw— anything but his eyes. Those eyes were breaking me, and I didn't know I could be more broken than I already was. "It has to be me. There is no one else."

His grip tightened on the back of my neck, his fingers threading into my hair as his other arm banded around my back. I had no other choice but to look at him, no other choice but to hear him. "You barely survived the In-Between."

"No, *you* barely survived the In-Between. I just got stuck is all." Really, it was semantics at this point, but the argument needed to be made.

Inexplicably, he somehow invaded even more of my space, pressing harder into me. "You're not leaving me, do you understand? I don't care about this world. I don't care if everything falls apart. You are not leaving me alone to live without you. Until the world stops turning and the sun stops burning, remember?"

I wanted to be mad, I really did. But all I felt was heat, his warmth, his soul boring into me. "But—"

"But, nothing. You are not leaving me behind. You're not doing this by yourself. I won't let you leave me. Not when I've just found you. Not when—" His sentence broke off as if he couldn't say another word. Instead, he dropped his lips to mine in a hard, fierce kiss.

I couldn't say why the almost violent touch of his mouth to mine relieved me, but it did. The fear, the fury, the uncertainty faded away once his lips made contact. The rough burr of his stubble against my hand as I cupped his face sent shivers down my spine. Bastian's hold on me got tighter, and he lifted me off my feet, bracing the both of us against the SUV as our kiss consumed us.

Three days.

It had only been three days since I'd lost him. Three days since I'd searched the In-Between in the hopes of finding him. Three days since his breathing stopped, and he whispered how much he loved me as he faded away. He couldn't live this life without me? Well, I couldn't do it without him, either.

I couldn't walk this road by myself, always wondering if he was going to... to...

Every bit of it came crashing down on me all at once. What we'd survived, what I'd lost, what could be in my future if the worst were to happen and I lost him again. Because there would be a time when I wouldn't be able to call him back, when I wouldn't be able to save him.

When I would be alone, too.

Bastian readjusted his grip, his fingers fumbling with the fly of my jeans, and I dropped biting kisses to his jaw, his neck.

My fangs ached in my mouth, practically begging to tear into his flesh, but I held back. At the touch of my fangs against his neck, he groaned, his large fingers hooking in the waist of my jeans and yanking. I felt more than heard the button ping to the ground as the zipper ripped apart.

I wanted him out of those clothes. I wanted his skin on mine—his blood in my mouth. My hands roamed, yanking up his shirt so I could feel every part of him I could reach. And then I was on my feet, my front pressed against the side of the truck as he roughly shoved my jeans to my knees, the cool air kissing my skin just as he had been a moment before. A second later—though it felt like an eternity—his warmth returned as he snaked his hand up my shirt. Tugging my bra out of the way, he cupped my breast with one hand as he notched himself at my opening with the other.

"Promise me," he growled in my ear. "Promise you aren't going without me."

I rocked back, aching to take him inside of me, but his grip tightened, stilling my hips.

"Please," I begged, tipping my head back to rest it on his shoulder. Everything ached, my heart, my sex, my fangs.

"Promise me, and I will. I'll give you everything. Just promise me."

And I was supposed to say no to this how again?

"I promise," I breathed, and he pushed inside, filling me in one stroke.

His other hand collared around my neck, directing my chin so he could press hot, fevered kisses to my lips as he moved in the most delicious rhythm. It was angry and hurried and so fucking beautiful, my heart felt like it was too big for my chest. I moaned into his mouth, and he groaned into mine. I didn't care where we were or who could walk in and see us. It was as if there was no one else on the planet but us.

Without warning he pulled out, and I moaned at the loss until I felt him yank my jeans the rest of the way off. Maybe he tore them off—I didn't know, nor did I care. Then he spun me, hauling me up his body so he could fill me again. The heat of his body hit my front in an almost blistering way, and I couldn't deny the ache in my fangs another second. I tightened my legs around his hips, tore his shirt over the top of his head, and struck. The thick, decadent lifeblood gushed into my mouth as his strokes got rougher, more needy, more desperate.

I fucking loved it.

One swallow, and I felt every kiss he'd ever thought of pressing to my skin. Two swallows, and I experienced every lick he'd wanted, everywhere he wanted to taste me. Three, and my climax raced toward me, the pleasure barreling into me with the force of a freight train. Pulling my fangs from his skin, the moan that came out of me could probably wake the dead. Tingles raced up my legs all the way to my scalp as Bastian thrust his fingers in my hair and jerked my mouth to his in another blistering kiss. A moment later he groaned out his own climax, and I swallowed that down, too.

Our heavy breaths mingled as we rested our now-sweaty foreheads together. My brain was officially scrambled, but I did gather that I was indeed naked from the waist down in the garage with what was probably my ass print on the side of the truck. Also? My pants were probably toast.

I mentally shrugged. *Totally worth it.*

Smiling, Bastian pressed another kiss to my lips before easing out of me and setting me on my feet. We located the remnants of my jeans and underwear, which turned out, wouldn't work to cover my ass in any sort of way. Hell, I'd wondered how he'd gotten them over my boots, I just hadn't figured he'd ripped them apart completely. Bastian reached behind his neck and yanked his black T-shirt the rest of the way off, handing it over. Surprisingly, I hadn't ripped it to shreds. I slipped off my T-shirt and dropped his over my head. The hem hit about mid-thigh, which would have to do.

Bastian tugged me behind him, checking that the coast was clear before leading us out of the garage and to what I now thought of as our room. We showered together, washing away the day's grief and our doubts, and we didn't talk again about the plan in my head that would most certainly fail.

We lived in that happy bubble for a little while.

And then it came crashing down on us.

10

"Please tell me you're kidding," Emrys breathed, sitting back in her chair like my stupidity was contagious.

I just held Bastian's hand tighter and shook my head. We were in her office, sitting in the very chairs where I had fed from Bastian for the first time. My fingers traced the crescent tears in the leather as I held back a smile. "I'm not, and if you'd have seen it, you wouldn't be kidding, either."

"I saw enough up at the lake to know you're dealing with complex magic that you have no idea how to harness. You want me to be pulling those souls out of her? Me and what bleeding army?"

It was cute that she honestly thought that I believed she was some fragile little thing. "Oh, please. You could probably do this in your sleep. Quit playing with me."

Normally, I'd be a little scared of Emrys. She was my boss, a badass druid, and had just a tad too much of gray in her soul to keep me on my toes. But my sister was rocking and rolling the planet for fuck's sake. I didn't have time to be afraid of Emrys.

I had bigger fish to fry.

"Contrary to popular belief, lass, I am not the end all be all of magical power. What was done to that girl took a whole coven of witches. I alone am no coven." Emrys steepled her fingers like the conversation was over and she'd delivered the final blow.

"So, you're telling me that you, plus Simon, Bastian, Bishop, and Dahlia—plus whatever mojo that Fae, Jimmy has— can't compete with a coven of witches half of ya'll's ages? And mind you, I'm being nice with that estimate since I know you and Thomas are older than Jesus himself. Go ahead and pull the other leg while you're at it."

She sat back, a ghost of a smile crossing her lips before the seriousness returned, her odd reddish eyes flashing with warning. "I'm not pulling your leg. I'm telling you the facts. The fact is that without Azrael's help I don't think we can pull those souls from her. And more than that, I think if we try, it could kill her."

Risking Darby's life wasn't something I was too keen on doing, but I feared waiting wasn't a better option, either.

"Then we need Azrael's help," I conceded, throwing my hands up. "She can't stand that much power inside her, she's a hair's breadth from losing her fucking mind. So, if we need to summon him, or lasso him, or what the fuck ever, it needs to get done. Bishop called me at eight this morning to tell me how she had destroyed her whole kitchen. There's only so much she can annihilate before it starts actually obliterating her life."

I felt the swish of wings a moment before my father spoke, his appearance making both Bastian and Emrys nearly jump out of their skin.

"You called?" Azrael asked from the doorway.

I tossed an irritated glare over my shoulder. "Yeah, I did. Lots. Good of you to show up."

Bastian found my hand and squeezed my fingers, likely trying to get me to shut up. But he didn't realize just how many times I had pleaded in my head for Azrael to help. Hundreds, maybe thousands of times over the last two days and he'd stayed gone. When our brother showed up, when that stupid note was in the grass, when Darby was breaking her living room apart. I had begged and pleaded with him to come and help us—help her—and still he'd stayed away.

"Sorry," he said, tilting his dark head to the side as he assessed Bastian. "I was working."

He and I both knew he could do his job from anywhere. In fact, he had done this job from a squat prison underneath thousands of pounds of rock and rubble and water where he'd stayed for close to twenty years. And now when we needed him that's when he decided he needed to be on site to collect souls?

I call bullshit.

Azrael's eyes flashed purple for a moment before they hid behind his usual glamour of dark brown. "Collecting souls is not my only job. You'd know that if you had taken me up on my offer to teach you. Instead, you decided to stay for *love.*"

He rolled his eyes in derision, but I knew it was fake. Azrael might not have known real love like what I had, but he knew enough to worry about his kids. Knew enough to not force me to come to heel. He knew enough to send me back to Bastian when I'd been stuck in the In-Between.

Stop trying to make us hate you. You might be a dick, but you aren't a monster. You know what love is, I don't care how old and jaded you are.

Both Bastian and Emrys stood, the pair of them bowing at the waist in deference to my father. Sure, he was the Angel of Death, but bowing? The act seemed to make Azrael uncomfortable, and so did the silence that hung in the room.

Rolling my eyes, I stood and introduced my boss and my... Bastian.

"Azrael, meet Emrys Zane and Sebastian Cartwright." I carefully left off who these people were to me, but since my father could read my mind, it was really unnecessary.

"A pleasure," Azrael said, nodding to them both. "I understand that Darby isn't handling things very well."

Well, that is the understatement of the fucking century. Good of you to finally give a damn.

Was antagonizing the Angel of Death a smart play? Probably not.

Was it exactly what he deserved for being the vaguest parent known to mankind? Absolutely.

Azrael speared me with a glare but continued like he hadn't heard me mentally berating him. "I would like to help. I believe with your assistance I may be able to extract the souls that Mariana has trapped inside Darby."

That was code for "I let Darby absorb those souls because I was too chickenshit to go up against the woman who stole my ring, put me in that prison cell, and dumped a couple kilotons of rock, rubble, and lake water on top." Darby had told me what that ring had showed her, and the fact of the matter was, was that all of this could have been avoided if Azrael had ever —just once—fought back. He let this happen, let this bullshit unfold because... because I had no idea why. And now he wanted help?

Of course he did. And we'd accept it because there was no other way, and he'd learn exactly fuck all from this experience except that he could get away with doing whatever the hell he wanted to do and fuck the rest of us.

"You know, you and your brother think quite alike," Azrael murmured, spearing me with a look of wrath. "Blaming me for the things I *had* to do. You don't see me doing that to you."

Without much thought, I was on my feet and in his face. "That's because it's your fault, you fuck. *You're* the reason I had to do those things. *You're* the reason I'm here. *You're* the reason I turned into a monster. You did this, fucking around with arcane women who had no idea what a curse being your child would be, and then you leave them holding the bag. Then you come back into our lives like you're some benevolent savior when it's your fault our lives are shit in the first fucking place. Get fucked, you asshole."

My lip curled on its very own and I contemplated spitting right in his face. Instead, I whispered the truth. "Your son killed my parents, he killed me, and then he had his minion kill the very last person on this planet that gave a shit about me. You have no right to come into this house and insult me like that. No. Right. I don't care whether you're a god or not."

That's when I realized I was looking Azrael in the eye—like *right* in the eye. I had totally meant to get in his face, but not like this. Azrael was tall—taller than even Axel, who had to be six and a half feet of ghoul giant. Looking down, I quickly understood what had given me the boost.

My feet were dangling a foot over the plush carpet. I was floating.

I.

Was.

Floating.

In the air. I was floating in the air like someone had shoved a helium tank up my butt and cranked the lever wide. Okay, so that was a gross analogy, but the imagery still worked.

And Azrael?

Well, he had a cat that ate the canary smile like everything was going according to plan. Naturally, it pissed me off and made me forget for a second that I was essentially flying. Okay, so not exactly flying, but *Peter Pan* had nothing on this shit.

"What the fuck are you smiling at?"

His hands rose, and he pressed them to the top of my shoulders, resettling my feet back on the floor. "Not a thing, kid. Not a thing."

Jerk.

"Next thing you know," Azrael said, chuckling, "you'll be sprouting wings like your dear old dad, and then we'll really be in trouble."

"Can we get back to the task at hand already?" I muttered, not even looking at Bastian or Emrys, and sort of thankful it was them and not Harper who saw this whole thing. She would have shouted the house down, made a whole scene, and then I'd never live it down.

Azrael opened his mouth to say something—likely to give me more shit if I were to guess—when the whole house rocked under my feet. Books rattled off the shelves and the lights flickered.

"Well, fuck," my father groaned, his hair turning white and his wings coming out in full force. "I thought we had more time."

Time? Time for what?

An instant later, Bishop La Roux appeared in Emrys' office, bypassing every ward and magical protection we had on the place. In his arms was a seizing Darby, her body shaking in time with the tremors of the house. Only, the house wasn't going to withstand the onslaught. The hardwood floor splintered under my feet, knocking me to the unstable ground. Bastian grabbed me by the waist, pulling me up with a rough tug.

"Outside," he shouted. "Everyone outside!"

Bishop and my wayward father disappeared, taking Darby with them. As we ran from the room, light fixtures swayed before breaking from their fastenings and falling to the floor.

Books toppled from their shelves, art slipped and fell from their nails. Harper screeched in Axel's arms—the big man held her like a football tucked under his arm as he sprinted down the stairs. Simon protected Dahlia with a silver tray that he had picked up from who knew where, and Thomas had ahold of Clem and Emrys, dragging them from the house with a speed I almost couldn't track through the shattered French doors, with us hot on his heels.

And then we were outside, slipping in the wet grass as we tried to get away from the house. Too bad the outside wasn't much better. The ground pitched and rolled, great fissures in the earth cracked wide open, threatening to swallow us whole. We converged on Bishop, my still-seizing sister, and Azrael in full Angel of Death mode, his wings spread wide and his eyes flashing purple for all the world to see.

"We can't wait," Azrael ordered. "We have to do this now."

11

We have to do this now.

That was all well and good, but I didn't have that first clue as to what we were doing, or how we were supposed to pull the souls from Darby, or keep her alive once we did. I was still having trouble standing up for fuck's sake. The ground was still bucking in time with Darby's convulsions, the soil cracking under our feet with each shake.

The thing that made my heart sink and gut go into freefall? I wasn't sure she was breathing. Darby's lips had an unhealthy blue tint that spoke of a solid lack of oxygen. I wasn't like her. I couldn't give away power or save people from the brink of death. I felt useless and impotent and…

But Azrael sure as hell seemed to know what he was doing. He gave Dahlia and Emrys a nod, crooking his finger as the three of them surrounded Bishop and Darby, latching their hands together. Bishop clutched Darby close to his chest, shaking his head like he was having an internal debate.

"You have to. If you're in there with her, you won't make it.

You want my daughter to blame herself more than she already does?" Azrael growled, his purple eyes flashing. "Let her go."

Bishop squeezed Darby once more before he gently placed her on the quaking ground and crawled from the circle like he was walking to the gallows.

"Sloane," Azrael called. "Get that ring off her thumb. Hold it in your hand and stand beside her."

I moved to do as told—shocker, I know—when Bastian latched onto my upper arm and drew me back. "You just told us whoever is in that circle with Darby will die, or was that bullshit?"

Azrael rolled his eyes before spearing Bastian with a violent purple glare. "But Sloane isn't alive, now, is she? Any other objections? I only have a child dying right before my eyes."

Bastian's grip loosened, and I tossed what I hoped was a reassuring glance over my shoulder as I shakily made my way to Darby's side. Prying the obsidian ring off her cold thumb, I held it in my hands and raised them to Azrael.

"Keep holding it, and don't move."

Well, that sounds ominous.

And it sounded like a whole lot of "not a good idea," too, but I kept that to myself and held still. I felt the power crackle on the air before the first zing of a soul hit the ring in my hand. A blindingly bright light nearly seared my retinas as the soul circled the cool metal in my hand, swirling like a tornado before it winked out of sight. The metal warmed slightly as it absorbed the soul, the ring rocking in my palm before it settled again.

What I thought was funny—not in a funny "Ha-ha" way and more "WTF" with a side of "Holy shit"—was that this was one single soul, and by my calculations, there were about a hundred thousand more coming. I met Azrael's eyes. His brow furrowed with concentration, his irises blazed violet, glowing just like one of those souls. But the sweat on his brow and slight ration of fear in his gaze was what made my whole stomach sink into the ground. Mariana's spell—even after her death—was too damn strong. Too strong for a fucking death deity.

Oh, shit. Oh, fuck, oh, shit, oh, no.

"Bishop, Simon, Bastian, get over here," Azrael ordered, and the men raced for him, joining Emrys and Dahlia in this macabre circle.

As soon as the guys joined the circle, the heat of the ring in my hand went from simply hot to raging inferno levels. Darby shook once more before her whole body lifted off the ground, the earth stilling as she bowed like she was being broken in half. Then she let out a scream that would haunt me until I was gone from this earth. Her eyes opened, the blazing white light of thousands of souls erupting from her lids as a scalding beam broke from her chest.

A gale-force wind tore through the air, nearly knocking us all off our feet, but I managed to stay right there—right next to Darby. Fire sprung up in a circle around both Darby and I, cutting us off from the rest, as lightning crackled through the sky. Then it was as if the heavens broke. Rain poured down on us, and all the while, Darby screamed as she hovered over the ground, the souls pouring from her chest like a dam breaking.

Then those souls reached for the ring, the brilliant tornado of thousands of trapped spirits whipped around the warming metal. And then I was the one screaming. Each soul warmed the metal, each one raising the temperature of the ring ten-fold, until it was glowing white and burning the flesh from my hands.

I wanted to drop it. Wanted to throw it away or chuck it

into the darkest, deepest volcano. But Azrael had told me to stay still, so for Darby, I did. Tears streamed down my face as the blistering agony raced through my body, the tremors of pain rocking me to my core. The light in my palm suddenly died, and along with it, Darby's limp form slammed back onto the ground. The ring of fire petered out, the rains dousing it as if it were all meant to be. Blinding pain shuddered through me as I knelt on the soggy grass.

My limbs refused to obey my commands as I stared in horror at the monstrosity in my palms. What had been an obsidian ring was now a trio of metallic sigils burned into the skin of my hands. The metal and stone had burned away, and now all I was left with was the growing horror that someone had played a horrible trick on me.

"What did you do?" I whispered, still staring at the three markings, each one I recognized from the In-Between. They had been on the blue door that had led me out and back to Bastian. "What did you do?" I asked again, louder this time as realization dawned.

Those souls had been in Darby and now… now they were in me.

The silence from Azrael was telling, and I tore my gaze from my hands to spear my father with a pleading stare.

"What did you do?" I whimpered, tears clogging my throat.

Sorrow and what I could only assume was pity raced across his features. "What had to be done. Gather yourself. We leave in an hour." Then that bastard winked out of sight, leaving me with a cryptic pronouncement and a boatload of agony.

The silence from everyone was more telling than anything else, each of their quiet stares full of pity. Maybe they knew what was going on. Maybe they knew why Azrael had done what he had, but I sure as fuck didn't. Bastian broke from the circle first, his rough hands cupping my cheeks as he knelt in front of me, his bottle-green eyes boring holes in me.

He knew what was going on. He had to know. Didn't he?

"Sloane? Love?" *Are you all right?* That last bit sounded like a gong in my head, even though his lips hadn't moved.

I couldn't speak, the tears clogging my throat as a wave of helplessness pulled me under. Was I all right? No, I could honestly say I was not.

"Sloane?" a voice croaked from behind me, and I turned to see an incredibly pale Darby sitting up, as if the act was the most torturous thing she had ever done in her entire life. Hell, if Bishop hadn't been helping her, I doubted she would have made it vertical. "What—what happened?" Her gaze flicked from my face to my hands to the open yard around us, the ground still marred with deep cracks and burnt grass. Then they fell on my hands again, Azrael's sigils burned into my palms taking the sole of her focus.

"Oh, no," she whispered, her eyes welling with tears. "What did he do?"

That was the question for the ages, and one no one had deigned to answer.

Shrugging, I shoved every bit of pain and worry down deep where it wouldn't bubble up my throat and choke me. "He didn't say."

He had, however, mentioned something about us leaving in an hour, and I had no idea what "gathering myself" meant.

None of this was going to plan—not that my plan was fleshed out exactly—but this was so far out of my scope, I practically had whiplash with how fast everything had turned. Bastian cupped my cheeks in his hands, the warmth a comfort in the midst of all this uncertainty. His expression had a healthy dose of fear and not a little bit of trepidation.

How do I tell her? His thoughts sounded in my brain. And

then the truth unfolded inside his mind, showing me all the things Azrael hadn't meant him to see while they were connected in the circle.

We weren't just leaving the house in an hour—oh, no. We were leaving this plane of existence altogether. Azrael intended to take me to the Underworld. And that hour time frame he'd given me to prepare myself?

That was the best-case scenario.

"No." As far as answers went, it fit the bill, but it didn't quite cut it when it came to explaining all the reasons why going to the Underworld was a terrible, no-good idea for someone like me. All the fears that I'd shoved down slammed into me in a wave, threatening to yank me under.

When I'd originally had the idea, it hadn't actually been real for me. I knew it was a possibility that I would have to go there, but—

"I'm going with you," Bastian growled, the tips of his fingers pressing into my scalp as he held my head in his hands. "You promised me, Sloane. Remember? You swore."

"What?" Simon breathed from behind him, and then he charged forward, ripping Bastian away from me and hauling him to his feet. A blackness settled over Simon's irises and sclera—the effect practically demonic as the smaller death mage lost hold on his rage. "Are you crazy? Is that it? Kick over and leave me behind? I don't bloody think so."

Darby had explained Azrael's decree after her father had died. That someone who had been brought back couldn't come back twice. That there was nothing he could do—that there was no way for Killian to return to the living a second time.

I'd promised Bastian I'd take him with me, essentially killing him and selfishly separating him from his only living family. I really was a monster, wasn't I?

"Stay out of this, Simon. You know damn well you'd do the

same for Dahlia. And there's no proof that arcaners have that same rule applied to them. I'm going, brother, and there is nothing you could say to stop me."

Thomas roughly pulled the brothers apart, shaking them both like he was trying to knock some sense into them. "Want to clue the rest of us in? Not everyone mind-melded with a death god for fuck's sake."

"Azrael is taking Sloane to the Underworld," Simon answered, his face twisted in derision. "My idiot brother wants to go with her, even though he most likely will be trapped down there." He tore Thomas' hand off his flannel shirt and shoved Bastian's shoulder, adding a little of his power behind it so Bastian stumbled. "You promised me when Mum and Dad died that you wouldn't follow them. You're a liar, brother." Simon pointed a finger right at Bastian's face, a black swirl of magic racing up his arm. "You're a fucking liar."

Bastian pinched his brow as his shoulders hunched. "I made that promise when we were children, Simon. Tell me. If Dahlia were in the same position, would you let her go alone, knowing that she might be trapped there, too? Would you kiss her on the lips and bid her goodbye, knowing she might not come back to you? Or would you follow her and damn the consequences? Because living another thousand years without her would be the worst torture you could imagine?"

Simon looked like Bastian had slapped him right across the face, an expression that turned pained when Dahlia threaded her fingers through his. His gaze broke from his brother's, and he stared down into her whiskey-colored eyes, his pooling with tears as reality set in.

"It's not fair," he whispered.

Dahlia smiled at him, a sweet bitter smile that spoke of her own pain. "It never is."

"Why?" Darby whispered, still staring at my rapidly healing

hands, the metallic sigils becoming permanent fixtures in my flesh. "Why would he do this to you? After all you've lost."

That I couldn't answer—not really. I got flashes of it in Bastian's brain, but I didn't understand.

I wasn't sure I ever would.

12

Simon wiped at his leaking eyes before striding across the grass and pulling me up by my biceps. "He gave you an hour and we've wasted enough of it. You have to get ready."

Dumbstruck, I allowed him to pull me by the forearm back to the house. How did one get ready for a trek to the Underworld? Was I supposed to load up with weapons? Did I need a sword? Did guns work down there?

"Clem, get their leathers ready," he called over his shoulder as we crunched over broken glass and fallen books.

The house looked no better than it had a week ago after our little invasion, and I had to wonder how many times it had broken apart and been put back together by magic over the years. Simon muttered to himself for a second before picking through the debris, yanking me behind him to the staircase. An irritated trill pulled my gaze to my feet, and an angry set of glowing green eyes pierced me with an annoyed glare. Simon yanked me again, and Isis wound around his feet, almost tripping him.

"Damn and blast, Isis. It's not my fault you went and hid under the bed. The whole bloody house was going to fall on us, you mangy feline, and you can't die."

She couldn't? Well, that was new information—and sort of comforting if I was being honest. The world without a little skeleton kitty in it seemed just a bit awful to me. I pulled my arm out of Simon's hold and picked up the bone cat, cuddling her in my arms as I continued following him up the stairs.

"Did evil Simon leave you behind, my sweet girl? What a bad daddy." Scratching at her nonexistent fur, I smiled evilly when Simon shot me a look over his shoulder as he muttered something about children these days.

Children? Pfft.

Considering Simon looked and acted younger than quite a few of my classmates when I was actually in college, he had little to no room to talk, but I didn't say that out loud. We entered Simon's domain, and he twisted his wrist before snapping the fingers of his right hand. Candles on the dusty surfaces flared to life, somehow not toppled in the commotion. Simon pressed on a wooden panel, and much like Emrys' office, the panel swung inward to reveal a whole other room.

This room was lit, too, with half-burnt black candles, their wax pooling on the stone floor. As soon as I crossed the threshold from Simon's room into this new place, the chill of the air had me shivering around Isis.

"Simon?"

I wanted to ask where we were. I wanted him to tell me a happy lie, but I knew as soon as I crossed into this new room, that we weren't in the house anymore. I hugged Isis tighter before setting her at my feet, the unease in my gut pulling me back toward the open door.

"Oh, stop it," he chided, not even bothering to turn around from his inspection of a massive shelf with dusty bottles and even dustier books. "If I wanted to brick you in the wine cellar, I'd have been more creative about it."

"Referencing Poe isn't making me feel any better, you know."

Simon shot an equally evil smile over his shoulder as his fingers perused the shelf by feel alone, pulling a huge tome into his arms without even bothering to look at the title. "That's what you get for agreeing to take my brother to his probable death. Now, do you want him to come back with you or do you want him stuck there? Because if you answer wrong, I really will brick you in the wine cellar. Just so we're clear."

My whole body practically wilted into the stone floor. "You can do that? You can…"

I wanted to cry I was so happy, the relief hitting me square in the chest.

"I believe so, but we don't have time to dally. And…" Simon winced as he trailed off. "You're going to need to lose a toe. It should grow back almost instantly, but yeah."

"What?"

"Normally it would be fingers, but those take longer to grow back, and we don't have that kind of time. The toe will just have to do. Though, it will give you less time to work with."

"Better make it three," Thomas insisted, filling the doorway. "Axel and I are coming, too."

I scoffed, staring at Thomas like he'd lost a head. "I'm not losing three toes. One for Bastian, sure, but you two? Hell no. And why—"

"We're coming, girlie," Axel said from behind him, shouldering through the doorway like the giant he was. "Emrys informed us of Azrael's real reason for getting those souls out of Darby all quick like. Essex is coming for you both, kid, and I'm not forgetting what I promised you. I owe you and yours for what you did. Not to mention, Darby's the reason I never have to look at my murdering father ever again. I ain't leaving ya'll unprotected. No way, no how. So, cough up some toes."

With everything that had happened over the last few days, I'd forgotten that the leader of the Monroe nest had been Axel's dad. With that added wrinkle, there was no way either of these idiots were going to let Bastian and I go to the Underworld—of all places—alone.

Ugh. Fine.

Bile rose in my throat as I started unlacing my boots. "Left or right foot?"

Was I really going to do this? Like for real? Just cough up some toes for Simon to use in some weird death mage woo-woo, no questions asked?

Evidently, I was.

"You're left-handed, correct?" Simon asked as he lifted a gleaming cleaver off a dusty table, littered with candles and an honest-to-god shrunken head and a mummified bird of some kind.

My stomach dipped and I took a step back. "Yeah?"

"The right will do."

I'd been half-joking when I'd asked, but Simon was serious, his normally jovial expression dialed to cold, calculating awful. Perfect.

"Hold her."

Then Axel and Thomas had ahold of my arms as Simon knelt at my right foot and brought the cleaver down.

Funnily enough, I didn't feel it at first. The blade was so sharp, it was a simple breeze against my flesh, and really, considering what I'd just gone through, I kind of figured I was due a lucky break.

As it turned out, the sharper the blade, the longer it took to hurt. About two seconds later the pain hit, and the howl that came out of my mouth scared the shit out of even me. My legs buckled, Thomas and Axel taking the bulk of my weight as they eased me to the ground. Simon buggered off to go do whatever spell he had dreamt up in his fool skull, and I cussed a blue streak as the pain subsided enough for me to actually form words.

"You son of a cunt-bag motherfucker. You piece of rancid gutter shit. *Fuck* you."

Then for the second time in my life, I puked on Thomas' boots.

I'd love to say I managed to hold it together after that, but after I emptied about a pint of blood and Clem's famous chicken and dumplings on Thomas' handcrafted Italian leather boots, I went ahead and passed out. Really, that was fair. I'd sort of had a rough day, and as soon as Azrael got back, it was about to get a whole lot worse. I figured I was due a little gastrointestinal pyrotechnics.

Thomas didn't think this was at all funny, but I woke up from my little snooze to the roar of Axel and Simon's laughter. Simon himself was laughing as he weaved a fair bit of dark magic, the swirls of his power coiling like snakes up his arms.

"That is two pairs of boots she's ruined in a month. Not even a month. A week!"

I knew Thomas was a vain bastard, but I'd just sacrificed a toe so *he* could help *me* out. I deserved some slack. And no one told him to throw me off a water tower. That was *his* fault.

"Aww, come on, Thomas." Axel chuckled as he strapped blades and other such weapons into the pockets of a rather nifty cargo vest. "Don't you remember the last time you lost a limb? No one is holding onto their lunch. Not even you."

"And the water tower incident was your fault," I croaked. "You know I'm afraid of heights."

Thomas shot me a glare, his jade eyes glittering with wrath.

Yeah, if we survived this, he was going to make me pay for that, and probably not with money—not that I had any. Clem breezed into the room with an armload of leathers and a pair of boots. She handed off the boots to Thomas without so much as a word before kneeling to pass me the leathers.

I hadn't paid that much attention to Clem over the last couple of days, but the redheaded revenant seemed less bubbly than usual. Her odd gray skin and red hair appeared duller than the norm, and her smile—not that I thought this was a happy time or anything—was gone. Even in the height of battle when she was wielding her favorite shotgun, she'd been smiling. It had only been since Simon had died and come back that she'd been this way.

"Hiya, Sloane," she whispered.

"Clem."

"I cleaned the blood from the battle out of the stitching, and I had Emrys beef up the protection magic. Bastian is coming with your weapons and such."

I reached out a hand to her shoulder, the cool temp of her skin startling me just a bit. Clementine was the only revenant I knew of, so I didn't know if the cold skin was a problem or not, but I was worried. *Or* I was using her as an excuse to not think about traversing the Underworld with the love of my life and my sperm donor.

You know, *whatever*.

"You okay?" Stupid question, right? But it was all I had.

She blinked at me before her gaze went to Simon and returned to me. "He'll be okay, you know. If you and Bastian don't come back. Dahlia and me and the gang will make sure of it. But Bastian? He won't be okay without you. So if it comes down to it—and you want to choose saving him instead of keeping your promise—I'd keep the promise."

A tear leaked out of my eye before I could hold it back.

Wiping it away, I muttered, "Did Bastian tell you to tell me that?"

She shook her head. "I've been with those boys for eighty years. I know them better than I knew my own flesh and blood when I was alive. There's nothing I don't know about them. Simon? He's a survivor—always has been. Bastian? He does everything for love. Love of his family, love of his brother, the Night Watch, as rag-tag a bunch as we are. I've never seen him like this before. If you left, you'd take his heart with you."

There was nothing I could say to rebut that, so I simply nodded. She helped me hobble back out of Simon's dungeon lair and into his room, assisting me in the rather awkward clothing removal as I tried to balance while still regrowing toes. Truth be told, if the initial pain and the unbearable itch of them regrowing wasn't so horrendous, I might not have minded so much.

Okay, so that was a total lie. I minded. A lot. But if it meant Bastian could come out of this unscathed? I would lose a thousand toes. Though, I really didn't want to think about what Simon needed those toes for or what Bastian, Thomas, and Axel were about to consume.

Nope. Don't go there. That way lies up-chucking.

By the time Clem helped me wriggle into my leathers, my toes were all grown back except for the nails. Also, toes without nails? Supreme grossness.

So long, open-toed sandals. I'll miss you.

I had just tied the laces of my boots when Bastian poked his head around the screen. Once I could stand on my own, Clem had left me to dress myself, so it was just me, him, and a boatload of silence behind a dressing screen.

"Thomas and Axel talk to you?"

If he meant did they hold me down while Simon procured spell ingredients? Then sure. "Yep."

"You didn't talk them out of it?"

I almost laughed but couldn't quite manage it. "Was I supposed to? I was kind of under the impression the only way I was going to talk them out of it was to behead them. Seemed better to have them watch our backs, don't you think?"

But I had a feeling—no matter what pretty words I used to dress it up—that I was signing their death warrants, anyway.

Bastian must have seen as much on my face because he crowded me—like he was prone to do—and cupped my cheeks in his hands.

"We'll make it out of this, love," he whispered before dropping a soul-searing kiss on my lips. Letting myself fall into that kiss, I could almost believe him.

Almost.

13

"Her toes, Simon?" Bastian yelled as he tried to shove me behind him. He had just learned of his brother's newfangled spell ingredients, and it was safe to say he wasn't pleased. "Plural?"

Simon rolled his eyes as he strained a viscous liquid into three glass vials. "She's fine. Do you want to come back to the land of the living or not? No offense or anything, but I wouldn't want to go into the Underworld without backup. It was three measly toes, and they grew back in ten minutes."

I winced. Those measly toes had been missed. "I volunteered, Bastian."

Would I have rather *not* lost the three largest toes on my right foot? Absolutely.

Did I regret it? Time would tell.

But I didn't want the brothers fighting—especially not right now. Not when we were so close to leaving. Every moment that passed, I braced myself for an attack—the whispers of Essex's return threatening each breath that gusted through my lips.

Simon completed his concoction and fit a cork stopper in each vial before threading a leather cord around the spout. Passing the vials off, he immediately smacked Axel, who seemed ready to unstop the bottle and drink the contents.

"Honestly, Axel? I know you're a ghoul, and cannibalism is your thing, but..." Simon trailed off, giving a full-body shiver. "It's not for drinking. It's for wearing, you idiot."

Axel leveled him with a scowl. "Well, how was I supposed to know? You just gave me food. I thought I was supposed to eat it."

My stomach lurched at the idea of Axel chowing down on flesh. "You haven't..." I couldn't think of the right way to ask. Aunt Julie had been just chilling in his giant walk-in refrigerator for months now, and even though I hadn't thought of how I wanted to honor her passing, Axel using her as an appetizer was just wrong.

Axel seemed embarrassed but also like he knew what I was going to ask. "No, I haven't been snacking on your aunt, Sloane. Not only would that be wrong on all kinds of levels, but I also prefer, umm... fresh meat."

I was in serious danger of puking on Thomas' boots again, but the fact that Julie's remains were safe did fill me with a bit of hope.

"Wear them. Don't let them break," Simon instructed. "The whole point is to make the Underworld believe you're supposed to be there, so it doesn't kick you out or try to kill you to make you stay. Since Sloane is already dead, the tincture in that vial should mask you at least for a little while."

Bastian reluctantly looped the bottle around his neck, tucking it under his body armor to keep it safe.

"But," he continued, "time works differently down there. A day in the Underworld would be just a few moments up here.

These vials will get you a day, tops. Any longer, and I can't promise the efficacy."

I took a moment to digest that bit of knowledge. I knew we were under a time crunch, but now with the added stakes of Simon's potion not working, I felt more than a little uneasy.

"And here I thought I was just taking my daughter to the Underworld," Azrael muttered as he breezed through Simon's dungeon lair without so much as a "How do you do." "Now I find out we have stragglers."

"You plan on stopping us?" Thomas asked.

Azrael opened his mouth to counter, only to be interrupted by a woman's voice yelling for us to wait.

"Don't go yet," Darby insisted, appearing at Simon's bedroom door. Her pallor was no better than it had been in the moments after her body had evacuated a hundred thousand souls. Her skin was just as pale as mine, and her hair had lightened to almost white in the midst of everything. I had to wonder if she was closer to death than any of us were comfortable with. Her breaths heaved through her lungs like she'd run all the way here—which given that Bishop was nowhere to be seen—might actually have been a possibility.

"You're supposed to be resting," Axel growled, pinching his brow. "I could have sworn I told you to stay hooked up to that IV and down Dahlia's herbal remedy. Are you ignoring everything everyone is saying today, or is it just me?"

Darby shot him an irritated glare, her shoulders still heaving as she held up an intact saline bag with the tubing still attached to her hand. "I'm still hooked up, but if you think I'm letting ya'll leave without me hugging my sister—especially after she saved my fucking life—well, I can't fix that level of stupid."

She marched over to me. Well, marching was an overeager estimate for what she was doing. A wobbly hobble was closer to the mark, but she did it with gusto, so I didn't say anything to the contrary. Her hands reached for mine, squeezing my fingers as she studied my face. "You know, I thought I wouldn't miss reading everyone's thoughts, but right now, I kind of wish I still could." She opened her mouth, tears welling in her eyes. "I'm sorry you have to do this. I'm sorry you have to fight this battle for me. I'm—"

I cut her off with a hug, tempering my squeeze so I wouldn't crush her fragile body. I couldn't handle her apologizing for things that were totally out of her control. Not today and probably not any other day, either.

"I don't blame you. I wouldn't ever blame you. And, hey. Maybe I'll look in on Killian for you," I offered. "Tell him you said hi."

Darby's answering laugh quickly turned into a sob, and she returned my hug with a fierceness I hadn't expected from someone on Death's doorstep. "If you see him, can you tell him he was a wonderful dad for me? And then come back, okay? But if it's a question, I'd rather you just come back."

Swallowing the lump in my throat, I nodded into her shoulder. She pulled away, wiping at her eyes and nose. "Now get moving so you can be home before I know it or some other timey-wimey bullshit."

"What? No hug for me?" Azrael joked, staring at my sister in a way that said his words were less a joke and more of a request.

Darby stared at him, the betrayal still radiating from every part of her. It was no secret that the pair of us blamed him for our misfortune, but she resented him far less than I did. Maybe it was because she had seen his life through his ring. Maybe she empathized better than I did.

Or maybe it was because she hadn't died yet. It was all fun

and games until you got stabbed in the heart by a brother you knew nothing about.

Not that I spoke from personal experience or anything.

Instead of hugging him, Darby held out her hand to shake. Azrael stared at her hand, giving it a wry smile before taking it in both of his own. He gazed lovingly at her face for a moment, then he pulled her to him, placing a gentle kiss to her forehead.

As soon as his lips touched her skin, her whole body sagged. At first, I didn't understand, but instantly, her skin flushed with color, the gray pallor disappearing. Her hair bled of the rest of its color, changing to the same shade as mine. She wrapped her arms around his waist, squeezing him for just a moment, and then she let go.

Tears were in her eyes when she stepped back, and she gave him a silent nod before turning and leaving the room, her hasty departure sending a niggle of unease through me. Tough, since I was full to the brim with those niggles already, but she managed it.

"Time to go," Azrael muttered, his throat a little clogged.

Yep, not worried at all about what I just saw. Not even a little.

"I take it you still have the entrance path lit?" my father asked Simon.

Simon himself blushed deeply as Azrael raised a single dark eyebrow. "It's possible that the path through is lit with torches."

I narrowed my eyes at the death mage, wondering just how he knew about the whole toe thing. He pulled everything together so quickly, he had to have done it before, right?

In answer to my mental question, Simon lifted the shrunken head, an audible click reverberating through the room as a dusty bookcase swung into the space to reveal a drafty stone corridor. Torches flickered in the domed hallway, the scent of gentle decay and the musty odor of a place long-since sealed wafted into the room.

"See, no one has gone through that door in a century or more."

Simon had a door to the Underworld just chilling in his creepy dungeon lair? Honestly, I couldn't say it was surprising. Not at all.

Azrael gave him a fatherly smile. "And the illustrious Clementine?"

Simon's lips pressed together so hard they turned white before he raised a petulant eyebrow. "There are other doors. More heavily guarded ones. Ones that eventually get you caught and locked up for decades."

The story of Clem's resurrection was starting to become clearer in my mind.

"I see. Do take care to guard it after us, will you?" I supposed that was Azrael-speak for "Essex was on his way here, so maybe don't open it for the nefarious bastard, mm-kay?"

My father gave me an indulgent smile and nodded to the open door. "Time to go," he repeated, only this time he wasn't about to start bawling. I considered this a good sign.

Bastian crossed the room and hugged his brother, slapping his back hard enough to rattle Simon's teeth before he came back to me and grabbed my hand. We then followed Azrael as he led us through the door, the chill making me shiver as our steps echoed through the hallway. Thomas and Axel trailed after us, their footfalls adding to the quiet cacophony that was our trek to the Underworld.

No one said anything for a long while, the echoes of our footfalls creating a gentle rhythm that was slightly unnerving. This little hallway seemed no different than Simon's dungeon, the cool, dry air less telling than it should have been. I mean, this was the Underworld. Shouldn't there be like a flashing neon sign, or a black hole or something that said, "Hey, you're dead" around here somewhere? I wasn't asking for something off the Vegas Strip, but a teensy feeling in my gut would have done the trick.

That didn't come until much later.

The only clue I got that something was amiss was when Axel and Thomas' steps faltered. Or rather, when those faltering steps turned into Thomas collapsing in the middle of the corridor and Axel growling at him to stay the fuck down.

"I'm fine," Thomas said tersely, pushing himself to standing with the liberal help of the stone wall. Granted, his legs gave out within a few seconds, but it was the macho principle of the thing, right?

Axel stood tall, staring at Thomas like he'd lost his mind. "Yeah, and I'm the Easter bunny. You've been stumbling for ten minutes, you idiot. I think when you shrivel to dust, they're gonna notice."

"I'm *fine*," Thomas repeated before a cough racked his whole body. Dutifully, he covered his mouth, only for his fingers to come away coated in red. "I just need a minute."

Azrael crowded the men, kneeling to assess Thomas in that unnerving way of his. "Would you have my daughter blame herself for your death?"

He'd asked the same thing of Bishop only an hour ago, and like Bishop, Thomas looked like he'd just swallowed bile.

He wasn't the only one. I'd promised to protect Thomas—and he, me—once upon a time. I wasn't sure I could live with myself if he died trying to pay me back for something I was going to do anyway.

Sighing, he answered, "Of course not."

Azrael raised an imperious eyebrow. "Then get your head out of your ass and allow your friend to take you back to the door. Beings like you are too old, too powerful to be masked by a little death. You knew this when you walked in here. I commend your bravery. Your stupidity, however, is going to get you into trouble one of these days." He hauled Thomas to his feet so the vampire could throw an arm over Axel's shoulder.

"Run. Fast."

Both Thomas and Axel gave me a rueful look, and then they were gone, Axel hefting the vamp over his shoulder as he took off.

I watched them go far longer than I should have, and Bastian stayed with me, our eyes on the corridor until we couldn't see them anymore.

We walked for ages.

We walked so much, I could have sworn we had been in this corridor for days, weeks even. When we came to a door—as glorious a sight as that was—Azrael opened it without a second's hesitation.

I, however, needed a bit of coaxing.

It didn't matter that this was a way out of the dumbest, longest, most boring hallway known to the universe, walking into the actual Underworld didn't sound like a vacation to me. And no, it didn't matter that the place looked like a carbon copy of a suburb circa 1965. In fact, that was the supreme reason I didn't want to step one toe—pun totally intended—over the threshold.

Azrael was not down with my foolishness and latched onto my hand, yanking me—and by default, Bastian—into the creepiest little neighborhood I'd ever seen. Maybe it was because I'd watched one too many horror movies, but a completely deserted subdivision pinged my not-okay radar.

Hell, I'd take the dirty streets of Ascension over the too-manicured lawns and sweet daisy wind chimes.

Hard pass.

Add in the too-bright sky with no visible sun and no way to see the horizon, complete lack of a breeze and… Not just no, but *hell* no.

"It's just Purgatory. Get a grip," Azrael grumbled, pulling me by the hand as my reluctant feet slowed us down.

"Purgatory a la *Supernatural* or *The Good Place*, because those are two very different things from two very different shows, and—"

Azrael stared at me like I had a recently formed hole in the middle of my forehead. "I've been locked in a prison for twenty years, Sloane. Under rocks and dirt and an entire lake. Cut me some slack and elaborate."

I dithered—actually dithered—waffling my hand from side to side. "Well, *Supernatural* would mean that all the monsters are sent here when they die, and we have to fight them to stay alive zombie-apocalypse style. *The Good Place* would mean that things are mildly inconvenient, and we have to become better people to ascend to the actual good place."

Bastian snorted out a laugh from behind his fist, while Azrael continued to stare at me like I was an alien.

"What? I didn't have much of a social life when I was alive. TV shows were my jam. At least I didn't bring up *The Vampire Diaries* or *Wynona Earp*. Their versions just don't seem as plausible."

Azrael just shook his head and turned, marching down the middle of a street that could have been copied straight out of *Pleasantville*. Grumbling, I stomped after him, wondering why there couldn't have been a speedier way to get where we needed to go. Wasn't he the Angel of Death? Didn't he do this shit in his sleep?

"Just because I am who I am doesn't mean I run things down here," he grumbled, shaking his head as he answered my unasked question. "Truth be told, I'm more like a messenger or a bus driver. People up there fear me because I'm the first person they see after what is likely the worst day of their existence. Humans and the arcane alike fear me because I seem so final. Arcaners try to extend their lives, try to stay on that little rock as long as they possibly can. Little do they know there is so much more. Take your friend Thomas for example. He's been alive since the Qin Dynasty, and still, he fears me. Over two thousand years on the planet, and he still worries what will happen when he dies."

Ho-ly shit. Thomas was that old? I had an inkling he was older than dirt, but I didn't know he was BC-era old.

"And you think just because I play ferryman, I have any control whatsoever down here?" He shook his head again, still marching. "I control fuck all."

Out of the corner of my eye, I thought I caught a glimpse of blonde hair, but as soon as I turned my head, it was gone. One of those mid-century modern daisy wind chimes with the too-happy faces and unbearably loud colors was moving, even though I couldn't feel a breeze.

Sure. Nothing to see here.

Bastian frowned, mouthing a "You okay?" at me, but I shook my head. This was one of those times where I wished I could speak inside his head like he sometimes did to me. Though, I was pretty sure that was a remnant of dear old dad's powers if I was being honest.

"Okay, so we have to take the scenic route," I replied, trying not to freak out. "Care to share how long you think that will be, or how the hell we get out of here?"

He shrugged, still stomping toward who knew where in this creepy-as-fuck neighborhood. And the creep factor went up to a thousand the first time I heard the giggle. It was cheery and feminine, and exactly what I did not want to hear in the middle of a deserted Purgatory with Grumpy McGrouch as my tour guide.

Honestly, I wanted a bazooka or some napalm or something, because I figured any minute a giant sandworm was going to bust out of the ground and eat me whole.

"Sandworms? And what the hell is *Beetlejuice?*" Azrael griped, shaking his head *again* as we came to a street sign. A completely useless street sign to be clear.

The street we were on? Purgatory Lane.

The cross street? Purgatory Avenue.

"It's not like you've been reassuring me that we aren't going to get stabbed to not-death in the middle of this creepy neighborhood that seems to have no end. What the hell am I supposed to think when wind chimes start moving on their own and I hear disembodied giggles? That things are going to turn up tea and roses? Let's not forget that I'm only here in the first place because of you!" At this point, I was jabbing my finger into a death deity's chest as I stared at him right in the eyes.

I was floating. Again.

Then those giggles sounded again—a fuck of a lot closer this time—and my feet found the pavement all on their own.

Azrael's eyes widened as he stared just past me, the giggles turning softer as they got closer.

"It's right behind me, isn't it?"

Bastian and I froze—or rather, I froze, and Bastian whipped around, pulling me behind his back as he faced whatever it was. Instead of a sandworm or a monster wielding a machete, there stood a blonde woman with flowers weaved through her curls and a serene expression on her practically cherubic face.

But her features wavered like mine sometimes did, turning from a pretty blonde hippy to a severe raven-haired woman.

She assessed the three of us with her exacting gaze, her form flickering back and forth between the happy blonde and angry brunette, only… the longer she flickered, the more the features seemed to settle until she turned into a strange mixture of both.

Bastian shuffled us back, doing his best to keep himself between the woman and me. Given that he was the only non-dead one of us, I figured this was probably a horrible idea on his part. But the woman simply smiled through her assessment, staring at Bastian as if he was simply adorable and she wanted to pinch his cheeks or something.

"My, aren't you precious?" she cooed, breaking out into a bout of giggles that equally filled my heart with joy and creeped me all the way out. "You remind me of my husband in that way. But you're not supposed to be here. I don't care what you try to use to disguise yourself. Your time is not quite up." She peeked around Bastian to peer at me. "And you, my dear, should have been here ages ago. I take it it's his fault?" She lifted her chin at Azrael before sticking out her tongue at him. "Is there anyone you haven't brought back yet?"

Azrael huffed out a withering chuckle. "Essex?"

The woman rolled her eyes. "Of all your children that you have brought to me, why haven't you hauled that dumbass down here yet?"

"The ru—"

She waved her hand at him dismissively. "Yes, yes. The *rules*. You know, you're the only one who follows them anymore. And if there were anyone to break your rules for, it's that miscreant." Her gaze flickered back to me. "I'm Persephone, by the way. It's very nice to meet you, Sloane. I've heard a lot about you. Not from this one," she grumbled, casting her gaze from Azrael back to me, "but your parents. They really are lovely people."

She could have bowled me over with a feather, but she chose a brick instead.

"You've met them?" I whispered, my eyes welling.

What is with them leaking all the damn time?

There were other questions I had, too, but they were ones I couldn't ask. Not with what I was now. My mother and father and hell, even Otis wouldn't recognize me now. I might have done some good, might have saved some people, but in their eyes, I'd be a monster.

I was sure of it.

"Of course I've met them. I greet all the new residents of Elysium personally. Azrael escorted them directly. They didn't even have to wait in line."

Don't know where you're going, huh? No shortcuts, huh? What a crock of shit.

"Are they…" I couldn't even finish that question. *Are they okay? Do they know what I am now? Do they hate me? Can I see them? Are they safe? Is Otis okay?*

Bastian wrapped an arm around my shoulder and pressed a kiss to my forehead. Maybe it was because I was shaking. Maybe it was because I was holding in my sobs with the efficiency of a toddler who'd just gotten their first spanking. Or maybe he knew just how bad all this hurt, how much I missed them, how much I hoped they didn't hate what I'd become.

"They're wonderful. They look in on you from time to time. Your mother is so proud of you. You know, she was quite the blood mage in her prime. Fought in the 1812 Blood Wars to boot. She sent many people our way over the years—just like you."

I wanted to feel relief—I really did. But it just didn't come.

"Since you're here, would you like to meet my family?" she asked, her odd eyes flashing back and forth from a lush grass green to a purple so dark it might as well have been black.

Did I? Honestly, the answer was a solid "Not particularly," but I had a feeling if I said so it would offend her. That fact was no more evident when Azrael prodded me in the ribs.

Oh, right. They can read my thoughts. Way to go, Sloane.

"Sure," I said, my voice a solid monotone. "I'd love to meet the family. It sounds like fun."

Persephone snickered. "I like her. I get why you brought her back. Way better choice than that dunderhead you call a son. Tell me again why you've let him live so long?"

"You know I don't break the ru—"

"Rules," she said, rolling her eyes. "Yes, yes. I remember. Okay, everyone, follow me."

Persephone led us to one of the creepy too-perfect houses, the manicured lawn and exactly perfect driveway a testament to the fact that no one lived here. I'd had a good home in a nice neighborhood. The houses were well-kept, and the lawns mowed. But there were imperfections, too—that's what made them perfect. There was the errant weed or bike not put away. There was sidewalk-chalked driveways and toys left out. And the sounds. The memory of those sounds called to my soul. Dogs barking, lawn mowers humming, people talking about nothing. It was a soundtrack of a wonderful childhood.

And even though it had been a lie, I still cherished it. Maybe that made me stupid, but I didn't care.

This neighborhood was scary to me because of its ordered perfection, and I figured that was the point.

Persephone opened the front door to reveal an elevator, the large cubicle big enough to fit us all and then some. It was one of those super-fancy elevators that required a key. She pulled a golden one out of her pocket, stuck it in the slot, and pressed the button for the penthouse.

Yeah, and that wasn't terrifying or anything.

In the back of my mind, I knew I was meeting Hades, sure, but the reality of it was a sight more surreal than anything I'd anticipated. It was one thing to binge Hades and Persephone romance novels as a young teen and quite another to be meeting them in the actual flesh.

The elevator ride was mostly silent and awkward, with Azrael looking like he was being taken to the gallows, and Bastian and I trying not to hysterically giggle at the highly inappropriate time. We were taking an elevator to go meet the King of the Underworld for fuck's sake. Not only did that not make any sense at all, but I was also running on the assumption that we most definitely were not supposed to be here.

Hell, if Azrael's face was anything to go by, we were about to be screwed seven ways to Sunday. And not in a good way.

The elevator dinged, the little "PH" on the floor indicator lighting up before the doors opened. Persephone breezed through them with no question in her mind that we'd follow her. Truth be told, we didn't have any other choice. It was either meet whomever she wanted us to or go back downstairs to the neighborhood that never ended.

At least if Hades smited me, I wouldn't have to traipse through there anymore. *Is it smited? Smote? What is the correct term for getting blown to smithereens by the King of the Underworld?*

We emerged from the elevator before Persephone flitted out of sight, following the sound of a dog whine and the tell-tale sound of happy puppy nails on tile. Everything about the penthouse felt like money. Like all the money in the universe was used to build this place. The floors were the whitest of marble, veined with what had to be pure gold. The walls were papered in rich linen with the faintest hint of a shimmer to them. Sconces dotted the entrance, the light from them pure magic.

I'd felt like I shouldn't have been here *before* I witnessed this level of luxury, and now that I had, I had the distinct feeling that I was somehow dirty. My hands were clean, and I had no visible signs of walking for what felt like days, but me in combat leathers and shit-kickers absolutely did not belong here. I met Bastian's gaze, and it seemed he, too, felt distinctly like Pig Pen from *Peanuts*, complete with that miasma of dirt following our every move.

Reluctantly rounding the corner, we caught sight of the goddess curled around a giant of a dog, its three heads trying to lick her face as she giggled.

"Honestly," she said, mock-scolding the hound, "I was only gone for a few minutes."

"A few minutes too long," a man said, striding into the room, his deep voice practically reverberating through my skull.

If Azrael was tall, this man was an actual giant, and formidable didn't even begin to cover it. The first thing I noticed about him—after the height, of course—were the scars that crisscrossed his cheeks, running down his jaw and into the collar of his shirt. The second was the impossible darkness in his eyes. I'd thought I'd seen black before, but this was something else. His hair was white like mine, which offset his dark skin like stars in the sky, the strands falling over his shoulders and down his back. He was beautiful and terrifying just like his wife.

And I could only assume this was Hades. Mostly because it seemed to take him a long while to notice us, his focus taken by the woman cuddling the three-headed dog. I'd always wondered if the famed Cerberus was actually three dogs in one body or a collective mind with three heads. It had bothered me to no end when I'd studied Greek mythology, though the mythology part seemed less and less of a myth nowadays.

"A bit of both, actually," the man rumbled, meeting my gaze with his pitch-black stare. His accent wasn't quite British nor was it American. It wasn't thick or hard to understand, but it held a gravity that spoke of several millennia of languages amalgamated into a singular dialect.

I jolted when he answered my question, which made him smile at me like I was adorable.

"You were wondering if Cerberus was three dogs or one. He's both."

Well, that clears everything right up.

Hades huffed at my internal cheek, giving me a wry smile. "He has three minds, but they run on a collective knowledge. Each head feels different emotions, sees different things, but all the information is shared, so he's both."

That actually did clear everything up.

"Glad I could help. Seph, what have you brought me?" he asked, crossing his arms over his enormous chest.

Persephone gave Cerberus another pat on each head before

straightening to look at our unruly little trio. "A wayward god with some serious familial issues, his daughter, and her not even remotely dead lover."

Hades frowned, not bothering to stare at anyone but me, which was super unnerving and not a little scary. "And she has hundreds of thousands of souls stuck inside her because?"

"Yeah, *Dad*, share with the class," I asked, whipping my head to the side to spear Azrael with my death glare. "Why do I have an inordinate number of souls just chilling inside my body?"

Azrael sighed as he pinched his brow.

Hades chuckled. "Wait, don't tell me. Essex, right? Please tell me again why you haven't reduced him to ash by now. You know none of us would think less of you. Even me."

Considering Hades had been literally eaten by his father, that was a pretty bold statement. Though, it was a complete mystery why Azrael hadn't killed Essex by now. It wasn't like he didn't have the means.

"You know why," Azrael answered. "The ru—"

"Rules." Hades cut him off. "Yes, I remember your faithfulness to those silly things. Don't you know by now that some rules were meant to be broken?" Hades paused, assessing me. "Though, your penchant for bringing people back from the dead does get tiring. Luckily, your daughter has sent us plenty of souls to make up for it."

"I brought one person back. One. *She* brought *him* back. That one is not my fault."

Hades blinked at him, his white eyebrow lifting in a way that was both comical and terrifying. "And what do death mages do again? Who do they make deals with for resurrections? I can't remember."

Azrael let out an irritated sigh. "Those are one-for-one trades. Those don't count, and you know it."

"Whatever you say." Hades gestured down the corridor. "Please come in. My home is your home. Would you like some food?"

Without waiting for an acceptance, Hades turned, walking hand in hand with his wife as they led us toward a mammoth dining table set for six. Already seated was a woman with a big black dog resting its head in her lap. Every few seconds she would tear pieces of meat from the drumstick on her plate and feed it to the beautiful animal.

Persephone motioned to one of the open seats. "Sit. Eat. You all must be tired after that trek."

Etiquette had never been my strong suit, but when it came to being offered food from gods, I couldn't tell if accepting would have me turned into a monster or not.

Before I could rein in my mouth, I asked, "This isn't like the Fae realm, right? Eating offered food isn't going to make it so I can't ever leave or something?"

Bastian elbowed me in the arm, but I just shrugged at him.

Excuse the hell out of me for being the smart one here.

The woman with the dog started laughing, wiping tears from her odd, blue-tinged skin. Her hair was black, pin-straight, and adorned with tiny, jeweled keys. In her ears were these strikingly beautiful gold earrings that looked like twined snakes.

Big black dog, snakes, and keys? I was putting money on this being Hecate.

"You'd be right." She smiled at me and also gestured for me to sit down. "Come eat. No one plans on making you a prisoner, and the fruit salad is quite delicious."

Awkwardly, I sat across from the woman as she inspected Bastian. He sat at my left with far more grace than I had, placing his napkin on his lap and keeping his mouth shut. Beside him was Persephone who gleefully passed him a large bowl of fruit with candied nuts and what smelled of a coconut and lime sauce. Hades passed me a platter filled with a gloriously fragrant meat. It looked like turkey legs—like the ones you'd get at a fair—only this was so much better. I passed Bastian the platter as Hecate handed over a basket of bread.

Soon, we were all eating. Hades, Persephone, and Hecate ribbed Azrael good-naturedly, but all the while, he seemed more and more uncomfortable—as if he'd rather be anywhere but here. He picked at his food, feeding most of it to the dog at Hecate's side. When he got quieter and quieter, Hecate engaged Bastian in a rousing debate over the merits of totems in casting work—a subject I found fascinating but still had no idea what they were talking about. As my plate emptied, Hades quietly got my attention. And by quietly, I meant he spoke inside my head.

You and I need to have a chat. Come to the balcony for a drink.

It was unnerving when Bastian's thoughts resounded in my skull, but Hades was a whole other animal. I was pretty sure my teeth rattled. There was no other choice, really. I got up, pressed a kiss to Bastian's cheek, and followed Hades out a set of glass doors that led to a giant balcony.

It was no secret I was afraid of heights, so when I stepped outside, I stuck close to the wall and kept my eyes on my feet. We were in that elevator for what felt like forever. There was no way I was going to look down from this height.

No way, no how.

"How can a dead woman be afraid of heights?" Hades asked as he mixed a cocktail at an ornate bar cart next to a pair of teak patio chairs. In a few moments his ministrations produced what appeared to be a mojito, the mint plucked fresh from a lush potted plant. He offered me a glass and I sipped dutifully, thinking of a good answer.

"Have you ever tried to…" I began, still trying to think of a way to explain.

"To end it? No, I can't say I have. But I get your point. You associate heights with pain and therefore you fear them."

When he put it like that, it made me feel sort of stupid. I was already dead, so death was sort of off the table. Plus, I was in the Underworld. I literally could not get deader if I tried. I took a hesitant step toward the stone railing, looking out on the world below. Banding the building in a lush mote was a dense forest dotted with ancient ruins, their jagged spines reaching for the sky. Past that was a river that had several forks, each one leading in a different direction.

"I wonder what you'll do when you get your wings."

I nearly choked on an ice cube and had to pound on my chest to get the damn thing to go down. "What? Wings?"

Hades smiled at me bemusedly. "You'll take over for Azrael, right? That job comes with wings, you know."

Taking over for Azrael? "Sure. Maybe in a thousand years or so I'll get used to the idea of flying around on wings. For now, though, the thought of flying anywhere—*ever*—sounds like a horrible idea."

"I see. Do you understand what he does?"

I waffled my hand. "In theory. I've read the mythologies. Doesn't mean that's the truth, though, does it? The Greeks never liked the thought of a peaceful death."

"None of the living like death much. They fear it and paint it as the end, but it never has been. There are those—even his own children—that see what he does and hate him for it, begging for more time when all your father is, is an instrument of Fate. But he never gained balance. Never thought to carve out happiness for himself. When I was younger, I made the same mistakes. Until I found Seph, that is."

He sipped his drink in silence, letting me digest what a

lonely existence Azrael had had. It made me sad for him, made me curse Essex for enacting a revenge that had never been fair.

"I want you to have balance and rest. The dead aren't going anywhere. When it's your time to follow in Azrael's footsteps, I want you to realize that balance, that love will see you through on your darkest days."

He was talking like I would be taking the job now. "I've got time, though, right? You're talking like this is happening tomorrow."

Hades gave me an enigmatic smile. "Not tomorrow."

Well, that wasn't cryptic at all.

"Since I've got you here, you know a way to get these souls out of me so I don't have to continue traipsing through the Underworld like a newbie?" I paused, deciding whether or not I wanted to ask this next bit. "And maybe go visit a few of your residents?"

Originally, I'd planned on trying to swing by to make sure Killian was where Azrael said he was after I was purged, but now that I knew that Persephone had seen my parents with her own eyes, well... It was probably a pipe dream, anyway.

"I *could* take those souls out of you right now, but then you would need to go home. If you were to travel to Elysium and send them to their rest yourself, you could possibly visit a few of the residents there. Plus, I figure if I give you an incentive, you might actually learn something about this place."

There was only one problem. Bastian was alive. Sure, he'd died once before, but it wasn't his time—Persephone had said so herself. What if it took too long? What if Essex attacked while we were gone? What if Bastian never made it out of here? What if Thomas and Axel never made it to the door?

What if...

"What if you worry about those things once you can actually do something about them? Go to Elysium, kid. You're too young to be worried about so much." Then he stood, offering me his mitt of a hand to shake. I took it without hesitation. "I look forward to working with you soon, Sloane."

"Not that soon," I quipped.

I hoped I wasn't lying.

16

Eventually, Bastian came to collect me, breaking my reverie of the vast and obscenely beautiful land below. I could almost see Elysium. The path wasn't exactly easy, but this bird's eye view at the very least gave us a heading. What I wouldn't give for a compass or a map or even a reliable tour guide.

I was staring at the broken spires snaking their way up through the trees when I felt a welcome kiss on my neck. At some point, Hades had left me to my ponderings, and now Bastian was here kissing my neck as I gazed upon a beautiful but a little terrifying landscape.

"You ready to go, love?" he murmured, wrapping an arm around my middle.

Was I ready to go? I wasn't so sure.

"Would it be so bad to stay here? To live here?" The question was out of my mouth before I really thought it through. I could do this—balance my love for Bastian while holding a job that was necessary and vital. We could live here, make a home where my awful brother couldn't attack us.

Absorb the beauty of a place like this and just be. It wasn't a fully formed idea, and I had not a single clue about whether it would work or not, but Hades had planted the seed in my mind.

"I think if we could come and go as we pleased, it wouldn't be so bad. But I think if we couldn't, we would miss everyone, don't you?"

He was right, and it hurt. It hurt for so many reasons, but the number one was that I knew it would make every single person we loved regret letting us go. Turning in his arms, I fit my nose into the crook of his shoulder.

"I don't want to leave them behind, either," I admitted, leaving off the fact that I felt almost at peace here, felt almost home. But the Night Watch was my home, too.

Bastian was my home. And Thomas and Clem and Simon and Dahlia. Axel and Emrys and Darby. Harper. Ingrid. Hell, I was even almost warming up to Bishop—even though I still thought he wasn't good enough for my sister.

If I could avoid leaving them behind, I would.

"I have a choice to make," I murmured into his skin, not wanting to look at his face as I told him my selfish plan. "I can let Hades remove the souls trapped inside me, set them free in an instant, and the three of us would immediately go back home. *Or* we can traverse the Underworld and take them to Elysium where they are meant to be."

Bastian pushed me back, his bottle-green eyes staring right down to my soul. "And by going to Elysium, it means you could maybe see your parents, talk to Darby's dad, give him her last goodbye."

It had to be a joint decision. I couldn't make it on my own with no one's input. That just wasn't fair. "Yes, that's about the gist of it."

"Do you honestly think I could say no to you?"

I shoved at his shoulder a little, jostling him. "But it's not just me here. It's all of us."

He reeled me in, pulling me tight to his chest as he pressed a kiss to my temple. His fingers toyed with my braid as he shook his head. "If it were me wanting to see my parents, what would you do?"

I did not like that he was this insightful.

"You would snatch me by the hand and march to the doors, hammering at them until Hades himself let you in. You would scour the whole of this realm just to make me happy. Don't act like you wouldn't make the same sacrifices for me as I would for you, love."

It really was annoying when he was this damn perfect. "Are you sure?"

He raised an imperious eyebrow at me.

"Fine," I muttered, pressing a kiss to his lips. "You're sure."

When it was time to leave, Persephone directed us to a different elevator, her trusty three-headed dog at her side. She rubbed at the fur on the center head as she pressed the ornate call button.

"If you get a chance, come back and see me," she instructed. "I'd love to talk a bit more, get to know you. Plus, it's so refreshing to see a new face around here."

Smiling, I said, "Of course. We'll come back around this way on our way out."

Her smile was genuine, but it had a tinge of something more, something bittersweet. Then the elevator dinged, and we piled on without her.

"I'll see you soon," she said, the statement far more ominous than intended, and the door closed, cutting us off from the pretty penthouse and thrusting us downward.

Far faster than my stomach would have liked, we reached the ground floor, the mechanical ding of the elevator announcing our arrival. The doors opened to reveal a lush forest, the likes of which I glimpsed from the top floor. I'd assumed the trees were dense, but I had no idea that the place was out of a Grimm fairytale.

The trees twisted and turned, their trunks crooked and jagged as if someone had constructed them from a fever dream. The imperceptible sun seemed unable to reach us under the canopy, the darkness a touch too ominous for me.

"This is creepier than the suburb, for sure," Bastian said, but Azrael and I scoffed at him.

"No way. Maybe you haven't seen enough horror movies, but that 'hood was about a millisecond from being a *Hitchcock* movie," I countered, an involuntary shudder quaking through my body as I walked.

Azrael had the good sense to nod. "A whole world full of nothing or a dark forest. I'll take the forest, thank you."

I bumped Azrael's shoulder with mine—or rather, I bumped his elbow with my shoulder, but whatever. "Good man. It's always important to side with the daughter in these types of situations. We're always right."

"I'll remember that." He paused, staring at his shoes before speaking again. "Did you have a good talk with Hades?"

I shrugged, kicking a rock as I went. "It was a little bittersweet and a lot confusing, but I couldn't say it was the worst thing I've done today. You didn't seem like you were comfortable there. I thought these people were your family?"

He grumbled intelligibly. "They are, and they aren't. We've known each other so long, it seems like it sometimes. But they're different from me. They see the aftermath of what I do, and..." He stuffed his hands in his pockets. "They are fulfilled here in a way I have never been. They have made this place their home, and I have always been on this outside with one foot in both worlds."

I bumped him again. "Maybe you could find a nice lady and settle down. One you hopefully don't impregnate immediately and actually get to know. That could be nice, right?"

He rolled his eyes at my jab. "I knew them all before I—never mind."

Snorting, I skipped ahead and began walking backward so I could taunt him. "Had s-e-x with them?" I whispered behind my hand. "Does that help your delicate sensibilities?"

He lifted his face skyward, probably asking whichever god that controlled patience to throw him a bone. "Why don't you ask the question you really want to ask? Did I love your mother?"

That had my feet stalling. It had been a question that had flitted through my mind, but one I didn't give much thought to. Or at least I thought I hadn't. Until that very second, I hadn't realized just how important his answer was or why I needed to know.

"Did you?"

A soft smile graced his lips before he stared right into my eyes. "Yes. I loved your mother as much as I was able. She brought me so much peace when I was with her that I wanted to stay, but..." He shook his head. "I wasn't what she needed. Rosalind needed someone stronger, someone who would stick around for the hard stuff. As much as I loved her, I—I couldn't be there. Not all the time. And it wasn't just the job that kept me away. Being around the living is hard for someone like me."

A sadness hunched his shoulders as he kicked a rock on the trail. "We ended it when she got pregnant with you. She said that the love of her life was in her belly, and she wasn't going to let her settle for scraps as she had. At the time, I'd thought I'd been a good partner, but I realized then that I would let you down. Peter came into her life when she was four months along and was there in every single way I couldn't have been. Loved her in all the ways I couldn't. And in the end, he died trying to protect you from my mistake. They both did."

Pivoting on a foot, I stalked farther into the trees, trying to keep sight of the path in the gloom. I'd been kidding. Why did he have to go and make me feel sorry for him, huh? I'd been just fine hating him this whole time. Why did he have to make me see myself in him?

Because that was the kicker, wasn't it? Azrael saw himself as other, as different, as a monster. When it came to stepping up and staying, he left because he thought it was better for everyone else.

I wonder where I've heard that before.

"I guess you got more from me than just hair color."

I snorted. "Yeah, a brother from Hell *and* generational trauma. Thanks a bunch, *Dad*."

He began moving again, bumping me with his hip as he passed. "What can I say? I'm a giver like that."

At least I know where I got my sarcasm from.

He let out a gleeful laugh. "Oh, no. That was a gift bestowed upon you from both sides. Your mother"—He shook his head—"she was the reigning queen of sarcasm. Do you know how we met?"

Obviously, I didn't. Mom hadn't spoken one word about him my whole life.

"It was on the battlefield. She had just ripped through an entire battalion with a blood-boiling curse—just popping people's brains like balloons. Given what it is I do, I was there to reap the souls. Even under cover of night and my natural glamour, she still saw me. Even tried killing me, too, until she figured out who I was."

He stared off in the distance at the memory, a fondness

taking over his whole face. "She was magnificent. Had a tongue just as sharp as her spells. And the fire she had, the fierceness with which she protected you…"

It was tough to see my mother through this lens—the battle-hungry and bloodthirsty mage—when all I had known of her was the mom who complained about charcoal stains on my white sheets. He knew her in a way I never could, and I wished that I could have grown up just catching a glimpse of the woman he described. Still, I missed the mother I had. The one who giggled with me about high school shenanigans, the one who patched up bloody knees and gave me the best hugs.

The one who did everything she could for me, all the time. Even if I hadn't met the warrior, I still got the best mom. The very best one.

"She was a good mom," I croaked, and if tears raced down my cheeks, well, then that was allowed.

"Yes. She was. And she chose a fabulous partner to raise you. I will be forever grateful for that."

Swallowing hard, I forced my feet forward. "He was a good dad."

For some reason thinking about Dad hurt a lot. Maybe it was because he hadn't known what he was getting into with me and Mom.

"Yes, he did," Azrael countered, dashing that misconception as fast as it slipped through my thoughts. "He knew from the start. Your mom made sure of it. Peter was with her every step of the way, through everything. They didn't have any secrets—not even about you."

I couldn't say why that filled me with a sense of relief. Maybe it was because it felt less like an unwanted betrayal on my part—that he'd died in my defense and didn't know why. But he knew.

He knew and he'd stayed.

For me.

For us.

Bastian startled me when he grabbed my hand, pulling me to a stop so hard, I nearly fell. Then I heard it—the rustling in the trees. The branches creaked as if something heavy were resting on them, and that filled me with an inordinate amount of dread.

Stupidly, I looked up, meeting the golden eyes of a bird. Or, maybe not. Owl-like eyes blinked at me from a distinctly feminine face that was a startling mix of both woman and bird, her sharp beak hooked and lethal. Her dark hair hung in a rope down over her shoulder, mixing liberally with her feathers, and instead of arms, she had wings.

My brain supplied the species: *Harpy*.

And she wasn't alone.

Oh, no, this bird lady had friends. A whole fucking flock filled the trees above our heads, their feathers ruffling as they stared menacingly down on us.

We were officially in deep, deep shit.

17

I'd sort of figured my luck was bad, but a whole flock of harpies just lying in wait to murder me? That was next-level bad luck of epic proportions. Honestly, it wasn't even fair.

I didn't know if it was because I'd looked up or the fact that Azrael took that moment to make a noise, but at the sound, the whole fucking group decided it was high time they took the plunge—each one sailing off their perches to dive bomb us. The collective screech was enough to make my ears bleed.

Without so much as a nod toward decorum—because let's face it, harpies were completely out of our wheelhouse—Bastian and I took off running.

Here's the thing they don't tell you about harpies in school—yes, I know they don't cover magical beings in Biology, just go with it—they are fast.

Like really fast.

Like could flip off a Peregrine falcon while in their sleep as they zoomed past it yawning, fast.

So, it didn't matter that I was a little more juiced up than usual—not that the effects of having that many souls just chilling under my flesh had given me so much as a blip of the problems Darby had—I wasn't getting away from these ladies without some serious injuries. Also, fun fact about the Underworld? Bastian's fun ability to slow time didn't work here.

Trust me, he tried it.

Bastian grabbed me by my arm, whipping me around so I was curled over his shoulders, and then we went exactly nowhere. There was no dip in my belly or slew of trees speeding past us. We weren't that lucky, but considering I'd already figured my luck was shit, it didn't exactly surprise me. Plus, being thrown over his shoulder did give me a very up close and personal look at what a harpy looked like when she went in for the kill.

Wings spread wide, she used them to slow herself, reaching her taloned feet toward my face with the expert skill of a practiced killing machine. The best I could do—and yes, I knew that my best in this situation was fucking suspect—was to knee Bastian in the chest. He stumbled, dropping us both to the ground in a bruising roll.

It hurt.

A lot.

But it did have the intended outcome of me not getting a face full of harpy claw, so at least there was that.

"Azrael," I screamed, shoving myself to my feet and yanking Bastian up with me.

But I didn't have the time to look for him—not when I heard the deafening screech of another bird lady. She was close —too close for my liking—and I latched onto Bastian, rushing through the twisted trees in a zigzag while trying not to die.

Yes, I know. I'm already dead. But whatever. Semantics. Regrowing shit fucking hurts.

Ahead looked like one of those ruins I'd spied from Hades' balcony, and I sprinted for it, hoping the cover would serve us. We were ten long steps from the stone façade when the blistering heat of agony ripped into my back. No, not just ripped.

Tore.

Gouged.

Every horrific word there was in creation couldn't possibly describe the feeling of a harpy's talons burrowed into your flesh. Then I was lifted off my feet by that dreadful *fucking* foot, hanging by my right shoulder as she attempted to carry me off.

I'd never in my life been so happy to be left-handed. Without much planning on my part, I latched onto the long dagger at my thigh and slashed up blindly.

Also, a good thing to know about harpies? They didn't waste time in the trees once their prey was acquired, nor did they keep going after prey once said prey started fighting back.

Want to know how I know?

Because as soon as I slashed, I miraculously managed to hit my target, and she dropped my ass like a hot potato. Truth be told, falling hurt a fuck of a lot less than I'd remembered. Maybe it was the sharp tree branches and twigs and leaves that broke my fall, but at least I didn't go splat on the forest floor. I did manage to break an arm, cut myself on my own dagger, and take a branch upside the head, though, so that was fun.

I laid there for several seconds, waiting for the breath to come back to my lungs as I stared at the Sloane-sized hole in the canopy. Harpies raced through the air overhead, peeling off at their sister's pained cry. So, those bitches were bullies then —cutting and running as soon as someone fought back.

I'd have to remember that.

Groaning, I peeled myself up off the ground, managing to

sit up without yelping in pain. Just fuck harpies and forests and the whole of the Underworld.

"Sloane," Bastian yelled, the sound reaching my ears from a decent distance. His voice was hoarse, like he'd been calling my name for quite a while.

"Here," I croaked back, my voice not even remotely loud enough. I cleared my throat and shouted louder, hoping he heard. At my shout, my whole right side took the opportunity to do a little shouting of its own, the pain radiating through me hard enough to make me gag.

Yep, in my initial assessment of my injuries, I'd missed the two broken ribs. *Good times.*

And where the fuck was Azrael? Wasn't he sort of a bigwig around here? Couldn't he have just snapped his fingers and got them to quit their bullshit?

Bastian reached me before I got the gumption to stand, the sight of his slightly bloody but otherwise unharmed self the most welcomed thing I'd seen in a hot minute.

"Jesus, fuck, Sloane," he muttered, dropping a marginally painful kiss to my forehead. "I thought… I don't know what I thought. She just snatched you right up and I…"

"I'm okay." I most certainly was *not*. "I'm alive." Again, debatable. "We're together now." Accurate.

"Where are you hurt? Do you need blood?"

The answers to that were: everywhere and yes. But drinking from him wasn't a good idea right now, especially if those harpies decided to sack up and return. He needed to be able to run, and although I didn't think me taking a few sips would be a detriment to his health, I sure as shit didn't want to risk it. Especially not here.

"I'm fine."

He huffed at me, clucking his tongue like I was an

impudent child. "I have eyes, Sloane. I can see the bloody bone sticking out of your arm."

Yeah, I'd been trying really hard not to think about that.

"Let me give you a few sips of blood. We don't have time for me to carry you all over this blasted place."

"But—"

He grabbed my face gently, forcing me to meet his gaze, but his tone was the most commanding thing I had ever heard in my life. "But nothing. Drink."

At the order, my fangs began to ache, the need to feed so necessary I nearly passed out at the scent of him. It was all around me, filling my nostrils of woodsmoke and spent magic, spices and Bastian. My mouth practically started watering, and when he positioned his neck so it brushed my lips, I was done for.

I struck, my fangs piercing his flesh with the most seductive pop. Images hit me instantly, flashing one after the other in a reel of what could be. Things that hadn't happened, hadn't even been dreamt up. But each one had a tinge of darkness to it. Each one had just a hint of death lurking in the background. I swallowed once and the visions changed, lightened. Taking one last pull, I withdrew my fangs, the warmth of healing flooding me with contentment.

Bastian's fist closed around my hair, the soft pull of it opening my eyes. His were bright and blazing, copper with a dose of power I'd thought was lost down here. "Is that what you see? Was that you?"

Confused, I shook my head. Reflexively, his fist tightened a bit more, drawing my face nearer.

"When you drink from me, is that what you see? That future? It is the future, isn't it?"

He'd never shared a vision with me before. "You saw it, too?"

Silently, he nodded, the wonder stamped all over him.

I thought of all the times I'd drunk from him and the path we'd traveled. "It's *a* future, but I only see that with you—the possibilities. I don't really know what they mean or if they'll come true. So far, though, they have."

A smile dawned on his face, the beauty of it zinging right down to my cold heart.

"Good," he murmured, pressing a soft kiss to my lips. He lingered there, tasting me in a way that made my whole body sing before breaking his mouth from mine and hauling me to my feet.

"When we get out of this, I'm taking you to bed for a month. The whole world can burn for all I care. It'll be you and me and a few of those positions you dreamt up."

I couldn't help the shiver that vibrated through my body, answering him without me saying a word.

"Glad you're on board. Now let's go find Azrael, shall we? I don't want to trek through this mess without a tour guide—no matter how unhelpful he's been."

Groaning, I let him pull me in the direction of the ruins. Maybe if we got under some decent cover, I could call for Azrael or something. Granted, the thought of that bout of good fortune made me wary.

It wasn't like we'd been lucky so far.

The trek was without incident, though every snap of a twig or flutter of a branch made us go on red alert. We'd been surprised by the harpies because Azrael hadn't thought to warn us about the dangers here. Granted, we hadn't asked, but that was beside the point.

A chill swept through me as we entered the cover of the ruins, the cracking stone façade, and broken statues far more ominous than the open forest had been. The forest had tried to reclaim the structure. Moss and thick ivy covered most of the walls, creating a sort of canopy above us. The broken statues were all fighting poses, the metal weapons still in the cleaved arms that littered the lush floor. We picked our way through them, arriving at an open courtyard, practically brimming with more shattered marble. It reminded me a little of the Terracotta Army in China, only this army was defeated, destroyed.

"Try to call for Azrael, and then let's get out of here. This place—"

"Gives you the creeps?" I finished for him, sweeping my gaze over the pained faces of the fallen army.

"That's a word for it," he muttered, nodding.

Without wasting any more time, I called for Azrael in my mind, taking care to show him where we were. Normally, I hated when he just dropped in, but at this point I would gladly welcome him popping in from nowhere. When he didn't seem to answer the call, I opened my eyes, trepidation filling my gut.

I was stumped. What were we supposed to do now? Go find him? And did he need me saving him? If the harpies got him, he sure as hell would.

In the middle of my contemplation, a sound piqued my ears, and I grabbed Bastian so fast it was as if my body got the message a good five seconds before my brain did.

"Close your eyes," I hissed, careful not to raise my voice above the faintest hiss of a whisper.

Confused, Bastian just stared at me. Without missing a beat, I let him go and unzipped my leather jacket. Beneath it was a soft cotton undershirt, and I took the fabric in two hands and ripped it, revealing my bra and a whole lot of skin.

"While I'm enjoying the show, wha—" I put my hand over his mouth, cutting him off.

"Shut. Up," I whispered, and wrapped the mangled shirt around his eyes. "Do not move. Fuck, don't breathe. And for fuck's sake, do not take that blindfold off. No matter what."

Letting him go, I shrugged my jacket back on and zipped it up as quietly as I could. I considered pulling the dagger at my thigh, but worried I wouldn't have enough hands. I needed to lead Bastian out of here.

Said man was clutching the air trying to find me, and I gave up my debate to grab his hand.

No weapons it was.

He pulled at me, drawing me to him so he could whisper in my ear, "What is it?"

I wanted to say "Duh," but I refrained. Barely.

A shit-ton of broken statues? Check.

In the Underworld? Check.

A faint hint of a snake's rattle? Double check.

We needed to get the fuck out of here, and now, and I knew that as soon as I said one word, Bastian would be more than a little on board.

"Gorgons," I breathed in his ear, that single word making his whole spine go rigid.

Yeah, and that luck that I'd thought was *so* bad?

Well, it, too, had officially run out.

18

Those stone statues that I'd thought were creepy before? Well, as I picked through them, trying to lead Bastian clear without him stumbling or impaling himself on one of the abandoned swords, their ick-factor went up ten-fold.

Because the damn things weren't statues at all, and the utter carnage made me want to hurl.

The other thing that made me want to curl around a toilet bowl? The heavy slither of a serpent's body trailing through the high grasses and ivy. I'd never been a fan of snakes. Okay, on jewelry? Absolutely. And pythons didn't wig me out too much, but the sound of a rattle?

Hard no.

Add in the utter destruction that a gorgon's gaze could do, and I was doing my level best to hightail it out of there. But picking through the wreckage wasn't exactly an easy task with a blind Bastian in tow. No matter how athletic or nimble he was, taking away his sight so suddenly left him frustrated and unable to adapt. I contemplated tossing him over my shoulder. I could do it, sure, but the fact of the matter was that I didn't know if I could do it and not accidentally get petrified in the process.

At the first clear spot, I took off, trying and failing to *not* let our feet pound against the dirt-strewn courtyard. Our deafening steps echoed throughout the place, summoning the rattle of one incredibly irritated snake lady. I almost tripped over my own feet as her tail whipped toward us, Bastian hanging onto me the only reason I didn't send us tumbling to the ground.

Her laugh chilled me to the bone, the throaty yet feminine chuckle both beautiful and deadly all at the same time.

"Smart of you to blindfold him," she purred, the patronizing tone a sure sign that we were cornered.

I couldn't look—not and survive—so I squeezed Bastian's hand and pressed my eyelids closed, standing as still as one of those broken statues.

"However, it is unnecessary for you to close your eyes. I don't hurt women. My stare will not affect you like it will him. Tell me, do you blindfold him because you don't trust him, or because you do?"

Confused, I kept my eyes shut, shuffling the both of us backward and away from her voice.

"You aren't the first to think of a blindfold, dear, so answer my question. Do you trust him or not?"

Croaking, I answered, "Of course I trust him."

The heavy slither of her tail got closer. "Then why the blindfold?"

Because I knew if it came to him or me, he'd choose me. Bastian would put himself in between danger and me every single time.

"It's because I do trust him that I blindfolded him. I trust him to be brave, to be strong, to put me above himself—even if it meant his death. I trust him to love me more than he loves himself, and I trust that if he were to die—in this life or the next, I wouldn't be able to make it without him."

Bastian wrapped an arm around my middle. It was just as comforting here as it had been every single other place he'd done it. "Love, remind me to slap a ring on your finger as soon as we get out of this, will you?"

Then he took advantage of my complete shock and stone-still body and whipped me behind him—getting in between me and the gorgon. My eyes popped wide, meeting a woman's gaze at the same instant. I waited for the pain, or anything that would tell me I was turning into a life-sized Sloane statue, but it didn't come.

"You weren't lying," I whispered, agog at the gorgon's beauty. It didn't matter that she had snakes writhing through her dark-auburn hair or that the bottom half of her body was encased in scales.

"About harming you? No. I could harm him, though. In fact, I really want to. So why don't you get out of my way?"

There were several stories about Medusa. Some said she'd always been a monster, just a mortal one. Some said that she'd been a priestess of Athena, and Poseidon raped her. That Athena had been so disgusted, she'd cursed her. Others said it had never been a curse, that the power to turn a man to stone had always been a gift—a way to make sure no man would ever harm her again. Given that she was trying to hurt Bastian, I figured the last two were closer to the truth.

"Please don't," I whispered, taking a step backward and shoving Bastian back with it. Raising my hands in surrender, I kept moving, shoving him away from her as best I could. "We don't want to hurt you—"

"Liar," she said, showing me fanged teeth as she smiled

serenely. "If you thought it would save him, you'd chop off my head and stuff it in the darkest hole you could find."

Huffing, I conceded. "Okay, fine. But I don't want to. Does that count for anything? I don't want you dead. I don't want to cause you harm. I just want to get the hell out of here so I can send these souls to their rest, and maybe find my father in the process so I can possibly go home and have a life. I'd also like to do that without the love of my life dying on me. Is that so much to ask here? To just let us go?"

The woman—who I assumed was Medusa but didn't know for sure—let out another throaty laugh. "Oh, the gods just love you, don't they?"

I shrugged, shaking my head. "It's a mixed bag. So, what do you say? Let us out of here, and we both go our separate ways?"

Medusa gave me an assessing once-over, pursing her lips in contemplation. "You could have pulled the 'Do you know who my father is?' card but you didn't. Why?"

Snorting, I rolled my eyes. Azrael hadn't quite managed to save my ass any other time in my life, why would he start now?

Only, just as soon as I thought that, said father appeared, flaming scythe in hand and wings spread wide, landing in a crouch in between the gorgon and me. He stood, his wings shivering in agitation, leaning toward the threat as he seemed to get taller, broader, making himself a solid wall of fatherly rage.

"You will let my daughter go, Medusa, or so help me, I'll carry you to Tartarus myself."

I couldn't see her face anymore, but her simpering tone still held a big enough threat. "I want the boy, not your daughter. You know I cannot harm a female. Or Death, it seems."

Azrael growled in response, the sound making me quake in

my boots, even though he was on my side. "You can't have him. Ever. Do you hear me?"

A slither was all he got in answer, but he wasn't satisfied. "Out loud, Gorgon. Swear it."

Medusa huffed, her tail rattling as it whipped in what I assumed was frustration. "*Fine.* The mage Sebastian Cartwright will not be harmed by me or my sisters by word or deed. Happy?"

"If you actually meant it, maybe. But you don't." A set of chains formed in Azrael's free hand: the two manacles barbed so they would pierce the flesh caught in them.

Her tail whipped in answer, a shuddering breath wheezing through her lungs. That's when my feet moved, getting in between her and my father, my back to her as I held out my hands to him.

"Don't." *Don't* what, I couldn't exactly say, it just felt wrong. All kinds of wrong.

Shifting to face her, I stared into her eyes. I hadn't noticed before, but her pupils were slit like a snake's, the thin irises a pretty hazel color. I'd avenged women just like her, ripped the souls from men who'd done more wrong than good, ones who had hurt people. Her gaze reminded me of the people I'd managed to save.

"Let us go. We mean you no harm and never would. Promise our passage is safe, and we'll leave in peace."

Medusa cast her gaze downward. "I swear. He will not be harmed by me or my sisters. You have earned my respect, and I would not injure you or your heart."

With that, she turned, slithering away and trailing her giant snake tail behind her.

"Thank you," I murmured to her retreating back, noticing the deep scars crisscrossing her arms and back for the first time.

Her hate for all those statues made a hell of a lot of sense. If I'd been in her shoes—or scales—I'd likely hate every person who entered my domain, too.

A touch on my shoulder made me jump, but it was only Azrael. Back to normal size and flaming scythe gone, he stared at me.

"What?"

He swallowed, before reaching out and folding me into a hug. He smelled faintly of brimstone and poppies, and I hugged him back.

"I'm glad I made it this time," he croaked, squeezing me just a little too hard.

I was, too, and it made me hate that I'd thought he wasn't right before he showed up. A stab of guilt ripped through me, and I fought off a sniffle. I would not cry, dammit, but the relief was hitting me hard.

He reluctantly let me go as I pushed away, the sorrow coloring his features plain as day. "I've done a lot of things wrong. I'm glad I got that right."

It was hard to come up with a response to that. We hadn't healed enough as a family for me to pat him on the back and give him a "good job" pep talk. But it was a start.

Clearing my throat, I managed to ask, "Where were you? We lost you in the middle of the harpy attack."

Before he could answer me, Bastian let out an irritated growl and asked, "Can I take this bloody blindfold off now?"

Both Azrael and I snorted out indelicate laughs, and I picked across the statue rubble to untie the tatters of my shirt. As soon as I saw bottle-green, he clutched me to him, kissing me so fiercely I thought the top of my head was going to pop off. He broke the kiss as he wrapped me in his arms, dropping pecks onto my hair.

"Scared the bleeding life out of me. If I weren't in the Underworld already, I would have died ten times by heart attack by now. Bloody crazy, you are, you know that?" He lifted his head. "And you," he said, staring past me to look Azrael in the eye. Bastian seemed to be gearing up to give my father a piece of his mind, but in the end, he only nodded. "Thank you for showing up when you did."

Azrael rubbed the back of his neck, his cheeks pinking. "Welcome, but I almost didn't make it. Those harpies are more vicious than I remember. You guys took off before I could reason with them, and by the time I got free, you two were in the one place you shouldn't have been."

I winced. So maybe the running was a bad idea.

"Harpies test wandering souls by keeping them from getting to the river. And Medusa is supposed to test the mettle of men, not kill all of them. Every soul—except for a special few—has to cross through here. Someone needs to talk to Hades about her."

I winced, thinking about the scars on her back. Maybe that kind of job wasn't fit for a woman who had seen as much misfortune as she had.

"You might be right," he muttered, a wave of sorrow pulling at his features.

Personally, I couldn't imagine being attacked over and over and just letting people go. Maybe keeping the men who would harm her out of Elysium was exactly where she should be. I didn't know the right answer, and it made me glad that it wasn't up to me to decide.

"Come on," Azrael said, tipping his chin to the exit. "We have a ferry waiting for us."

For the first time, I looked in the direction of his chin. An ivy-coated archway led to a shore with black waters lapping at its edges. Beached was a boat, the curled bow and stern both a serpent's head.

I swallowed, barely able to croak out a pitiful affirmative before my feet followed suit.

Elysium was just beyond the water, and with it, my parents.

Finally.

19

Tears filled my eyes as my feet touched the smooth wood of the boat's floor. A smiling ferryman pocketed the single gold coin, payment I hadn't thought to bring, but Bastian had. Since he was the only non-death deity—or deity adjacent—he'd been the only one who'd had to pay to travel down the river.

My stomach had dropped when the ferryman had asked. Of all the ways to be prepared for a trip to the Underworld, money hadn't even crossed my mind.

Those tears I'd been staunchly holding back before, slipped down my cheeks as I sat down on the polished bench, the wood worn from eons of use. Bastian sat next to me, his warmth seeping into me as all the doubts came crashing down once again.

What if the boat sinks? What if we never make it? What if—

"If you think any harder, the boat will capsize," my father muttered, sitting on the bench in front, but rather than facing the direction we were going, he chose to sit facing me.

It didn't matter that he was joking, his sly smile a

testament to that fact, it still made me want to punch him. "I think it's healthy to have backup plans."

"Neurotic is more like it. You're on the ferry to Elysium for Fate's sake. Maybe take a minute to breathe before you imagine perishing in a fiery boat crash?"

In my imaginings there had been no fire, but I suspected he was taking poetic license. In response, I stuck out my tongue at him before resting my temple on Bastian's shoulder. Childish? Sure, but it was the best I had.

Azrael gave me an indulgent grin before focusing on Bastian. "You plan on spending the rest of your days with her, correct? Plan on making a life with her?"

Dear sweet mother of all that was holy. This reminded me of the times my dad had grilled my dates before deigning to let me leave with them.

Bastian only smiled at him. "I plan to marry her, to live my life such as it is with her. I plan to die with her—whether that comes today or in a thousand years. I promised her that we'd be together until the sun stops burning and the world stops turning, and I mean to keep that promise. Is this the part where you warn me off?"

Azrael smiled wide. "No. This is the part where I give you my support because my blessing is not needed nor required. You have that, too, but it's not necessary. I'm just glad she found you—or rather, you found her. There aren't many people in this universe that I'd want for her—not many that I'd think were good enough. I'm glad you pulled your head out of your ass, mage."

Such flowery words turned crude in an instant. Yes, I really was his daughter.

"Thank you," I said, the flowery part still fitting, even if he torched it with the ass talk. My parents had never gotten the chance to meet Bastian, never got to see me settled, see me in love. I hoped they would get to see me happy—if just for a moment—like Azrael had. I wanted them to see that I was okay. That their sacrifice hadn't been for nothing.

That I'd lived—even though I was different.

I swallowed hard, casting my gaze to the glittering waters. I hoped they were happy and safe. That what my horrible brother had done hadn't scarred them.

"One thing I need to know—for my own peace of mind," Azrael began, drawing my gaze off the horizon. "If you took this job—my job—would you be fulfilled?"

I thought of a future where I brought people to their families, where I eased the suffering of the ill and infirm. Where I confirmed the valor of a soldier or reaped an evil person before they caused further destruction. Could I do what Azrael did? I thought I could. The young ones would hurt, I was sure of it. The innocent would sting something awful. But taking those that would do harm?

Piece of cake.

Joking, I asked, "When has killing people ever been a problem for me?"

Azrael sighed, shaking his head.

"Fine. Parts of it would suck, but that's because I have a heart, okay? And as long as those who did harm found an unfortunate end, I suppose it won't be so bad."

If I got to keep my family, that is. I sent that thought to Azrael, making sure he understood. I would want to keep Bastian and Darby, the Night Watch. I'd want to stay in their lives—however long I could. Granted, by the time I took the job, most of them would be long dead, but I wanted assurances.

If I get to keep them, I'll take it. But your life—the way you lived it—was lonely. I want more than that. I deserve more.

Azrael's violet eyes welled, and he nodded once. *You shall have it, my daughter. All you want for you and yours is in your grasp.*

This was the first time Azrael had spoken inside my head, and his voice had the same tenor as Hades, the vibrations nearly rattling my whole body. Smiling, I rested my head on Bastian's shoulder, letting the breeze kiss my face as the boat cut through the water.

Before I knew it, Bastian was shaking me awake. The boat was beached on a rocky shore, the littering pebbles winking at me in the bright sun. He pulled me to standing, steadying me as I climbed out of the boat.

Beyond the water's edge was a gleaming city surrounded by little pockets of odd-colored sky. I didn't understand at first until I rubbed the sleep from my eyes and really looked. What I thought were pockets were small little worlds, little heavens, each one as singular as the people who resided there. They each dotted the horizon in a glittering mass of worlds, too many for my brain to count.

How were we supposed to find my parents—or even Killian for that matter—in all of this? And the souls inside me? Would they know where to go?

Bastian gave my hand a reassuring squeeze, leading me to a large information sign that would hopefully give us some sort of direction.

"If you think this is bad, you should see Hell. It's a certified mess there and all the rings? No, thank you," Azrael said, shuddering. "I stay on the outskirts if I can help it."

Good information to be sure, but it didn't help me find what I needed. I stared at the sign—the directions were more confusing than I'd thought they'd be. My parents' names weren't anywhere on it.

I fought back tears as the world ebbed and flowed around me, the hopelessness hitting me exactly where I was sore. Swallowing down tears, I turned to Azrael. "Maybe we should let these souls out. If I can't find my parents or Darby's dad, at least I can do that."

Azrael nodded before wincing. "This is going to hurt, but you'll heal fast here."

"Wha—"

Before I really understood, he grabbed my hands with one of his and drew a blade from his hip with the other. In an instant, I felt the slashing pain of his knife meeting my flesh, and then the burning ache of the souls escaping their prison. Granted, I much appreciated that it didn't feel like my entire body was being flash fried, but I couldn't say it was altogether comfortable, either.

The scream that escaped me had the residents of Elysium crowding around us, the offers to help drowned out by my pain. And then it was over, the metallic sigils still there, but the full ache in my hands gone.

Confused and more than a little sweaty, I rested against Bastian as he gave withering looks at my father.

"Was that necessary? You could have warned her."

Azrael shrugged. "I thought it was better to treat it like a Band-Aid—the ring's wards kept the souls contained, but there wasn't a better way to get them out other than just cutting the skin."

Bastian huffed. "Like you've ever ripped off a plaster a day in your life. Fun fact: it hurts no matter how you do it. The quick way is just more traumatizing."

Azrael sucked in a breath through his teeth, wincing. "Sorry."

I was stuck on the sigils still burned into the skin of my palms. At my questioning gaze, Azrael shrugged. "It marks you as one of mine. It actually could have gotten you past the harpies and gorgon, but I forgot it was there. Usually I have my ring, and that grants me passage, but…" He shrugged, trailing off.

He'd given me safe passage and left himself without? If my brain wasn't so addled, I could have asked him why, but I was just so tired. I had to think that was a bad thing—being tired in the Underworld. I'd already slept once, and that had been with a host of souls in my body.

I stared at the information board—the text just as confusing now as it had been before I released the souls. I mean, I was dead, right? Shouldn't it be at least a little helpful? We were in heaven, weren't we?

Honestly, I was about to throw a full-on tantrum when Bastian came through with logic.

"Why don't we ask someone?" Bastian asked, frowning at the tremendously useless information board. "There has to be someone here who knows where your parents are or where Killian is, right?"

He transferred my weight to Azrael, who clutched me to him like he was close to absorbing me.

"I'm tired," I muttered, my head lolling up to look at his face.

"I know. Shouldn't be too long now, and you'll be right as rain."

"That sounds bad," I slurred, having a hard time holding my head up. "Am I dying again?"

It wouldn't be the first time, but since I was in the Underworld, this time it would probably stick.

My father looked down at me, glittering lights surrounding his head as a smile bloomed across his features. "Not dying. Changing. It won't be long now."

"I'm scared," I breathed, the fear making it hard to draw in my next breath. Or maybe my lungs just weren't working, I couldn't tell.

"Don't be. It's been a long time coming. I'm sorry, Sloane. I thought we'd have more time. I thought I'd be able to show you everything you needed to know. But I want you to know you were loved and wanted. And I've never been prouder than I am of you and your sister. Will you tell her that for me? When you see her again? Will you tell her that I love her, that I never regretted a day being your father?"

My sluggish brain didn't understand, my body hanging in Azrael's grip as his eyes pleaded for me to listen. "You sound like you're saying goodbye. Are you leaving?"

Was that my voice all childlike and small? Had I ever sounded like that?

"Not leaving, but you will eventually. You'll continue being the beautiful woman you've become. You'll tie your life with the man you love. You'll be a sister and a friend, you'll have a full long life, and I fear I won't be around for it. For either of you. I know I haven't been the father you needed, but I'm glad you both had some mighty fine men to take my spot. I'm glad you learned the lessons I couldn't teach you. And that you both found love when I couldn't bless you with that, either."

Fear clutched tight to my middle. "I don't want you to go."

His smile was wobbly, or maybe that was the tears in my eyes—I didn't know which. This felt horrible, like I was losing someone else, like I was losing a part of me.

"I'm not going anywhere. I'll always be with you," he whispered, kissing my forehead.

But that felt like a comforting lie, and I was too tired to make him tell me the truth.

20

At the touch of Azrael's lips to my skin, a flood of what I could only describe as life filled me, solidifying my legs and straightening my spine. He'd done the same thing to Darby what felt like ages ago, healing her in a way I'd never seen before.

Had I been dying like she'd been? Azrael said I wasn't, but a part of me didn't believe him.

I didn't know what was going on, but my bullshit meter was going off big time.

Azrael gave me another tired smile. "You'll know when you know, kid. Don't be so quick to find all the answers. They'll come when they're supposed to."

What a cryptic and patronizing answer, Dad.

"I like you calling me Dad. Did you know that?"

Blinking, the weight of that statement hit me like a bomb. "No," I croaked. "I didn't."

"I found him," Bastian announced as he jogged back to us. "Not your parents, but one of those souls knows Killian. I figure we can check in on him, and he might know something, or we can ask someone else. What do you say?"

Truth be told, we probably should have left as soon as those souls were freed, but the carrot of helping my sister was almost too big to say no to. I looked at Azrael, his skin not nearly as vibrant as usual.

"What do you think? You said Essex could be coming to attack the house. Should we go back?" But he hadn't said that, had he? Simon said he'd seen it in his mind.

Azrael shook his head as he moved farther down a busy street, the foot traffic almost swallowing him up as he weaved through the souls. "Not yet. We still have time. Let's go see him."

Reluctantly, Bastian and I followed, the worry in my gut multiplying with every passing second. Catching up to Azrael, Bastian instructed him to take a left at the next street. We followed the directions Bastian had been given, arriving at a neighborhood that looked very familiar. It resembled the one I'd grown up in, the scent of hot dogs cooking on a grill and roses blooming a heady perfume of home. Ten houses down, we came to a pretty white house with a black mailbox. The name "Adler" was lettered neatly, but there were two pairs of handprints, one a man's size and one a little girl's.

I swallowed hard, debating on whether or not I had the courage to do this. If I could even get through talking to the man who'd raised my sister without bawling my fucking eyes out. Bastian nudged me with his elbow, jutting his chin at Azrael. He was paler than he'd been just a few minutes ago, and now he was wobbling on his feet.

I reached for him, but he lurched away, the door to Killian's house his heading. We followed, and I thought we might have to catch him if he fell.

What had he done?

Before we reached the door, it swung open, Darby's father filling the entrance. His blond hair was slightly messy, and he had on a ratty college sweater over jeans, with a pair of comfy slippers on his feet. His face fell a bit when he saw me, and it made my heart ache just a little.

"Mr. Adler? Killian?"

I'd only seen him the once, and he'd been bloody and bruised. The man before me barely resembled the one on the lakeshore, what seemed like so long ago.

"Yes?"

"Umm…" I trailed off, swallowing a lump in my throat. "My name is Sloane. I—I know your daughter, Darby. Well, she's my sister."

Killian seemed confused for just a moment before he invited us in. We piled inside his neat little living room, taking chairs when we were offered a seat.

"Wow. I didn't think I'd meet any of Darby's siblings." Killian pulled at his ear, a sign or nervousness as his gaze kept falling to Azrael. "Good to see you again, though you have looked better. Would you like some tea or something?"

Azrael gave him a weak smile. "No need. I'll feel better soon."

That felt like a lie, and I wasn't the only one who thought so. Bastian and Killian shared a glance that both said they thought my father was full of shit. I had to agree.

"I'm sorry to bother you," I began, trying to figure out what to say. Funny, we'd traveled all this way, and now I was trying to figure out my script?

Way to go, Sloane.

"It's just, I was coming here anyway, and I thought you might want to give me a message to give her since you two didn't get a chance to say goodbye."

There was more. Like how I was sorry we hadn't been able

to save him. I was sorry that the plan had failed him—that we hadn't thought to save him sooner. I wanted to tell him that Darby was going to be okay—that we'd be there for her.

Killian's smile was watery, and he nodded. "I—I'd love to give her a message. But… is she okay? I know she isn't. No one would be after that. So much became clear after. All of Mariana's spells lifted, and I saw the life we had before she left. I can't think of a better gift to be given than the time I got with Darby—the life we built. She grew into such a beautiful woman. If you don't mind, I'd like to write her a note?"

I blinked, surprised I hadn't thought of something so simple. "Of course. Take your time."

Killian stood, pacing over to a rolltop desk and began scribbling on a legal pad. While he did that, I returned to my inspection of Azrael. His skin was now solidly in the gray range, his black hair fading to white before my very eyes. His irises began to get a purple quality to them as he continued to study his hands. It was as if he was losing his glamour.

That couldn't be good.

I flicked my eyes to Bastian, and he, too, was staring at Azrael, like he might turn into a pillar of salt at any moment. Bastian must have sensed my stare because we then shared a worried glance.

What was going on? One second, he was fine, and the next he was like this.

Killian rustled some papers, ripping them from the legal pad and folding them together. He rose from the desk chair, his warm blue eyes on me. "I can't thank you enough for doing this," he croaked, his eyes getting watery. "If this doesn't work, could you just tell her I'm proud of her?"

I hadn't even considered Killian's note not working, but the reality of it was too probable to discount. "Of course I will."

Azrael rose shakily, almost stumbling as he lurched toward

Killian and grabbed his hand. "I said it before, but it bears repeating. Thank you for being her father. Thank you for raising her. Thank you for the sacrifices you made. I'll never forget it."

Killian surrounded Azrael's hand with both of his, a sort of knowledge coming over his face that I didn't understand. "It was my honor."

Azrael gave him a jerky nod, straightening. He seemed to gather himself and turned. His gait was smoother, a little less fragile than before. And he walked right out of Killian's house, leaving the three of us to stare after him.

"Is he going to be all right?" Killian asked, and I couldn't peel my gaze off the now-closed door to answer him.

"I'm sure he'll be right as rain soon enough," Bastian replied, doing what I couldn't.

Because I didn't know if Azrael would be okay, and I didn't know why he'd deteriorated or how someone like him would decline so quickly.

"It was good to talk to you, Killian, but I fear we must be off."

I heard Bastian say those words, but all I could do was stare at that damn door, only breaking my gaze to bid Killian a hasty goodbye. Bastian gently latched onto my elbow and guided me to the stoop. But once we got there, I could hear things I most definitely should *not* be able to hear.

Especially from the man I was listening to.

Just a little longer. I can make it a little longer. Stupid Fate. Why couldn't she have thrown me a bone on this one? I just wanted... It doesn't matter what I wanted. But Sloane won't understand that it was meant to be, that my choices were limited. That my failures were the rules I'd been given.

I couldn't breathe. I couldn't swallow. I couldn't do anything but listen to that litany and let the knowledge that something was really, really fucking wrong wash over me. Shaking myself, I managed to snap out of it, and a bout of rage flashed through me like a brushfire.

"Why are you cursing Fate? And why in the high holy fuck can I read you? *What* did you do?"

He'd kissed my forehead just like he'd done to Darby. A gentle little flutter against my skin and then I'd felt better. But unlike with Darby, Azrael looked like he was dying.

Was he dying? Could he even die?

"I told you," Azrael responded, giving me one of his patented raised eyebrows. "You're changing. And don't read my thoughts—it's rude."

I blinked at him for a solid five seconds before my eye started twitching. "Says the man who has read nearly all of my thoughts in every single interaction we've ever had. But you never answered the Fate part. Why are you cursing Fate, and what did you do?"

Just a little longer. Just a little longer. Just a little longer.

"Why do you keep saying that?"

Azrael shook his head, but the act made him almost stumble. He reached out a hand, using a cute white picket fence to keep himself vertical. "I told you not to read my thoughts."

"And I told you to stuff it. It seems we're at an impasse on that front."

He cleared his throat—or at least he tried to. That turned into a cough that racked his whole body and almost took him to his knees. Bastian and I lunged for him, easing him to the sidewalk as we waited for him to catch his breath.

I barely held in a sob as I watched a god withering away right before my eyes. "What is going on?"

He gave me a halfhearted chuckle. "Just my past catching up to me."

I didn't understand until I saw a flash of white hair out of the corner of my eye. I could feel him, his presence like a black spot on my brain. "He was never going to attack the house, was he?"

Azrael smiled. "You're entirely too smart for your own good, you know that? Help me up?"

Bastian and I pulled Azrael to standing, his touch sipping just a little of the power he'd bestowed on me.

Just a little. You'll get it back. Just need to look strong for a second.

Then he shoved me, hard. Hell, it was practically a throw. My ass hit the pavement as the glitter of a familiar blade cut the air right where I'd been standing just a moment before.

"Ruining my fun again, old man?" my brother growled, brandishing the same blade that had taken my life and so many others. "No matter. I have plenty of people to kill."

Then the world slowed, and my heart stopped, and the sun died. Because Essex flicked that blade out again, the point aimed for Bastian's throat. But then Bastian wasn't there anymore—he'd sailed over the fence Azrael had just used to prop himself up.

And in his stead stood my father with Essex's blade buried in his chest.

21

At first, what I was seeing didn't make any sense. It just couldn't. There was no way Essex Drake—the man who'd murdered me and my parents and so many others—could just come down here and steal from me. There was no way he could just try and kill me again.

No way he could take this much.

I stood there, frozen—when I'd gotten to my feet, I couldn't say—watching as Essex held the hilt of the blade, his eyes wide with an emotion I couldn't track before it morphed into a sneer. The blip of pain there and gone in an instant.

"A little out of order, but it will make things easier on the back end, I think. How does it feel, Father? To know that I will take all your children from you? To know that I got my revenge?" His lip quivered, the unmitigated joy playing havoc with the muscles of his face. "Tell me, did you realize when you stole my children—my wife—from me that this day would come? Did Fate tell you when you would be reaped, too?"

Azrael latched onto Essex's hand—the one still holding the hilt—and stepped forward, pressing the blade farther into his body. "Do you think I don't know your game, boy? I know all about your deal with Nemesis. Did you think my sister wouldn't tell me?" Azrael let out a low chuckle, a wet cough drawing blood to his lips. "She agreed to your proposal and gave you safe passage here because Fate deigned it so. You are not in charge of destiny any more than I am. And I did not *take* your family from you. You did that when you started killing your own." Then he lifted his chin, nodding to a woman and child as they stood staring in shock at the tableau.

"Essex?" the woman called before she covered her mouth with her hand, disgust making her shake her head. Her dress seemed straight out of the Middle Ages, with belled sleeves and an outer, more durable dress corseted over a lighter under layer. Her hair was a deep red, the curly strands threaded through with flowers and braids. She even had a haphazard flower crown that was staying on her head by a wing and a prayer, the handiwork of the child at her side.

The little girl was a copy of her mother except for her hair, the strands a familiar shade of white. She held daisies and dahlias and roses in her little hand, squishing the stems as she stared at what I could only assume was her father.

Essex looked, just for a second, before he did a double take.

"Bronwyn? Clara?" He shook his head as if the sight of the pair was something he'd never thought he'd see in a million years. "I—I don't understand."

"What have you done?" she asked, aghast as she moved the little girl behind her skirts, the girl's flowers forgotten on the cobblestone road.

Shakily, Essex turned back to Azrael, confusion and pain and rage amalgamating throughout his whole body. "How?"

"Did you think I wouldn't care for them? They were yours, and I couldn't prevent their deaths, but I could keep them safe. All you had to do was wait—your time was coming. You would have been with them soon enough. And now you have made it so this is the last time you'll see them—see all of them."

Several people stepped forward, each one staring at Essex with hurt on their faces. Whispers of their thoughts flitted through my mind like Azrael's had, memories of their deaths, the pain they'd felt at his hand. Sweeping my eyes over the crowd, I could see so many. So many deaths, so much torment, so many people lost.

And he had been the author of it all.

This crowd, this moment was just the beginning of his punishment. This was the knife in his heart. Because he would never see his family again, and after what he had done, they didn't want a single thing to do with him, anyway.

Quick as a flash, Azrael reached out and wrapped his fingers around Essex's throat, his other hand still on the hilt of the blade in his chest. Brilliant bright light peaked from under my father's fingers as Essex's pallor grayed slightly. It took a second, but he finally got the gumption to yank himself away, leaving his blade in our father's chest—watching with a chaotic mind of sorrow and regret and avarice.

I saw the instant he chose himself—the exact second Essex realized he had nothing to hold onto anymore. He stumbled, staggered, and then he took off running, damn near disappearing in the crowd. I stood frozen for a moment, unsure if I should keep him from escaping or—

"Go, Sloane. I've got Azrael," Bastian shouted, giving me the answer I needed.

Essex had always put his revenge over everything else. I refused to follow in his footsteps. Instead of following my brother, I pointed my feet toward Bastian and Azrael.

"What are you doing?" Azrael croaked, blood coating his pale lips as it leaked from the side of his mouth. "He'll get away."

I shook my head as I gave him a wobbly smile. "No, he won't," I insisted, brushing a strand of hair from Azrael's face. "He's headed for a gate. I'll catch up to him soon enough."

"You—you're staying with me?"

His voice was so small, so vulnerable, it opened my chest wide and left me bleeding. A smattering of glass was where my heart should have been, the damage too great to ever be repaired. I sucked in a shuddering breath, the words to comfort him lodged in my throat.

But I could count on Bastian.

"We both are," he said, assuring Azrael, who was getting paler by the second. "We wouldn't leave you alone."

Azrael's odd violet gaze shifted from me to the man I loved. "I'm glad she has you." A wet cough seized his chest, sending spasms throughout his whole body. His eyes rolled back in his head before he managed to find himself again, those eyes that matched my own, focusing what would likely be the last time.

"You knew, didn't you?" I whispered, the weight of it all crashing down on me at once. "That this was going to happen when you brought me here. That—"

Azrael's smile was sad. "I've never been one to argue with Fate. Maybe you'll be better at that than me." He swallowed thickly, before spearing me with a gaze that was so final, I felt it in my bones. "Better do this now before I run out of time. Love you and your sister. Remember to tell her."

I was in the process of nodding when his hand found my throat much like he'd done to Essex. Only he didn't seem to steal anything from me. No, he gave me something. My entire body buzzed with power, with knowledge, with a vitality that seemed almost too much for my skin to contain.

Memories—his—raced through my mind. What he had seen, what he'd done. What I was now. He'd been right this whole time—he'd had to follow the rules because his fate had been sealed.

But mine wasn't.

An itch bloomed in my back, almost making me cry out, the need to keep my eyes on Azrael the only thing that kept me upright. The irritation turned into a burn, and that burn morphed into a pain so fierce that the urge to scream was almost too much to bear. A blisteringly hot ache settled through me, and with it, a weight that nearly brought me over backward. A shiver worked its way through me, starting at my head and flowing all the way down to my toes, and all the way out to—

I shifted, the black things racing just out of my field of vision as I turned. My hand went to my shoulder, the feathers there smooth and soft and—

There are feathers on my back. I have wings. There are wings on my back. Actual wings.

I stared down at the man who had given me life—twice—my gaze landing on the smile frozen on his lips. My stomach lurched, my heart—the one I'd thought was just broken—shattered even more. He was gone. And I couldn't bring him back, and I couldn't deal my way out of it, and I—

A sob ripped up my throat, the agony of loss more than I could bear. My fingers closed around the hilt of the blade, ripping the offending thing from him so I could clutch him to me. My mother had done this same thing, held my lifeless body to her chest. I'd thought that memory hurt, but this…

A hand found my shoulder, a tiny one that I had no choice but to answer. Clara Drake stood there, tears on her small face. Her mother stood with the child's hand in hers. Bronwyn swallowed hard, a sob almost leveling her. When she could speak, she asked, "Can I—can we say goodbye to him?"

Thoughts raced through me. Clara and Azrael sitting in a

meadow, her weaving flowers in his white hair. He didn't glamour himself with the child, and she'd loved playing with it because it matched hers. But it wasn't just Clara. It was all of them. It was our family, and each of them wanted to say goodbye.

"We'll take care of him," Clara insisted. "I'll take him to the field. He likes the flowers there."

There was no way to say no, so I nodded, moving away from Azrael as the others filled the gap I left. Bastian came to me, holding me up as the sorrow threatened to pull me all the way under.

"Sloane, look at me."

Doing so almost gutted me, but I did it. But for the first time, those bottle-green eyes weren't the balm they usually were.

"We need to go after Essex."

Yes, we did need to do that. Too bad I didn't know if I could.

"Love, I need you to remember the family you have left. He'll steal them, too, if we don't get moving."

And that's all it took. I latched onto Bastian's hand, and we took off running, pushing faster as we sprinted through the city with a singular focus.

It turned out we had an easier go of it than Essex had. The crowd parted for us, but had refused for him. Hell, some of them threw their shoulders into him on purpose, hurling food and objects at him. One soul even started beating him with her umbrella. Essex stumbled, digging in his pockets as he tried to run, the sound of his chaotic mind a whirling mess of blame and toxic thoughts.

He still thought he could get back to the gate. Thought he could win. Sure, he hadn't accomplished all he needed to, but there was still time.

Wrong on all counts, buddy.

Then he found whatever it was that he'd been searching for, yanking it from his pocket like he'd struck gold. With a twist to his fingers, he winked out of sight, popping up in a clear spot of the street fifty yards ahead.

Motherfucker.

I'd only seen that power in one other person, a sorcerer that I'd chased all over the ass-end of Tennessee. My eye practically twitched as I remembered the man I'd had to chase up a water tower just to trap.

I hated heights.

Pushing faster, we shortened the gap, sprinting like the hounds of Hell were after us. We'd almost gotten close enough to reach him when he turned that fucking dial again. Only this time he didn't just end up fifty yards ahead. He was so far away, there was no way we'd be able to catch him—not if he did that again.

Essex turned to look at us and twisted it again, winking out of sight. Shaking, I tried to make my mind focus on the task at hand.

Essex. Running. Now.

Those feathery extensions on my back got the message before I did, flapping once and shooting me—and by extension, Bastian—into the air like a goddamn javelin.

Did I mention I was not good with heights?

My stomach lurched, threatening to evict everything in it as I stared in horror at the ground that was *much* too far away for my liking. My eyes managed to find Bastian's, his body hanging from my lone hand.

This was not safe. *What if I drop him, what if… The gate. Essex is heading for the gate.*

I saw it in my mind, the stone walls and arched ceiling. The near-constant *drip, drip, drip* of water that made me equally creeped out and have to pee all at the same time. I wanted to go there—needed it more than air in my lungs—wanted Bastian's feet firmly planted on the ground. And then it was as if I was holding my breath—like every molecule of oxygen had been sucked from my lungs, as I was squeezed in a vice so tight I thought my eyes would pop from their sockets.

When I could breathe again, I sucked in huge gasps of cool, musty air, my brain just not comprehending the fact that we were standing in the middle of the too-long hallway that led to the Underworld.

Bastian's groan was music to my ears as I reached for him with both hands, hysterical laughter bubbling up my chest as adrenaline flooded my body. We were on the ground, he was alive, and the gate was close. The pounding of footsteps echoed through the corridor, their vibration a siren call of vengeance.

They pulled me to my feet, and I followed them—or at least I tried to. Those wings that had been so awesome before—*not* —didn't exactly fit in this hallway, the scrape of the wall yanking feathers out at the root. What had Azrael done to make them go away? That last time I'd seen him with wings, he'd just shivered a little, and they had gone *poof*. Emulating this was marginally successful, the things tucking up and back instead of disappearing all the way, but I'd take it.

"Almost there, love," Bastian growled, his thirst for justice just as big as mine.

Those steps were so close, I could practically taste the blood on my tongue. I wouldn't swallow it, but the thought of ripping Essex's throat out was a balm to my soul. We rounded a corner, the largest turn in the whole stretch of the corridor so near to the entrance it made my entire body shudder and my stomach drop.

Essex was in our home.

Again.

Pushing as fast as I could, I let go of Bastian's hand as we came to the end of the hall. Essex had just busted through the door, diving for the cleaver on Simon's macabre altar table as soon as he saw it.

Essex brandished it like the weapon it was, and Simon and Dahlia stumbled back. The bastard had caught them by surprise, but what he hadn't accounted for was my sister. While Simon and Dahlia backed away, Darby pulled a gun from her hip and fired without a second's hesitation. Essex moved at the last second, so her shot wasn't lethal, but it caught him in the shoulder.

Still, it had the intended result. Essex dropped the cleaver, his hand no longer able to hold the blade, and then he was on his ass.

And then *I* was on *him*, flying out of that hall like a missile. I landed just like a harpy, feet down, my boots pounding into his gut with a satisfying squish. Reaching down, I snatched him from the floor, raising him up above my head, fangs bared.

I was going to rip his throat out and watch him bleed out on this floor. Then when he was well and truly dead, I was going to try and conjure some of those chains Azrael had tried to capture Medusa with and haul his sorry soul down to Tartarus. And if I needed help, I'd ask Hades or Persephone.

Yes, that was precisely what I was going to do.

"Sloane?" Darby breathed, only slightly pulling my focus from the man who'd earned every bit of pain I was going to dish out. "Sloane!"

"What? I'm a little busy here," I griped, turning my chin to stare at my sister.

Her hands were raised over her head, her gun being taken from its holster by an incredibly tall man in a suit. There were others in the room as well, men and women I didn't know, who were frisking Simon and Dahlia for weapons, and others who were holding giant orbs of magic like they were cocking a gun. Thomas and Axel were in magical cuffs, and Bishop was face-down on the floor, an agent's knee on his back and magical ropes around his arms. Another agent pointed an odd-looking gun at Bastian, a canister of glowing liquid at its base that looked very familiar. My brain caught up and I recognized it as a very powerful sleeping potion.

A slight gentleman with a purple paisley tie cleared his throat, stepping forward like he was in charge. Maybe he was.

"As I stated before while you were otherwise indisposed: Arcane Bureau of Investigation. You're all under arrest."

I had a feeling no one in the history of the ABI had laughed at Director August Theodore Davenport III, but there I was, cackling like a lunatic as I still held Essex by the neck. Tears almost poured out of my eyes as the hilarity hit me full force.

"Fates, you are adorable," I said, wiping my eyes. "Hate to break it to you, but unless your jurisdiction covers deities, you're shit out of luck."

Davenport scrunched his nose like he smelled something rotten. "Deity," he said scathingly. "And what deity are you supposed to be? The god of vampires? Or maybe you're one of those new gods that presides over avocado toast or something."

The ABI Director appeared around my age, but his mind was much older. I'd peg him around the eight or nine hundred range. Still, he sounded like a damn Boomer.

I flashed him my fangs, my wings spreading wide. "Tell me —have you ever heard of the Angel of Death? Don't answer that. I know you have. Well, Essex and I are his kids. He used to have a bunch, but Essex here killed them all. Even me. But see, Daddy didn't like that, and he brought me back." I turned my chin, staring Essex down. "All that power that you wanted, that you killed for, that you tried to steal? Belongs to me now."

I flicked my gaze back to Davenport. "So no, I won't be put under arrest, and neither will my friends. And Essex here, well, his time is up. I'm going to rip out his throat and watch him bleed. Then I'm going to chain his soul and haul his ass down to Tartarus. And if I see so much as a flicker of one of those spells, I'll take every single one of you down with him."

The other agents in the room seemed to get the message far faster than their boss, the orbs of magic winking out of sight and the guns properly stowed as each one took a collective step away from my friends.

"You can't be Death," Davenport countered like he was the end all be all of god assignments.

I smiled, letting just a hint of power leak out of my eyes. "I can, and I am."

He sputtered, shaking his head. "But Azrael—"

"Do. Not. Speak of my father as if you know him, August. You do not. I know in your precious little head, you think of him as a confidant or a shoulder to cry on, but I can assure you, Azrael is retired."

And retired was a nicer way of putting what Essex had done to him. My stomach pitched, and I tightened my grip on my brother's throat, the pain of saying goodbye to Azrael far sharper than I ever thought it would be.

"I suggest you stand down, Director, and remember where you are. This is the entrance to the Underworld. You're in my house, so to speak."

"But... but you're a murderer," he cried, staring at me like he hadn't meant to blurt that out.

I scoffed, enjoying the little choking sounds Essex was making. "So are you, but if it makes you feel better, think of it as on-the-job training."

Davenport got really flustered then, like a toddler about to throw a fit. "You can't kill him. We need him."

"Oh, I assure you, I can, and I will." Inspecting the director's thoughts, though, I decided to expose the meat of the issue. "But what, pray tell, do you need this miserable, lying, murdering sack of dog shit for? Plan to install him in your newest ABI branch and let him run amuck? Maybe kill a few more agents, break a few more prisoners out of jail, conspire with Director O'Shea to open a goddamn rift in the planet so she can steal the power of the dead? What the fuck could you need him for?"

Davenport's shoulders fell in defeat. "He has answers. Knows who's dirty. Who's been bribed to keep their mouths shut. He knows where the bodies are buried."

And they wanted him alive so he could dish, sleeping in a nice cushy cell with cable TV and a nice comfy mattress. I didn't think so. "No deal, sorry. I've seen the way your agency runs its prisons, and they leave something to be desired. You can't keep hold of the prisoners you've got."

Davenport ground his teeth, his brain grasping at straws to sweeten the deal. And make no mistake, he was making a deal —he just didn't know it yet. "Essex Drake would not be going to prison. He would go to a black site, sedated with enough sleeping potion to kill a fucking rhino, and strapped to a table until his brain has been mined of every detail, secret, and cover-up for the last four centuries. Then, you may do with him what you wish."

"I can do what I wish now," I said, yawning. "What's in it for me?"

Davenport growled under his breath before sucking in air

through his nose like an irritated Southern mother. "Fine," he ground out. "I will expunge the records of Agents Bishop La Roux and Sarina Kenzari, releasing them from their contracts if they so wish. I will grant immunity to Darby Adler for her crimes against the Knoxville coven and the Monroe nest. She will be deputized as the new Warden of Knoxville and will accept the duties that entails. Also, I will grant blanket immunities for all past crimes to Sebastian and Simon Cartwright, Dahlia St. James, Harper Jones, Axel Monroe, Thomas Gao, Emrys Zane, and that little revenant girl ya'll keep in the kitchen."

He almost had everything, so I lowered Essex to the floor. He was turning an awful shade of purple, anyway.

"Get it to me in writing within the hour." My mama—and every episode of *Law & Order*—didn't raise no fool. "Binding contract that states you may not have possession of Essex Drake for longer than one month, his body and soul to be claimed by me and only me."

"Done." He'd given too much away too quickly, and he knew it.

"And Davenport?"

He winced, his shoulders hunching.

"One more thing."

It made me sick to my stomach, but Bastian and I returned to the Underworld empty-handed. The fact that I got Davenport to agree to publicly acknowledge every agent and civilian Essex had murdered, and pay their surviving families reparations for up to one century, still didn't make me feel any better. Sure, it was the absolute least they could do, and agencies were typically stingy with the pennies, but inside I wanted to curl around a toilet and evict my lunch.

I had not even an inkling of what I might be walking into, and I didn't think my heart could handle it.

"If you think any harder, you're going to explode and we've already got the wings to deal with," Bastian chided, fitting his arm around my waist as we walked into the building, my wings barely fitting through the double doors.

The last time Bastian and I had been to this building, we'd entered from a very different door. This time we took the direct route. A smiling doorman skirted around a counter, reaching for my hand with both of his. He shook mine once before moving to Bastian's.

"Sloane, Sebastian, it is so good to see you. Mistress Persephone had me set aside your keys for you and asked that I show you to your apartment. It's one floor down from theirs." He said this *sotto voce* like this was a very big deal. I had a feeling it really was.

He pressed the golden call button, and the elevators opened. I stared at the too-small elevator and then looked at my shoulder.

"Meet you guys there?"

Bastian's gaze had the same track mine had. "Yes, that might be best."

Snorting at the absurdity of it, I kissed his lips.

"See you in a minute." Then I walked right back out the doors, letting the wings I couldn't figure out how to put away haul me up to the second highest floor in the tallest building I'd ever seen in my life.

Good times.

"Are you kidding me?" I hissed, trying for the fifth time to follow the instructions Hermes had written down, but his handwriting was so bad it was no wonder doctors everywhere had the worst penmanship. "Can't I get the training wheels version?"

"Oh, for Fate's sake," Persephone muttered, slapping her book down on my new couch. "I'll read it." She snatched up the paper I had been helplessly trying to decipher, took one look at it and yelled at the top of her lungs, "Hermes!"

A fine-boned man with the body of a long-distance runner appeared a second later. Dressed in a gold caftan and a wide-brimmed hat—a completely different outfit from what he was wearing an hour ago—he minced to Seph with a smile on his face.

"You rang?"

She waved the paper at him. "What is this? No one can read your handwriting, you weirdo."

"Those are detailed instructions."

"That no one can read."

It had been four hours, a very inventive round of grief sex, and a messy bath, and I was completely done with these wings already. The only upside to the damn things was that they didn't tear my clothes—*don't ask me how*—and they made drying after a bath a snap. Yes, there was currently a mess of feathers everywhere in our new bathroom, but who needed towels?

"Can you just walk me through it step by step?" I asked, praying he would decide to help.

Hermes checked his watch, counted on all of his fingers, and then shrugged. "I've got three minutes, so I'll take this slow."

Three minutes was slow?

He snapped his fingers in my face. "Focus. Take a deep breath and let it out. Then imagine the wings disappearing into your back. When I first got mine, I pictured it all horror-movie style with the cracking ribs and blood and stuff. They winked right out of sight, no muss, no fuss."

My expression was skeptical, but he nodded at me. "Promise. The more gruesome the better."

I followed his advice, complete with the bones snapping and blood flying, and wouldn't you know it? The weight of them disappeared almost instantly.

"Look at you," he exclaimed, latching onto my hands and spreading them wide. "A quick study. Okay, I've got to run. I'll see you guys at the coronation later, though, okay?"

I swallowed thickly and nodded.

Coronation.

Had I known when I took this job that there was an actual ceremony involved, I might have skipped it. Just the thought of me in public, in a dress, in front of a boatload of actual gods? It sounded like the worst form of torture. But someone —*Seph*—promised me food, and I was a sucker for a good buffet.

Plus, they were unveiling Azrael's statue, and if nothing else, that needed to be celebrated.

A god dying was rare, so rare, in fact, that the entirety of the Underworld mourned the loss of Azrael with a passion that warmed me a little. In his mind he hadn't been loved or wanted, but with the vehemence in which these people grieved him, I knew that just wasn't true.

Azrael's statue would reside in the Elysium fields, a monument to all those he had brought to peace.

Then I would be paraded around as the new Angel of Death, which sounded like the absolute worst thing I could think of *ever*.

"Oh, it won't be that bad," Seph said, elbowing me in the side. "You look beautiful, your lover is hotter than blazes, and you've been promised as many appetizers as your stomach can hold. What more is there?"

I thought about all the worries I had stockpiled in my brain, but most of them centered around the very alive man I wanted to spend the rest of eternity with. The one that I wanted to see happy and free and not trapped down here.

Seph seemed to see the worries on my face. "Is it Bastian? Are you worried about him?"

I swallowed. I couldn't decide if he should live down here or up there. Couldn't figure out if being down here was going to hurt him or not. And what if something happened to his brother or any of our friends while we were gone?

Seph waved her hand like she was shooing my extremely valid worries away. "Oh, please. Why did you think I made him eat the fruit salad? I even told him I made it myself, so he had two helpings to make sure I knew he liked it."

Confused, I took a step back. "I don't know. Why did you make him eat the fruit salad?"

She smiled like I was cute. "It had pomegranate seeds in it. *Underworld* pomegranate seeds." She specifically stressed the "Underworld" part, but I shrugged. Rolling her eyes, she elaborated. "It makes it so he can come and go whenever he wants. You're welcome."

I sputtered, "But that was before Azrael—"

"Fate and I are good buddies. She filled me in. So quit worrying about it already, and get out of that bathrobe. We have a party to get to."

That "party" turned into a three-day event, complete with the statue unveiling, my coronation, and an incredibly raucous after-party that made me glad I was already dead so I couldn't experience the hangover.

Fun fact: when you were a new god, everyone wanted to buy you drinks, and these people must have had iron stomachs, petrified livers, or both.

"Where are you taking me?" I asked as I let Bastian lead me by the hand down a manicured street. I hadn't started my duties yet, but Hades had told me to take a few days, that the dead would always be there for me to call home.

"Balance," he'd said, and I didn't argue. Taking a well-deserved rest was something Bastian and I both needed.

So, there I was being escorted through a cute neighborhood, the houses unfamiliar until we stopped. In the living world, Bastian and I had stared at an empty plot of land where this house used to sit. He'd stayed with me while I grieved, while I worked through the awful loss and the blank spot in my memories.

"Do you remember what you said to me in Medusa's lair?" I croaked, not taking my eyes off the house I'd grown up in with its perfectly imperfect blue shudders that Dad and I had painted ourselves, and the slightly off-center birdbath that just would not go together right.

Bastian had asked me to remind him to put a ring on my finger. I'd thought he was joking at the time, but just in case he wasn't, I wanted him to. I wanted him for as long as possible, as long as he would have me.

"I do," he answered, his voice so close as he nudged my ear with his nose. "I've been waiting for you to remind me."

Swallowing thickly, I broke my gaze from my childhood home, and stared at the man I would be with until the end. "This is your reminder."

"Thanks, love, but why don't you take a look at your hand?"

Dumbly, I pulled my eyes from his to stare down at my hand in his. On my third finger was a thick band carved in an exquisite leaf design that spanned from the base of my finger to my knuckle. Resting on top of it was the biggest stone I had ever seen on a ring, the familiar violet color winking at me in the sun.

"How?" I breathed, awestruck.

Bastian chuckled. "It turns out Seph knows a good jeweler." Then he moved, cupping my face in his hands as he tilted my head back. "I want you forever. Will you be mine?"

Instead of responding to a question he already knew the answer to, I pressed up on my toes and kissed him, allowing the joy of this moment to wash through me as I tasted his mouth.

This was where we began, and I couldn't wait to walk into our future together.

Clearing my throat, I lifted my chin, gesturing to the house, a familiar eager bark baying from behind the door. "Care to meet the in-laws?"

"Absolutely," he murmured, bringing my hand to his lips before leading me toward our forever.

THE END

This concludes the Soul Reader Series.
Thank you so much for reading. I can't express just how much I have adored writing Sloane Cabot and her ragtag bunch of friends.

*However, if you would love to see a special glimpse of Sloane & Bastian's first feeding from HIS point of view, turn the page for an epic **Soul Reader Bonus Scene**. I hope you enjoy it!*

*If you loved Sloane and want to know more about her sister, Darby, check out the Grave Talker series, starting with **Dead to Me**.*

Are you ready for a new adventure?
Don't miss **Spells & Slip-ups!**

Want the skinny on future releases without having to follow
me absolutely everywhere on social media?
Text "LEGION" to (844) 311-5791

BONUS SCENE

Dear Reader,

I hope you enjoyed the Soul Reader Series. Sloane Cabot has a very special place in my heart, and I am absolutely ecstatic for you to read more about her and her favorite mage.

I have an extra special bonus scene for you as a thank you for reading. All you have to do is click the link below, sign up for my newsletter, and you'll get an email giving you access!

SIGN UP HERE:
https://geni.us/nw-bonus

Want more in the Arcane Souls World? Check out...

DEAD TO ME

Grave Talker Book One

**Meet Darby. Coffee addict. Homicide detective.
Oh, and she can see ghosts, too.**

There are only three rules in Darby Adler's life.
One: Don't talk to the dead in front of the living.
Two: Stay off the Arcane Bureau of Investigation's radar.
Three: Don't forget rules one and two.

With a murderer desperate for Darby's attention and an ABI agent in town, things are about to get mighty interesting in Haunted Peak, TN.

Grab Dead to Me today!

SPELLS AND SLIP-UPS

The Wrong Witch Book One

I suck at witchcraft.

Coming from a long line of famous witches, I should be at the top of the heap. Problem is, if there's a spell cast anywhere near me, I'll somehow mess it up.

As a probationary agent with the Arcane Bureau of Investigation, I have two choices: I can limp along and *maybe* pass myself off as a competent agent, or I can die. *Horribly.*

Worse news? I seem to have a stalker in the form of a sinfully hot, perpetually grumpy wolf who seems to have a keen interest in keeping me alive.

Whose idea was this again?

Grab it now!

To stay up to date on all things Annie Anderson, get exclusive access to ARCs and giveaways, and be a member of a fun, positive, drama-free space, join The Legion!

ACKNOWLEDGMENTS

A huge, honking thank you to Shawn, Barb, Jade, Angela, Heather, Kelly, and Erin. Thanks for the late-night calls, the endurance of my whining, the incessant plotting sessions, the wine runs, the trauma I put you through…

Basically, thanks for putting up with my bullshit.

Every single one of you rock and I couldn't have done it without you.

ABOUT THE AUTHOR

Annie Anderson is the author of the international bestselling Rogue Ethereal series. A United States Air Force veteran, Annie pens fast-paced Urban Fantasy novels filled with strong, snarky heroines and a boatload of magic. When she takes a break from writing, she can be found binge-watching The Magicians, flirting with her husband, wrangling children, or bribing her cantankerous dogs to go on a walk.

To find out more about Annie and her books, visit www.annieande.com